The Shakespeare Mask

NEWTON FROHLICH

Also by Newton Frohlich

FICTION

1492: The World of Christopher Columbus

"Captivating . . . (an) extraordinarily vivid first novel . . . Frohlich, an attorney, spent eight years researching this book, and brings remarkable realism to his chilling depiction of the fanaticism fueling the Inquisition . . . This is a convincing, detailed recreation of the Old World on the brink of discovery . . . ."

– Publisher's Weekly

NONFICTION

Making the Best of It:
A Common Sense Guide to Negotiating a Divorce

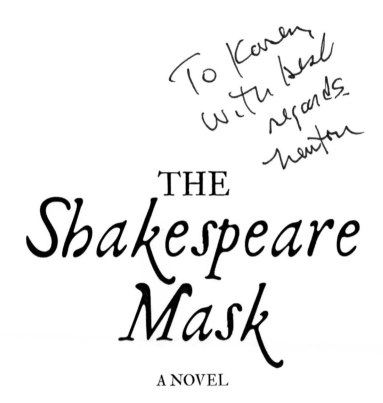

To Karen with best regards— newton

THE
Shakespeare
Mask

A NOVEL

NEWTON FROHLICH

BLUE BIRD PRESS

The Shakespeare Mask

© 2014 Newton Frohlich

BLUE BIRD PRESS

Edition ISBNs
Hardcover 978-0-9960484-0-8
Trade Paperback 978-0-9960484-1-5
E-book 978-0-9960484-2-2

First Edition 2014

This edition was prepared for printing by The Editorial Department
7650 E. Broadway, #308, Tucson, Arizona 85710
www.editorialdepartment.com

Book design by Morgana Gallaway

For Martha

And in Her Majesty's time . . . are sprung up another crew of Courtly makers, Noblemen and Gentlemen of Her Majesty's own servants, who have written excellently well as it would appear if their doings could be found out and made public with the rest, of which number is first that noble gentleman Edward Earl of Oxford.

George Puttenham
The Arte of English Poesie
London, 1589

PART ONE

Earl John

I

Time is like a fashionable host
That slightly shakes his parting guest
by th' hand,
And with his arms outstretched
as he would fly,
Grasps in the comer.

Shakespeare
Troilus and Cressida

*O*n a cold December night in 1554, John de Vere, the sixteenth Earl of Oxford, steered his wife through the
crowded courtyard of Hedingham Castle. Grown men
knelt to kiss his hand, women curtsied and held out small gifts
as he made his way toward the keep.

"Earl John!" a farmer called out. "Please, save us!"

"All will be well," Earl John said. "All will be well." He glanced
back toward the gate. Hundreds more were camped out there, a
count he based on the campfires scattered across the surround-
ing hills.

Someone jostled him. He whipped around as his hand flew to
his sword. But it was just another farmer.

Earl John tightened his grip on Margery's arm and kept
walking.

A pig roasting in the courtyard bonfire reminded him of last week's hunt. He'd spent the whole day teaching his four-year-old son to hold a bow and arrow. That night a wild boar had invaded his camp—John skewered the animal with a flimsy French rapier he found on the ground. Edward, of course, was awestruck.

Would that all his problems were so easily solved.

His biggest one had come about because of Mary, damn her. He'd supported her claim to the throne, but then she announced her intention to marry the king of Spain and force a return to Catholicism. He wouldn't have it! Certainly not for the few parcels of land she said she'd return. He already owned more than a hundred tracts, a mansion in London, not to mention God knows how many castles, priories, and abbeys all over England.

Now the rebellion against Mary had exploded. Robin Dudley, a Protestant nobleman, had marked Earl John for assassination. He sighed and looked at the villagers standing about in their sheepskin coats, all of them looking to him for their salvation.

"Mr. Christmas!" he shouted to his clerk. "More food, firewood, and beer for these good folk."

Earl John waved and resumed his walk to the keep. It was up to him to preserve the Oxford name, property, and titles—a legacy that went back five hundred years. And tonight could be his last chance.

He peered up at the walls of the keep that towered eight stories high. A servant said little Edward liked to watch his father through the archers' slits. He saw a flicker of light and smiled. Good—perhaps his son had learned another lesson about how an earl treats his people.

Once the keep's massive wooden doors were bolted behind him, Earl John threw himself into a chair near the great hall's trestle table and ordered three cups of warm wine. He and Margery were sipping their drinks when her stepbrother, a Cambridge don of about fifteen, joined them. Earl John waved him into the third chair.

"Welcome, Arthur."

Arthur Golding kissed his stepsister, shook Earl John's hand—the young scholar's was clammy—and set his book on the table. Earl John picked it up: a collection of Calvin's Protestant sermons. He tossed the book back to the table and signaled to a servant, who ladled soup into bowls for the three of them and left.

Earl John got right to the point. "What did Cecil say?"

"Smith has agreed!" Arthur beamed. "He's said he'll take Edward at your convenience."

Margery looked up from her soup. "Take him where?"

Earl John glanced at his brother-in-law. "Where will they stay?"

"Smith lives in South Buckinghamshire," Arthur said.

"Good," Earl John said. "Not a Dudley for miles."

Margery's eyes moved from her husband to her stepbrother and back. "Milord, please," she said. "What's going on?"

Earl John inspected his soup as if he'd just discovered barley. After a long moment, he looked up to his wife. "We must move Edward to a safer place, so I asked your stepbrother to make inquiries about his staying in the home of Sir Thomas Smith."

"But he's only four—"

"He'll be five in a few weeks. Did we not decide to employ a tutor when he turned seven? What's two years?"

"But—"

Earl John slammed his fist on the table. "When I want your opinion I'll ask for it. Until then, be silent." He turned to Arthur. "What other news?"

"The queen's burning Protestants again. She's even exhuming

dead bodies and adding *their* bones to the fire. They also say she imprisoned Lady Elizabeth."

"Arthur, are you sure Smith's suitable for Edward?"

"Sir Thomas Smith has not only mastered law, history and Greek and Roman literature, he speaks Latin, Greek, Hebrew, Spanish, Italian, and French. At twenty-seven, he held the first chair in civil law at Cambridge. They made him vice chancellor when he was thirty, and he was so successful at it that they made him master of requests for King Edward's protector."

"King Edward's protector was a thief."

"But he bought Smith a mansion, which cost four hundred pounds. They say it overlooks the Thames and has a splendid view of Windsor Castle. On a clear day you can see St. Paul's."

"If Smith's so smart, why's he tutoring a five-year-old?"

"He *is* smart. He's not terribly . . . diplomatic."

Earl John snorted.

"Queen Mary said she was forced to fire him," Arthur said. "Though still she gave him a pension."

"How much?"

"Ten pounds a year."

"That's nothing," Earl John said. "You said Edward was too young for a Latin tutor, but he needs male company, so I'm sending Fowle as well."

Margery half-rose from her seat. "My lord—"

"Margery, *sit*."

She sat.

"Didn't I tell you to keep quiet?"

She slumped in her chair. Arthur patted her hand.

"I can't wait to see Smith's library," he said. "He has four hundred books, forty or fifty in English and the rest in Greek and Latin. History, philosophy, drama, rhetoric. He invented a new way to pronounce Greek and he's also a wordsmith. They say he's determined that England shall have a language *everyone* can speak."

"If he makes a scene, he'll call attention to Edward."

"Earl John, he's just the man to direct the education of the future Earl of Oxford. And Sir Thomas is not only a brilliant scholar, he's close to Cecil as well—the man who'll govern England once Lady Elizabeth is queen."

Earl John smiled.

"My Edward *is* a remarkable boy. Last week, he memorized all the letters of the alphabet. This week he memorized the numbers." He put down his spoon. "I'll summon Lewyn."

Arthur sat back. "Who?"

"Servant of mine. Flemish fellow. Edward took a liking to him, so I made him his companion. Christian name's William—well, not exactly Christian, I suppose. Lewyn's a Jew. Must be a hundred of them in London now, even if it *is* against the law."

Earl John called to a servant. "Bring in Lewyn." He turned back to Arthur. "I want Edward to speak French, Italian, Spanish, German, and Dutch in addition to Greek and Latin. With all the talk about routes to the Orient, languages are England's future. I also want him to speak proper English, not some bloody backwater dialect." He turned to Margery. "Lewyn will escort Edward under strict orders not to let the boy out of his sight. He'll sleep at the foot of his bed, taste his food, watch him like a hawk."

She bit her lip and nodded.

"Earl John," Arthur said, "may I accompany Edward as well? I'd like to meet Smith."

"Fine, but no one else. I don't want a crowd drawing attention to him. If someone kidnapped Edward . . ."

Margery looked up. "No guards?"

"Arthur will take a sword—that is, if he knows how to use

one—and Lewyn will carry a pistol. Arthur, I want you to dress in the clothes of a peasant. Edward, Lewyn, and Fowle, too."

"I love disguises," Arthur said.

"What's the name of Smith's estate?" Margery asked.

"Ankerwycke."

"Does he have a wife?"

"He does." Again, Arthur patted his stepsister's hand. "Why don't you write her a letter? I'll take it with me." He turned to Earl John. "Cecil says his wife brought good property to the marriage, a place he's renovating not far from here. Smith intends to move in as soon as Elizabeth's queen."

Margery looked hopeful, but Earl John shook his head.

"I don't want Edward living in Essex till Bloody Mary's off the throne. Safer that way."

A tall man of about eighteen with dark brown hair falling over his forehead stepped into the hall.

"Here's Lewyn."

Earl John watched William Lewyn stride toward the trestle table.

"God's blood, I like that boy. Nothing intimidates him, not even me." He took a sip of wine and squeezed Arthur's shoulder. "You know, I haven't thanked you enough for your efforts. I think Edward and Smith will get along just fine."

"Earl John, you don't have to thank me. Arranging the education of someone as brilliant as Edward is a privilege."

2

O wonderful, wonderful,
And most wonderful
Wonderful, and yet again
Wonderful, and after that,
Out of all hoping!

Shakespeare
As You Like It

On a cold January morning, five-year-old Edward rode toward Ankerwycke, the twenty-room brick manor house surrounded by acres of pastureland and woods owned by Sir Thomas Smith. Edward sat in the saddle in front of William Lewyn. His legs too short to reach the stirrups, he leaned against Lewyn's wiry frame to keep his balance.

"My boy," Arthur said, riding to his left, "Sir Thomas is a self-made man, something you've not experienced before."

"What's a self-made man?"

"His father was a farmer. Sir Thomas left home when he was twelve, went to Cambridge on a scholarship, took a first in everything, went to Italy, studied at the University of Padua, and when he returned he was placed in charge of Eton, the high school for young men like you. At court, people noticed him."

Thomas Fowle nudged his horse closer. Edward liked his red-headed Latin tutor, a good teacher who smiled a lot.

"Understand all that, Edward?"

"Most of it."

Fowle laughed. "You don't miss much, do you?"

"I *like* stories."

Arthur touched Edward's shoulder. "He can't pronounce the words correctly until he's heard them spoken, but he always knows the meaning."

Edward ran his fingers through his curly brown hair and straightened in the saddle. Ahead, Ankerwycke's gate was open. Earl John always said every gate must be locked.

Arthur raised his hand and the three horsemen halted.

"My boy, before you stands your home for the next few years. That river sparkling in the sun is the Thames. Across the water is Windsor, the only palace with a heating system worth the name. And downriver are the spires of St. Paul's Cathedral. When Bloody Mary no longer tortures our land, we'll visit London."

"Promise?"

Arthur smiled. "Promise."

By the time they crossed the last field, it was midday. An elderly servant who'd been taking in the sun in front of the house led them inside to a long wooden stairway. Halfway up, he stopped and turned to face Edward, who saw he was missing some teeth.

"My lord, your room's next to the one occupied by Sir Thomas's father. He's dying, so keep your voice down. A man about to meet his maker needs quiet."

"Yes, sir."

Edward quickened his pace as they passed that room. He'd seen animals die but never a person. He turned and looked for Arthur, but neither he nor Fowle were in sight. Lewyn squeezed his shoulder.

"Your uncle and Fowle are sleeping at the other end of the hall."

Edward followed the servant to his room. Lewyn unpacked his bag—which didn't take long—and handed him fresh clothes. He was washing his face when Fowle came in.

"Sir Thomas is in his laboratory, distilling medicines."

Lewyn winked, bowed, and swept the door open. He took Edward's hand, and together they followed Fowle to Sir Thomas's library.

They found Arthur already there.

"Look, my boy! Look!"

Bookcases packed with leather-bound tomes lined the walls, floor to ceiling.

Edward smiled. Upstairs he'd felt homesick but kept it to himself—Earl John said boys don't cry. This, though—this was a wonderful place. There must be a thousand stories here. And he was getting pretty good at learning to read on his own. Last night, Aesop's Fables.

"This collection is the largest I've seen outside of Oxbridge," Arthur said.

Edward looked around the room. Bookshelves were everywhere, even over the doorways and beneath the windows, and framed maps hung in the few places where there weren't any. An oak desk and a tall red leather armchair were by the window, a round table covered in books in the center of the room.

Beneath the table, on a red Turkish carpet, he spied a tabby cat and a flop-eared spaniel snuggled close as kittens. Eyes wide, the animals stared at him. He stared back. Maybe they could be his friends.

"*Fasti.*" Arthur took a red leather book from a shelf and pointed to the gold letters on the binding. "It was written by Ovid—you're going to love Ovid." He replaced the book and wandered along the shelves, Edward's hand still in his. "Plautus, Juvenal, Horace, Lucretius, Cicero, Saint Augustine . . . you'll love them all." Arthur's voice rose with excitement as he pointed to book after book. "Caesar, Chaucer, Homer, Josephus, Heliodorus, Livy, Plutarch, Seneca, Virgil, Apuleius, Castiglione!" He stopped. "I take it back. You're not going to *love* them, you're going to *need* them."

Fowle inspected the shelves on the other side of the room.

"He's got books on everything from philosophy and history to astronomy and astrology . . . angling, poetry, Welsh and Danish customs."

Arthur resumed his stroll along the shelves, Edward by his side.

"My boy, our work's cut out for us. Most of these books are in Greek and Latin, the rest in French and Italian. Few books are translated into English. It'll take years to—"

"Arthur, the printing press is only a hundred years old," Fowle said. "Give us time."

"I know, but in the meantime this young man will soak up languages like a sponge! Then he can read each work in its original language."

"It'll be fun," Edward said. Lewyn smiled, and Edward smiled back.

Fowle reached for a book. "Here's Aesop's Fables. You were reading that last night."

"I liked it a lot," Edward said.

Arthur laughed. "When I was five it was my favorite, too."

Edward's gaze moved from shelf to shelf. At Hedingham, Earl John had taught him to ride and hunt and then promised to teach him how to fence and use a spear so he could compete in the tournaments. But Edward had never seen his father read a book. "By the time you're twenty-one," Earl John had said, "you'll know everything you need to take your place in Parliament, manage our properties, and read law at the Inns of Court." He'd never mentioned this—all these stories, all these subjects, all these languages. Edward ran a hand over one of the volumes—it felt wonderful.

Arthur plucked a book from a stack on the table and opened it. Edward moved closer and saw a portrait of a man in a suit of armor.

"My boy, that's the Duke of Urbino. This is an engraving of his portrait painted by Titian, an artist who lives in Venice."

"Who was the duke?"

"I don't know much about him except he was murdered. Someone poured poison in his ear."

"Who?"

"Luigi Gonzaga."

"Why?"

"You know, I'm not sure—but we'll find out, won't we?"

He turned to the maps on the walls. Other maps lay in frames on the floor and leaned against bookshelves. More were rolled up and jammed into a wooden umbrella stand.

"Sir Thomas knows the explorers, sailors, and mathematicians who made these maps," he said. " In Windsor, there must be a hundred paintings of things explorers brought back from their voyages—animals, birds, people. When it's safe, Sir Thomas will take you to see them."

Safe. Earl John said Queen Mary was Catholic—just like him and his father. But his mother's family was Protestant. He wondered if Arthur and Fowle were Protestants, too. Were they afraid? He was about to ask when a brown-bearded man with a big nose entered the room.

"Sir Thomas," Arthur said, "please forgive us for intruding. Your servant instructed us to come here. I'm Arthur Golding, and this young man is my nephew, milord Edward de Vere."

Edward extended his hand.

"Milord," Sir Thomas said, "I regret I was unable to greet you when you arrived. I was in bed with my wife. It's that time of month." He turned to the others. "I'm determined to beget a son like this fine fellow. My efforts seem hopeless, but still we halek."

"What's halek?" Edward whispered to Fowle as soon as Sir Thomas walked to his desk.

"Later," Fowle said, his face red.

Sir Thomas looked over. "Milord, when I was provost of Eton I developed a pedagogical technique I'm eager to try out on young nobles such as yourself."

"What's a pedagogical technique?"

"A teaching technique. I want you to meet people who write and think about important matters, so they'll inspire you to write and think, too. I'll explain more about it when it's time for you to meet them. For now, let's take lunch. Tomorrow we'll begin."

*A*nd begin he did. He'd learned his numbers and he could read, but Sir Thomas taught him so much more—about the world of nature, the medicines he made in his laboratory, and all the languages Edward could imagine: French, Italian, Hebrew, Greek, Latin, English.

Sir Thomas also encouraged him to write. Edward liked the stories he was learning in Italian, so he made up one about an Italian girl and a boy his age. They liked each other, but one family was Protestant and the other Catholic, so their families were sworn enemies.

"It's hard for someone your age to write about love," Sir Thomas said. "It might go easier if you model your characters after people you know."

Writing distracted Edward from thoughts of home and his

father. On the ride from Hedingham, he hadn't been able to imagine life without him—Earl John was everywhere, even in his dreams. But Sir Thomas gave him new dreams, and little by little he was getting used to life at Ankerwycke. Still, he couldn't wait to visit Hedingham and tell Earl John everything he was learning.

"*E*dward, your first guest is about to arrive," Sir Thomas told him one morning when he was reading in the library. "Listen carefully and answer all his questions. Mr. Digges is a mathematician. If he likes you, he'll bring his grandson the next time he comes here."

The meeting must have gone well, because Mr. Digges returned the next day with his grandson, whom he called Junior. He was five years older than Edward, who was now eight, but they became friends—a rare experience for Edward. On the few occasions when a boy from some neighboring village had visited Hedingham, he'd always called Edward "milord." Junior didn't— he said Sir Thomas had told him not to.

"Edward, do you know how to skip pebbles on the water?"

"I didn't know you could do that."

"I'll show you."

They explored the bank of the Thames, skipping pebbles on the river and talking nonstop. They rode ponies Sir Thomas kept for him. One day after they returned to the stables, they threw themselves on the grass to rest while Lewyn took the horses inside.

"Last night my grandfather told me something," Junior said. "Two things, actually. He said people used to think the earth was the center of everything and the sun went around it, but a Polish astronomer in Italy—or maybe an Italian astronomer in Poland?— anyway, he said no, it's the *earth* that goes around the sun."

"Well, he was right."

"Mathematicians and astronomers said he was right and told him to put what he discovered in a book, but he refused. He said if he put it in a book, the rulers would kill him, because if the earth isn't the center of everything, then they wouldn't be as important."

"Some grownups are stupid."

"I know. Grandfather says a lot of people are, especially the ones in charge."

"What happened to the astronomer?" Edward plucked a piece of grass and chewed on it.

"He waited until he was dying, then he put his idea in a book. That way, they couldn't hurt him."

"What if people never found out he discovered the idea?"

"Grandfather said if you have courage like Copernicus, and you're lucky—"

"And die before they find out?" Edward laughed.

"Right!" Digges, laughed too. "Everything will turn out for the best."

*A*nother guest was Bartholomew Clerke, a Greek and Latin scholar Sir Thomas knew from at Eton. Bartholomew was studying at Cambridge, and Edward looked forward to his visits because he told the funniest stories. He said he got all his stories from Italy, where actors played them out right on the street.

"Edward, I'm translating some of the Italian books I brought back into Latin."

"Sir Thomas said I have to master Latin before I take my seat in Parliament, and so I can study law at the Inns of Court."

"You also have to master French. All debates in Parliament are in French."

Bartholomew's visits were a perfect opportunity to practice languages, and Edward followed him around like a puppy.

"I want to write stories someday," he said, "just like the ones you tell me."

"Is that so?" Bartholomew smiled. "And what kind of stories will you write?"

"Something funny," he said. "They don't laugh enough around here."

*E*dward's most frequent but least favorite visitor was Sir William Cecil. Sir Thomas and Cecil had been classmates at Cambridge and spoke to one another like brothers. Cecil acted like he knew everything, but he wasn't wise like Sir Thomas. Edward loved Sir Thomas. He didn't see how anyone could love Cecil.

"Edward," Sir Thomas said, "I was never able to get along with Queen Mary. But Cecil knows how to talk to her. I resent his ability to do what I can't, but I'm also in awe of him."

"How can you like and not like a man at the same time?"

"Most people have at least two sides to them. Your job is to find out on which side their heart feels most at ease."

*M*any a morning Sir Thomas woke Edward before dawn and they went hawking in the fields with Lewyn.

Sir Thomas and Lewyn would take a portable perch and several hawks to the field and attach leather leg straps and bells to the legs, tail, or neck. To keep the birds quiet, they placed a hood on the head.

"How old do they have to be before you can train them?"

"They can be taken from the nest or as fully adult haggards."

"What's a haggard?"

"A wild female hawk captured after it has plumage. We train it on a long line to fly to our glove for food, then increase the distance. When the hawk responds from a hundred yards, we know we can trust it to fly free."

"I'd like to read about it."

"Good boy." Sir Thomas beamed. "I have a copy of a treatise written by the Holy Roman Emperor Frederick II. He lived three hundred years ago, but it's still the foundation of falconry." He executed a formal bow in the direction of a bird standing all alone. "Edward, permit me to introduce you to my favorite peregrine. I call her Elizabeth."

"Why Elizabeth?"

"Because she's the one female I've never been able to tame."

*T*hat night, Edward used what he'd learned about training hawks in writing a story but applied it to a man training his wife. Usually he showed Sir Thomas whatever he'd written, but he decided to keep this story to himself. It had been inspired by Sir Thomas and his wife.

During the four years he'd lived at Ankerwycke, Sir Thomas always complained about his wife's inability to become pregnant. Fowle said it wasn't Philippa's fault, and Edward could understand that. But somehow Sir Thomas couldn't. As kind as Sir Thomas was to him, he treated Philippa as if she were a haggard.

I'm taking you on a trip," Sir Thomas announced one morning. Lewyn saddled horses for the three of them—Fowle was coming, too—and they rode toward Essex.

"Where are we going?"

"To Hill Hall, the house I'm renovating. Earl John doesn't want you to live there yet, so our visit will be brief. But you won't be afraid, will you?"

"Why would I be afraid?"

"A lot of the people Queen Mary burned lived in Essex."

Edward was quiet, but as they neared Hill Hall he looked for smoke. Once he thought he smelled burning flesh, but he never saw anyone on fire.

At last Sir Thomas pointed to a large manor house. When he dismounted there was a smile on his face.

"I'm going to need those rooms for all my future children." His smile slipped a little as he looked at Edward. "Come. Let's look round."

Sir Thomas took him to Hill Hall often after that. The best visits were in springtime, when the fields of saffron walden bathed the manor house in the glow of yellow blossoms.

*W*hen Edward was nine years old, Sir Thomas invited him and Fowle down to his library for some important news.

"Edward, Queen Mary's dying. When she leaves this world, her stepsister Elizabeth will become queen. Elizabeth's promised to appoint my friend Cecil as her chief adviser, and since Cecil promised to arrange a position for *me* at court, I have a plan for you. Fowle, pull that chair closer."

Sir Thomas leaned forward over his desk. Fowle pulled up. Edward waited.

"Both of you are going to Cambridge, which occasionally admits special children called 'impubes' who aren't required to attend classes with the older students. They take their meals in their rooms and can bring a personal tutor with them. Would you like that, Edward?"

"Yes, sir." He didn't know what life would be like at Cambridge, but he had faith in Sir Thomas. Besides, Fowle and Lewyn would be with him.

"Good. I'll write to your father for permission. As for you, Fowle, I assume you're only too pleased to return to our alma mater."

"Yes, sir!" Fowle was beaming.

"Then it's settled."

Sir Thomas beamed. Edward wanted to cheer, but he was nine years old now. He nodded and smiled.

*E*dward's time at Cambridge proved short. He and Fowle shared a room, while Lewyn lived with servants below stairs and joined them for meals. The routine was similar to that of Ankerwycke, except here there were other students.

One afternoon he heard one of them say a girl and her "fellow" had spent their time together halecking.

"What's that mean?" he asked the boy.

"Don't you know anything? Means fucking."

"Oh," Edward said. After dinner that evening, he asked Fowle about it. Fowle's face turned red, but Edward knew he'd give him an answer.

"Haleking is when a man and a woman copulate. To copulate is to make a baby."

"I know *that*. But *how?*"

"You're very curious for someone so young."

"I'm nine."

"All right." Fowle sighed. "A man and a woman make a baby when he takes his member. That's this"—Fowle gestured at his crotch—"and puts it in a hole in a woman's body near where she pees."

"And out comes a baby?"

"It takes time. Nine months, to be exact."

"Then out comes a baby?"

"Not always. Sometimes people halek and it's fun, but no baby comes."

"How do you know the difference between when it's just for fun and when a baby comes?"

"You don't, but if you want to be sure you won't get a baby, you put a venus glove over your penis."

"What's a venus glove?" Whatever it was, it sounded intriguing—but awkward, considering where it was supposed to go.

"Rich men use it mostly. I'll show you pictures—Sir Thomas has a book of them. If I recall correctly, the book contains over two dozen illustrations of the different positions a man and woman can use." For some reason, that seemed to amuse Fowle. "You can try them when you're older."

"Can I see the book?"

Fowle dragged the stepladder to a row of shelves, climbed it, selected a book from the top shelf, and climbed back down.

"This contains sketches made by an Italian painter and sculptor, Giulio Romano, who studied under Raphael." He handed Edward the book. "You remember Romano?"

"He worked for the Gonzaga dukes in Mantua." He opened the book and studied a few pictures. "Luigi Gonzaga murdered the Duke of Urbino by pouring poison in his ear." He frowned, turned the book sideways. "Is that what's happening in this picture?"

A few months later, they were in his room at Cambridge when Fowle told him Queen Mary had died.

"She said she was with child. The 'baby' turned out to be a tumor."

Sir Thomas, who was waiting in his house in Canon Row, in London, for the position Cecil had promised, wrote often.

Edward, I have good news. Your father escorted Elizabeth to London to be crowned. As Lord High Chamberlain, he held the canopy over her head at the coronation. Lady Elizabeth told Cecil she'd make him her principal secretary, so it's only a matter of time before I hear good news, too.

Every day, Edward badgered Fowle about Sir Thomas' appointment.

"I don't understand why it's taking so long. What could have happened?"

"What often happens at court, Edward. Sir Thomas made the wrong enemy. He humiliated Queen Elizabeth and she never forgot."

Edward let out a frustrated breath. "What could be so bad she wouldn't forgive him?"

Fowle sighed. "An affair. When she was young." He pushed a book across the table toward Edward. "Now, focus. I want to discuss this translation with you."

Finally, another message from Sir Thomas arrived. Edward opened it with excitement.

I'm on my way to Cambridge to collect you, Edward. The renovation of Hill Hall is complete . . .

Edward scanned the rest of the letter.

"He didn't get the appointment."

Fowle put his hand on his shoulder. "I know how sorry you must feel for him."

Edward thought for a minute. "I'm not, really," he said. "I get to go back to Hill Hall with Sir Thomas, and I'll only be thirty miles from Hedingham and Earl John."

Walking along the Cam, he heard more news. On her first tour of her realm, the new queen was going to visit Hedingham.

3

Why then,
The world's mine oyster,
Which I with sword
Will open.

Shakespeare
The Merry Wives of Windsor

*E*dward, now twelve years old, was on his way to meet the queen. As soon as he was out of sight of Hill Hall, he stuck a hawk's feather in his cap.

As they approached Hedingham, the castle looked dressed for a party—flags fluttered on the turrets, long banners hung from the walls. Servants, farmers, and villagers waved and shouted his name. He felt as if he were a king.

He'd visited Hedingham before, on May Days and for Midsummer and Twelfth Night celebrations. But today Earl John and his mother stood outside the gate waiting to welcome him—and the queen.

Edward jumped down from his horse. His mother kissed him on the cheek and dabbed her eyes. Earl John crushed him in a hug.

Even the servants looked grand. Every one of them was clad in the livery Earl John had bought last spring, Oxford blue and tawny colors with the boar's head insignia on the left shoulder.

Musicians blared sackbuts, pounded drums, blew trumpets, strummed lutes. Jugglers and acrobats formed human towers. Maidens handed out cakes and ale. He couldn't remember feeling so happy to be home. Even his stepsister Katherine smiled at him.

Mary, his eight-year-old sister, grabbed his hand and tugged him toward the Great Hall. "Father's players are rehearsing, let's watch."

He looked across the hills. The queen's caravan of three hundred wagons was just now making its way over the farthest rise. He took Mary's hand, and into the castle they went.

At once he recognized the morality play his father's men performed every Christmas. The plot wasn't original, but people said the queen loved all drama. He spotted Yorick, the actor who always played the clown in productions of *The Earl of Oxford's Men*. When he was little, he'd cling to Yorick's back while he circled the hall on his hands and knees.

"Yorick, what happened to all your hair?" he shouted. "You haven't got a strand left for me to hold on to!"

The actor gave a whoop.

"That's because you pulled it all out when I gave you piggyback rides!" He ran to Edward and gave him a bear hug.

He was wrapped in Yorick's arms when the queen entered the Great Hall.

Escorted by an entourage of way too many to count, the twenty-nine-year-old queen circled the room, turning this way and that, her green gown trailing, her curly red hair dancing.

Edward thought she was the most beautiful woman he'd ever seen.

When she reached him, she smiled. "What a handsome buck you are. You must be Edward." Her jaw tightened. I see you survived Sir Thomas' whip."

"Sir Thomas taught me well, Your Majesty. He didn't need a whip."

She smiled and touched his cheek. "And what have you learned?"

"I read books and write stories, Your Majesty. I can create English words and phrases using Greek and Latin roots, using hendiadys and the other tricks of Greek rhetoric."

She cocked her head. "Law and order," she said.

"Pomp and circumstance, Your Majesty."

"Sound and fury." She slapped her riding crop on her sleeve.

"The long and the short," he said.

"Delightful!" She beamed. "We'll resume our duet at supper. You shall sit on my right."

"Thank you, Your Majesty."

"And in the morning, unless I'm too tired, we'll go riding. Last month the doctors thought I had smallpox. Sometimes I think I'm going to fade."

"You could never fade, Your Majesty." He smiled.

"Thank you, kind young sir." She curtsied. "This morning, I felt weary. Now, not at all. She turned toward the door, curls bouncing.

As if drawn by a magnet, his eyes followed her. He could still smell her scent. Only a woman as beautiful as Elizabeth would have the nerve to wear such a heavy musk. She moved gracefully through the crowd and then stopped, turned, and stood on her toes. Was she looking for him?

The sound of music distracted him from his reverie. A young boy was playing a lute and singing a madrigal about love.

April is in my Mistress's face,

And July in her eyes hath place.

Within her bosom is September,

But in her heart a cold December.

Seated on the queen's right at the banquet, Edward gave up trying to follow the play. She kept touching his cheek and feeding him sweets.

"The last time I saw you, you were a baby," she said.

"I'm afraid I don't remember that," he said. She laughed, but his attention was caught by the string of pearls entwined in her hair. He told her how grand she looked, and she blushed.

"Edward, what are you reading?"

"Ovid's *Metamorphoses*."

"Have you read his *Art of Love*?"

"No, Your Majesty, I haven't."

"You must, even if you're too young to make love. Have you read *Fasti*?"

Before he could say he had, the lute player began another madrigal about love. The queen touched his fingers.

"Edward, you must read *Venus and Adonis* and *The Rape of Lucrece*."

"I will, I promise." He glanced down at her hand. "Right now I'm reading Cardano's *On Melancholy*."

"Everyone's talking about it. Tell me what he says."

"He writes about guilt and sadness, Your Majesty."

"I know about that." She gazed across the sea of faces in the Great Hall.

"I've met Cardano, Your Majesty. He visited Sir Thomas. He told me he worries about people who suffer from melancholy—he said they don't know if it's better to live or die, to be or not to be."

"What a dreary thought for someone as young and handsome as you." She flipped her curls and grinned at him. "Have you read Ronsard?"

"'The world's a stage'."

She took his hand.

"Sometimes I think all I do is act." She looked away until a passing servant brought more wine. Then she fed him another sweet.

"Edward, have you considered traveling to Italy when you're older?"

"Sir Thomas wants me to study at the university in Padua."

"I wish I'd gone when I was young. Promise me you'll live in Venice and when you return you'll tell me all about it."

"I will, Your Majesty. But first I want to fight for England and bring honor to my name, just as my forbears have!"

"If not for the Earl of Oxford, Richard III would never have been defeated at Bosworth Field, and I wouldn't be queen." Her expression was serious as she raised her cup of wine. "I, Elizabeth Regina, hereby promise to grant Edward, Earl of Oxford, his wish to go to battle—but not too soon. Battles are stupid and wasteful, even if the blood spilled is for me."

People in the dining hall were watching. At once, they stood and began to chant, "Oxford! Oxford! Oxford!"

When the chant was over, Earl John, seated on the queen's left, followed with a chant of his own. "To the queen! The queen! The queen!"

"Edward, you must promise to visit me in London."

"Of course, Your Majesty. I will right after I return to Sir Thomas."

The queen frowned.

*T*hat night, unable to sleep, he thrashed in bed
        "Lewyn, are you awake?"

"Now I am," he said from the other side of the room. "By the way, I heard the queen said you were the handsomest, brightest young man she'd ever met."

"She told me to read Ovid's *Art of Love*."

Lewyn howled with laughter.

"What's so funny?"

"Don't you remember the book of sketches Fowle showed you? The one by Giulio Romano with all those positions?"

"How could I forget?"

"Ovid's *Art of Love* tells you how to *perform* each position. The emperor exiled him from Rome over that."

"I want to see the book as soon as we return to Hill Hall."

"You'll have to talk to Sir Thomas." He grinned. "When the queen says she likes a lad, he'd better prepare!"

"Prepare for what?"

"For haleking."

"I'm only twelve!"

"I didn't say you'd see her tomorrow. But later . . ."

"You really think she meant *me*?"

"She wasn't talking about the clown."

"You've got her wrong, Lewyn. She said she banned women from the Cambridge and Oxford residence halls because women distract men from their learning."

"Now do you understand why people say she's fickle?"

Edward lay back and thought. Earl John had said the queen was twenty-nine, but there was something childlike about her. He also said that after King Henry executed her mother, she lived in isolation with her governess. Only now was she coming alive.

Maybe it was as Sir Thomas said, that most people had two

sides to them. If that was true, which one had he met tonight—and which one would he meet next?

*H*e was about to depart from Hedingham when Earl John summoned him to his study, a large room with a deer's head hanging over the fireplace and a stuffed boar standing on a heavy table. The bookshelves were full, but the books looked dusty.

Earl John was seated at his desk holding two documents, fingering the red ribbons that fastened the pages together and rubbing the red wax seals beside his signatures.

"Dudley'll soon be here, Edward. The queen wants me to make peace with him." Earl John pulled a chair next to his. "Sit here. My lawyers told me to make a will. I want to explain it since mostly it's about you."

He sat next to his father. They hadn't been this close since Earl John taught him to kill boars.

"I won't bother you with the details. I take care of your mother, sisters, uncles, and leave everything else to you. One hundred sixteen parcels and enough income for you and for them, as well as everyone living on the properties. You'll have two thousand pounds of income a year, and by the time I die—which let's hope won't be for years—there'll be more."

"Thank you, Father."

"The document's endless, but the thrust of it is, if I die before you reach twenty-one, you and the property will be under the control of the queen. That's the law. But she'll turn you and the property over to William Cecil, her principal secretary and master of wards."

"I know Cecil." Edward made a face. "He's tedious."

"He'll take care of the cash and two-thirds of the land and buildings until you're twenty-one. The queen will give the rest to

Dudley to hold until you're of age. She and Dudley are lovers, but that's neither here nor there. By the time I die, you'll be old enough to inherit everything without Cecil or Dudley getting their hands on any of it."

Edward glanced at the stuffed boar on the table.

"As I said, the queen wants me to befriend Dudley. I agreed because if something happens to me before you're of age, I don't want him bothering you. I've also completed a contract of marriage for you. When you're twenty-one, you'll marry one of the Hastings girls—Mary or Elizabeth, whichever one you choose. Your sister Mary told me you liked them."

"I hadn't thought about it."

"Treat it as something to take care of later. Their family's good as ours. As for the rest of my will, I appoint you executor of my estate. By the time I die, you'll have read law and will understand everything."

*E*dward returned to Hill Hall. A few weeks later he was studying in his room after lunch on a hot August afternoon when the elderly servant who'd welcomed him to Ankerwycke eight years before knocked on his door and entered. He seemed upset.

"Is everything all right, Robert?"

"Yes, it is, milord. With me. And thank you for asking." He paused. "Sir Thomas wishes you to come to his study."

*A*s usual, the dog and the cat were asleep under the table when Edward entered the library. Sir Thomas put down his pen, dragged a chair next to his, and walked over and put his arm around Edward's shoulders. Edward could count on one hand the number of times Sir Thomas had embraced him.

"A messenger from Hedingham just brought word." Sir Thomas cleared his throat. "No one's sure of the cause, but . . . I'm so sorry to tell you, Edward—Earl John is dead."

The study was suddenly stifling.

"I . . . that can't be right," Edward said. "We just . . ."

"There's a rumor he was poisoned."

"No!" he shouted. "Earl John's too clever for that!"

"Try to be strong, son. I know how hard this is."

"He *can't* be dead!" He struggled to lower his voice. "When's the inquest? I want to be there."

"The queen's advisers say an inquest is unnecessary." Sir Thomas looked away for a moment and then turned back to Edward. "The funeral will take place as soon as you return to Hedingham."

"Everybody loves Earl John." Edward's voice dropped to a whisper. "Everybody."

"No one gets through life without making a few enemies." Sir Thomas rested a hand briefly on his shoulder. "I suggest you go to your room and rest. We'll meet at five, drink sherry, talk."

Edward was vaguely aware of being steered toward the door.

"I don't drink sherry."

"I can't think of a better time to start."

*H*e felt as if someone had thrown him into a river and he didn't know how to swim. Sir Thomas had told him to rest, but he couldn't even close his eyes.

He stared at the books on his desk. One was open. Had he been reading it? He couldn't remember. He stared at the ceiling for hours.

Eventually he got up, descended the stairway as if he were sleepwalking, knocked on the door to the study, and stepped inside.

The dog licked his hand. Edward reached down to scratch its ears. The cat rubbed against his legs and purred.

Sir Thomas filled two goblets with sherry.

"You must return to Hedingham," he said. "You're the Earl of Oxford now. You won't be able to stay, of course—you'll go to London, live in Cecil House."

The sherry burned Edward's throat.

"Cecil's house is a veritable dormitory for young nobles." Sir Thomas glared into his sherry. "They lose their fathers, Cecil gains wealth and power."

"It's so hard to believe," Edward said. "Earl John . . . dead."

Were those tears in Sir Thomas' eyes?

"Edward." He blinked. "If I had a son, I'd want him to be you."

Edward hadn't—he wouldn't—allow himself to cry. Earl John had said boys don't cry.

"Thank you."

"Now, I must prepare you for Cecil. You'll be under his control and it won't be easy."

"May I have more sherry?"

Sir Thomas filled his goblet. "I tutored Cecil at Cambridge, but he taught *me* things I'd never have learned on my own."

Edward tried to pay attention. He couldn't. Instead he studied the elm tree outside the window. The leaves didn't move. No breeze today.

"The balance sheets for Cecil's marriages are better than mine," Sir Thomas said. "His first, to the daughter of our favorite professor, opened doors for him. His second, to the daughter of the famous Cooke, was even more helpful. His wife, Mildred, is the most brilliant woman in England, after the queen. I also respect Cecil's audacity—it was his advice that caused your father to send you to Ankerwycke."

"Why won't there be an inquest?" His voice was loud again, but he didn't care.

"In a moment," Sir Thomas said. "First, I must tell you about Cecil. My madness is obvious. His isn't. And neither is he harmless."

"What does *that* mean?"

"Cecil is my friend, but his loyalty is to himself."

"Isn't that true of everyone?"

"Perhaps, but he's deceptive and sanctimonious. Beware."

"I will. Why won't there be an inquest?" He pushed his goblet toward Sir Thomas, who paused before he refilled it.

"Easy, Edward. Sherry has a way of biting you in the arse."

"Like Cecil."

He smiled. "Never lose your sense of humor—it'll get you through life's rough patches. Now, a few principles. For Cecil, there's no such thing as education for its own sake. He thinks a young noble's mind must be focused on serving the crown and protecting his property. He's going to train you to perform like a puppet. You're about to enter combat."

"Sir?"

"A mind like yours comes along once in a hundred years. To limit you to administering laws, however important, and dealing with property, no matter how vast, is a waste. *All* issues must be *your* issues."

"How can that be when I'm under Cecil's thumb?"

"He can't control your thoughts," he said. "Neither can he stop you from writing. Eventually you'll leave his house to study at Cambridge and Oxford and read law at Gray's Inn. A renaissance is sweeping Italy and France, but it hardly touches our shores. You must go abroad and bring back what you learn.

"Study languages and street life, new and old writing, food and music, military affairs and customs, the best and worst of whatever passes for culture. My year in Padua was the most important of my life, but *your* time there should be longer. Do you remember when Bartholomew Clerke spoke of a manuscript—*The Courtier*, by Baldassare Castiglione?"

"Yes, sir."

"It describes the matters every courtier must master to educate his sovereign. My hope is you'll produce a work of similar import for England. Let Cecil clutch his copy of Cicero's *De Officiis*. Your perspective must move *beyond* duty. One day, *you* may advise the queen."

"It seems there's an awful lot for me to do." He was trying to take in what Sir Thomas was telling him, but he still felt numb.

"Continue your study of Greek and Roman drama, politics and rhetoric. When Cecil objects, don't fight him. He's too powerful—work around him. And when the time comes, write anonymously. That's what noblemen do."

He drained his goblet and refilled it. Edward sat sipping and thinking as Sir Thomas continued.

"And be careful of the queen, Edward."

"What? Why?"

"She's precocious and brilliant, but she's unstable. Considering what happened to her mother, that's understandable. Nevertheless, be careful. More dangerous to you is the fact that Robin Dudley's room adjoins the queen's. They have other lovers, but their relationship endures. I wish she'd marry him and ensure a stable succession, but she refuses. In any case, watch out for Dudley."

"My father tried to make peace with him."

"Dudley wasn't interested in peace. Earl John had more land and money than Dudley, the queen, and Cecil combined. Now *you'll* be Dudley's target, and don't expect Cecil and the queen to help you. They're in awe of Dudley's venality."

"I'm not worried," Edward said. "The queen likes me."

"Of course she does. You're a likable fellow and she adores men, especially the young ones. Maybe she fantasizes you're the child she never had. Who knows? To understand her requires more skill than I possess, and God knows I've tried."

"I'll never be able to handle all three of them."

"I didn't tell you to *handle* them." Sir Thomas gave him a sharp look. "I told you to *watch out*. And remember, no man wins by being outspoken. Look where that got me."

"But I *want* to be like you."

Sir Thomas astonished him with a kiss on the forehead. "I'm not the best model. Be like Cecil—no one can deal with the snakes at court better than another snake."

Edward felt as if he'd fallen into a pit. "You don't give me much hope."

"I'm sorry." Sir Thomas looked across the field and then faced him. "Never stop studying. A life of the mind is the only life worth living. *Write,* and watch the outrage fly from your soul."

"I don't know if I can. This is . . ." He closed his eyes. "This is too much sadness to write out."

After a long moment he opened his eyes. His grief would have to wait.

"Sir Thomas, what about the inquest?"

"The inquest will take care of itself. Now, one more thing. A month ago, your father signed a contract of marriage for you to wed one of the Hastings girls. He wrote me the property aspects were attractive and thought it was a fait accompli. But don't expect Cecil to honor it—he has a daughter of his own."

He hated his new life already.

"I know how you feel, Edward, and after Earl John arranged it all so well. But when he appointed Dudley a trustee of your lands, he put a fox in charge of the henhouse."

Edward looked straight at Sir Thomas. "Dudley killed my father, didn't he."

"Poison *is* his preferred method." Sir Thomas sighed. "Someday maybe you can speak out. But not now—it's far too dangerous."

"I feel so . . . lost."

"Then let me offer you one ray of hope. Eight years ago, when I lost my position at court, I thought my life was over—until an amazing five-year-old boy came into my life." He smiled. "Edward, hope has many fathers. One day it can fly in on swallow's wings."

PART TWO

Sir William Cecil

4

We know what we are,
but we know not
What we may be.

Shakespeare
Hamlet, Prince of Denmark

*A*ccompanied by his uncle Arthur, Thomas Fowle, and
William Lewyn, twelve-year-old Edward still felt alone.
Earl John's death weighed on him like a stone.

Behind him rode 140 Earl of Oxford servants, villagers, and
farmers in two long columns. The blue and tawny colors seemed
more somber now, the boar's head shoulder insignia less cheer-
ful. Each man wore a black sash and armband.

At the funeral he suffered a new wound. As his father's body
was lowered into the grave, his mother leaned on Charlie
Tyrrell, Earl John's administrator. His sisters were worse.
His stepsister Katherine, who was married and lived nearby,
refused to visit. His sister Mary refused to even admit Earl
John was dead.

"Father went away," she said. "And mother took a trip."

The villagers were restless, agitated.

"Tell them their lives will go on as before," Arthur said.

My God—these harvests are the worst in memory. How can I tell them everything will be all right?

Edward turned in his saddle. All escorts were in the Strand, and Arthur was pointing to Cecil House. Four turrets and a dozen statues decorated the walls. The gardens were lavish. He tried to study the plants, but he felt as if his brain were wrapped in fog.

He shook his head and took another look. Now he understood what Sir Thomas meant when he said Cecil was nouveau riche. Fishponds and gaudy statuary were scattered all over the lawn. Across the street from Cecil House was a mansion once owned by Lord Somerset, and next to the old Savoy Hospital was an apartment house for the well-to-do. The law courts, Whitehall, and Westminster were all within walking distance. The Strand was too valuable for the poor.

England's economy was dead, but the people were well-dressed. Protestants in the Netherlands and France flocked to London for employment and safety. On his way there he'd seen former Catholic churches with their stained glass windows whitewashed, and he knew stolen Communion chalices now graced the tables of the rich. All trace of the old religion had been extinguished, and these once-colorful houses of worship were now puritanically drab.

He'd been shocked at such desecration but knew he was fortunate. Though Earl John was Catholic, he hadn't supported Bloody Mary, for reasons of faith, and his Protestant mother limited her devotion to making sure he said his prayers. Sir Thomas had taught him that religion was an intellectual exercise, and now he understood.

A light rain began to fall. He handed the reins of his horse to a Cecil House valet and watched servants lug his bags of books inside. Cecil's library was the best in England, but Sir Thomas said having one's own books in one's room was an advantage. His servants unfastened the saddlebags of sherry Sir Thomas had given him as a going-away present. The elixir worked like magic when sleep eluded him.

The rain began to pelt, and still Cecil failed to appear. Arthur refused to let him dismount.

"Protocol demands he greet you personally. Your superior rank requires no less."

Edward thought it absurd, but he waited. Surely life was more important than pomp. If it were it up to him, he'd march up and pound on the door.

Sometimes his loss hurt so much he could touch it. His father seemed to be everywhere he turned. Sometimes he swore he could smell Earl John's sweat after a day's hunt.

"No sign of plague here." Fowle ran his fingers through his soaking red hair.

"My boy," Arthur said, "we should never have come here. Cecil was wrong to insist."

"Did you see those slums outside the city walls?" Lewyn said. "My uncle in Antwerp told me they're a breeding ground for sickness."

Edward frowned. "So why doesn't the queen build proper homes for the poor?"

"Because her clerks *say* the land can't support more wells." Arthur shrugged. "I think they don't want more poor folks in the city, but what do I know? I'm just a scholar who translates religious texts."

"Why do they lock the gates of the city every night? Who would want to enter a plague-ridden city?"

"It's not about keeping people *out*. It's about keeping people *in*. Folks in the country don't want city people to bring their disease."

Edward looked across the street. Behind the grand buildings was the Thames. And Arthur said Ivy Lane, at the corner, ran down to a boat stop where wherries picked up passengers. If he had his way, he'd escape right now.

At last the front door opened and two liveried servants emerged. One invited him and his companions to enter, and the other said Sir William Cecil was engaged in matters involving the queen.

Edward ordered his men to deliver the sherry to his room and then entered Cecil House and followed the servant up the staircase. Fowle was staying the night and then going on to Cambridge to become a Protestant minister. Arthur and Lewyn would remain with Edward.

"Milord," the servant said, "Sir William requests that you meet him in the library after you've settled."

Edward and Arthur followed the servant to Cecil's library. Five times the size of Sir Thomas', it was furnished with upholstered chairs and Turkish carpets. The bookshelves were said to hold two thousand books and manuscripts. A gallery with a ladder on wheels made the books accessible. Arthur stood there, staring up, hands clasped as if in prayer.

A huge desk commanded the room. A fire blazed in the fireplace and framed maps hung where the walls weren't covered by shelves. The servant invited them to sit in the two chairs facing the desk and said Sir William would be with them shortly.

Cecil entered a few minutes later. In his mid-forties, he leaned on a cane with a silver handle. His black beard and thick head of hair were flecked with gray. His black robe, in the style popular in Puritan London, didn't hide his large belly.

"Milord," he said with a smile, "welcome to London."

"Thank you, Sir William. This is my uncle, Arthur Golding." Arthur bowed.

"Welcome, Arthur." Cecil's voice reverberated as if he were

delivering a sermon. He patted Edward's back and limped to the high-back leather chair behind the desk and sat with a groan. Sir Thomas had told Edward that Cecil suffered from gout.

"Milord, I hope your journey wasn't too wearing," Cecil said.

"It was wet." He knew his tone was curt but didn't care. He was chilled and soaked to the bone.

"Milord, I've some matters to bring to your attention. Under the law of guardian and ward, when a lord of the realm such as your dear father dies leaving an underage son, the queen may give one-third of his property temporarily to whomever she chooses."

"My father told me."

"Her Majesty is giving that third of your land to Robin Dudley."

Edward sat up straight and looked directly into Cecil's eyes for the first time. "Can she really do that?"

"Yes, but only until you're twenty-one. She also has the right to sell her power to make decisions concerning your marriage. But in your case, I think Her Majesty will make that decision herself. Questions?"

Yes, but he'd think first and speak later.

"Good!" Cecil clapped his hands. "Then let us proceed to matters which, I assure you, are important for the maintenance of good order. I know the sumptuary rules are not respected in the countryside, but now you live in the capital, where such rules are strictly enforced."

Edward slumped. "What sort of rules?"

"First, clothing. You possess more than twenty pounds per year of income, so you may wear satin doublets but not satin robes. You also possess more than a hundred pounds per year of income and you may wear velvet but only in doublets and outerwear, and neither crimson nor blue. Those colors are reserved for knights of the Garter and nobles of similar rank. I intend to nominate you for election but only when the time is right. Clear?"

"Clear." His brows drew together—*this* was essential for the maintenance of order?

"I will leave for another occasion the rules pertaining to other fabrics and to the issue of pleats. Instead I shall issue a word of caution: under no circumstances may you wear a hat. *Caps* are made in England, *hats* are not. To encourage consumption of locally made products, Parliament requires that everyone wear a cap."

"I'm so glad you've told me," he said. "I should hate to have worn a hat by mistake." If this were a play, the audience would be rolling in the aisles.

Cecil was smiling, but Edward was certain he wasn't amused.

"Milord, you may ask why I deliver an exposition on matters that appear trivial."

"I *was* wondering."

"As the seventeenth Earl of Oxford, you are England's premier nobleman. Your title dates back to the birth of our nation. In England's firmament, no one else is the seventeenth of *anything*. What you do and say are subjects of study and emulation. Need I say more?"

"I think I've quite a clear understanding."

"Now then, let's move on to the rules pertaining to food. If your income were ten pounds a year you'd be limited to two courses per meal plus soup, but owing to your generous income, you may dine without limit."

To think that the queen did nothing without first consulting this man.

"As for fish—"

"Fish?"

"Yes, milord. I have no doubt you are acquainted with the fact that since Henry VIII, no one may eat fish on Friday without risking three months in prison. Our church will agree to treat veal, chicken, or any other fowl as fish, but only for a fee."

"How accommodating."

"Now then, the plague. Milord, the plague is rampant in London. Every year there are more deaths than births. London's geographical area is only two miles from north to south, traversable by foot in less than an hour, and you may be tempted to flee. But do not—I repeat, do *not*. Avoid crowds. Follow the law. Set an example. You're the Earl of Oxford. Never forget."

"I won't."

"Good, good. Now, I've not yet had the opportunity to make an inventory of your lands. At this time, I should like to ask your uncle if he would do that. Arthur, will you oblige?"

"Of course, Sir William."

"I'd also like you to collect all rents due Edward and deposit them in his account. Will you oblige me in that regard as well— for a generous fee from Edward's account?"

"I'd be happy to."

"Good, good."

Edward smiled. Finally, Arthur was being paid for his efforts. Earl John had given him precious little. As the youngest of eleven children from the poor side of the Golding family, twenty-two-year-old Arthur hadn't a shilling to his name. He had to give Cecil some credit.

"Now then, Earl John owned more than a hundred parcels of land running into the thousands of acres and containing numerous structures of varying sizes and purposes—"

"My father told me."

"Did he also tell you to expect two thousand pounds a year in income from those lands even after expenses?"

"Yes, but is the two thousand before or after Dudley's third is subtracted?"

"Good question, milord. I'll investigate and advise. Now, I suggest we move to a less agreeable matter. My informants advise that your stepsister Katherine intends to challenge your right to inherit Earl John's titles and property."

Edward's temples began to throb. He felt as if he'd been in this meeting for hours. "On what grounds?"

"Bigamy. She claims your father's marriage to your mother was invalid because he was already married to *her* mother. Earl John neglected to have that marriage annulled before he wed your mother."

"Is her claim valid? Can she prevail?"

"Her claim *is* valid, and ordinarily she *would* prevail, but in your case she won't. When I informed Her Majesty, I persuaded her to declare your stepsister's claim against the interests of the Crown. As soon as your stepsister files suit, the queen will file a notice to quash, and the matter will be closed."

Again, Edward was impressed. Was there anything Cecil didn't know? "The queen has that power?" he said.

"She controls *all* matters relating to young nobles."

"But why, if the claim's well-founded?"

"Because it's not in her interest that a matter relating to your father when *he* was young be brought to the attention of the public. When the *queen* was young she also, shall we say, sowed wild oats. Since your sister's claim might resurrect memories of her majesty's indiscretions, she *will* quash that claim." Cecil pulled himself to his feet. "Milord, I suggest we take lunch. I'm famished. You must be, too."

Edward followed him out, deep in thought. Sir Thomas had said he must be careful. He was being protected, but only because the queen's needs mirrored his. From now on he'd consider the short term but would always base his decisions on the long term.

5

*O, what men dare do! What man may do! What men
daily do, not know what they do!*

Shakespeare
Much Ado About Nothing

"Milord, may I introduce you to Lady Cecil?" Arthur
said. "Mildred, this is Edward de Vere, the seventeenth Earl of Oxford. And this young man here is
Thomas Nowell, your new tutor."

Edward bowed to Lady Cecil and shook Nowell's hand as a
waiter entered the dining room with a carafe of sherry and crystal glasses.

"Nowell's leading our search for Anglo-Saxon manuscripts,"
Arthur said. "He discovered *Saxo Grammaticus*, the foundation of
our nation's literature, and is translating it from the Old English."

Now, this sounds interesting. "Please, tell me a little about your
work with this manuscript," Edward said.

"Milord, the manuscript reveals a fascinating character, Prince
Amleth of Denmark. His oath to avenge his father's murder is as
powerful a statement as I've read."

"Sadly, I can't read Old English."

Nowell smiled. "Then tomorrow you shall begin learning."

"Dear," Lady Cecil said, "I know how much you were looking forward to surprising Edward, but Her Majesty's clerk just sent her regrets. She won't be visiting us, I'm afraid."

"Is she unwell?" Cecil said.

"The note didn't say."

Cecil speared an oyster on the half-shell with his two-pronged silver fork and devoured it.

Edward smiled at the very thin Lady Cecil.

"Thank you for inviting the queen. I should have loved to see her," he said. Then he turned his attention to Cecil. "I was wondering about the maps in your library. Sir Thomas says maps are the key to England's future."

Cecil chuckled. "I know all about Thomas' dreams." He picked up another oyster. "I also know such voyages are courageous and satisfy our need for trade. But stealing Spanish gold erodes moral fiber and in time will lead to war with Spain."

"Does the queen agree?" Arthur said. "If I may be so bold."

"No, but Her Majesty and I agree to disagree. Piracy is piracy in my book, even if it's funded by the queen."

"Sir William." Arthur wiped his lips. "Edward's tutor, Bartholomew Clerke, asked him to underwrite a translation of Castiglione's *The Courtier* and to write a preface in Latin."

"At twelve?" Lady Cecil laughed.

Edward poked at an oyster.

"Thomas Bedingfield *also* asked Edward to be his patron." Arthur was glowing. "Bedingfield's translating Cardano's *On Melancholy*. And Geoffrey Gates as well—he wrote an important work, *On Defense of the Militarie Profession*."

"Now *that's* more like it," Cecil said, "though neither Her Majesty nor I wish to encourage talk of war. England can ill afford to waste its blood and gold."

"Then you'll be pleased to know Edward agreed to be patron of Anthony Munday's *The Mirror of Mutabilitie.*"

"From the sacred scriptures?" Lady Cecil practically swooned. "Edward, how wise you are! But if you patronize so many books, what funds will be left for *you?*"

"Two thousand pounds a year is more than enough for my needs as well as the needs of a few scholars." He was losing patience. Cecil and his sumptuary laws, Lady Cecil and her *funds.* Shopkeepers, both of them.

"And what a deep voice you have! You could give a speech in Parliament!" Lady Cecil smiled at him and turned to Arthur. "Have you completed your translation of John Calvin's sermons? I've been waiting for that."

"Thank you for asking, Lady Cecil, but now I'm translating Aretino's *Wars Between the Goths.*" Arthur turned to Cecil. "If I may, Sir William, I'd like to dedicate it to you."

"How kind of you."

"I'm also translating Justine's *Tragus Pompeius,* but I'm dedicating that to Edward. In return he's agreed to translate Ovid's *Metamorphoses* into English."

"*Edward's* translating *Ovid?*" Lady Cecil smothered a giggle. "Surely you jest."

Arthur took a big sip of wine and let out a small sigh. "I know Ovid's treatment of love is risqué, Lady Cecil, but I can't do it myself. Besides, Edward's humor is more subtle than mine."

Cecil looked from Edward to Arthur. "Is that . . . appropriate, for someone of his tender years?"

"He has the maturity."

Edward suppressed a smile, and the table fell silent as waiters took away oyster shells and served stuffed mushrooms.

"Of course," Cecil said, "I don't see how I could permit the Earl of Oxford's name to appear on a book, especially *that* book, even as the translator."

"I couldn't agree more." Arthur was grinning. "It *is* impossible for someone of his position. Nevertheless, the work is important for England's scholarship and should be translated. So I'm putting *my* name on it."

Cecil laughed. "Who'd believe that?"

"What they believe is immaterial. My name will be on the cover, Edward's will not, and Ovid's work will see the light of day in English."

Cecil rubbed his beard. "Clever." He shrugged. "I suppose it couldn't hurt."

"Thank you, Sir William." Arthur glanced at Fowle. "Now, while Edward's moral development has been carefully supervised by Mr. Fowle, Sir Thomas, and myself, Fowle leaves tomorrow morning for Cambridge to complete his studies for the Protestant ministry."

"Well done, you." Lady Cecil was purring again.

Fowle blushed.

Edward studied Cecil. The man had already downed a fourth glass of wine and the waiter was filling a fifth.

"Splendid," Cecil said. "That reminds me—I've not had a moment to tell you, but Sir Thomas will also be moving on. Her Majesty agreed to appoint him ambassador to France. It's a far cry from educating a remarkable young man, but just as important."

Edward smiled. When he left Hill Hall, Sir Thomas had seemed so forlorn. "That's wonderful news," he said. "I've often thought the queen has been overly harsh towards Sir Thomas."

Cecil was squirming. Edward knew the queen's affair was not a subject for comment—even a nobleman could lose his head for it.

"Edward," he said, "what are you reading now?"

"Last night I was much taken by Ronsard. Are you familiar with his work?"

"As a matter of fact, I'm not." Cecil signaled for more mushrooms. "But I know how much Sir Thomas loves his Frenchmen."

"It's not yet published. Sir Thomas lent me his copy. Here's a passage:

> *The world's a theatre and mankind the players,*
> *And fortune, who is mistress of the stage,*
> *Lends costumes and Heaven and Destiny*
> *Are the great spectators of human life;*
> *With differing gestures and in different tongues,*
> *Kings, princes and shepherds play their parts*
> *Before the eyes of all, on the common boards."*

"Poetry," Cecil said. "I haven't time for it."

"Have you tried writing lines of your own, Edward?" Lady Cecil said.

"I have, especially since my father's death." Edward turned to Cecil. "I've found poetry to be a great catharsis."

"Would you care to recite something you wrote?"

"With pleasure. I call it *Loss of Good Name.*

> *Fram'd in the front of forlorn hope past all recovery I stayless*
> *stand,*
> *to abide the shock of shame and infamy."*

He paused. "I was feeling rather sad that day. Melancholy isn't always cured by stiffening one's upper lip."

"Please go on." Lady Cecil gave him a pleading look.

"Very well, but just a few lines. I hadn't intended to perform.

Help Gods, help saints, help sprites and powers that in the heaven do dwell.

Help ye that are aye wont to wail, ye howling hounds of hell;

Help man, help beasts, help birds and worms, that on the earth do toil,

Help echo that in air doth flee, shrill voices to resound,

To wail this loss of my good name."

The room fell silent. Even the sound of Cecil's fork was stilled.

"Sir William," Edward said, "thank you for convincing the queen to quash my stepsister's suit."

"To be honest, it was the queen's idea." He gave Edward an appraising look. "But now, *I* have a thought to share with *you.* I appreciate that Sir Thomas's Frenchmen can make a strong impression on a young man's mind. I also know poetry can be a comfort—and it's certainly all the rage at court. Nevertheless, you must focus on serious work. Poetry simply isn't—"

The door to the dining room opened, and in walked a little girl of about five, holding the hand of her governess.

"Anne," Cecil said. "Please, come here, child. I have someone for you to meet."

"Yes, Papa." The girl walked over to Cecil and stood between her father and Edward.

"Anne, this is Edward."

She shot a quick glance at her mother, who nodded. The girl curtsied. "How do you do, milord?"

"How do you do?" The way she looked to her mother reminded him of his sister Mary—as did the way she avoided her father's gaze.

"Anne, you may go now," Cecil said.

"Yes, Papa." She curtsied, took the governess's hand, and left.

"Lewyn," Cecil said, "I understand you speak Hebrew. My wife and I take the view a literate Protestant must read the Bible in the language in which it was written. Would you be so kind as to tutor Anne in Hebrew?"

Edward flushed. All those languages he'd learned, and he'd never once thought to ask Lewyn if he spoke Hebrew. He must learn that language as well.

"I'd be delighted to, Sir William."

"I'm sure we can agree on the appropriate compensation. You'll still be required to sleep below stairs, of course."

Lewyn glanced at Edward, who nodded. Lewyn shouldn't remain bound by his long-ago promise to Earl John not to let Edward out of his sight.

Cecil turned to Arthur. "I'd like you to prepare a schedule of study for Edward's time here, before he moves on to Cambridge and Oxford."

"Actually, Sir William, I've already taken the liberty of doing that." He extracted a sheet of parchment from his pocket and handed it to Cecil.

"I'll review it tonight," Cecil said, "and we'll go over my revisions in the morning. I intend to add strenuous training in Protestant worship and Scripture study. Edward must read a different Epistle and Gospel in French *and* Latin every Sunday. I'm sure you agree, Mildred?"

"Of course, dear."

"Now, you must excuse me." Cecil tossed his napkin onto the table and stood. "Emissaries from Russia have arrived to press their case for the czar's marrying the queen." He sighed. "They don't speak proper French or English, just stand there chattering away amongst themselves. Of course, she'll never marry him, but our wool industry needs markets and it's cold in Russia. I'll make small talk until they leave."

Back in the library, Edward had wondered how he could endure nine years of Cecil. Now he was wondering how much he could learn just by sitting at his table.

"Edward?"

"Yes, Sir William?"

"I was too hasty. Your poem about the loss of good name was well-written." For just a moment, the man seemed to soften. "Sir Thomas said your mind was a sponge, and I can see how impressive is the breadth of your interests. Write your poems. Observe your theater. Study your Ronsard. You're brilliant enough to do all of it and still administer Her Majesty's realm." Cecil turned to Fowle.

"You and Arthur, and my dear friend Smith, did a fine job with Edward. On behalf of the queen, I thank you. I shall continue whatever pension Earl John paid you—how much was it?"

"Ten pounds a year. And thank you, Sir William."

"Don't mention it. The de Vere estate will cover it for the foreseeable future."

Edward looked at Cecil and smiled. Smooth. No wonder the queen valued him.

"I'm pleased you feel that way about his poetry," Arthur said, "because I have *more* exciting news. Edward's working on a larger poem he calls *Romeus and Juliet*. It's based on something he wrote in Italian about young lovers who reject the authority of their parents and friends."

Cecil sighed but looked amused. "You'll be the death of me, Edward. Of course, he can't publish under his name. He's England's premier nobleman."

"I know." Arthur was grinning again. "For this one, Edward has invented a pen name."

"Which is?" Lady Cecil sat back in her chair.

"Arthur Brooke," Edward said.

"I know several," Cecil said. "Which Arthur Brooke?"

Edward made ready for some fun. "Sir William, the more apt question is: *what* is Arthur Brooke? What's another word for *ox*?"

"I don't have time for games." Cecil looked grumpy.

But Lady Cecil wanted to play. "Ruther."

"Exactly, Lady Cecil. Now, repeat *ruther* several times, quickly."

"Ruther, ruther, ruther." She giggled.

"Notice when you said *ruther* a few times, you heard *Arthur*, not ruther".

"Oh—so I did!" She giggled again.

"So, from Arthur we have *ruther*, which means 'ox.' Presto, we have the *ox* in Oxford. Now, let me ask *you*, Sir William—what do you do when you cross a brook?"

"I *ford* it." Cecil was warming to the game.

"So there you have it. With *Arthur* we have the ox. With *Brooke* we have something for *ford*."

"Stretching things a bit, aren't you?"

"Of course, but that's what word games do. And it *is* amusing, isn't it? If the author can't be Oxford, Arthur Brooke will have to do."

The door swung open and four waiters entered carrying platters of chicken. Cecil rubbed his hands.

"The Russians will have to wait. Fun always gives me an appetite."

Edward tucked in his napkin. "It all smells delicious I'm eating more today than I ever have."

"I can't wait to read your *Romeus and Juliet*," Lady Cecil said.

"I'll send you a copy when it's ready," Arthur said. "Meanwhile, I'll give you a copy of another poem he's published—"

"*Published?*" Cecil paused, drumstick in midair. "When did he do *that*?"

"Two years ago."

"When he was *ten*?" Lady Cecil gave Edward an adoring look, followed by a wink.

"As you now realize," Arthur said, "Edward *is* remarkable."

Edward helped himself to more chicken. Their admiration, at least, was something he could get used to.

"I'll say." Nowell studied Edward. "Milord, what's the subject of *that* poem?"

"Just a minute." Cecil put down his drumstick, minus a large bite. "Arthur, I assume you did *not* publish that one under Edward's name. What name *did* you use?"

"For Edward's first published poem, entitled *Ovid's Tale of Narcissus*, we used *T.H.*—the initials of the printer, Thomas Howell."

Lady Cecil chimed in. "I assume, Edward, your poem uses material from Ovid's *Metamorphoses*, the large work you're translating with the help of your uncle?"

"Correct, Lady Cecil. My *Narcissus* is only a hundred and ninety-two lines, mostly in pentameter."

"It's a fine piece of work." Arthur's pride was obvious. "He used the less risqué material—as you observed, he *was* only ten when he wrote it."

Cecil wiped his fingers, laid his napkin aside, and rose. "I simply must see to those Russians. We can't have Ivan the Terrible declaring war on England because I became enchanted with pen names. Arthur, do be careful. Edward *is* our premier and the Lord High Chamberlain of England."

Edward rolled his eyes. "I will, Sir William."

Cecil was hauling his body out of his chair when the door opened to admit a messenger in the queen's livery, who handed him a red leather pouch with trailing red silk ribbons. He ripped off the seal and read. "God's shoulders."

"What's wrong, dear?" Lady Cecil said. "You're white as a sheet."

"Elizabeth has smallpox."

The room went silent. Lady Cecil hid her face in her hands.

Edward felt sick. Smallpox? The queen? He thought of her lovely face, her smile.

Cecil grabbed his cane and lumbered toward the door.

"Dear? Be careful. Don't go near."

"Yes, Mildred."

*T*he sound of his cane echoed down the hall as Lady Cecil spoke.

"Only yesterday the queen observed that the plague was subsiding, deaths in London down to fewer than fifty a week. Poor Elizabeth—she's not yet thirty."

"Poor England," Arthur said, "with no clear succession."

"Arthur!" She rose to her feet. "You know it's forbidden to refer to the succession."

She turned to Edward and forced a smile. "I know I speak for Sir William when I say how much we enjoyed learning about your writing. We look forward to many happy years in our home."

"Thank you, Lady Cecil." He paused but decided to risk it. "But what *will* happen if the queen—"

"Edward, please! *Any* comment on succession is forbidden on penalty of *death*. I beg you. Say nothing."

"But I—"

"Edward, dear." Her smile slipped. "No buts."

As she swept from the room, Arthur, Nowell, Fowle, and Lewyn gathered around him. Arthur placed a hand on his shoulder.

"Don't worry. The queen's indestructible."

"On the other hand," Nowell said as he glanced around, "her death could be followed by civil war. Life in England could become a hell on earth."

Arthur steered Edward to the door. "We've all had too much wine to talk about this sensibly. I'm going to take a nap. I suggest you do the same."

Edward felt a tug on his sleeve. It was Nowell. He motioned him back into the dining room, now empty of guests, and shut the door.

"Milord, I thought you'd like to know about that little scene with Anne."

"Cecil's daughter?"

"Milord, she's going to be your bride. Just an intimate ceremony of a thousand in Westminster Abbey, with the queen—assuming she's still with us—in attendance."

Just as Sir Thomas had warned him.

"How can you be sure—"

"Milord, this is indispensable for Cecil. He's not a nobleman, and *you're* the premier earl of England. If Anne is to marry you, the queen *must* elevate Cecil's status. She'll make him an earl or a baron." He sighed. "I'm afraid it's unavoidable."

"But my father already made a contract for me."

"Sorry, milord. When it comes to the queen's ward, she can do whatever she wishes." He lowered his voice. "And if you're having trouble keeping up with Sir William, don't berate yourself. Even with a cane, he's two steps ahead." Nowell opened the door and stepped into the hall. "Now, when shall we begin to translate *Saxo Grammaticus*? I can't wait to introduce you to Amleth. He reminds me of you, you know."

෴

*T*hat night, a note from Arthur was slipped under the door of his room.

Tomorrow morning at eight, Sir William wishes us to meet him in the library. Bring Lewyn. If the last few weeks taught us anything, we may need a witness.

At eight, he appeared in Cecil's library, Lewyn and Arthur in tow. Cecil soon joined them.

"I've revised Arthur's tutoring plan." Cecil sat down and placed his cane at his side. "Pardon my tardiness—I just received word of the queen's condition."

"How is she?" Edward said.

"No change, but I'll tell her you inquired." Cecil pulled Arthur's schedule from his pocket. "I suggest you commence earlier than eight. Begin at seven, with an hour of dancing. Smith never acquired social skills, and he paid dearly."

"Dancing?"

"Her Majesty loves to dance." Cecil dabbed his eyes, studied the ceiling, and took a deep breath. "Poor Elizabeth. Where were we?"

"Dancing at seven?"

"Just so. After breakfast you'll resume your studies in French, followed by an hour of Latin and a half-hour of writing and drawing. You've demonstrated a facility for writing, so exercise in penmanship is important—in italics as well as secretary script."

Edward smiled. "Just so." The old boy either didn't mind or didn't notice the mimicry.

"After lunch, you'll rest. Arthur, your memo proposed cosmography at one. Smith believes mapping the heavens and earth is indispensable, and so do I. Likewise the study of astronomy, geography, and geology. After all, this *is* the sixteenth century.

"I noticed you added another hour of Latin at two and another hour of French at three. I agree. While his day is long, he shall also have another session of exercise with the pen at four."

"Thank you, Sir William," Edward said.

"I thought that might please you. This isn't too strenuous, is it?"

"I already write two hours every morning beginning at five, and two every night before I retire." He shrugged. "I don't need much sleep."

"Then I trust you'll not object that I added another item. Each evening before supper, Lady Cecil and I insist he spend an hour in prayer. We think he should focus on the Epistles and the Gospels in English, Latin, French, and Greek."

"I've studied the Epistles in the Greek," Edward said. "Sir Thomas saw to that."

Cecil's lips tightened. "I didn't expect otherwise, milord, though I dare say Sir Thomas' purpose was to master the Greek *language,* not religion."

"I dare say."

"Now then, most of your free time will be devoted to horsemanship. The queen requires a young companion to ride with her every day. Dudley maintains three hundred horses for that purpose and you'll be invited often." Cecil handed the memorandum to Arthur, who scanned it.

"You added *shooting, more dancing, walking, other commendable exercises, and additional time for prayer.*"

"Quite."

"A rather full day."

"He's swimming in deep waters. Lady Cecil was tutored by Roger Ascham, as was the queen. We can't have him educated at the appalling level that prevails in our grammar schools."

A knock on the door was followed by the entry of a blackrobed clerk carrying a leather pouch. A document poked out, ribbons hanging.

"Surveillance report from Paris, Sir William. Your son's in trouble again."

Cecil sighed. "You may go, Harold."

"Very good, sir." The clerk backed out of the room.

"Excuse me." Cecil grabbed his cane and limped out of the room, slamming the door behind him. They caught a few muted, angry words.

Arthur shook his head. "He employs three spies just to follow his first wife's son."

The door opened. Cecil limped back to his chair. "Your suspicion was well-founded, Edward. Your income *will* be reduced by the third of your lands transferred to Dudley." He sighed. "One of the properties in that third is Hedingham Castle."

Edward fought to keep his voice calm. "He'll account for the rents when my lands and castle are returned to me, yes?"

"Yes, but heirs seldom come out ahead." Cecil shook his head. "Your father's desk will be transported here, but that's all I was able to do."

*A*fter the meeting, Edward went to his room and stared out the window overlooking the Strand. He was now to live under the thumb of the most complicated man he'd ever met—stimulating, yes, but controlling. God only knew what would happen if he didn't adhere to his *schedule*—a schedule that seemed built around a queen who might not survive. To top it off, he was to be married eventually to a mouse of a girl, and the man who murdered his father was living fat in Earl John's keep.

He filled a tumbler with sherry, drank it, filled it again. He pulled a piece of parchment out of his pocket and glanced at a poem he'd been working on:

. . . like a woeful witch I wove the web of woe
The more I would weave out my cares, the more
they seemed to grow . . .

One thing was clear. He *had* to write.

6

Youth, the more it is wasted,
the sooner it wears.

Shakespeare
Henry IV, Part I

*A*t Cambridge, Edward found himself surrounded by foppish young men who seemed to think they'd live forever. He was only fourteen but determined to treat every night as the death of each day—he never forgot that Earl John had died in the pink of health.

The frenetic regimen wasn't new to him. At Cecil House, he'd followed Cecil's schedule like a dog chasing his tail—until the day Lady Cecil gave birth to a baby with a humped, crooked back.

The tragedy plunged the household into a state of perpetual gloom. Even if little Robert could walk, doctors said, his gait would be hobbled. So rather than carry out his Cambridge studies at Cecil House, Edward decided to live on campus. Anything to escape the constant sadness and the confines of Cecil's house. He still had to follow a schedule, but at least here he had a chance to think, to dream, to write without constant interference.

His day began when the bell struck 4 a.m. After private prayers and mass, he joined the others in the hall for lectures that continued nonstop, aside from a break for meals, until early afternoon, which was free for recreation. Edward's favorite was archery, practiced on the field between the college and the River Cam.

Lectures resumed at three, followed by supper at five. On feast days he stayed with the other students to sing, talk, or play cards—dicing and gambling were forbidden—and then returned to his room to study. He seized every opportunity to separate himself from the others so he could write and explore his own ideas.

At times he missed Cecil House. He'd shared a suite of rooms with Ned Manners, the newest ward there. Until Ned, he'd not had a best friend—Arthur and Lewyn were as close as he'd come. When he'd made ready to leave Cecil House, he asked Ned to join him, along with his older cousin Tom Howard. As the three rode down the Roman road to Cambridge and approached the River Cam, Edward sucked in a deep breath of free air. It was good to be gone.

He couldn't wait to see King's College Chapel. A hundred years old, it was a place where things were changing. Erasmus, Europe's leading scholar, had studied there before he produced a New Testament to replace the Latin Vulgate Bible. At last people were eliminating superficial ritual and expressing attitudes of the heart. Edward naturally thought of how this might spill over to matters other than worship. If he could escape the confining rules of rhyme and write in free verse, his stories would be more real, express more depth of feeling. A whole new world of communication might ensue.

On his first night at St. John's, he toasted his freedom with Manners and Howard in their living room.

"When Nowell told Cecil he was returning to research," Edward said, "he said he was leaving because he'd 'done all he could do with me.'"

They all laughed.

"Let me guess," Manners said. "Cecil decided you were a lazy lout?"

Howard snorted. "Isn't he?"

"Of course not," Manners said. "Cecil had to know he was joking. I heard him brag that Edward's mind expands in direct proportion to his schedule."

"Here we go again," Howard said. "Basking in the glow of Edward's brilliance."

Edward grinned. "Jealous, are you?"

"No, just annoyed."

"Don't be offended, Edward," Manners said, "but you do have a tendency to inflate."

Edward rolled his eyes. "Thank you, Manners. As always, your conciliation is appreciated."

"I know. That's why Cecil insisted I accompany you to Cambridge."

"As my good angel to fire out the bad?"

"Exactly." He smiled. "When I commence the practice of law, I'll send you an invoice."

"Don't overdo," Edward said, "lest I kill you off with all the other lawyers." He took a swig of sherry. "Starting with my sister Katherine's."

"Ah, here we go." Howard refilled their glasses.

"Did I tell you how I plan to retaliate? I'm writing my own version of *King John* in which a bastard dominates the play. I'm also transforming my *Romeus and Juliet* into a play of similar name. At first I thought I'd model the friar after Nowell, but he's really a blend of Nowell and Sir Thomas. As the queen says, 'Two for the price of one.'"

"Name-dropper." Howard drained his sherry and poured himself another.

"Gentlemen," Edward said, "four years from today—if Cecil doesn't force me to marry his daughter—I shall confirm my father's contract and wed Mary Hastings." He leaned back and closed his eyes. "I can picture it—her shapely form, her lips . . ."

"Cecil's webs don't break," Manners said. "Besides, Mary Hastings is too tall for you."

"I find being short an advantage. My deep voice makes more of an impression that way." He was quite warm now, basking in the glow of freedom and sherry. "Did you know Mary Hastings' father, the Earl of Huntingdon, is next in line to the throne by virtue of his descent from Richard III? If I wed Mary, our son could be king."

"Any more bedtime stories?" Howard said.

"But it's *true*."

Just then Edward glanced out the window and saw Arthur galloping toward their building. "What's *he* doing here?"

"*I*'m parched, Edward. Something to drink, please." Arthur collapsed in one of the soft chairs as Edward poured water for him. "My boy, I bring good news. Not only has the queen returned to health, she quashed your stepsister's lawsuit."

Manners pounded him on the back.

"To Arthur." Edward raised his glass. "For bringing such good tidings."

"Thank you, my boy. Since our translation of Ovid wasn't back from the printer, here's a copy of my translation of *The Abridgement of the Histories of Tragus Pompeius* as a souvenir of the occasion. I dedicated it to you."

He embraced his uncle.

"Now, if only I didn't have to marry Nan, everything would be perfect."

"Edward, I implore you. That's a long way off. Accept your fate and go quietly."

"But Nan's like a sister to me!" He shuddered. "Marrying her feels like incest—they can force me to marry her, but I'll never sleep with her."

*T*he queen arrived in Cambridge on August 5, accompanied by an entourage that included Robin Dudley. He now possessed one-third of Edward's holdings and was thus worthy of being elevated to the nobility, so the queen had appointed him Earl of Leicester.

To celebrate the Cambridge graduation of two knights, one doctor of divinity, and nine nobles including Edward, a ceremony in the chapel led by Cecil as chancellor of the university was followed by a play presented in Latin. The next day featured a debate on the superiority of a monarchy to a republic followed by a play, *Dido*. But before the last event, an anti-Catholic play, the queen claimed fatigue and the performance was canceled.

In the morning she made ready to leave. Undeterred, undergraduates followed her to the outskirts of Cambridge, pleading to entertain her one more time. The queen relented, and that night they performed an impromptu lampoon of Catholic bishops being held in jail. Actors paraded onstage carrying a lamb they ate as they walked, but when they fed a live dog sacramental Catholic wafers, the queen leaped to her feet.

"Didn't I issue a proclamation outlawing discussion of religion and politics on stage?"

Edward's eyes were fixed on her. Her reddish hair seemed on fire. She wore a new kind of cosmetic that made her complexion look like cream. She was slim, athletic, everything a woman should be.

Nevertheless, he felt as if her presence here was hypocritical—she'd issued a decree forbidding women from setting foot on the campuses of Cambridge and Oxford. He said as much to Manners.

"Edward, did you ever consider that maybe the queen doesn't think of herself as a woman?"

"What else could she possibly see herself as?"

Manners grinned. "A hermaphrodite?"

"That's absurd! The queen's *not*—"

"She swears she'll never marry."

"And how do you know she'll keep that vow?"

*T*he next morning, before anyone was up and about, a message was slipped under his door. The queen wanted to ride with him—she'd be at the stables in an hour. They'd never ridden together before.

When he reached the stable, she was waiting, two horses saddled. Soon they were splashing across the River Cam and then cantering across the field.

She said nothing, and he followed her lead. It was rather pleasant, simply enjoying her company.

At last, she signaled that she wanted to rest. He jumped from his horse, extended his hands, and her supple body slid through his arms until her feet touched the ground.

Then, her face directly in front of his, he saw why she wore that new paste—to cover the small scars and pockmarks left by her bout with smallpox.

He felt a wave of pity. She was still attractive, but she'd been so beautiful. And vain—how she must be suffering! Even now tears streaked the paste and made craters of their own.

"I didn't want you to see me this way, but I so much wanted to ride with you, Edward. It's been too long. I've missed you."

"And I've missed you, Your Majesty."

She smiled—no more tears. "You've been busy studying."

"I hear you've been busy as well, Your Majesty."

They laughed.

He spread his doublet and they sat on the grass close together. She was wearing a light-green riding costume that set off that glorious reddish hair. He worried that her costume would be stained, but she didn't seem to care.

"This is the first time I've gone riding since the pox." She lay back on the grass. He knew what he wanted to do but he didn't dare.

Silence engulfed them except for the sounds of birds. But it was enough. They listened.

"Your Majesty, may I ask for your help? I'm troubled."

"Of course you may. You have only to ask."

"Sir William insists I marry his daughter Anne when I reach my majority." He paused. "It's not for seven years, but I can't get it out of my mind. I don't want to marry, I want to write."

"Do both. A man can do whatever he wants."

"But she's . . . so childlike. Her parents control her utterly. They make her that way, she'll never be different. Wouldn't it be better if I didn't have to violate my marriage vows?"

"*Better*? You're a *man*. A woman obeys her husband, but men needn't extend the same courtesy. Just look at my father."

Edward kept quiet. Her father had executed her mother so he could marry someone else!

"No man is perfect," she said, "nor need he be. My father was a good king, but did you know he was also an artist? He composed songs. Now let's talk about something more important." She sat up. "When are you going to Italy? If you're going to write, you must. To drink, one must go to the well."

"Cecil insists I marry and produce an heir first. Only after that will he consider Italy. Even then he says he's worried about my being captured en route and held for ransom."

"You'd be protected by your entourage. I'll speak with him."

"Thank you, Your Majesty."

She got to her feet.

"They'll be wondering about me. This was fun. We must do it again."

He helped her mount her horse. *No, Your Majesty, it wasn't fun.* He'd enjoyed her, but she'd made it clear he was indeed doomed to marry Nan. The queen held the lever—all he could do was bend.

*T*wo years passed. Edward was sixteen now and preparing for another graduation, this time from Oxford. He often daydreamed about the queen, but today he wondered what she'd think of the musical play he'd written for the graduation ceremony.

The first of his plays to be performed, it was to accompany the award of honorary M.A. degrees to seven nobles: himself, two knights, two government officials, and Cecil. Edward had again chosen to live at the university—anything was preferable to living in a household with crippled Robert, puppet Nan, and the controlling Cecils.

Neither Manners nor Howard had gone to Oxford with him. During his two years here, Richard Edwards was his companion, and together they'd produced the play—Edward writing the dialogue, Richard the music.

Cecil had appointed the much older Richard to be director of the Children of the Chapel Royal. The mild-mannered musician had simply appeared at Oxford and sought Edward out.

"Sir William informed me his brilliant ward–you—intend to

write a play," Richard said. "He asked if I'd co-author a musical with you for the graduation celebrations."

In addition to his talent as a musician, Richard was full of advice about theater.

"The Oxford venues are enclosed, like the ones at court. I suggest we use a lute rather than the blaring trumpets used in outdoor productions." He paused. "And I suggest we take our plot from Chaucer's *Knight's Tale.*"

"Please, go on."

"Palamon and Arcite, two cousins who are prisoners of war of Theseus of Athens, fall in love with Emilia, Theseus' sister-in-law. Arcite is banished. Palamon escapes from jail with the aid of the jailer's daughter, who loves him. Theseus learns of the rivalry of the two kinsmen, decides to hold a tournament at which the victor will win Emilia and the loser will be executed. Arcite wins the tournament but dies in a riding accident. Palamon and Emilia, now free to marry, live happily ever after. We can call it *The Two Noble Kinsmen.*"

"*Palamon and Arcite* would be better for the Oxford crowd."

Richard's smile came quick. "Well, you'd know best, wouldn't you?"

*A*s soon as the applause died down from the queen's entrance, the two-part play began. But just as the last actor made his entrance onto the makeshift stage, there came a deafening crack—then another, and another.

Edward, seated next to the queen, was frozen in horror for a moment. The stage collapsed in pieces—first the supports and then the floor, plank by plank. Actors fell through the gaps, some shrieking as planks fell on them or they fell on jagged pieces.

He leaped to his feet and moved toward the stage. There was

blood everywhere, limbs twisted, faces contorted. Three were dead, five injured. He was devastated.

After the casualties were taken away, he and Richard sat with the queen.

"Edward," Richard said, "the show must go on."

He buried his face in his hands. "I don't see how."

"Substitute actors and another venue," Richard said. "That's the tradition. The show must go on."

"I know how you feel, Edward," the queen said. "But Richard's right."

*W*hile rehearsing with new actors, Edward heard shouts. He ran to the window and saw two frenzied hounds barking, fighting. Two drunken undergraduates hung out the window, cheering the dogs on—then one leaned out too far. His friend made a wild grab, and both students tumbled out the window and to the ground.

With their broken bodies still in the dirt, again the queen insisted the play go on.

That night, tense and worried, Edward attended the performance. When the curtain finally fell, he was exhausted, but Richard was ebullient.

"Edward, your first play's a success! Your characters don't just say lines—they think and feel!" Richard threw his arms around him and kissed him on the forehead. "What an achievement!"

They were on stage, behind the curtain. He felt the warmth of the older man and realized it was the first time anyone had truly hugged him since Earl John. He was still in Richard's arms when the curtain was drawn back.

"Make way for the queen!"

Richard dropped to his knees, kissed the queen's hand, and

backed off the stage. The actors also stepped back. But Edward was rooted to the spot as the queen rushed to him and kissed him on the lips.

He grasped her hand and kissed it as Cecil came up behind her. He didn't say anything, and the actors dispersed.

"Congratulations, Edward," the queen said. "I loved your play."

"Thank you, Your Majesty. You remember my colleague, Richard Edwards, the director of the Children of Chapel Royal." He turned, but Richard was gone. "I don't know where—"

"That's all right, Edward." She smiled at him. "I *adore* your lyrics. So many new phrases! You must lie awake nights thinking them up."

"When I'm not thinking about Your Majesty."

Cecil coughed. Neither the queen nor Edward took notice.

"What phrase did you invent last night?"

"*Play fast-and-loose.*"

"Who, me?" She laughed.

Edward felt his face flush. "No, Your Majesty." He grinned. "Never *you.*"

"The next time you invent a phrase, I'd like you to send it to me by courier."

"I'll be happy to."

"I loved your altering each actor's speech to match his character. I've never seen *that* done."

"I'm pleased I could show you something you haven't seen before."

She blushed. "And blank verse—how sophisticated! And quite courageous, rejecting conventions."

"No one ever called me courageous."

"Well, you are." She turned serious. "I do have a few suggestions. You use too many terms from your days at Cambridge. You can't expect an outside audience to understand them."

"What terms?"

"I knew it! You weren't even aware you used them." She laughed and shook her curls. "Now, *I* liked the terms. I'm simply suggesting you consider whether a word or phrase will be understood by those members of the public who haven't attended Cambridge—which, let me assure you, will comprise most of them."

"For example?"

"You referred to a 'study where he keeps.' Anyone can understand *study*, but *keeps*? You and I know that's where a Cambridge student can be *found*, but how many others will?"

"Very true, Your Majesty," Cecil said.

Again they both paid no attention to him.

"I don't know where your talent will take you, but I *do* know it will be a long and fruitful journey." For a moment, the queen looked proud—which for some reason made him uneasy. "Therefore, always consider how you'll be understood by the broadest number of people. The audience in England is small now, but it will grow. One day we may even have public theaters."

He'd dreamed of that—a public theater, where everyone would see his work, not just courtiers and scholars. "I don't know what to say."

"Aha! Then I, too, accomplished something today—I reduced England's most promising playwright and poet to speechlessness."

Cecil chuckled. The queen took Edward's hand and kissed the palm.

A page carrying a red leather message case approached the queen and dropped to one knee. "Your Majesty. Urgent. From London."

She removed the message from the case, read it, nodded. "I must return to London at once." She gave Edward a last, brilliant smile, and as she walked off the stage with Cecil tagging after her, she perched her right hand on her rear—leaving Edward alone on the stage, wondering if queens ever did that. So far as he knew, village girls didn't do that.

But the queen liked his play! If people didn't know how students spoke at Cambridge, let them learn.

That night, the scent of her musk haunted his dreams.

A few months later as he prepared for his first day of reading law at Gray's Inn, he received bad news: Richard had died of the plague. They hadn't worked together since Oxford, but he felt his passing deeply.

7

If you can look into the seeds of time,
And say which grain will grow and which will not,
Speak then to me.

Shakespeare
Macbeth

Ned Baynam, apprenticed to Cecil's tailor, was taking measurements for Cecil's new robe. Edward sat nearby, reading.

"Care for a bit of fencing?" Ned said one August afternoon.

Edward glanced outside—it was only seven, plenty of light left. He put down his law book and outside they went.

They were just beginning when out of the blue—just as Edward lunged—someone ran into the courtyard and charged between them.

The intruder, Cecil's undercook, screamed as the point of Edward's rapier thrust deep into his thigh.

The bleeding was profuse. Neither Edward nor Ned could stop it.

"God's blood!" Edward yelled back toward the house. "Somebody call a damned doctor!"

By midnight, the undercook—Tom Brincknell—was dead. He was the father of a three-year-old, and his wife was pregnant.

"This is serious, Edward," Cecil said. "You require the services of a lawyer."

"It was an accident!" Edward paced the study. "You heard Baynam. It wasn't intentional and I wasn't careless—Brincknell was drunk and ran between us! It could just as easily have been Baynam's weapon that struck him."

"Nevertheless, you were armed and he wasn't. Follow your lawyer's advice and plead self-defense. Don't leave it to a jury. The penalty's too grim." Cecil leaned forward, hands pressed together. "I beg you, be reasonable. In just a few years you'll be married—"

"Nan's lovely, Sir William, but she's too silent for my taste."

Considering that Nan's parents kept her in a constant state of intimidation, her reticence was understandable, but he couldn't say *that*. Over the last seven years, Cecil had become like a father to him. He was still controlling, manipulative, preoccupied with money, but Earl John's death had left a gaping hole, and in many ways Cecil filled it.

Edward sighed. "All right," he said. "I'll get a lawyer."

*W*aiting for Cecil to return with the verdict, he paced the small attic room. The official in charge of the inquest required his confinement to the third floor of Cecil House. He was writing—nothing could keep him from that—but he was bored and the August heat was oppressive.

As he paced he took care to step around the stacks of books. He needed to finish reading the ones on the bed, copy the portions he'd underlined into his journal, and read the ones on the floor. But worry over the inquest sapped his energy.

Writing was still his most reliable friend. In fact, except for Ned Manners, writing was his only friend. The two new Cecil wards—stupid Sheffield and lazy Eddie Zouch—didn't compare to Ovid, Petrarch, Plato, and Chaucer.

He opened the shutters, planted his hands on the windowsill, and leaned out. Behind the houses across the street flowed the Thames. If he could jump to John Gerard's garden and make it across the street, he'd hire a wherry, row to the south bank, buy a horse, and head for Dover. He'd be across the channel before anyone even knew he was gone—

Ridiculous. He'd never survive a leap from such a height. Even if he did, he'd be a cripple like Robert.

He rolled up the sleeves of his doublet and let the sun bake his face and hands. His gaze drifted across the river to the Cardinal's Hat and the brothels of Southwark. He shrugged, walked to his bed, lay down—and heard footsteps.

He sat up and turned to the door. At last this melodrama was about to end.

He'd never denied that his rapier struck Cecil's undercook, but Baynam had also testified that the incident was Bricknell's fault. No, he didn't like Bricknell, who'd lurked nearby whenever he talked to Nan, but why should that matter?

The footsteps grew louder. Edward got to his feet. Cecil wore slippers because of his gout, but these footsteps weren't padded. God knows it wasn't his fault. He hated violence. Earl John was the one who took pride in the family's descent from warlike Vikings.

If only Bricknell hadn't been drunk . . . Knees shaking, he stared so hard at the door he could almost see soldiers on the other side. The hinges creaked. He took a deep breath.

The door swung open and there was Arthur, holding a sack. Without a word, his uncle crossed the room, shoved aside the paper, pens and pot of ink that servants brought every day, and placed the sack on the desk.

"My boy, I present to you the galleys of your translation of Ovid's *Metamorphoses.*"

"I thought you said you needed to rest."

"The inquest does disturb my sleep, but when Seres sent me a note the proofs for the first volume were ready, it seemed like a message from God, so I ran to his print shop and here we are." Arthur flung his arms wide in the black robes that hung on his skinny frame. He looked like a scarecrow.

"Take my chair, uncle. You don't look well."

Arthur sat. Edward took a seat on a wooden bench and faced him.

"My boy, I want you to promise me you won't get into something like this fencing fiasco again. I know it was an accident, but sometimes . . . you're like a volcano, dormant one moment, explosive the next."

"I promise I'll only fence in closed rooms so no drunk under-cooks can throw themselves on my sword."

They laughed and laughed. God, what a relief—he couldn't even remember the last time he'd laughed.

Arthur picked up the title page. "The ink's still wet—be careful. The challenge is to correct a printer's errors in setting type as well as our errors of content."

Edward wondered what process he'd follow to edit galleys. Not that he was going to change anything. As Arthur continued to leaf through the pile, the aroma of ink filled the room, masking the faint stench of garbage wafting up from the Thames. Except for the queen's perfume, Edward thought he'd never smelled anything as sweet.

Arthur reached the bottom of the pile.

"It's all here, my boy." He closed his eyes. "Lord, thank you for giving Edward the wisdom to do Your work."

Edward raised a brow as Arthur remained still, eyes closed, waiting. Finally he sighed and opened his eyes.

"Very well," he said. "You don't pray, but you do know your Ovid. Let's get to work." He handed Edward the title page. "*Metamorphoses.*"

Edward read. "*My soul would sing of metamorphoses, but since, O gods, you were the source of these bodies becoming other bodies, breathe your breath into—my book of changes—*'"

"'*And may the song I sing,*'" Arthur continued, "'*be seamless as its way weaves from the world's beginning to our day.*'" He looked up. "You did such a splendid job. The words are beautiful."

"*We* did a splendid job, uncle. You *and* I."

"No, my boy, this translation is yours, though I must say you took more license than you should have. But after a few corrections, all will be well."

"It's finished, Arthur. I won't change a word."

"Do you forget my name's on the manuscript? I'm the one who has to face the critics."

"Arthur, it's not my fault Cecil insisted you put your name on the cover."

Edward stuck his thumbs in his vest, lifted his chin, stuck out his belly, and peered down his nose. "*Edward, never forget you're the Seventeenth Earl of Oxford and Lord High Chamberlain of England. The taint of commerce must never sully your noble name.*'"

They both laughed at his imitation.

"He *does* worship a nobleman's status too much," Arthur said.

"He's too damned eager to condemn me to anonymity."

"England's mores condemn you, not Cecil. But class is the cement that binds us. Consider my lot. *I* have to face the wolves of academia. You can't possibly know how vicious they can be, but surely you understand the risk to me."

Arthur leafed through the manuscript until he found the page he was looking for. "See here, you invented words."

"What of it?"

"You can't do that."

"I know what I wrote, and—"

"That's just the point, my boy. You didn't write it, you translated it." He looked down. "Is this how you show respect for our precious Publius Ovidius Naso? *In a land where corsies whewl, where orpid buggs sty awkly in the queach, where froshes yesk, and flackering pookes*—'" Arthur put down the page. "How can I defend *that* against the backbiters of Oxford and Cambridge?"

"You said if I enhanced meaning I could take liberties."

"Take *liberties*, not take advantage. Edward, no writer wrote more salacious material than Ovid. His *Art of Love* is—well, let's just say you can't add your excesses to his."

Edward looked at his uncle and sighed. "Forgive me. I *do* understand the risk you're taking. I also know your translations of the Geneva Bible and the works of Chaucer and Plutarch are classics. I'll take another look at the manuscript."

"Thank you, Edward. My colleagues resent the income I receive collecting your rents. The slightest mistake will bring them down on my head." He patted his shoulder. "I know you're a good boy. I'll never forget the day Oxford awarded you a master of arts— proudest moment of my life."

"And in the presence of the queen."

"And we can't embarrass her."

"I showed her every racy passage. She laughed."

"You're two of a kind. Audacious and outspoken." Arthur dug in his pocket and extracted a folded sheet of parchment.

"Which reminds me. I was making an accounting of your rents. Rummaging in Cecil's files, I came across this."

He poured himself a glass of the sherry servants smuggled to the attic—Arthur rarely drank wine or beer—and scanned the paper.

"What did you find that's so shocking?"

"According to Cecil's appraiser, the value of your lands the queen gave Dudley is 809 pounds, nine shillings, and eight pence, including 178 pounds in *increased* rents. Now, the queen admitted she gave him a bit *more* than the one-third she was entitled to, so if the amount of *income* accruing plus the value of the lands themselves are projected over the nine-year period until you're twenty-one, they'll owe you over seven thousand pounds."

"I hope I can get all that back from them."

"You'll be up against Cecil, Dudley, *and* the queen—a skilled lawyer, a skilled talker, and a polished thief. But that's your money in their pockets."

Edward realized his jaw was clenched. He also realized he'd forgotten about the inquest for the past few minutes and asked his uncle about it.

"My boy, I'll never understand why Cecil permitted an inquest. He could've made this go away with the snap of his fingers. I think he wants to make you feel obligated—pretend to work a miracle on your behalf, then take credit for it."

"Cecil told me Parliament's always looking over his shoulder. He said he's afraid of them and that's why the matter couldn't be dropped."

"Afraid? That man has ice in his veins." Arthur brightened. "You know, you deserve a gift to commemorate your first book. What would you like?"

"You don't need to give me gifts. It's enough God gave you to me as my mentor."

"You, thanking God?" Arthur faked a swoon.

"But you're right about the inquest. I've no peace of mind."

"The queen's also worried, though I told her what happened, why you weren't to blame for what happened to Brincknell. She saw it my way." Arthur grasped his shoulder. "You're ready to move from translating to creating. Last time, we talked about your writing a long poem or another play. Visit Ovid, he's a gold mine of plots. And Chaucer's a bottomless pit for characters. What about writing your version of *Troilus and Cressida?*"

"Base something I write on someone else's work?"

"If someone objects, remind him that using another author's characters or plots proves you know how to read."

Edward laughed. Then he began to make notes. "*Troilus and Cressida. Titus Andronicus.*"

"And *Pericles,*" Arthur said.

"What about *Coriolanus?*"

"And *Antony and Cleopatra.*"

"Don't forget *Julius Caesar,*" Edward said. "Plutarch is filled with information and opinions."

"Exactly." Arthur glanced at the books on the floor and the bed. "I daresay this room contains enough material for a hundred plays. The queen will want to present all of them at court. Printers will clamor to publish them, producers will beg to stage them—"

"So what? I can never use my name." He sighed. "I want recognition, Arthur. What writer doesn't?"

"Don't be glum, Edward. Who knows? Maybe the queen will help you. Now, where were we? Oh, yes, take a look at Boccaccio."

"*Boccaccio for characters,*" he noted.

"And Dante. And Petrarch."

"*Dante and Petrarch.*"

Arthur smiled. "On second thought, let Cecil take all the time he wants for his inquest. As the queen observed, isolation can be an opportunity."

"This morning I felt so melancholy I considered jumping out that window and rowing to freedom."

"Don't even think about it! You could have broken your neck, you know."

They were quiet for a moment.

"So when are you going to Italy?" Arthur said.

"Cecil says it's too risky. Someone could take me hostage."

"Cecil's only interested in your marrying Nan and producing a grandchild. If he continues to oppose your trip, remind the queen Chaucer traveled. She'll melt."

"I know she wants me to go. She said so."

"Then be patient. You're always in such a rush."

"I thought I'd write a long poem about the rape of Lucrece. People expelled a king whose son raped Lucrece—I want to write about the abuse of power. I also want to write a long poem about the love affair of Venus and Adonis."

"Love and death. What else is there?"

He laughed. So did Arthur.

They were still laughing when Cecil entered the room.

8

"How hast thou purchased this experience?"
"By my penny of observation."

Shakespeare
Love's Labour's Lost

lack robe billowing, Cecil swept into the attic room and walked straight to the window, where he stared out at the Thames as if he'd never seen it.

Edward glanced at the door. No soldiers—a good sign?

Cecil turned and faced him.

"You're free."

"Thank you, Sir William!" He kissed Cecil on both cheeks. Cecil patted him on the back. Behind Cecil, Arthur winked.

"However did you manage it?" Arthur said.

"I don't take kindly to questions of technique." Cecil sat at Edward's desk and placed his elbows on galley proofs. "But I will tell you the verdict was *felo-de-se,* which, as you know is Latin for putting an end to one's own existence, in this case running on the point of a rapier. In a word, the jury found Brincknell committed suicide."

Arthur smothered a smile.

"The ways of the law are wondrous indeed."

"Spare me your sarcasm. Now I'd like a word with Edward—in private."

"Of course. But if you please, I gave Edward a list of books. Would you be so kind as to ask your clerk to purchase them?"

Cecil studied the list: Plato, Tully, Cicero, books in French.

"Is this all?"

Deadpan, Arthur said, "I'm fairly sure Edward has sufficient funds."

Edward's turn to swallow a smile. He owned more land than anyone in England, and thanks to Arthur, all rents were up to date. Of course, Cecil was always ready to spend it. The more of a ward's funds he spent, the greater his commission. Yesterday, a mountain of extravagant items he hadn't asked for had been delivered to the attic, from doublets of cambric, leather, canvas, and black satin to ten pairs of Italian leather shoes to God knows what they were but they were silk and there were a dozen of them.

*T*he inquest was . . . challenging," Cecil said once Arthur had left.

"If you hadn't ordered Brincknell to spy on me—"

"I'll ignore that impertinence."

"Don't ignore it, *do* something about it! I won't tolerate surveillance."

"I'll try to be less . . . thorough."

"I'll take that as a promise."

"More important," Cecil said, "Nan's reputation could have been ruined. I insist you formalize matters."

"Sir William, your daughter's only ten years old."

"You can wed her when she turns fourteen, which scarcely leaves me enough time to make arrangements. Not the least of which will be asking the queen to elevate me to the peerage."

Edward slumped. He was no match for this man and never would be.

"Spare me the melancholia, Edward. I saved you from a murder charge. Be grateful."

Anger surged through him, and he straightened. "I refuse to marry Nan because you crave advancement! I want to *write*, Cecil."

"You promised that if I arranged the printing of your Ovid translation, you wouldn't write for the public. Just compose some trifle and circulate it among your peers, there's a good fellow—"

"I also have a long poem in mind."

Cecil shook his head so hard his chin wobbled.

"Forget that. You're studying law."

"Arthur thinks the poem will find a large audience."

"I've told you a dozen times! *No one in your position writes for the public.* It's not done. Write for your peers—your forbears offer enough material for a hundred works! Write about *them*." Cecil's eyes were shining. "The first Earl of Oxford was descended from Charlemagne and rode by the side of William the Conqueror! The second—"

"Sir William, spare me. I'm well aware of my family's history."

"Very well, I've expended quite enough time on your affairs. I've work to do." At the door, he paused and turned. "By the bye, Edward, while preparing for the inquest I found two letters you wrote. They appear to be drafts." Cecil sighed and assumed a rather pained expression. "You signed the first with a flourish beneath your signature, which is entirely proper given your noble status. But beneath your signature to the second, you drew a crown over your name and slashed seven bars across the flourish."

"Sometimes I dream I'm a philosopher king."

"Flirtation with a claim to the throne is dangerous—not only to you but to Nan and your future children."

Edward shot up from his chair. "If your servants would stop snooping in my trash basket, you wouldn't be agitated!"

Cecil raised himself to his full five foot five. "You'll never be Edward the Seventh. Is that clear?"

"You think I *want* to be?" He was shouting. "I want to be a writer!"

"What if some *public* theater staged your plays? They perform before inebriated louts in the courtyards of inns."

"I'll remain anonymous, but I refuse to stop writing. I can't. I won't."

Cecil heaved an enormous sigh. "Well, thank you for meeting me halfway by studying law." He paused. "And I must say, your *Palamon and Arcite* was memorable."

Cecil was remarkable. He changed like the weather.

"I'm now calling the play *The Two Noble Kinsmen*."

"Good. People don't like foreign names." Cecil sighed. "Just don't use your own name."

"I won't." He gave a short bitter laugh. "I'm used to disappointment."

"Nothing a happy marriage can't fix."

"A thousand times, but Nan's not right for me."

"Clairvoyant, are you?"

"I'm talking about love." Abruptly, all the wind went out of his sails. "Maybe if you read some of my work, you'd understand."

"Try me."

He looked up. Cecil stood there, hands folded, patient. Was he serious?

Edward quickly cast about the room. Books on the floor. *Metamorphoses* on the desk. Cecil waiting expectantly. He grabbed a scrap of paper and read:

Love is a smoke raised with the fume of sighs;
Being purged. a fire sparkling in lovers' eyes;
Being vex'd, a sea nourish'd with lovers' tears:
What is it else? a madness most discreet,
A choking gall and a preserving sweet.

"Well, it's certainly . . . poetic," Cecil said.

Edward sighed. But what had he expected? Still, he had to try. "I need a wife who's . . . different from Nan. I wish I could make you understand."

"She's perfect for you." And with that, Cecil turned and padded out of the room.

Edward slumped to the bed. As long as Cecil and the queen were his guardians, he was their prisoner, and before long Cecil would be his father-in-law. He pulled himself to his feet and settled into the chair Cecil had vacated—the cushion was still warm. He squirmed.

A mind troubled is like a fountain stirr'd.

He got to his feet, went to the window, and looked out. What a lovely country. One day he must write about England—but not yet. Too much de Vere blood drenched its history. Until then, he'd write about the Romans, the Greeks, the Italians.

The air was warm. Wasn't it grand how the sun dispersed the darkest clouds?

He remembered he'd promised Bartholomew Clerke a preface in Latin to his translation of *The Courtier*. He sat down at his desk. He dipped a pen in the pot of ink and began a draft in English:

What more difficult, more noble or magnificent task has
anyone ever undertaken than—Castiglione who has drawn

for us the figure and model of a courtier—the highest and
most perfect type of man—[H]e has been able to lay down
principles for guidance of the very Monarch himself.

He sat back. The queen confessed her yearning to be a better
monarch. Why not use this to instruct her, and in the process
warn her about some of the people who surrounded her?

Castiglione has depicted persons who cannot be Courtiers—
some notable defect—some ridiculous character—some
deformity of appearance—whatever is heard in the mouths
of men in casual talk and in society—set down in so natural
a manner that it seems to be acted before our very eyes.

He supposed he ought to flatter her as well. He needed her
more than he needed Cecil. Again, he dipped his pen in ink.

Our translator has wisely added one single surpassing title
of distinction to recommend his work—[in] dedicat[ing] his
Courtier to our most illustrious and devoted Queen—for
there is no pen so skillful—no—speech so clear—[than]
obtain[ing] the protection of—our own Queen.

The devil with Cecil. Once and for all he'd announce *he* was a
writer. He reached for another sheet of parchment.

He scrawled his signature across the top of his preface to
Clerke's translation and stared at his name and title: *Edward,*
Earl of Oxford. Then he signed a personal salutation: "*Lord Great*
Chamberlain of England, Viscount Bulbec and Baron Scales and
Badlesmere, to the Reader—Greeting."

Let Cecil chew on that.

Once his preface was signed with his own name and titles,

his literary identity would be established. Publication of Clerke's book was assured—he'd already paid the printer.

Feeling better, he was looking at the blank page in front of him, thinking what to write, when he heard soft footsteps. He opened the door—it was Cecil again, but this time he wore a smile. Now what?

"Edward, I almost forgot. I spoke to the queen. I don't know when, or under what circumstances, but she's told me she will permit you a brief period of military service."

"Wonderful." He wanted to write, but he had an obligation to his forbears. Besides, who knew what he'd witness on the battlefield. He thought of *The Iliad*. "Thank you, Sir William. When do I go?"

"I know you long for the sound of battle, so after two years of reading law at Gray's Inn, you shall serve as aide to your uncle in whatever military matter he's engaged."

"You spoke to Sussex already?"

"I have. But I hope I won't regret this. The Catholics in the north are organizing and it's only a matter of time before they rebel."

"I can hardly wait."

"Your enthusiasm reflects your lack of experience."

In the fall, he read law at Gray's Inn while continuing to live at Cecil House. The law satisfied his craving for the practical *and* the abstract, but its absurdities alienated him. To endure a disquisition by some attorney on the legal consequences of suicide was more than he could bear. He got through it only by trying to fit the idea into a play.

Plays, now—those were filled with tolerable absurdities. He attended each weekly performance in the Gray's Inn and Temple

Inn auditoriums. Acted by students, based mostly on Roman and Greek mythology, they suffered from poor pacing and often he struggled to keep awake—the students insisted on rhyming everything—but he still learned a great deal.

He watched George Gascoigne's *The Supposes*. His cousin's dialogue derived from stereotypes of Italian comedy preferences for off-color jokes and women protagonists. His would be better. He'd resurrected the story he wrote as a child about a man who tames a woman like a hawk, and he was modeling the shrew after his stepsister Katherine.

*I*n December 1568, his mother died. He rode to Kingston-on-Thames to attend her funeral. As her casket was lowered into the grave, he was surprised to find he felt nothing at all. She'd had so little to do with him—her husband, Charlie, had actually returned the horse he gave them as a wedding present.

He peered into the hole in the ground. People said she was beautiful, but Earl John never gave her a look. He must have known of her affair with Charlie—or had the affair come about because of Earl John's neglect?

That thought left him uncomfortable. He put it all out of his mind as he galloped back to London—he could hardly mourn someone he'd never known.

*H*e was in his room at Cecil House with Ned Manners, sipping sherry and celebrating his nineteenth birthday, when he received the message. His uncle Tom Radcliffe, the Earl of Sussex, was inviting him to York to be his aide-de-camp.

He went at once to tell Cecil, who already knew.

"The old general has his hands full with that rebellion," Cecil said. "The situation's so dangerous he had to send an armed escort just for you."

"Don't worry, I won't be captured. I wouldn't dream of burdening you."

"The papists have six thousand soldiers, Edward, almost as many as Sussex. You could lose your life."

Edward's reaction was to go straight to his room and write the administrator of Hedingham. When he showed up with a band of reinforcements following, his uncle would know he was no overindulged courtier.

*E*dward's escort arrived in the morning. He'd never ridden so far so fast—they'd only stopped to eat, piss, and change horses. When they reached York, he was ushered into his uncle's headquarters. The encampment consisted of gardeners' shacks in a park in the middle of town.

He'd met the Earl of Sussex only once, at a family gathering when he was a child. But now his gray-haired uncle greeted him warmly and then gave him the grim details.

"We're seven thousand strong, surrounded by almost as many Catholics plus the city's entire population of angry civilians. We're in a dung heap of trouble, hemmed in and stuck eating dried beef and drinking warm beer. Now the queen informs me she can't send reinforcements."

"None?"

Sussex walked to the door of the shack, stared out for a moment, and returned. He probably had more important things to do than explain this untenable position to a freshly graduated law student.

"You've got quite the physique," he said. "And the queen told me about your riding skills. But it's your voice that'll help me, Edward. The men can't read, so I give them orders by voice. The queen said you thunder when you speak."

"Why doesn't she send you reinforcements?"

Sussex snorted. "She has to send everyone she has to Henry Carey. *He's* defending against a Spanish invasion, which means I can't do shit against thousands of Catholics defending their home."

"Where *are* the Spanish forces?"

"Still in the Low Countries soiling their pants. I wouldn't be surprised if they never show up, but *we* still have to fight every Catholic in York."

"If the Spaniards come ashore, what will they do?"

"What else? Return us to Catholicism and put Mary Queen of Scots on our throne. She claims she doesn't know anything about the revolt because she's been under house arrest for ten years, but Cecil intercepts her letters. She's in it up to her eyeballs."

"Stupid of her to write about it."

"It's a bad situation, and it's getting worse." Sussex drained his mug of warm beer.

"I tried to stop you from coming, but you'd already left Cecil House. I'll assign as many guards as I can to protect you."

"I'm good with a rapier." As soon as the words were out of his mouth, he regretted them. This wasn't some swordfight in Cecil's courtyard.

A commotion outside drew them to the door. A hundred soldiers plus horse stood at attention just outside, fully armed men from Hedingham dressed in blue and tawny.

"We're here, milord!" they shouted.

"Here!"

"Here!"

Edward called to a few by name the way Earl John used to, and they cheered.

Sussex looked impressed. "I take it they're yours?"

"From my farms and villages. I didn't ask for permission, since I wasn't sure they'd come."

Sussex clapped a hand on his shoulder.

"Let's find them a place to sleep." Sussex shouted orders to a sergeant, and then he and Edward came back inside. "Now, let's celebrate. Not every day a man gets unsolicited help."

Edward reached into his saddlebag for a sack of sherry.

"I was saving it for victory," he said, "but let's drink it while we can."

*F*ood dwindled, but forays to the city were too risky. Everyone remained in the encampment, sleeping in huts, washing with water from the few wells. The days dragged on. Hope ebbed.

Edward came down with a fever. His uncle gave him fenil powder, and he sat in cold well water to get the fever down. Every day was torture, every night was worse.

Lightheaded, he wondered what would happen to England if it couldn't quell the rebellion. Half of all Englishmen were still Catholic. The queen refused to coerce them beyond ordering them to attend Protestant services once a week, but her tolerance didn't seem to have accomplished much. Yet if Spain ruled England—and the king of Spain would hold sway over Queen Mary—*all* tolerance would disappear. An inquisition would commence. On the other hand, if England overcame the rebellion, the Protestant reaction might be almost as vicious.

Edward stopped thinking about Bloody Mary on the throne

and the hideous prospect of an inquisition. It made his head ache, and he was too sick for that.

*A*nother night, another day, and he was finally able to stand. He washed and dressed, consumed stale bread and warm beer, and then his fever returned. Sussex cursed their strategic position while Edward sweated and shook.

One morning it occurred to him the Catholics of York had not attacked. What were they waiting for?

He soon got the answer, when spies returned from the city. The Spanish weren't coming. Despite all the talk, despite the burnings and torture Mary had inflicted eleven years ago, the king of Spain had called off his invasion. York's Catholics were beside themselves.

"Assemble the men," Sussex said. "I've got to make a speech. When people are desperate, sometimes they attack. We need a show of force to dissuade them."

"What can you say to convince them?"

"Well, now, if the facts are on my side, I shout facts. If I'm in the right, I shout that. And if I haven't got either, I just shout."

"What have you got this time, facts or right?"

"Neither, but when *our* soldiers start shouting at the Catholics, maybe the Catholics will lock their doors and give us some damn peace."

*E*dward assembled the soldiers, and Sussex gave his speech. The old general wasn't an orator, but the men responded with enthusiasm. It was amazing what words could do.

The next day, Catholic houses in York sprouted white flags. The

Duke of Norfolk announced he was going to throw himself on the mercy of the queen. When he left his estate to surrender in London, farmers grabbed the tail of his horse to try to stop him, but it was no use. Even the other leaders of the revolt fled.

"Westmoreland made it to the Low Countries," Sussex said as they ate their meager breakfast. "And spies say Northumberland's in Scotland."

"So much for the wolfish earls. What about Mary?"

"She wrote Cecil she'd tell all Catholics to stop rebelling if he frees her. She also promised to return to Scotland."

Edward smiled for the first time in days. "I can't imagine Cecil responded well to that."

"He told her the offer comes too late. She even offered to give him her little boy James as a hostage. He rejected that, too."

"Now what'll happen to her?"

"What happens to anyone who supports a rebellion—she'll lose her head, and so will Norfolk. But first there'll be reprisals." Sussex unrolled a sheet of parchment. "And I'm the one who has to carry them out."

His uncle handed him the instructions. The parchment bore the queen's signature, but the language was Cecil's.

He handed the paper back in a state of shock.

"Three hundred victims, one from every village?" He felt sick. "To 'hang them on a tree and let them swing 'til birds pick their bones clean'?"

"Don't look at me that way, lad. I didn't give the order."

"What about Mary? People love her, and she *is* a queen."

"For now, she'll remain Henry Hastings' prisoner. Cecil will have her killed later, when things quiet down."

"And Her Majesty? How is she?"

"In Windsor Castle. London's not safe." Sussex got to his feet.

"Now I have to find three hundred fathers and sons." He looked Edward over. "You want to come? It's an invitation to a nightmare."

He had a fever, but he could stand. "I'll come, Uncle." He downed the sherry and followed the old general from their hut.

*A*s instructed, the selections were arbitrary—this was meant to "maximize deterrence." Edward thought that was the stupidest phrase he'd ever heard.

Every scene was much the same. A father or son stood on a cart, hands tied behind his back. A rope was placed around the neck and the cart was dragged away. The screams of mothers, sisters, and sweethearts echoed in his dreams.

The whole thing took four and a half weeks. When a woman from York brought sherry as a peace offering, he and his uncle shared it. When it was empty, Sussex went for a walk. Edward took the parchment he hadn't used to write orders. He remembered what soldiers said and turned it into dialogue for his *Henry V*:

"*Fortune is painted blind, with a muffler afore her eyes.*"

"*I would give all my fame for a pot of ale and safety.*"

"*Men of few words are the best men; and therefore he scorns to say his prayers, lest a' should be thought a coward.*"

"*The queen's a bawcock, and a heart of gold, a gal of life, an imp of fame. I kiss her dirty shoe, and from heart-string I love the lovely bully.*"

*C*ecil and Nowell were right: war *was* hell. The queen was right, too—no battle was worth it, even for her. The only thing that kept him from going mad was putting the words on paper.

PART THREE

The Qveen

9

Things sweet to taste prove to digestion sour.

Shakespeare
Richard II

On a cold December day, Edward approached Westminster Abbey with his best man, Ned Manners, by his side. Cecil's guards drifted in and out of sight. They'd been patrolling the port in Southwark when he tried to escape after the September wedding date was announced. He walked to the Thames in the dead of night, hired a wherry to Southwark, collected a horse he'd bought, and galloped to Dover. He was looking for someone to sail him to Flanders when Cecil's men caught him and brought him back to London.

Christopher Hatton, his latest rival for the queen's affection, stood outside the Abbey, hoping to be noticed. Robin Dudley briefly locked eyes with Edward and turned away. Edward couldn't care less. The queen only had eyes for him—he rode with her every morning, danced with her every evening, and basked in her compliments: "No one has your command of words, Edward"; "No one but you can discuss Ovid's *Art of Love* like an author"; "Only you understand what Cardanus says about melancholia, Edward."

He entered Westminster Abbey. The archbishop's deputy guided Edward down the aisle to an anteroom behind the altar, and Ned closed the door behind them. A commotion in the nave caught their attention: The queen was taking her place. The crowd filed in behind her, and Ned clapped Edward's shoulder.

"Come on," he said. "Best get it over with."

The ceremony was a blur. When it was over, Edward and Nan emerged from the abbey to cheers and were hustled into a carriage bound for Cecil House.

"I was so nervous," Nan said. "Did it show?"

"You were fine," he said.

He kept his eyes on the carriage window. Nan turned and stared out the opposite side.

They rode the rest of the way in silence.

Nan continued to live at Cecil House, and Edward rented rooms at Savoy House across the street. When he'd turned twenty-one, he took his seat in Parliament, so his days were filled with tedium.

Only at night did he come alive.

While working on *The Famous Victories of Henry the Fifth,* he decided to split the story into several plays. *Henry V* would be the first of a chronicle of English history, and the Earls of Oxford would play leading roles in all of them.

He refused to write about Henry VII. After the Fifteenth Earl of Oxford had helped him gain the throne, the monarch turned around and fined the family fifteen thousand pounds, claiming the Oxford uniforms too closely resembled his own.

Edward invited young writers from Cambridge and Oxford to stay at his apartment—all brilliant, all penniless. He paid printers to publish Thomas Twynne's translations of Petrarch and Virgil.

He paid for Bartholomew's translation of Cardanus' *Comfort* and Bedingfield's translation of Castiglione's *The Courtier.* He hired Angel Day to be his secretary. Arthur continued to be his tutor—Edward needed his translation of *Tragus Pompeius* to write *Henry VI.*

He worked through much of the night. When he was writing, he didn't need a lot of sleep. If the apartment became too noisy, he went to Vere House, near the London Stone. He planned to sell the family mansion when he got his property back.

He always ate lunch at Cecil House—it seemed the politic thing to do. Besides, Cecil had gotten him used to fine dining, and no one offered a better table. Of course, it came with his wife.

"How did you pass the morning?"

"Mother and I prayed, then we went for a walk. How did you spend your morning, Edward?"

"I read and wrote."

She never complained. They hadn't consummated their marriage, but she either had no interest or was too timid to say anything.

Occasionally, eight-year-old Robert Cecil joined them. Cecil said he was a genius. The queen called him her *Bosse,* her "hump." But the boy's drawf-like body distressed Edward, who on such occasions beat as hasty a retreat from the table as he could manage. Usually he fled to Cecil's library, where he read about Copernicus, the Ptolemaic view of the universe, or geography to restore his faith in science. He also read Plato, Erasmus, Cicero, and Petrarch's *Lives of the Noble Greeks and Romans.* He toyed with the idea of writing *Julius Caesar* and *Titus Andronicus,* though he feared *Titus Andronicus* would be too gory for the queen's taste.

But they all required foreign settings. He craved verisimilitude and so decided to shelve these ideas until after he had a chance to visit Italy.

He spent a few days at Hill Hall every month. Sir Thomas was in Paris, but Edward took comfort knowing Hedingham was just thirty miles away. He petitioned the master of wards to return his property, but Cecil claimed his men were still making appraisals. He also claimed the amount Edward owed the queen for his father's land and buildings far exceeded what she and Dudley owed him.

They presented him with a list of his expenditures—he owed the queen three thousand three hundred pounds. They insisted he secure the debt with bonds guaranteed by friends.

At least he had Earl John's desk.

*W*hen the Duke of Norfolk was sentenced to death for participating in the Catholic rebellion, Edward asked Cecil to petition for a pardon. After all, the Howards were family, even if the duke was an arrogant, jealous fool.

Cecil refused, so Edward contacted Martin Frobisher, a ship's captain from Wakefield he'd met at Sir Thomas' house. Frobisher agreed to sail the duke to Spain, provided Edward could get him out of the Tower.

"Do you know anyone who could help me?" Edward asked.

"Milord, I can't even get permission to explore a north-by-northwest route to the Orient. What makes you think I can engineer an escape from the Tower?"

He asked a half-dozen others, but with no success. In June, Norfolk was beheaded.

"*T*he queen was here yesterday, Edward," Cecil said when he asked him into the library not long afterward. "We engaged in a little tête-à-tête about her marriage proposals."

Edward nodded, cautious.

"She's not eager to take a husband, but she knows her obligation," Cecil said. "I wonder, dear boy—do you know yours?"

So that was it.

"I made my position quite clear before the marriage," Edward said. "I'll never sleep with Nan."

"Spare me, Edward. She's a beautiful woman, and until she bears a son, the Oxford name is in jeopardy."

"My cousins can inherit."

"They're unmarried, and your lands are crucial to England's defenses." Cecil folded his hands on the desk. "My boy, you must live as man and wife. There's simply no alternative."

"There is. My position won't change."

"Neither will mine."

The longer they stared, the stronger he felt. What could Cecil do, force him to copulate? He had yet to bed any woman, and he wasn't going to start with Nan.

Finally, Cecil sighed, stood, and left the library.

A few weeks later, the queen invited him to Havering-atte-Bower, another of his father's country estates. He assumed the invitation was for a Christmas celebration, but just to be sure, he asked Ned Manners to inquire.

"Well, it's not a Christmas party."

"How do you know, Ned?"

"You're the only one invited."

"Perhaps she wants to celebrate my wedding."

Ned rolled his eyes. "Without your wife?"

"Maybe she intends to discipline me," Edward said. "When I wrote the preface to Bartholomew's translation of *The Courtier*, I signed my—"

"The queen doesn't give a fig how you sign your name." Ned grinned. "She played the same game with Hatton. Prepare yourself for a merry Christmas, my friend."

"What the devil are you getting at?"

"Get your head out of the clouds, Edward!" Ned slammed his book shut. "The queen wants you in her bed."

Edward couldn't say anything for a minute. Then, finally, "She's forty! She was beautiful a few years ago, but . . ."

"What are you going to do when she climbs on top of you, politely decline?"

"Her face is covered in little scars, Ned—her maids put *paste* on it!"

Ned was shaking his head. "You ought to know by now, no one says no to the queen."

*E*dward returned to Savoy House and buried himself in the play he was working on, *The Troublesome Reign of King John*. He found it hard going.

Several hours later, Arthur tapped on the door.

Edward looked up. "You brought notes?"

"I did," Arthur said. "My boy, you violated Aristotle's unities of time and place! Seventeen years in one king's reign—I'm not surprised you're having trouble." He held up a scrap of paper. "And your use of rhetorical devices is effective, but there are *dozen* of quotations from Horace and Ovid. You have to—"

"Can't you say something nice? I feel melancholy."

"Feelings are not my brief, my boy." Arthur flipped through his notes. "The play's too long, your language is dated, and I count three thousand made-up words. Oh, and for God's sakes, get rid of John wanting to abdicate—the queen will have your head."

"The queen." He glanced out the window. "Yes, there is that."

That was a week ago. Now he sat in the queen's bedroom, waiting for her to complete her morning ablutions. It didn't seem proper, but her maid said she'd insisted. He tried to calm himself by reading the labels on the jars. *Egg whites. Powered eggshells. Alum. Borax. Ground poppy seeds. Mill water.* All mixed together to make the paste, he assumed. He didn't want to think about the paste. But when she swept into the room, her face looked lovely until she sat next to him and he saw it close up.

"Your Majesty, it's Sunday," he said. "Would you like me to accompany you to church?"

She waved a hand. "Sermons are excuses for clergymen to lecture women. Sometimes I think my stepsister Mary was right—all Puritans should be burned at the stake." She smiled. "Do you know they want me to ban all mystery plays? Good God, I can't live without plays."

"I know exactly how you feel."

"Cecil insists that I marry. They suggested Eric of Sweden, Archduke Charles of Austria, and Philip of Spain." She made a face. "I can't marry a Catholic, and I refuse to take my stepsister's leavings."

He relaxed. She wanted to talk. He liked listening to her.

"Some even want Robin Dudley, but he's as bad as my father."

"Your Majesty, some say it was Cecil behind Dudley's wife's accident."

"No, it was Robin, all right." She shook her head. "No woman breaks her neck falling down two steps. Besides"—her eyes danced—"I don't need to marry Robin to sleep with him." She glanced at his untouched glass. "I thought you liked sherry?"

He took a sip. "Your Majesty, your predicament is awful." He thought of Nan. "Believe me, I understand."

She refilled his glass. "They say Catherine de Medici is pushing her sons again. I told Smith to take another look at the oldest one—imagine, me asking Thomas Smith for help."

Edward smiled. "I was so grateful you appointed him ambassador to France."

"Why not? I like learned people." She drained her glass. "Smith wrote me Charles is wise for his years. Good God! He's still half my age."

"And I doubt Charles has a mind of his own," he said. "His mother is so controlling."

"Thankfully, he doesn't need a *mind* of his own, just a penis." They both laughed.

"I sent your uncle to Vienna to inspect the archduke, Edward. He said the archduke speaks four languages, so he's learned." She sighed. "But again, Catholic."

"It'd be civil war," he said. "After the northern rebellion, we know that for a certainty."

"The *piece de resistance* was when the archduke asked to 'inspect' me. What am I, a cow at a country fair? I told Tom to send him one of my approved portraits, and the archduke could take it or leave it. He left it, for which I'm glad."

"Earl John used to say if one waits long enough, things take care of themselves."

She picked up one of the mirrors that littered her table, glanced at her face, and grimaced.

Could one be in love with a mind? Nan never had a thought of her own, but the queen was clever and fun, her figure still slim. She smiled at him. He squirmed, stood up, and stretched.

"I sent Walsingham to Spain to talk marriage with Philip again," she said. "At least he's not a French prince. Did you know one of them—Henri, I think—wears two rows of rings on each finger of both hands?"

Again she patted the cushion next to her. Again he sat down.

"Your Majesty, this marriage business is so difficult for you," he said. "I wish there were something I could do."

"You're sweet to care." She blew him a kiss—he spotted a couple of blackened teeth. "And so innocent. That's why I love you."

"Your Majesty, have you heard John Dowland's new song, 'Vivat Eliza'?"

"Yes, it's lovely. Puritans say I commissioned John to write an 'Ave Maria' to show people how to worship me." She took his hand. "I know I'm driving Cecil mad, but so long as they can't agree on whom I should marry, I think I'm safe. What do you think?"

"I think you probably are."

"We must play William Byrd and Thomas Tallis on the virginals."

"I gave Byrd one of my houses. Battails."

"How generous of you, Edward."

He shrugged. "It was the least I could do after he wrote some songs for me."

She shivered, though the room was overheated. He patted her hand.

"My doctors tell me I'm suffering from hysteria," she said. "My melancholia can last for days."

"Mine too. Aristotle said it can last as long as a season." He shuddered.

"Your Cardano, though—he truly understands. I can't thank you enough for recommending his book." She sighed. "I wonder if migraines are the result of my mood."

"Perhaps you should consult the doctor."

"So long as I don't have varicose veins, I'll be all right," she said. "That's what killed my father—of course, weighing much too much didn't exactly help."

They laughed. She poured more sherry for both of them.

He glanced down. She'd once prided herself on wearing simple black dresses, but her maid told him she owned hundreds of gowns now—all cut low like the one she was wearing. Pearl ropes looped around her neck like vines. Where were the diamonds that dominated her latest approved portrait? He'd heard she was threatening to include a spider motif in the next one.

"What are you writing, now, Edward?"

"History plays. The first one's about Henry V."

"Write amusing plays. The Puritans will bore us to death or burn us . I'm not sure which is worse, and I need to laugh."

Surely this was his chance.

"I'd very much like to go to Italy and study their improvisational technique, commedia dell'arte. Of course, Cecil's against my going there until I've fulfilled my 'marital obligations.'"

She looked away. He spoke faster.

"Commedia actors take a character, a static role—a nasty old man, a stuffy soldier, a crooked doctor, a crazy *zanni*—and improvise his lines. They perform right on the street."

"Can you really learn just by watching?"

"I would think so, but there's a playwright in Mantua who has a school for drama—the Gonzaga duke's his patron. The man's written a fifty-volume manuscript on every aspect of theater from makeup to diction to gestures to lighting. It's not published yet, but Arthur thinks he'd let me read it."

"How exciting! Oh, I'd love to go with you, if I could."

"I'd also like to watch the playwright work with his company, Your Majesty. His name is Leone de Sommi."

"I'd marry a handsome Italian in a heartbeat—now, that *would* be cause for my assassination." She laughed, but her eyes showed no mirth. "Someday one of those nice English boys they send to France for indoctrination will come back to England and kill me."

"Your Majesty, Walsingham will protect you. He trains his men well."

"Ever since the Pope announced it's permissible to murder me, I haven't been able to sleep a wink." She grabbed both his hands. "Sit closer, Edward. I need you."

Ned would know what to do—*he* had no idea. But perhaps it didn't matter. She took his hand and pulled him to his feet. Then, still holding his hand, she walked him to her bed. She let her robe slide off her shoulders and fall to the floor. All she had on underneath the robe was a thin shift! Mesmerized by the sight of the muscular yet feminine body beneath the silky material, it took him a second to realize that the Queen of England was undressing him.

In moments they were in her bed, and worry turned to fear.

What if he got her with child? No, that wouldn't happen—he wasn't aroused.

But then she began to stroke him in ways he could never have imagined, with effects that astonished him.

His eyes widened and then shut tight. He could barely contain himself.

He knelt over her, the way they did in Giulio Romano's pictures, and spread her legs. In a moment he was inside her, and as he began to move, so did she. His pleasure mounted but then became excruciating. It was for her, too—he could see it in her face, now beautiful beyond belief. When the explosion was over, he kissed her and flopped onto his back.

She turned on her side and stroked his shoulder.

"Edward, you really must sleep with Nan. You'll enjoy the practice."

He felt plunged from a glorious height.

"I'm sorry you were disappointed, Your Majesty."

"Not at all—you're quite the best virgin I've had. First times are usually far more difficult."

So this wouldn't be the last time. He smiled—why practice with Nan when he could have this? The queen knew so much. And what fun learning from her would be. He'd always been a quick study.

"I've been thinking," she said. "If I'm willing to marry someone half my age from France, why not marry a handsome young nobleman from England?"

He blinked.

"Nobody seemed to think Dudley's wife would be a problem, least of all Dudley," she said. "So, I got to thinking—marrying you could be even easier. Cecil would agree—he always does, after he's compensated."

"Your Majesty, I don't know what to say—"

"If I were you, I wouldn't say anything. Let events develop. *Semper diadem*'s my motto, the same as my mother's. Of course, nothing's really the same. The only constant is change."

Quick as a rabbit she straddled him.

Maybe it wasn't love—no play, no poem would call it that—but it was sublime. She'd done things that weren't even in Romano's sketches. But a half-hour later, when she moved to try again, he hesitated.

"Edward, what's wrong?"

"I don't want to make a baby."

"That's so sweet." She lay her head on the pillow next to his. "After my father executed my mother, he declared me a bastard.

I wouldn't wish that on anyone, so if I become pregnant we'll just have to marry."

He took her advice and said nothing.

*H*e left for London wondering if she was serious. He had no doubt that she could buy Cecil's agreement to an annulment or that Nan would be happier with someone else. But did the queen really want to *marry* him? He was sure he could do things for England, perhaps more than his forebears. He might even be happy—she was bright, witty, educated, and God knows she was experienced. Perhaps they could cure each other's melancholy.

Until yesterday, all he'd wanted was to go to Italy and write. Did he now want to be the queen's consort? Or perhaps king?

10

If women could be fair and yet not fond,
Or that their love were firm and fickle, still,
I would not marvel that they make men bond,
By service long to purchase their good will. . . .
Unsettled still like haggards wild they range,
These gentle birds that fly from man to man . . ..
Yet for disport we fawn and flatter both,
To pass the time when nothing else can please . . .
And then we say when we their fancy try,
To play with fools, O what a fool was I.

The Earl of Oxford
Woman's Changeableness

*E*dward was riding with the queen to meet Matthew
Parker, the Archbishop of Canterbury. The road was slip-
pery with snow, but she insisted they return to Havering-
atte-Bower by horseback. If she meant to prove her riding skill,
she succeeded—even the guards had trouble keeping up.

She pulled her horse closer to him. "None of us rides as well
as you," she said.

Now he knew why they'd ridden ahead of her guards. She
didn't want to be overheard.

"Edward, the day before my poor mother's head was chopped

off, she placed my hand in Matthew's and said, 'Elizabeth, you can count on this man.' Matthew was her confessor, my father's, too, and in time I chose him as mine." She turned to face the road ahead. "You can confide in him."

He tightened his grip on the reins. Even if she were pregnant, she could place the child with a nobleman who'd give the baby his name. She didn't *need* to marry him. Apparently, a great deal depended on how things went with the archbishop.

*M*atthew Parker, with ruddy cheeks and a broad smile, was waiting for them at the front door. The queen kissed him on the cheek, Edward shook his hand. As they made their way to the library, Parker laid a hand on the queen's shoulder for support.

"Edward," the queen said, "Matthew's well cared for by his wife, Margaret. He was the first clergyman to marry, even before the law permitted it. He even supported Northumberland in the Northern Rebellion."

She'd told him that on their ride to Havering. Lately, she was repeating herself—was she nervous?

They sat close to the fire. A stiff wind rattled the windows.

"Edward," the archbishop said, "the queen tells me you write plays. She saw your first when you were graduated from Oxford. She's very proud of you."

Edward glanced at her and smiled. "I'm very grateful."

"When I was vice chancellor of Cambridge, I got myself in trouble over a play," Parker said. "I permitted students to perform *Pammachius*, which derides the ecclesiastic system. It's important to shake things up, don't you think?"

"I do, provided it's done carefully." He put on a serious expression. He was being tested.

"I quite agree." The archbishop's gaze was piercing. "It's always good to seek a middle ground. Catholics and Protestants could benefit from finding a mean, don't you think?"

"Indeed I do," Edward said. "I would love to see our country at peace with itself."

Parker smiled. "I don't credit myself with knowing all the answers—"

"You're too modest, Matthew," the queen said. "I wish you'd accept appointment to the Privy Council. The reformers don't want bishops and the Catholics don't want change. Cecil can't get anything done."

"Given my age, Elizabeth, I can't decide anything more important than the color of vestments."

"Don't be silly. You're the architect of our religious settlement. Thanks to you, the Church of England has an identity distinct from Catholicism *and* Protestantism."

The conversation continued until the wee hours of the morning. When they went to bed, he and the queen slept in separate bedrooms. In the morning, they returned to London.

*T*here were two more meetings in as many weeks, and then the queen announced her courses resumed. She did not need to tell him there would be no marriage. Edward felt hollow. It had been only a dream, but a marriage to the queen had captured his imagination. If there were ever a time for him to leave the country and lick his wounds, this was surely it—so he broached the subject of Italy with Cecil.

"Edward, you haven't created an heir," he said. "What if you were captured or killed? What about Nan?"

At sixteen, Nan still had her whole life ahead of her. It was future grandchildren bearing the Oxford name that occupied Cecil's mind.

He knew he should go to the queen, but for once he felt tongue-tied, not to mention angry. He wrote a poem about her changeableness and commissioned William Byrd to put the words to music.

She read the poem. She heard the music. She didn't say a word.

Back to Cecil? He'd just get more of the same.

So instead of confronting him, Edward staged a prank.

One day at lunch, after being elevated to lord treasurer, Cecil confessed he was worried about a shipment of gold being transported to London from the south.

"It's guarded by only two men," he said.

Edward looked up. "I'm sure they'll take the safest route, Cecil."

As soon as lunch was over, he went straight to Savoy House and sent messages to Danny Wilkins, John Hannam, and Denny the Frenchman to hold themselves in readiness. Their families had been in the employ of the Oxfords for years.

On May 15, armed with muskets and wearing masks, the four of them stopped the wagon of gold.

"Transfer the gold to our wagon," Edward shouted through his mask. "Then you're free to complete your journey on foot."

The hapless guards did as they were told. When they reached the capital, Danny, John, Denny, and Edward were waiting for them on the front steps of Cecil House, the gold stacked next to them in packages tied with red ribbons.

"Bring the gold inside," Edward told the guards.

When Cecil saw what had happened, he surprised the four by laughing and inviting everyone inside for refreshment.

"You know, Edward," he said, "I may have an opportunity for you to earn some gold."

"You don't say."

"I still owe you fifteen thousand pounds for marrying Nan—a terrible embarrassment, but the affairs of state weigh heavily on my shoulders. In any case, the Spanish ambassador and I have been negotiating a treaty of peace between our sovereigns. When he learned of my debt to you, he suggested that in return for a more *understanding* approach by England, you could collect the sum I owe you directly from Spain's agent in Dunkirk."

"Sounds like a bribe."

"Fifteen thousand pounds just happens to be the sum due me from Spain. This merely shortens the whole transaction."

"That's an enormous amount of gold to transport."

"You wouldn't have to do it yourself—you'd engage other persons of loyal disposition, such as the men who accompanied you to Gad's Hill."

"It still sounds risky."

"You? Worried about risk?" Cecil laughed. "That doesn't sound like the Edward I love."

Cecil had never applied *that* word to him before.

"I do know someone who might help me," Edward said.

"Who would that be, if I may be so bold?"

"Ned Somerset."

"The Fourth Earl of Worcester?" Cecil said. "Splendid chap. Fine family."

"Would the Spanish ambassador provide us with safe passage from Dunkirk to Calais, then back to England?"

"That goes without saying."

"When would we make the crossing?"

"In summer, when the channel's calm. I'll contact you as soon as I can. In the meantime, we should organize a ship."

"I can take care of that."

"Good, good. That would be most helpful."

"Thank you, Sir William."

He meant it. The Court of Wards still hadn't returned his lands. Every week he had to plead for funds. His debt to Cecil's clerks was enormous, but with this sum he could pay his debt, obtain his lands, and finally free himself of financial concerns.

*T*he next month, the queen summoned him.

"Edward!" Her smile was radiant. "I'm holding a reception for the French ambassador. Cecil says it's important we ally ourselves with France more closely. Since the ambassador loves dancing exhibitions, I'd like you to perform at the reception. You're the best dancer I know."

"I'm not a dancing cow, Your Majesty."

"I never said you were. I'll be your partner—"

"It's out of the question."

Her smile fell. Under all that paste, he detected a flush of anger. "Surely you can't mean—"

"Try me," he said.

She stormed out of the Presence Room.

He fully expected her to punish him, but instead she left on a progress to Cornwall and the West Country.

The next day, Cecil invited him to the library.

"You'll soon receive a visit from Antonio de Gueras, a Spanish agent. The purpose will be to introduce himself. The next time you'll see him will be when you collect the gold at the port of Dunkirk. Have you the ship?"

"Captain Frobisher's holding himself in readiness. As is Ned Somerset."

"Splendid!"

*T*hree weeks after the queen left on her progress, Edward sailed for Calais with Ned Somerset and the Gad's Hill three. They spent the night at Wivenhoe, his estate near the port.

"Edward," Ned said as they lingered on deck after a light supper, "I'm curious. Where does one find ideas for plays?"

Edward glanced over at him. "I suppose my history plays are an excuse for writing about the Oxfords. The first Oxford fought by the side of William the Conqueror at Hastings, another fought with Henry Tudor at Bosworth Field, and so on and so forth."

Ned nodded. "Sounds like a rich source—if you're a gifted playwright to begin with."

"When I was recovering from a fever I contracted during the Northern Rebellion, I spent weeks on my back reading Amyot's French translation of Plutarch's *Lives of the Noble Greeks and Romans*. I got some interesting ideas for plays from that."

"I looked at Plutarch once. He wrote about lives, though, not history."

"Plutarch wrote that character is revealed in small circumstances, not in glorious exploits."

Ned grinned. "Between your family and Plutarch, you should have plenty to write about."

"That's only the beginning." He looked over the rail, out toward the horizon. "After my father died, I became convinced he was murdered. I even know who's behind it, but I have no proof. I'm going to write a play about that, too."

"Didn't the queen tell you to write comedies?"

"The play isn't all dark. Cecil's in it—I call the fellow Corambis, which means 'two-hearted.' Cecil's motto is 'one heart.'"

Ned laughed.

"Serves the old boy right, but it all sounds a bit much for one play, don't you think?"

"As long as it holds their interest, I don't think the audience will mind. Besides, if the queen likes it, I'm content."

"That was quite a spat you two had."

"She'll recover, she always does. Besides, my play has a few choice words about Dudley that are sure to make her laugh."

"I don't know why you're not in London writing."

"I know." He sighed. "I've decided to give my marriage to Nan a chance. I finally realized I have no choice."

"It's about time."

"Actually, that gave me another idea—"

"Enough!" Ned laughed. "You'll make me sorry I asked. Write the ideas you've started working out—worry about the rest later."

"Ned, I can't *stop* ideas. I get them all the time. Some don't work and I throw them away. The ones I turn into plays are the best."

"I wish I had half your imagination."

"Anyone who's ever crafted a work of art will tell you the process is one part imagination and ninety-nine parts hard labor. You do more rewriting than writing, even when you're using something that happened in real life. The Gad's Hill gold robbery ended up in my *Henry IV* as a prank pulled off by Falstaff and his merry band, but it took four drafts to get the scene right."

Ned looked at him seriously. "You could use a vacation—or travel."

"Meeting new people, finding new books, seeing strange places, learning foreign languages and customs . . ." He grinned. "Imagine how many more ideas I'd have if I traveled."

"Then go to Italy. You're always talking about it."

"To me, Italy means freedom, beauty, everything. Cecil won't let me go."

"Maybe if you reconcile with Nan he'll change his mind."

"I feel as if I'm locked in a bottle, Ned."

"Is that why you're wasting time going to Dunkirk?"

"I told you, I'm broke. Cecil and the queen hold my lands. I need money to write, stage plays, travel, help friends. Cecil fights me over every little tract. Fifteen thousand pounds' worth of gold sets me free."

"But if Cecil gets in trouble, so will you."

"Why didn't you say that when I asked you to go with me?"

"You would have listened?" Ned shook his head. "You fight with the queen. You rob Cecil's shipments. Sometimes I worry about you, Edward."

"When I was young, my highs and lows lasted only a short time. Lately, they can go on for a month, even a season."

"Edward, did it ever occur to you your melancholy might contribute to your artistry?"

"Aristotle wrote that great art comes from melancholy people." He glanced at his friend. "As for the queen, I won't let her yank my strings any longer."

"What are you talking about?"

Edward sighed. "I've been in her bed."

Ned let out a whistle. "Now I understand," he said. "When I told her we were off to have a little fun in the Low Countries, she wrote me from Cornwall. Edward, she wants me to detain you in Bruges until a messenger arrives with her thoughts."

Edward shook his head. "She's as mad as I am."

"She insists you wait for her messenger. For that matter, *I* insist. Don't worry, the gold won't spoil."

*T*he boat crossed the channel at its shortest point from France, and the pilot threaded his way through the swampy approach to Calais. Edward and Ned complied with the queen's order and went straight to Bruges. The harbor there was silted, but storms created a natural channel.

"What's that smell, Ned?" Edward said as they entered the bay.

"That's a spice boat. What do you want to do till the queen's messenger arrives?"

"I'd like to see the print shops. The first books in English were printed here by Claxton. I'd also like to see the Memlings and the Van Eycks. Scholars still write that Van Eyck invented oil painting, though we now know painters were using oils five hundred years ago."

"Sometimes people can't change their minds even after they're beaten over the head with facts."

A week later, he and Ned were drinking in a cafe on the dock in Bruges when Tom Bedingfield's boat approached. Tom was standing at the bow, waving a leather pouch with red ribbons fluttering from it.

"Edward!" he shouted. "I've got a letter for you."

Tom was thirteen years older, the second of Sir Henry Bedingfield's five sons and the translator of Cardano's *On Melancholy*. He and Edward had spent many an evening getting drunk at the Pye.

Tom leaped ashore. "I wish I could keep on going straight to Italy," he said.

"No one's stopping you."

"I can't—my book's the talk of London. But you can."

Edward stared at him. "What—"

"The queen wants to tell you herself. All I'm to say is forget about Dunkirk and return at once. Now, buy me a drink. I don't have local money."

Edward waved the waiter over and ordered another bottle of white wine. As soon as it was served, Tom drained the goblet.

"Now I feel better."

"Stop stalling and give me that letter."

"First, a few details." Tom sat back and gestured to the waiter to bring a refill. "After Somerset here told the queen what you and Cecil were up to, she decided to make a few changes in your itinerary. She summoned me to Cornwall, gave me this letter, and ordered me to deliver it to you."

"What changed her mind?"

"She said it was the poem you wrote in your preface to my translation of *Cardano*. You know, the one that—"

"Tom, I wrote it." He began to recite:

> *The laboring man that tills the fertile soil,*
> *And reaps the harvest fruit, hath not indeed*
> *The gain but pain, and if for all his toil*
> *He gets the straw, the lord will have the seed.*
> *So he that takes the pen to pen the book,*
> *Reaps not the gifts of godly golden muse;*
> *But those gain that who on the work shall look.*
> *And from the sour the sweet by skill shall choose;*
> *For he that beats the bush the bird not gets.*
> *But who sits still and holdeth the nets.*

"Now tell me," Edward said, "what does that have to do with the queen?"

"With pleasure! When I entered her Presence Room in Cornwall, *On Melancholy* was in her lap. She said she didn't want *Edward to till the soil and never see the gain.*" He handed over the letter.

"She said to tell you she has *plans* for you."

Her cursive handwriting was like his, the letters even and well-formed: "*Edward dear, please come home, but just for a moment. Then, you'll be off. I promise. And this time I intend to keep it.*"

He tried to conceal his elation. It was time he and the queen were discreet.

II

There is a tide in the affairs of men,
Which, taken at the flood, leads on to fortune;
Omitted, all the voyage of their life
Is bound in shadows and in miseries.

Shakespeare
Julius Caesar

*T*he queen's guards opened the door to the Presence Room. Edward entered, glanced around at the packed room, and smothered a laugh. Colors clashed. Jewelry dazzled. Floppy sleeves competed with sparkling doublets, cumbersome capes with pleated ruffs. Stockings stretched tight over bulging codpieces. Fops and social climbers vied for the queen's attention alongside the judgmental, the puritanical.

Which was worse: a monarch with unchecked power or a monarch hamstrung by Parliament? Was there something better? The Greeks had democracy, but he didn't see how that could work in a country where four out of five people were illiterate. It was a miracle these courtiers, these administrators of the realm, got anything done.

After three years in the House of Lords and two decades in the libraries of Sir Thomas, Sir William, the Inns of Court,

Cambridge, and Oxford, he felt separate from all of this. Despite his titles and ancestry, at heart he was an outsider. He was *from* this world, but it was no longer *his*. At first this understanding had made him feel sad—until it occurred to him that being an outsider had its advantages. He could know these people but not waste his time with them. He could listen to their schemes without participating, be privy to their plots without taking them seriously. And he could use all of it in his work.

The queen sat on her throne. Slowly he broke through the wall of people, through bouquets of perfumed ladies and knots of perspiring men. September in London seemed hotter this year—or was it his apprehension? At the last minute, would she change her mind? He tried to imagine Venice but couldn't.

Standing on tiptoes, he looked over the heads of the courtiers and maids of honor toward the queen and quickened his pace. Christopher Hatton towered over a group near the dais. As the queen's newest dancing partner, Hatton's fortunes were rising. Ten years older than Edward, he seemed to work hard at appearing youthful and attractive. His only profession was being seen.

He'd modeled a character in a prose poem after Hatton and included it in a collection about to be published. Would it temper the queen's infatuation with the man she called Sheep? He hadn't identified himself as the author—the satire was too scorching.

He passed more people and studied more faces. So many stuffy men to parody. So many balloons to burst. He'd almost reached the throne. He saw Francis Walsingham, the queen's new secretary of state, and waved. Walsingham waved back.

He reached the dais. The queen, holding papers, was talking to someone. Had she noticed him? She pointed to the captain of the guards.

"Everyone but the Earl of Oxford, out!"

The captain raised his spear. "Clear the room!"

This wasn't how a monarch should behave—so blunt, so melodramatic, singling him out like that. But the room was already nearly empty, and she was pointing to the chair beside her.

Edward sat.

At last, she looked at him. Her eyes sparkled.

"I have your itinerary. First you go to Paris, as my personal representative to the coronation and wedding of the king of France."

"May I ask when?" He would brook no more delays.

"The coronation is February 15, the wedding the seventeenth. That leaves you ninety days to put your affairs in order. Which brings me to my one condition."

What now? He didn't trust her.

"Edward, your wife has asked me for help. You must father a child before you go."

"Your Majesty—"

"God's shoulders, Edward! It's not complicated." She shuffled her papers. "Now, this is what I've arranged. Don't interrupt."

She needn't have warned him. He was too angry to speak.

"I ordered your Uncle Tom—he's the new Lord Chamberlain now—to arrange a gala at Hampton Court. Ostensibly it's to wish you bon voyage, but as soon as the festivities are over, you'll escort Nan to the room overlooking the hedge my father called a maze. Having contemplated the labyrinth of trouble you'll be in if you're kidnapped without fathering an heir, you will take your wife by the hand, get on that bed, and copulate until you make a boy."

He wanted to laugh in her face. "Your Majesty," he said in as even a tone as he could manage, "I can hardly guarantee the sex of the child."

"Don't test my patience, Edward. Cecil and I are worried about you."

"You two are relentless."

"Perhaps, but in exchange for your cooperation I'm prepared to be generous. Do your duty and, at the wedding reception in Rheims, the French ambassador promised me Jacques Amyot, the translator of the new French edition of Plutarch's *Lives of the Greek and Roman Nobles*, will sit on your right. Pierre Ronsard, your favorite among the French literati, will sit on your left."

"Wonderful."

"Save your sarcasm, there's more. The ambassador also assures me actors from Mantua will be present to demonstrate the improvisatory techniques of commedia dell'arte."

"Your Majesty, I'm speechless."

"A rare event—remind me to issue a proclamation. Now, I've delivered my side of the bargain. Are you prepared to deliver yours?"

"Of course, but—"

"No buts. I prepared a literary and cultural itinerary for you. Follow it and you'll accumulate enough experience, material, and technique for a lifetime of writing."

As she scanned her notes, he took a piece of charcoal and a sheet of parchment from the pocket of his doublet.

"My tutor Roger Ascham wrote to Johannes Sturm, the man they call Germany's Cicero. He's their leading Protestant intellectual, and after you visit Paris and Rheims, he'll host you in Strasbourg. He's consented to discuss anything you desire for as long as you wish. Then, when the snows melt sufficiently to permit you to cross the Alps, you'll take the St. Gottard pass and enter Italy."

He clapped his hands—he couldn't help it. She smiled the kindest smile she could, given the paste. Again she consulted her notes.

"Edward, you *must* avoid the Duchy of Milan. The Inquisition there tortures Protestants as well as Jews. And use the canals and rivers that make traversing northern Italy easier. You should arrive in Venice—*la Serenissima*—in springtime."

He laughed. "You sound like one of those agents who arranges grand tours for courtiers."

"You're taking the trip of a lifetime, realizing a dream I'll never fulfill. Please be so kind as to let me share your good fortune without your bon mots."

"Forgive me—only *mal* mots from now on."

She glared. He held up his hands.

"It's only my way, Your Majesty. I thank you from the bottom of my heart. You're thoughtful and generous and I don't know what to say."

"If the Queen of England planned my itinerary, I wouldn't know what to say either, especially when I learned she's considering the additional destinations of Athens and Constantinople."

"You really must love me."

"I'd like you to take time from your literary pursuits to be my personal emissary to Murad, Pasha of Turkey. Our Catholic brethren destroyed his fleet at Lepanto. While he licks his wounds, England is prepared to offer him a treaty in exchange for a military pact against Spain. You can pave the way by making him our friend. The people Walsingham calls his *intelligence* report that he loves falconry. Thomas Smith tells me you have an aptitude for the sport."

"Greece and Turkey will make my trip more risky."

"Another reason to do what you have to do with Nan. I asked Sir Thomas to send her the chemical waters he's concocted to strengthen women. I also asked my doctor to provide Nan with Paracelsus distillations. I've done my part, now you do yours."

"You've certainly thought of everything. You have no idea how excited I am—"

"Don't be too excited. Cecil says a thousand brigands want to take you hostage."

He gave her his most solemn look. "I'll try not to be kidnapped, Your Majesty. Now, Cecil's clerks say my debt to you exceeds nine thousand pounds. I either have to borrow more funds to make the trip or sell some of my lands in Cornwall—and I'll need your permission to sell."

"Dear boy, I mastered many details to arrange this trip, but information about Cornish real estate was not among them. Ask your father-in-law. I did write the future king of France and requested he provide you with letters of introduction to important persons in Venice. I also inquired if you might stay in the Louvre—if you can stand his mother, that is."

She sat back, her shoulders slumped.

"You seem gloomy today, Your Majesty. May I be of assistance?"

"You *are* intuitive, and yes, I'm gloomy. Everyone I ever thought of marrying is either wed or dead except the Frog Prince, and he's more pockmarked than I am." She took a sip of wine. "Edward, I'll miss you."

"And I you."

"Don't be impatient with Cecil. His Court of Wards needs time to appraise all your lands. Until Drake brings me more gold and jewels from the New World, your lands are my best financial hope.

"By the way, the French court is rife with gossip about whether the future king's bride will permit the king to style her hair for the wedding. That seems to be his condition for marrying her." She shrugged. "What can I say? They're French."

They both laughed.

"Also, Henri of Navarre will be at the wedding. Why is it every French king is named Henri?"

"I ought to write a comedy about that," he said. "Of course, we might also ask why every English girl is named Elizabeth or Mary."

"Because half of England loves me and the other half loved my sister."

They both laughed, and then her eyes became dreamy.

"Oh, Edward. How I wish I were going with you."

So many tasks to accomplish in ninety days, and the most important was the least welcome.

After the goodbye party at Hampton Court, Edward took his wife by the hand and they walked to Henry VIII's favorite bedroom. It was very late and he was tired. He glanced out the window. In the dark, he could hardly see the maze.

He closed the door, embraced Nan, and kissed her.

She *was* lovely, with a petite blossoming figure, thick brown hair, and deep-set brown eyes. She smelled sweet and fresh. They'd been married four years, yet he'd never really looked at her before.

"Nan, can we make a new start?" he said. "I do care for you, it's just that I never thought of you as—"

"Edward, please." She raised a finger to his lips and looked away. "I know you don't love me. I don't know if I love you either, not the way I should. I wish we were back at my parents' dining-room table. I always thought you were smart, confident, handsome, and funny. You were my hero."

"I didn't know you felt that way."

"And I wish we could play the way we used to."

"We played?"

"Don't you remember? You taught me to play tennis."

He did remember. "You were *good*."

"You also taught me to dance."

"You were good at that, too."

"I hope I can be good at what we have to do now." She looked down at the Bible she carried. "Nobody's told me how."

She placed the Bible on the table next to the bed and murmured something that sounded like a prayer.

Now more than ever he was glad of his time with the queen—at least one of them here would know what they were doing. But the queen had made it easy for him by taking the initiative. Nan, a creation of her parents' demands, could never seduce anyone.

Slowly, he helped her undress.

"Thank you, Edward." She forced a smile. "I was too nervous to undo the buttons."

When she was naked, he lifted the sheet and she slipped under the quilt. He didn't feel an ounce of passion.

As he undressed, she started reciting. "*The Lord is my shepherd; I shall not want. He maketh me to lie down in green pastures.*"

He got under the quilt and began to caress her breasts. Her nipples hardened. He saw her blush as she said, "He restoreth my soul," under her breath. He put his hand between her legs and gently spread them apart. Her eyes widened. "He leads me in the paths of righteousness."

Should he ask her to stop praying? But she was frightened. If prayers gave her comfort, he'd have to think of other things.

He thought of the queen.

"*Yea, though I walk through the valley of the shadow of death, I will fear no evil: for thou art with me; thy rod and thy staff they comfort me.*"

Rod and staff. He smothered a laugh.

He was inside her now. What a difference—he'd known the queen was no virgin, but Nan was tight as a vise. She didn't complain, but tears trickled down her cheeks. He wished he knew how to make it better for her, but that didn't seem possible. He closed his eyes and was back in the queen's bedroom. Finally, the explosion.

"*Thou preparest a table before me in the presence of mine enemies: thou hast anointed my head with oil; my cup runneth over. Surely goodness and mercy shall follow me all the days of my life: and I will dwell in the house of the Lord forever.*"

She knew so little about life. He didn't know much, but at least he *wanted* to know more. He rolled off her and lay there, wondering if he should say something. Before he could think of anything, Nan moved farther away from him. Thank God she'd run out of verses and felt no need of another psalm.

It was over.

*H*e'd had no doubt that Nan was a virgin, a status confirmed by a glance at the bed sheet the next morning. He said a prayer of his own that they'd made a boy—he never wanted to do this again. He wasn't naive. He knew the odds, but he'd done what the queen asked. Besides, nobody asked him to stay until Nan conceived.

Next on his list was to write a last will and testament. He left his property to his sister Mary and granted Nan the right to use it until she died or remarried, whichever came first. If they made a boy, the child would inherit everything and Nan would be provided for. If they made a girl, the usual provisions for the child and Nan.

*H*e assembled his entourage, from groom to harbinger to cooks (two). Counting Lewyn, there were eight altogether. He intended to stay away at least a year. The cost would be enormous, and Cecil dragged his feet on advancing funds. When he swore for the hundredth time that no nobleman should sell his lands, Edward decided to sell the property in Cornwall himself. Sir John Arundel agreed to pay 2,488 pounds for the Cornwall lands and manor house, in two payments on November 1, 1576 and 1577. The price seemed so good that he accepted, even if he'd have to wait two years for the first payment.

To his surprise Cecil not only approved the sale but offered to cover the travel expenses out of his own pocket until the purchase price was paid—even after he'd told Cecil that the cost of travel could approach 4,500 pounds.

"I'm proud of you, Edward. After Arundel pays, you'll only owe me two thousand pounds."

Was Cecil mellowing, or had bedding Nan done the trick? He was so relieved that he didn't remind Cecil the old boy still owed him fifteen thousand pounds for Nan's dowry.

He hoped his estimate of expenses was correct. He hadn't a clue what anything cost, in Europe or in England. He'd never managed his own money before.

His last task was to have a New Year's present delivered to the queen. If not for her, he couldn't imagine how he'd have gotten through the experience with Nan. He had no trouble convincing Cecil to add the huge cost to the balance he owed the Court of Wards. The gift was a ship made of gold and diamonds.

In January, he was off.

*H*e reached Paris safe and sound. The Louvre was grand and the Frog Prince didn't kidnap his brother Henri. The new king's mother was as unbearable as the queen had predicted, and Henri won the battle to dress his fiancée's hair.

For Edward, talking with Amyot and Ronsard and seeing the commedia dell'arte performance by the players from Mantua were the high points. He was even surer now that this impro-visatory technique would be crucial to his playwriting, for the serious fare as well as the comedies.

Before he left for Strasbourg, he sketched two plays. He added a reference to King Henri of Navarre, whom he'd met at the wedding. Another Henri—the queen would love it. He used Plautus' plot about a man searching for his long-lost twin brother, but it needed amusing touches, so he gave each twin the same name. Their servants, another set of long-lost twins, also shared the same name. For spice, he made use of an Italian play, *Gl'Inganni*, which hadn't yet been translated into English.

The other play—*Love's Labour's Lost*, also in the tradition of commedia dell'arte—included a braggart, a pedant, a curate, and a clown. The pedant would be the star—no one at court ever forget their Oxbridge professor who'd made a fool of himself with excessive displays of learning.

*I*n Paris, a letter from Cecil arrived with good news: Nan was pregnant.

"I can't believe it, Lewyn. On the very first try!"

"Young women can be more fertile."

"I'm sending Cecil and Nan presents. A pair of coach horses for her and a portrait of me in a French beret for Cecil. Maybe that will broaden his outlook."

PART FOUR

Italy

12

There is a history in all men's lives
Figuring the nature of the times deceased;
The which observed, a man may prophesy,
With a near aim, of the main chance of things.

Shakespeare
Henry IV, Part I

*E*dward stood at the bow of the *traghetto* as rowers pro-
pelled it across Venice's Grand Lagoon. His entourage
surrounded him, shouting and pointing.

"Venice looks like a juicy tart!"

"Nah, she's a lovely woman!"

In addition to Lewyn and the rest of his entourage, he had
two guests: Nathaniel Baxter, a Greek-language scholar, and
William Russell, the future earl of Bedford and Baxter's Oxford
University roommate. They'd promised to pay their way, having
no idea of the cost, but how could he deny them the adventure?

After weeks in the saddle, crossing France, Germany,
Switzerland, and northern Italy, he was tired. After the *traghetto*
docked. Edward strode across Saint Mark's Square without so
much as a glance at the palace. He'd present his credentials to
the doge tomorrow—right now he needed a bath, a meal, and a

bed that didn't roll. He wanted to see the city when he was alert. What he knew about Venice from Sir Thomas was more than enough to whet his appetite.

"The city's on land *and* water," Sir Thomas had said. "The canals narrow as they flow into the interior, and the sun's light is like none other on earth. As for the buildings reflected in the water, it's a stunning display of eastern and western architecture. You'll never wonder again why Venice dominates the world."

The king of France was providing accommodations at his embassy until Edward rented a *palazzo*. Henri said fifty thousand Venetians—nearly a fourth of the population—had died in the latest outbreak of the plague, and with many more having fled to the country, there was no shortage of places to rent. When Edward arrived at the embassy, he discovered that the ambassador had also fled and left only a skeleton staff.

He was asleep in an hour. As usual, he and Lewyn shared a room. He awoke at dawn, dressed quietly, and crept down the grand stairway in his bare feet. He helped himself to wine and bread in the kitchen and then went out into the garden.

He liked to take his breakfast where he could listen to the early bird. That song was best, Sir Thomas said—those that followed were repetitive. He'd already dressed for his ten o'clock meeting with the doge. Cecil said Luigo Mosenigo was crucial to restoring diplomatic ties Venice had cut when England turned Protestant.

Having heard that courtiers in Venice didn't flaunt themselves like the nobility in London and Paris, he went inside for a look at his attire in the foyer mirror. The red in his cape was too bright and the silver embroidery screamed. The brim of his hat was too wide and the feather excessive, but he had nothing quieter with him.

He left the embassy and hoped for the best.

~~

*T*he moment he entered the palace he felt like a peacock. Everyone here wore black.

When his turn came, he spoke Italian and talked too fast.

"Your Excellency, I am honored to present the compliments of my queen, who desires my visit to be a first step in restoring diplomatic relations with your magnificent city. Personally, I would be grateful if you would grant me the privilege of touring the arsenal—the queen tells me Venetian craftsmen turn out a new boat every day."

"Our shipyards turn out *six* boats a day, Your Grace," said the doge. "As for diplomatic relations, we shall give that matter due consideration when we have a better idea about what England has become. In the meantime, I am sure that increased trade between Venice and England would prove beneficial to all."

"Your Excellency, Her Majesty is pleased to agree, but would not a military alliance enable your ships to cross Spain's waters more easily?"

"Your Grace, our boats no longer require military assistance. We now transport our goods in Genoese boats—the ones you English call 'Andrews'—and the Ragusan boats you call 'argosies.'" The doge raised an eyebrow. "With regard to *England's* difficulty in traversing Spanish waters, may I humbly suggest that piracy is no way to make friends?"

Edward scrambled for a tactful response. "I would agree, Your Excellency, that England's piracy is . . . shortsighted."

"Your Grace," the doge said, "our ambassador in Paris reported that he attended a reading of your play *The Famous Victories of Henry the Fifth*. He said you translated it into French and read all the parts. Would you do that for us in Italian?"

Edward smiled. "With pleasure, Your Excellency. As soon as I complete my preparations, I'll notify your clerk."

*H*e returned to the French embassy to find Baxter and Russell awake. He dispatched them to find a *palazzo* to rent, asked Lewyn to obtain black clothes for a literary soiree that evening—an invitation had been waiting for him when he returned--and went to work translating *The Famous Victories of Henry the Fifth.*

Lewyn returned a little past nine. Edward dressed, and together they walked to 6129 Campo Santa Maria Formosa, the *palazzo* of Domenico Venier, a senator, poet, and leader of the Venetian aristocracy.

"How did you get the clothes so fast?"

"From tailors in the Jewish ghetto," Lewyn said. "This soiree is important, Edward. Venier's hostess is his courtesan, Veronica Franco. To win France's support in resisting the Moslem attack, the doge asked her to sleep with Henri on his way to his coronation. She obliged, and the next morning Henri agreed to contribute French boats. Veronica Franco is Venice's heroine."

Edward was still laughing when they approached Venier's *palazzo*. In front of the *palazzo* was a café, across the square Santa Maria Formosa. The voices of the choir drifted out of the open church door.

"Lewyn, let's rest here a moment, take some wine and enjoy the music." He sat down. "What other stories have you gathered regarding our charming hostess?" He signaled the waiter for wine.

"After Veronica Franco separated from her husband, she listed herself in the directory of Venice's courtesans. It contains her address, her fee, and instructions to make all payments to her mother."

Edward chuckled. "A novel approach to prostitution."

"That's because she's not really a prostitute—at least, nothing like what we have in England, which here they call *cortegiana di lume*. She's a *courtesana onesta*, or honest courtesan who is educated and musical as well as skilled in the art of love. Veronica Franco is the author of a volume of poetry and she's founded a charity for courtesans and their children. It's important that you treat her with the utmost respect."

"I can't wait to meet her."

"I'm sure you will." Lewyn hesitated. "Edward, Venetian custom requires Senator Venier to provide you with your own courtesan, not only for this evening but for the rest of your stay in Italy. He won't know you don't engage in extramarital relations, so you'll have to make that clear to him."

Edward looked across the square.

"Isn't the tenor in that choir remarkable?"

"Santa Maria Formosa's a Catholic church, Edward. Did you hear what I said?"

"Don't worry, Lewyn." He stood and clapped him on the back. "Let's go inside."

Venier's *palazzo* was small compared with English palaces. In the salon on the second floor, fifty guests assembled to greet the senator. Edward took his place at the end of the line.

Venier, gray-haired and ailing, stood at the other end of the room, leaning on the arm of a woman with closely cropped brown hair tipped with gold. Veronica Franco, Edward assumed.

Then he saw the young woman beside her.

She didn't look older than nineteen. She had lush black hair, sparkling dark eyes, and ivory skin. She was smiling, her eyes lighted like candles. He lost himself in the curve of her shoulders, the full breasts and hips, the small waist.

Before he knew it, he was facing her.

"Milord Oxford, may I present Virginia Padoanna?"

"Pleased to meet you, *signorina*." He felt Lewyn's gaze burn on his neck. What did he want him to do, dismiss her? "Your family name suggests you're from Padua. Am I correct?"

"Yes, my lord."

"You say *my lord* as if I were a king."

That smile again. "I'll address you any way you wish."

"How about Edward?"

"Hello, Edward."

"Hello, Virginia."

Hearing Lewyn cough behind him, he quickly greeted Venier and Veronica Franco. Venier lifted a glass of wine and proposed a toast to his courtesan Veronica Franco and her new book of poems, one of which she recited in a clear voice at his request. Edward thought it rather a good poem—certainly the audience did, applauding enthusiastically—but he had trouble concentrating on it, his head was full of Virginia. She had drifted closer, standing just a few feet away—close enough for him to smell her scent and hear the rustle of her gown.

"*Sei bella,*" he said.

"Thank you, but Veronica's the beautiful one. Tintoretto painted her portrait, not mine."

"Only because you're young. Soon, there won't be a painter in Venice who'll be able to resist you."

A waiter passed by with hors d'oeuvres. They each took a shrimp.

"I understand the theater season hasn't yet concluded," Edward said. "I'm eager to observe commedia dell'arte."

"For that, you must go to Mantua—Leone de Sommi's academy is the center of commedia dell'arte. Venice's theater is mostly masques and carnival for the masses."

"Is Mantua far?"

"After Padua, you take the canal to Verona. Mantua's just a short ride south from there."

"I'm a stranger to this area," he said. "I don't suppose—"

She smiled. "I'd be pleased to guide you."

"I'd like that very much."

Later that evening, he told Lewyn he intended to escort Virginia home.

"Not a good idea, my friend."

"Lewyn, the streets are dark. I have no choice."

"Venice has night police!"

"I'll see you in the morning," he said. "Tell Baxter and Russell I expect to hear good news about a *palazzo*. I'll need one for at least a year."

"A year?"

"I have much to do in Italy. Venice will be my base." He patted Lewyn on the back and walked away.

*V*irginia was waiting for him at the door. She'd removed her shoes—very high heels and soles were the fashion—and put on clogs. He offered her his arm and they strolled across the square.

"Do you live far?"

"By the Canale di Cannaregio at Campo San Geremia."

As they walked, he savored the silence. Normally he felt compelled to fill such a void with conversation, which he found tiresome. This was a comfortable silence, one that filled itself with the quiet sounds of their footsteps.

She stopped in front of a narrow four-story house. Across the square stood a large structure, perhaps an old factory.

"This is where I live."

"What's that over there?"

"The ghetto. Only Jews live there—the gates are locked at sunset and aren't opened until sunrise."

"They lock them up like prisoners?"

"Most cities don't allow Jews to live within their walls. Venice only granted them permission sixty years ago. At first they weren't forced to live anywhere, they only had to limit their occupations. It was lending money that caused them to be confined."

"I don't understand."

"Christians believed lending money was a sin, but when they needed money, they borrowed it from Jews. Soon Christians decided to lend money, too—and to minimize competition, they made the Jews live in the ghetto."

"You seem to know a great deal about them."

"Their situation's similar to a woman's. Veronica Franco wrote about that, and the male writers complained to the Inquisition."

"They sound like our Puritan zealots." He smiled and then hesitated. "Virginia, . . . may I kiss you?"

"Outside? Of course not."

His face fell.

She smiled and unlocked her door. "But inside, yes."

*W*hat followed was a night he would never—could never—forget.

It was as if he discovered what a man and a woman were intended for. Why had it taken it taken him so long to find out? The closest his mother had come to affection was to place him in the arms of a governess. The only other times he'd known a woman's touch had been that afternoon with his queen and the one devastating night with his wife.

He'd never known that sensuality like this existed.

Virginia's body yielded. Her smile warmed. She was passionate, tender, playful. Afterward, when they were lying in her bed, her head on his shoulder, her hair on his chest, it was as if she'd always been there.

*T*he next morning they ate breakfast in the kitchen downstairs, next to a salon where somebody was playing a virginal. She said the doge granted her the top two floors of the building.

While a maid cleared the dishes and put fresh linens on the bed, he took Virginia aside and offered to pay.

"Last night wasn't business."

His heart skipped. "What was it, then?"

"I'm not sure." She touched his cheek. "You're a writer and so am I. Let's call it a writers' meeting."

He laughed.

"I saw you looking at Tintoretto and Veronese," she said. "I'm sorry I didn't know them well enough to introduce you, but I do know Tiziano. Would you like to meet him?"

"How do you know Titian?"

"He loves only three things besides painting: books, and food, and women."

He clenched his fists and then forced himself to relax. He'd no right to be jealous. "Would you take me to him?"

"I'll send him a message. He doesn't live far." She kissed his cheek and walked him to the door. "If he can't receive us, I'll send you a note. Otherwise, please collect me at five."

∽

*H*e returned to the embassy to learn that Baxter and Russell had found a *palazzo*.

"On *Vicus Sagittarius!*" Baxter said.

"The owners of the *palazzo* fled the plague?" Edward said.

"They died. The lawyer says he'll have it scrubbed. And it's half a block—"

"From San Marco Square?" Edward said.

"How'd you know?"

"Everything seems to be." He grinned. "I'm going to Mantua tomorrow, but I'll be back in a few weeks. As soon as I return we'll move in. Tell the lawyer we'll need it for at least a year—"

"Sorry, old man," Russell said. "You can only have it till March. There's a buyer already lined up."

He'd been here only a day and already he never wanted to leave. Of course, there was still his mission to Greece and Constantinople.

"No matter. Gentlemen, if you don't mind, I have another request. Please find a banker named Baptista Negrone. I'm told his brother is his correspondent banker in London. I must borrow five hundred crowns. I don't know how much that *palazzo* costs, but after paying the rent and traveling, I'll need money."

"Delighted." Baxter turned to Russell. "Aren't we, William?"

"Indeed. Edward, Nathaniel and I want you to know how much we appreciate your taking us along. We've fallen in love with Venice."

"So have I, gentlemen."

He looked around, but Lewyn was nowhere to be seen.

*E*dward got lost in the winding streets on the way to Virginia's house. But helpful passersby directed him, and eventually he found Campo Germenia.

There she was, seated just inside the open door, reading a book.

"I was beginning to worry," she said. "I'll leave my clogs here—we'll go faster without them."

When they reached Titian's house, the painter answered the door himself.

Edward liked him at once. His long, narrow nose and bushy white beard reminded him of Sir Thomas.

Titian greeted Virginia with a quick kiss.

Edward decided his beard was absurd.

Titian led them to his atelier, two stories high with floor-to-ceiling windows that overlooked the Grand Canal. The artist was a rich man—not surprising considering all the portraits he'd painted of the world's rulers. But hanging on one wall he saw a different kind of painting.

It seemed to depict the affair of Venus and Adonis, but the woman was nothing like the Venus of classical Greece. Titian had depicted her as older, aggressive, and lusty, reaching for an adolescent Adonis in a hunter's bonnet. Adonis held a javelin, twisting away from Venus' grasp while Cupid looked on sadly from a corner of the painting.

Tiziano returned, carrying a tray with a carafe of wine, three glasses, and a bowl of olives. He glanced at the painting, then at Edward.

"You like?"

"Very much."

"I painted five or six of Venus and Adonis," he said. "This is the only one that varies from Ovid's version of the myth."

"Why did you alter it?"

"King Philip of Spain commissioned the painting after he wed Bloody Mary. When he returned to Spain, he took it with him. It's here for—how do you say?—a touch-up."

Walking back to Virginia's house, they held hands—she said she felt shy in the daylight, but now it was dark.

"Edward, are you sure you want me to travel with you to Mantua?"

He'd been expecting her to tell him she'd changed her mind. "Of course I want you with me," he said. "I'm going to Mantua to learn commedia dell'arte from the master, and I want to go there with the most beautiful, intelligent woman I've ever met."

"When you return to Venice, you'll write plays about everything you see, from the beaches on the Adriatic to the temples in Sicily to the magic of the Aeloian Islands."

"You'll be my guide through all those places?"

"As long as you promise to write about them."

"I promise." He looked up to the night sky. "And I'll finally write my version of Venus and Adonis. Thanks to Titian, I now know what to say."

"I don't understand."

"You will when I have the courage to tell you."

*A*fter they parted, he walked back to the embassy. There was so much he wanted to tell her, but *not* that Titian in painting *Venus and Adonis* had depicted the Queen of England and her subject Edward de Vere.

13

All the world's a stage,
And all the men and women merely players:
They have their exits and their entrances;
And one man in his time plays many parts.

Shakespeare
As You Like It

*B*efore they reached Mantua, they had to survive Verona.
Edward and Virginia were sitting on a bench by
the canal that ran from Verona to Milan, waiting for
the next passenger boat. Edward wondered if he should have
rented fresh horses for the last leg of the trip instead of purchasing them.

"I spend too freely," he said. "Before Italy I never cared about
money—now there are so many things I want to do with it."

"Travel makes us see things in a different light."

"I think I'd like to buy a *palazzo*," he said. "I could live here,
write . . ." He glanced at her. "But the queen controls my lands.
Until I buy them back, I could never afford it."

"You're a creature of England," she said. "Won't you miss it? All
your work is inspired by England's history."

"I *am* writing plays about England's history, but I also want to write about Italy. I saw some things in Verona that inspired me."

"Such as?"

"Remember that girl brushing her hair in front of the window? I'll add that. Little details give a play verisimilitude."

"Plutarch's rule."

"You know it?"

"Of course."

"I'd also like to write a play set in Venice, something about the Jews. We Englishmen know so little of them."

"Would that interest people?"

"I think so, but even if it doesn't, they ought to learn. And, well, I should be able to make any character interesting, whatever the background."

*I*n Mantua, he spied a grove of trees. Virginia unpacked the lunch he'd bought in Verona while he stretched out on the grass and made notes.

"Lewyn didn't approve of my going with you," he said.

She raised a brow. "Because I'm a *cortegiana onesta*?"

"He disapproves of all infidelity."

"How will you manage him?"

"I won't even try—I respect him too much." Edward tossed aside his notes and stretched out. "Besides, he'll get over it. He always does. And he gave me an idea for a play."

"About what?"

"Two best friends fall in love with two women, then become angry with each other for being disloyal. To preserve their friend- ship, one offers to give his woman to the other."

She turned back to their lunch and set out some plates. "You'd treat women like chattel?"

"Of course *I* wouldn't, but it happens all the time—and it's not just women, you know. Men treat each other that way, too." He shook his head. "England's raw."

"So is Italy."

He looked up. There was a tightness in her voice.

"Edward, a rich father in Venice keeps his wealth intact by investing only in the dowry of his eldest daughter. The others are forced to enter a convent or become a *courtesan onesta*. There are thousands of courtesans in Venice." She looked away. "A man has many options."

"One day, my plays will be performed at court," he said. "Maybe they'll strike a chord, encourage people to think differently. My uncle's the Lord Chamberlain, in charge of the queen's entertainment, so they're sure to be seen."

"Venier said *you* were the Lord Chamberlain."

"No. I'm the Lord *High* Chamberlain. It's a ceremonial position—I carry the canopy over the queen's head on state occasions."

She shrugged.

This was harder than he'd imagined. He thought she'd be pleased. Perhaps if he bought her something? He adored Virginia even more than Italy itself.

The silence stretched out.

"Didn't you love walking in the footsteps of da Vinci?" he said. "He was born just outside Verona, you know."

"I was born in Verona."

Stupid—she didn't need a lecture from him. He cast about for something else.

"What haunts me, even more than the Roman arena, is the Lazaretto. Imagine if your parents were diagnosed with the plague—your whole family quarantined in that compound by San Lorenzo's Well and left to die. That mass grave must be the largest in Italy." He reached for his pen. "I think I'll write about that as well."

"Is *everything* grist for your mill?"

He blinked. "You don't approve?"

She looked away, over the rolling hills. "My family is buried in the Lazaretto."

He sat up, reached for her. She didn't turn, and he let his hand fall.

"I'm so sorry," he said. "I didn't know. . . . How did you escape their fate?"

"I was visiting my cousins in Mantua. Afterward, my aunt and uncle there took care of me."

He reached for her again, and this time she leaned into his touch.

"I also lost my father," he said. "He was poisoned by a man who wanted his property."

She turned to face him.

"Your father was *murdered?* How you must have suffered?"

"You suffered, too." He took her hand.

"I've never met a man like you," she said. "I know business-men who are single-minded about their work and artists who are dreamy-eyed. But you're driven as well as dreamy—the best of both."

"You understand me after such a short time," he said. "You're right—my work is everything." He held her gaze. "Almost every-thing."

He longed to say more—that he loved her, that she filled and fulfilled him, that he wanted her to come back to England with him—but she knew he had a wife. He had so much to tell and was afraid to lose her in the telling.

"Come," she said. "It's time we moved on."

They sat in the waiting room outside Leone de Sommi's *studiolo* in Mantua, drinking wine and waiting. The assistant to the academy's director said Leone was in a rehearsal and couldn't be disturbed.

Since the picnic, they'd ridden in silence. For years he'd brooded about his father's death—now, for the first time, he thought about how others had suffered, just as much and perhaps more than he had. He vowed to be a better observer—if he couldn't empathize with others, how could he hope to infuse his plays with feeling?

"Virginia," he said, "what did your aunt and uncle say when you told them you intended to be a courtesan?"

"They were pleased. The alternative was worse—I wanted to be an actress." She shrugged. "They had no money for a dowry and actors make next to nothing. As a courtesan I had a chance to be independent, even rich."

"Do you regret not becoming an actress?"

"Wait till you meet Leone." She smiled. "Then you tell me."

"Women aren't even allowed to act in England," he said. "Boys play the female roles."

She laughed. "No wonder your Puritans are agitated."

He was laughing, too, when the clerk returned.

"The duke will be here tomorrow, milord. I would give you a tour of his art but he insists on showing it to visiting noblemen himself. He's very proud of his family's acquisitions."

Virginia smiled. "He hides the best ones in his bedroom."

Edward glanced at her, frowning.

"*Signor* Leone won't be much longer, milord," the clerk said. "He hasn't eaten since breakfast."

As soon as the clerk left, Edward took Virginia's hand. "I'm sorry I was so gauche about the Lazaretto."

"You didn't know."

He was making notes when Leone de Sommi arrived in the waiting room, white hair flying, black robes swirling, script pages flapping.

"Milord, my deepest apologies," he said in English. "Did my assistant explain?"

"Yes, and I fully understand, *signor*." Edward rose. "I believe you know *Signorina* Padoanna."

Leone kissed her on the forehead. "Virginia's like a daughter to me. When she declined a life on the stage, I lost the privilege of training a great actress."

She smiled. "How are you, Leone?"

"As well as an old man of fifty can be. And you are more lovely every time I see you, which is not often enough. How are things in Venice?"

"Very busy."

Of course she'd be busy.

"And Veronica, and my friend Vernier?" Leone said.

"Worried—the Inquisition has Veronica in its clutches. Jealous writers stop at nothing to preserve their position."

"Don't despair, Vernier will protect her." Leone wiped his brow. "It's very warm. Shall we take the juice of the lemon tree?"

They followed Leone into his office, a large room illuminated by windows that overlooked one of the lakes. The tables were laden with scripts and books, the walls lined with more books.

Leone collapsed in the leather armchair behind his desk, propped his slippered feet on a stack of scripts, and waved them toward an overstuffed sofa along the wall. Edward took a seat, and Virginia settled in close beside him.

Leone poured lemon juice from an earthenware pitcher into goblets made of Venetian glass and set the glasses on the table between them.

"Help yourselves, please. It's sweetened."

"*Signor*, I understand you wrote the play you're rehearsing. What's it about?"

"It's my newest, milord. I call it *Gli Sconoscinti*, which means—" " 'The unknown.' "

"You speak Italian?"

"I do."

"Thank God! Now I won't have to break my teeth speaking English. Hebrew's my mother tongue, Italian I've acquired. Two languages are enough for one old man."

"Leone, don't call yourself old." Virginia leaned across the desk and touched his hand. Edward wished she weren't so free with her touches, and then he stopped the thought. He loved her generosity of spirit, which naturally made her physically affectionate.

"Milord, the doge's representative in Paris wrote me he attended a reading of *The Famous Victories of Henry the Fifth*. How clever to alternate comedy and history scenes. I must try that."

Edward smiled. "I've been hearing about the interesting things you do here, *signor*. I'd like to see a performance or two of plays that use the commedia dell'arte technique. We have nothing like it in London."

"It's not so original as you might think, milord. In Siena, a stained glass window in the *duomo* depicts the seven ages of man: the infant, the schoolboy, the soldier, the old man, and so forth. That's probably where we got the idea."

Leone reached across the desk and patted Virginia's hand. "This young lady would have been the heroine in all my commedia dell'arte plays. What a future she had."

"Leone, please. I made my choice."

"You can always change your mind, my dear. Your Leone waits for you, arms wide."

"Thank you, but my place is with Veronica."

"What a woman our Virginia is!" He shook his head. "It's not enough she must make her way alone in a harsh world—she must also fight for *all* women."

"*Signor*, a woman rules my country, but she receives no respect unless she plays the virgin."

Leone laughed—a genuine from-the-belly laugh.

"Your Elizabeth is a greater actress than my Virginia."

Edward felt the heat in his face. He turned from them and glanced around the room. "*Signor*, how long has your academy been in existence?"

"Thirteen years, milord. Almost every town of size has some sort of theatrical academy now, but Mantua's was the first. Federico's father, Don Cesare Gonzaga, founded ours—he fancied himself a playwright. He's in heaven now and has thankfully left the writing of plays to others more suited to the challenge, but his Academy of the Enamored grows from strength to strength."

"*Signor*, forgive me if I offend, but something's been troubling me." He paused. "I thought Jews *had* to wear a badge, yet you seem to be exempt."

"The duke protects me. He did try to have me formally exempted, but too many objected. So I told him, 'Federico, I can live with insult so long as I have your personal dispensation.' And I do."

"Please tell me more about the academy."

"We have a master of dance, Isacchino Massarano, and a Flemish composer who is our master of musical instruments. Their presence leaves me free to write—comedies, tragedies, a poem in defense of women. But closest to my heart is my book, *Dialogues of the Theater.*"

"I'd love to read it. I was saddened to hear it remains unpublished."

"I'm afraid the cost of printing fifty volumes is too great. I could ask the duke, but I don't like to go to the well too often. I'd rather he save his money for the academy."

"I'd love to see one of your plays as well."

"Of course! Tomorrow night my students are performing *The Three Sisters of Mantua*, a tragedy about a marquis's daughters that's based on a true story."

"How long has your family been in Mantua?" Edward said.

"Seventy-five years, milord. Those who didn't burn in the fires of the Spanish Inquisition were expelled by King Fernando and Queen Isabella. The Duke of Mantua welcomed two hundred of us. Today, we are two thousand."

*A*t dinner Edward couldn't take his eyes off Virginia. The black gown she wore made her hair shine like the plumage of some exquisite bird. Still, the most wondrous thing about her was her smile. He felt he could watch her smile for hours.

He took her to bed immediately upon reaching their room. He was so passionate he had no control over himself and worried at first that he might offend her, but she only matched his enthusiasm. There was no end to the things she showed him—she made Romano's book of love sketches seem like a primer.

Afterward, she put her head on his shoulder as she had that first night in Venice.

"Edward, tell me about your queen."

He stroked her hair. "Before my one night with her, I'd never been with a woman. I was twenty-two, married a year, and hadn't even slept with my wife. Nan and I grew up together—she was like a sister to me."

"I understand."

If she really did, she was the first.

"A year after the wedding, the queen invited me to a country house," he said. "Before I knew it she'd got me in bed with her. It wasn't . . . what I would have chosen, but I'll admit there's something about her. Something seductive."

"Did you ever sleep with her again?"

"Never." He sighed. "I even thought we might marry—she said as much—for a brief time. But her interests are . . . changeable."

With each answer he gave, he felt as if a weight were being lifted from his shoulders. "The queen's condition for granting me permission to travel to Italy was that I bed my wife to produce an heir. I've never slept with anyone else—until you."

She kissed him. Her lips were like balm.

"Now do you see why I want to stay with you forever, buy a *palazzo* in Venice, and write?"

"Yet the queen has control of your lands and money," she said.

"But she doesn't have control of me."

For two weeks, he attended rehearsals of commedia dell'arte performances. He also read Leone's *Dialogues* and absorbed his disquisitions on playwriting. He spent every morning writing, every evening in Virginia's arms.

Duke Federico arrived—young, bright, obsessed with his art collection. He began by showing them the frescoes on the walls of his former stables, remodeled by a mistress into galleries.

"Here we are." The tall dark duke spread his arms. "This is my Salon de Troia. The frescoes are by the great Raphael, his students and colleagues. They depict the chaos, the cruelty, the waste and terror of war. I never forget the lessons of my frescoes. I always work for peace."

Edward found the frescoes remarkable. Unlike the religious art that decorated Italian noblemen's every wall, these secular works were physical, sensual. Horses reared, eyes flashing, mouths agape. Giants plundered. Achilles shook his spear as a Greek soldier clutched the corpse of Patroclus, who was stripped of the armor he'd borrowed from his lover Achilles.

As always, he made notes. He thought of the Northern Rebellion. Perhaps he could write another long poem, one that described his vision of the Trojan War—not just its madness and cruelty but its abuse of women. That should please Virginia.

Federico took his arm. "Milord, permit me to show you sculptures of Giulio Romano and his students and colleagues, the disciples of Raphael. Romano designed my palaces as well as many of my gardens—he even designed my plates and silverware. But my favorites are his sculptures. He covered them with paint and gold he purchased from Tiziano, applied wax and lac, and in doing so he made them come alive." The duke pointed to one of the statues. "You see, milord? It looks like human skin."

Edward stood in awe of the warm lifelike tones. "Vasari didn't mention Romano was a sculptor."

"Take pity on the poor scholar, milord. They're only human, and humans make mistakes." The duke smiled.

"It's wonderful to be here. I'm afraid England's devotion to the arts is somewhat lacking."

"Of course, milord. We capture our emotions through art, and in the process we help others to express theirs."

"I hope to do the same in my writing."

"I wonder," Virginia said, "whether the written word might not be even more valuable than a fresco or a monument. Monuments may crumble and paintings fade over time. Words don't."

Just when he thought he couldn't love her more.

"You are very wise, *signorina*."

If Raphael and Romano could train and inspire students of painting and sculpture, he must inspire students to write. He'd find the most promising ones at the universities, provide them with room and board, and try to hone their creativity. Another reason to preserve his money, assuming he could. He'd start a movement. At last, England would have a writing community worthy of the Renaissance. Sir Thomas would be so pleased, as would the queen.

Most evenings they dined with the duke. Leone did not join them—he observed Jewish laws regarding meals—but on one occasion he invited them to his table, where he introduced them to a colleague.

"This is Samuel Archivolti," Leone said. "Virginia was quite excited by his writing. I think you will be too, milord."

Archivolti, perhaps forty-five years old, was the thinnest man Edward had ever seen.

"What's your subject, Samuel?"

"Desire, milord. I write about its various aspects—hope, joy, suffering, despair—and urge suitors to marry and stay married, even if it's difficult."

"A noble endeavor. What forms do you use?"

"Letters and other prose, milord, though lately I've found the sensitivity and grace of the sonnet well-suited to the subject of desire."

"My uncle Surrey was the first in England to write sonnets in the Italian style. I think I'd like to try it myself at some point."

*T*hat night, their last in Mantua, Federico was called away to settle a dispute in a village and Leone was in Ferrara introducing actors to the duke. After dinner, Edward went to their room and wrote all night.

In the morning he was still at it—sweaty, tired, content. The plays were taking shape.

Virginia looked over his shoulder.

"You write like an Italian."

"I let the clerks print their records in secretary script." He got up and stretched. "Shall we take a bath together? Then we're off to Venice, where I promise I'll write even more."

"But first we must stop in Padua."

"I know—there are a few books I'd like to pick up."

*H*e bought out nearly every bookstore in Padua.

"I already have a copy of *I Suppositi* back in England, but I need it for a play."

She smiled. "Tell me about it?"

"It's about a man who tames his wife with the skills a nobleman uses to tame his hawks," he said. "I've had the idea ever since I lived with Sir Thomas. He treated his wife poorly, as did my father."

Virginia rolled her eyes. "Hasn't being with me caused you to feel any compassion for women?" She'd never spoken to him in that tone of voice.

"But it's an interesting idea," he said. "And I must write for my audience."

"You could try to elevate their taste." She was glaring at him. "But why bother? First you'd have to elevate your own." She walked out of the bookshop.

He moved to follow her but then glanced back at the shelves. Perhaps if he waited, her anger would subside.

He bought several more books: Veronica Franco's poems, a *novellino* by Massachio Salemitano, Fiorentino's *Il Pecorone*, and *Gesta Romanorum*. He'd need them all.

Arms filled with his purchases, he hastened to find Virginia.

14

Friendship is constant in all other things
Save in the office and affairs of love:
Therefore all hearts in love use their own tongues;
Let every eye negotiate for itself
And trust no agent.

Shakespeare
Much Ado About Nothing

When he returned to Venice, a letter from Cecil was waiting for him.

He was a father!

The child was a girl, but Edward didn't mind one bit. He'd never expected to feel like this when the baby was born: proud, exhilarated, tender.

Again Cecil pleaded with him to return. Edward fired off a reply congratulating Cecil on becoming a grandfather and asked him to send more funds. He hadn't realized when he rented the *palazzo* that the entire nine months' rent was due in advance. And his credit was no good here—only the booksellers accepted his promise to pay "soon." Baxter and Russell managed to locate Baptista Negroni, who promised to contact his brother in London. With any luck, he'd persuade Cecil that more money was needed—and soon.

Now, he was on his way to the French embassy. Lewyn had asked to meet him there, and the tone of his brief note was solemn. Virginia offered to accompany him on the walk. He didn't tell her he was worried about the meeting. He was just grateful for her company.

It was near autumn, and the weather was still warm and windy, like summer in London. He unbuttoned his doublet and enjoyed the passing breeze.

"The banker hasn't received my money from London yet."

"Don't worry, Veronica will advance you whatever you need."

He smiled. "I've never borrowed from a woman."

Her jaw tightened. "We're good for more than—"

"I'm teasing, my dear." He lifted her hand and brought it to his lips. "When the money arrives, where shall we go?"

"Sicily, provided we leave no later than the end of the month. Any delay and the weather will make the journey by sea impossible."

"What route do you have in mind?"

"We should cross the Adriatic, sail down the coast—oh, and we should certainly stop at the ports of ancient Illyria. We'll stay in Sicily a while, then continue on to Cyprus. On the way home we'll stop again in Sicily, just to re-provision."

Her tone warmed as she outlined their travel plans.

"Virginia, while I meet with Lewyn, would you look for a galley we could rent?" He squeezed her hand. "You're sure to find a better deal than I could."

She smiled. "Of course."

He'd finally found a way to make her smile. Now if only he could find some way to keep her.

"Before you go," he said, "something's been bothering me."

She looked at him, brows raised. He took a deep breath.

"Virginia, what if we have a child?"

She shrugged. "My aunt will help. I have only to ask."

"Simple as that?"

A sharp glance. "For a woman it's never simple."

He studied her for the thousandth time. Her form was as curvaceous as a pear, but it was nothing compared with her mind, her strength of spirit. Should he ask her now to come back to England with him?

No. He hadn't won her yet, not completely, and he couldn't bear it if she said no, and if she said yes, what would he do about his family?

They walked on in silence for a while.

"Edward . . ." She looked pensive. "Have you ever been with a man?"

"What? No!" He laughed. "Do I seem a Ganymede?"

"No, but . . . so many of your encounters with women have been unhappy. Perhaps for you, loving a man is more . . . logical."

"Not *every* encounter has been unhappy." He gave her his best smile. "Besides, love's not a matter of logic."

She laughed. "A priest might have something to say about that. Aren't you religious?"

"No. I read the Bible because it's filled with good stories. I have my Geneva Bible in my book sack right now. I always carry it with me in case I have to wait for something."

"Times are changing," she said, "at least in Venice. For every ten men who take a traditional view, there's one who thinks women deserve better treatment. Equality's only a matter of time."

"I believe it." Though he was sure that in England, at least, it would be a long time.

She kissed his cheek. "Here we are," she said. "Good luck with Lewyn. I hope he's not as upset with you as you think."

✺

*T*he embassy was deserted. Everyone was out, running errands and preparing for departure. Edward went straight to his room. Lewyn was waiting for him.

"How was Mantua?"

"Perfect," Edward said. "I learned everything I need to know about commedia dell'arte and more. Virginia introduced me to the director of the academy. He even let me read his manuscript on theater. I have pages of notes."

He stretched out on the double bed and clasped his hands behind his head. Lewyn sat down on a chair. Next to him sat a traveling bag.

"I packed your things," he said. "You can take them over to the *palazzo* before you leave for Sicily." He took a deep breath. "I'm sorry to say I won't be with you."

Edward shot up. "Where are you going?"

"I'm leaving."

"You're . . ." He looked down at the travel bag and back up. There were tears in Lewyn's eyes.

"Edward, when you married, you made a vow—"

"For God's sake!" Edward ran a hand through his hair. "When I married Nan my eyes were open but my dreams were elsewhere. You know that."

"Very poetic," Lewyn said. "But you married her nonetheless. And now you have a child."

"A girl—"

"Edward, she's your *wife!*" He looked down. "I sent a letter to Cecil. I've resigned from his employ."

"From *his* employ? What's Cecil got to do with this?"

"Before we left London, he . . . asked me to keep him informed. About you, about what transpired." Lewyn looked up, held his gaze. "I never dreamed my promise would pose a conflict of interest until . . . I should have told you."

"You don't have to *go*—"

"If I stay I can't keep this from him, not in good conscience. Don't worry, I pre-dated my resignation, effective before you met Virginia. I don't have an obligation to tell him about her."

Edward began to pace the small room. "Since when did you become so *legalistic*?"

"I thought it best for everyone."

"But you're my *friend*." His heart hurt. He couldn't believe this, couldn't bear it. "We've been together twenty-two *years*. You can't just walk away!"

"This is hard for me, too, Edward. Please don't make it harder. In addition to being your friend, I must be honest."

Edward spread his hands.

"Where will you go?"

"I have family in Antwerp."

"But what will you *do*? How will you *eat*? You can't even cut a diamond or paint a portrait."

"How I make a living will depend on what I find there." Lewyn frowned. "Don't worry about me—worry about yourself."

"What's that supposed to mean?"

"You've lost your way. You're away from home, you're excited—you've experimented. Useful to a writer, but it plays havoc with a family."

"Don't my feelings have any place in your world?"

"Sometimes feelings must give way to obligations. We love, we hate, we grieve, but—our families, our homeland, our laws? They're the glue that binds us, and we break that bond at our peril. I know your marriage hasn't been fulfilling, but with effort, it could be."

Seconds of silence ticked by.

"Why didn't you say all this before we left?"

"You don't like confrontations." Lewyn gave him a sad smile. "Besides, . . . would it have made a difference?"

He shook his head. "But. . ." His voice cracked. "You've been like a brother to me."

"And I watched you grow from a bright boy to a brilliant man." Lewyn's eyes filled with tears. "I was with you when your father died. I attended your first tournament, read your first poem, your first play. I wanted to be with you to the end."

Edward's voice went flat, cold. "You're mad."

"You're the one who's . . . Your behavior with Virginia—it's no different from your father's—"

"Leave him out of this!"

"I know you love him, but Earl John didn't always set the best example—"

"Take that back!" He was shouting.

"Edward, you know I'm speaking the truth—"

He lunged at Lewyn and punched him in the mouth. When he drew back his fist, there was blood on it.

Edward turned away, grabbed a handkerchief, and held it out to him. Lewyn pressed it to his lip.

"I'm sorry I struck you."

"You were upset. So am I."

"Isn't there *anything* I can do to dissuade you?"

"I don't see what it could be."

"Virginia's good for me. She's an amazing woman—"

"I'm sure she's amazing, but that's not the point."

"And what is?"

"Edward, how would you feel if *your* daughter did what Virginia does?"

"Virginia's had a hard life. We come from different worlds."

"That's also my point."

"If you only knew how much I learned in Mantua. And I never would have gone, never would have learned so much, if it weren't for her."

Lewyn stood and reached for his valise. "If I don't leave now, we'll weep, and I promised Earl John I'd never let you cry."

He embraced Edward, turned, and left the room. Edward followed him down the stairway and stood at the front door.

At the stop for the *traghetto* near St. Mark's Square, Lewyn paused once to look back. Then he turned the corner and was gone.

Edward stood there, perfectly still, staring after him. He'd known Lewyn wasn't happy about the affair, but from time to time he was unhappy about other things—the Gad's Hill prank, for one—yet in the end, they always laughed. Together.

He was alone now.

No word from Cecil. Near frantic over his dwindling funds and gloomy over Lewyn's departure, he decided to participate in a jousting tournament—or, to be precise, a parody of a tournament. He could use a bit of fun. A Venetian aristocrat had dreamed it up to celebrate the marriage of Irene, the Empress of Constantinople. Every worthy in Venice was there, including the Pasha of Aleppo and the Sultan of Persia.

He rented a horse, wore a violet costume, and carried a falcon device on which he had a motto engraved: "Valor Proceeds Arduous Undertakings."

To his surprise, his opponent was a woman. Virginia said Venice was changing—perhaps he hadn't understood how much. He wished she were there, but she said she was working with Veronica on her defense against the Inquisition.

The Countess of Edenbourg appeared at the far end of the field. Dressed in a bilious yellow robe, she rode a dappled gray hag and carried a Frankish lance. She pulled down her visor and galloped toward him.

They collided, and were both unhorsed.

He sat up, dust billowing about him. Unhurt, he raised his visor and looked for the countess. She was getting to her feet and opening her visor. They laughed and clasped hands. They were awarded a prize, the Horn of Astulf, paladin of Charlemagne. Someone said the horn contained magical properties to vanquish foes. The following week, the joust entered Venetian folklore. A *dottore* acting in a commedia dell'arte play described "Milord Oxford" and his costume, trappings, and titles, reciting every word in one long breath.

When Edward heard about it, he was embarrassed—until it occurred to him that this was to be *his* world, the world of entertainment. If he were going to act in his own plays, he'd better prepare himself to be the occasional object of laughter.

*H*e took long walks alone. On one rare occasion, Virginia joined him. "Virginia . . ." He had to ask. "Have you been with another man?"

"I told you, Edward, I'm working with Veronica. She has *two* lawyers now. The meetings are endless."

He wanted to believe her—still, he felt jealous. They walked beside the canals, which stank of garbage and sewerage. Venice's side streets were scented with jasmine and peach blossoms, but the city as a whole was far from perfect. They strolled across the Rialto square. He always stopped to study *Gobbo*, the statue of the kneeling hunchback.

He told Virginia some of the names he'd thought up for the characters in his Italian plays, including Gobbo, after the statue, and Bassano, the family name of five Jewish brothers exiled from Spain. She particularly liked Shylock, inspired by Sir William Lock, the promoter of Frobisher's voyages. Lock had hounded noblemen in London to invest in the venture, and he hooked Edward. If he lost his investment, he'd be *shy* of funds. Ergo, *Shylock.*

Only a hundred Jewish families lived in London—it was still illegal for Jews to live in England—but the Bassanos, he explained, were respected. He was using their name in his play to introduce Jews in a positive way, before he unveiled the more complicated Shylock.

*W*ith or without Virginia, walking the streets of Venice brought him peace of mind. Before he left London, he'd published a book containing nineteen of his best poems about love, death, and moral agony under the name of his friend George Gascoigne. Titled *A Hundred Sundry Flowers*, the book was well-received—until Puritans denounced it as lewd and per-suaded the censor to burn the rest of the copies.

He decided to publish a short novel written in Italy under the name of the novella's hero, an Italian nobleman named F.I., for *fortunatus infelix*—the unfortunate one. Everyone in England would see it as a play on Hatton, who signed *his* poems "Fortunate One." Since it was supposedly written by an Italian nobleman, the queen would find it easy to overrule the censor.

He was proud that he'd finally crafted a novel. He didn't know how many more he'd write, but he was proud of this one and by God he'd see it published.

*H*e wrote to Cecil again, demanding to know what was tak-ing so long to send the money. "I am not what I seem," he wrote. It was time Cecil understood him.

He took long walks in the evenings, with and without Virginia.

Night watchmen, on guard everywhere, made him feel safe. He went over scenes from the Venice play in his mind. Above all, he wanted his play to give the Jews their day in court.

If only Lewyn were there to see it.

No wonder he wrote at a furious pace—it was all he could think to do. Virginia aside, he was walking around with a hole in his heart that hurt like the devil.

He stopped in the street, turned, and headed back to his *studiolo*. He wanted to finish the play while he was still in Venice, and he was running out of time. His money would be here any day, and then it was on to Sicily.

The money *would* come. It had to.

He stopped at a cafe to drink wine, read his Bible, and make notes. The other day he'd underlined a passage in Deuteronomy: *"my doctrine shall drop as doth the rain, and my speech shall flow as doth the dew."* He copied the sentence, revising it to *"The quality of mercy is not strain'd. It droppeth as the gentle rain from the heaven."*

He'd remind Londoners of the importance of the battle in the Gulf of Lepanto as well. Too many ignored the outside world. Without access to the Mediterranean, English wool and weapons couldn't reach the south by sea, nor could Italian textiles and eastern spices reach England.

And wasn't it time English aristocrats stopped dressing like fops? Wearing black was a good way to start. He'd start the trend himself as soon as he returned. With luck, the queen would take note. She couldn't keep playing the virgin seductress. It was a lie, and it demeaned her. It demeaned all women.

*V*irginia still hadn't returned, so he worked night *and* day. He was weary of asking her when she'd be there. But he couldn't complain—she'd lined up a galley *and* crew. He'd have plenty of time to find out if there was another man—or men—on the voyage to Sicily.

On September 24, 1575, five hundred crowns arrived via Pasquiro Spinola, another banker he'd met at Venier's soiree.

The next day they made ready to sail. Virginia met him at the dock. "You look surprised to see me," she said. "Did you think I wasn't coming?"

She wore a new dress and a hat with a wide brim.

He kissed her. "Not at all," he said. "Just taken aback by your beauty, as always."

*A*s the galley crossed the Adriatic Sea, he felt himself the happiest man in the world. He wanted to share his elation with Virginia, but she seemed pensive, serious. So he waited.

As they sailed down the Illyrian coast, she turned to him. "I've thought about you so much in the last few weeks."

"And I you," he said.

"Tell me," she said, taking his hand, "what is it you want out of life?"

"I want to write." He smiled. "I want what I write to connect with people. To make a difference."

"Interesting but vague," she said. "What do you want for *yourself?*"

He was quiet for a long moment.

"I'm not sure," he said. "I only know I want what I do to be worthwhile. I want it to matter."

*E*ach town they passed brought fresh ideas, new images. "I've been thinking of that mansion we saw in Verona, the one across from the dock," he said, looking at the coast of the

Adriatic Sea. "The owner treated the square in front of his house as if it were his living room—easy to adapt that to the stage."

"Do you still intend to write about a man who trains his wife as if she were a falcon?"

"It *is* funny," he said. "But I think I've found a way to make it more pleasing to you."

"It's not just me, Edward."

Why must she keep bringing it up? Every time they spoke of it, he felt her drifting away from him.

"Remember the man who called Pisans 'grave citizens'? It wasn't because Pisans are serious, Virginia, it was because in Pisa they bury people in a cemetery where soil from Jerusalem is sprinkled on the coffins." He chuckled. "I'm going to have a character call the bodies in that cemetery grave citizens—of Jerusalem."

"People have a fine sense of humor, Edward, but only up to a point."

*A*fter a while, he wearied of these tiny coastal towns—he always seemed to arrive before or after a town changed hands as a result of some battle. Still, one town gave him an idea.

"Those statues we saw reminded me of the ones Giulio Romano sculpted in Mantua," he said. "I'm thinking of having a statue dragged onto the stage during a production, then come to life right in front of the audience."

"It's dramatic," she said. "I love it."

"I was beginning to think I could do nothing right."

"That's ridiculous. You're a brilliant writer, Edward, but I have opinions of my own."

"I'm going to call it *The Winter's Tale.*"

"What's the play have to do with winter?"

"Absolutely nothing, but what's French for *The Winter's Tale*?"

"*Le Compte d'Hiver.*" Her eyes lighted up and she grinned. "The tale of Count Vere! *Bravo!*"

"I always try to leave clues like that in my work—if I don't, I'm going to be consigned to an anonymous oblivion." He took her hands. "Now then, for your sagacity, you get a prize, anything you desire. What would you like?" Her smile was so warm, so loving, he forgot they'd ever argued.

"Anything?"

"Yes."

"I'd like to go to Sicily with you."

He tilted his head. "But you're already coming to Sicily with me."

"Why, so I am!" She turned and pointed. "Now, turn around, Monsieur le Compte, and look off the starboard bow—we've arrived in Palermo. *Merci* for taking me along."

Near Palermo lurked volcanic Mount Aetna, the legendary home of Scylla and Charybdis. After they docked and went ashore, he found a hotel and booked a room for them. At the desk, he studied a book he'd bought in Padua on the history of Sicily. It was here the Sicilians had rebelled against a French king. On an Easter Sunday they'd massacred eighty-four thousand French soldiers and invited Pedro, king of Aragon and Catalonia, to rule them.

It was perfect for a history play. To catch the attention of his English audience, he'd mention that the Spanish king's bastard brother, Don Juan, was also coming. The threat of a Spanish invasion was real. If he worried about it, so should all Englishmen. But audiences being what they were, he'd write the play as a comedy and call it *Much Ado About Nothing*.

After several hours of writing, he went down to the port for some wine, leaving Virginia to nap.

༃

*T*he tavern wasn't crowded—just a single English officer and a Spaniard drinking red Sicilian wine at separate tables. He chose a table between them and ordered a bottle for himself.

Afternoon darkened into evening. All three tables were on their second bottle of wine when the English officer turned to Edward.

"You're from England, aren't you?"

He glanced over. Fat and balding, the fellow looked to be in his mid-twenties.

"In fact," the officer said, "weren't you at St. John's, Cambridge?"

"I was." He extended his hand. "I'm the Earl of Oxford."

They shook hands.

"Milord, I knew you then as Edward de Vere. What a small world—and believe me, I've seen much of it."

"I envy you."

"Permit me to introduce myself," he said. "William Webbe."

"A pleasure, Mr. Webbe—come, join my table and tell me tales of your travels. I'm sure they're thrilling."

"That's one word for it, milord. I was captured by Moslem pirates, spent some time as a slave on a galley. After the Turks tortured me, I was ransomed. I'm recuperating here while I translate Virgil's *Georgios*. When I return to England, I'm hoping to find a position tutoring a fine Essex noblemen."

"Perhaps I can help you," Edward said. "Let me know when you're in London. You can reach me at Savoy House in the Strand."

"Very kind of you, milord. We St. John's men have to stick together, don't we?"

"Indeed." He ordered another bottle of wine for each of them.

"Gentlemen," said a Spaniard, "I couldn't help but overhear your conversation."

"You speak English," Webbe said.

"Of course," he said. "I have a Spanish education."

They laughed.

"Won't you join us?" Edward said.

"Don't mind if I do." Once he was seated, he ordered a fresh bottle.

"Spanish friend," Edward said, "we heard from Webbe, here— what's your story?"

The Spaniard took another sip of wine. His hair was white as snow, though he didn't look much older than Webbe.

"Miguel Cervantes, at your service." He feigned a bow. "Born in Alcala de Henares, father a surgeon, uncle the town mayor. I was valet to a wealthy priest until he became a cardinal and I enlisted in the Spanish navy's infantry. From there I was captured by Algerian pirates, forced to row in a galley until my family ransomed me. I'm going home in a few days."

Edward nodded toward the Spaniard's arm, which hung limply at his side.

"Did you injure it in battle?"

"I took two shots in the chest and one in the arm in the last moments of Lepanto. I like to say I lost my left hand for the glory of the right. I spent three years in a Naples hospital, and now if the pirates don't get me again, I'm off to Barcelona. And you, milord?"

Edward emptied his cup and refilled it.

"Please, call me Edward. Both of you."

Webbe raised his cup.

"To you, Edward."

"To the three of us."

They clinked glasses and drank.

"I hardly know where to start," Edward said.

"Stories begin at the beginning," Cervantes said. "Why don't you?"

"Well, then." He took a long drink. "When I was very young, my father was murdered, poisoned. At least, I think he was—no, I have good reason to be sure of it. I became a ward of the queen. I had to leave my home and live with her principal minister."

Webbe waved the waiter over for another bottle.

"I went to Cambridge and Oxford, read law at Gray's Inn—I even served as aide to my uncle, the Earl of Sussex, when he was putting down a rebellion in the north of the country."

"Good show," Webbe said.

"I suppose it was, until we massacred three hundred innocent civilians to teach the rebels a lesson. . . . Not much more to tell, really. I was forced to marry my guardian's daughter. We've just had our first child, a girl."

"Wonderful!" Cervantes raised his glass. "Congratulations, *signor*."

"Again, good show, milord." And again they clinked glasses and drank.

"The only thing of note about me is that I'm a writer," he said. "I've been published, my plays have been produced, my work has been enjoyed. Praised, even. But I can't put my name to my own work because I'm nobility—it's just not done. So there you have it."

For a long moment they all drank without talking.

"You said your father was murdered," Cervantes said, "but you've said nothing of revenge."

"If I kill him, *I'm* a murderer," Edward said. "I could lose my land, my titles. I might even be executed."

Cervantes shrugged. "A steep price, but it would not stop me."

"In any case, killing him would interfere with my writing," Edward said. "I won't have that. He's hurt me enough. He killed my father, I won't let him kill my soul."

He looked to Cervantes, whose only reaction to this ringing

declaration was another shrug. Webbe was busy pouring himself another cup of wine.

He had to prove himself. He climbed onto the table and lifted his cup high.

"I, Edward de Vere, Earl of Oxford, call on all manner of persons to choose any weapon and confront me on any field of battle, anywhere." The table wobbled, and he stumbled down. Cervantes laughed and bellowed for another bottle while Webbe stared, wide-eyed.

"My English friends, this one's on me." Cervantes raised his cup. "I, Miguel Cervantes, also wish to make a challenge. If God spares me from the pirates, I will become a writer like my friend the Earl of Oxford, and the hero of my very first novel will be modeled after him." They drained their glasses as Cervantes collapsed back in his chair.

"So how will your hero resemble me?"

"Fill my cup, Edward," Cervantes said, "and I'll tell you. You'll have to pour—I'll spill the whole damn bottle if I try."

Hands unsteady, Edward managed to slosh wine into each cup.

"Miguel, even *I* don't know what kind of a person I am. How would you?"

"I've drunk with you for over an hour. I think I know you well enough."

"Very well, let me fortify myself." Edward drained his cup and slammed it on the table. "Now let me hear your version of the Earl of Oxford."

"When I'm done, you may smash that bottle over my head. "

"I'd never do that—go ahead, speak your truth. I can take it." He glanced at all the empty bottles on the table. If he did smash one over the Spaniard's head, at least the fellow would feel no pain.

"You have every advantage in life—wealth, position,

education, high intelligence, talent—yet you cannot avenge your father's death."

"What would you have me do?" Edward half-rose from his seat, leaning over the table.

"*Write.* Forget your damned anonymity and write."

"And if the world never knows I'm the author?"

"Who cares? You don't write for money, you're already rich. You don't write for notoriety, you're the seventeenth Earl of Oxford." Cervantes banged a hand on the table, rattling the cups. "Quit your whining. Who cares who wrote the words, as long as they're heard?"

Edward slumped back into his chair. It was true—Cervantes saw his soul.

"When I was in that galley," Cervantes said, "I learned that freedom isn't something to waste. You can write, therefore you must." He turned to Webbe. "As for you, Webbe, I'm going to make you the model for my hero's faithful squire. A true Englishman, loyal to the end, even if a member of your upper class shits on your face."

Webbe chose this moment to slide from his chair to the floor.

"Yes, dear Oxford," Cervantes said, "you've inspired the hero of my novel. He'll use a sword, not words, but he, too, will travel the countryside, a nobleman intent on setting right every wrong he finds."

*E*dward barely made it back to the hotel. Virginia took one look at him and wrinkled her nose.

"Where have you been?"

"Nowhere special," he said. "And everywhere important."

With that, he collapsed on the bed.

15

Lovers and madmen have such seething brains,
Such shaping fantasies, that comprehend
More than cool reason ever comprehends.
The lunatic, the lover and the poet
Are of imagination all compact.

Shakespeare
A Midsummer Night's Dream

He was worn out from Sicily, but Virginia insisted they sail to Cyprus. He slept all the way to Famagusta and when they arrived went straight to the battlements that overlooked the port. He climbed to the top, made a note or two, and told Virginia he'd seen enough.

"We came all the way here so you could take a walk on the battlements?"

"That's the way it is with Petrarch's *little things*. Besides, I haven't even seen Florence, Siena, or Rome. Let's get started."

Virginia smiled. *"Andiamo."*

They returned to Palermo for a night and weighed anchor the next morning. The captain wanted to make it past the Aeolian Islands before a storm hit. Every sail was raised and the rowers did their best, but the wind and waves rose steadily and the captain ordered all sails furled—there was nothing to do now but row and pray. The crew members rowed ceaselessly until they reached the island of Volcano, where they found anchorage in the strangest place Edward had ever seen: inside an enormous rock on the beach. Anchoring was tricky—the line needed ample room to swing, but too much and the ship would be dashed to pieces in the small space—but the galley was soon secured.

He and Virginia made their way down the beach, passing pool after pool of muddy water that stank like horse piss. Eventually they came upon a shack. He knocked.

A man speaking a Catalan dialect invited them in. He offered one of his three rooms—he lived there with his wife and little girl—and said they were welcome to stay until the storm abated. Edward could have hugged the poor wretch. For two more days the winds raged. They passed the time by exploring the island, and at night Edward filled page after page with notes about strange animals, ugly flowers, steaming geysers, and insects that looked as if they could kill a grown man. And when the wind blew, the cracking, drumming, and sighing from the rocks sounded like music.

"Of course, it's the perfect setting for a play," Virginia said as they walked along the beach.

"I'll call the character Caliban, *outcast* in Catalan."

Finally, the storm subsided. On a calm sea under a sunny sky they sailed for Naples.

Two months had passed since Edward left for Sicily. He'd seen Cyprus and Volcano, Adriatic ports from Capodistria to Zipola with its Roman amphitheater, Bohemian ports like Fiume, Spolato and the palaces of Emperor Diocletian, and Ragusa. Now he was ready to return to Venice, which they reached on the last day of November.

Winter hadn't yet arrived, and if they moved fast they could make it to Florence, Siena, and Rome, and still be back in time for Carnival. No word from the queen awaited him, so he paid his bills and counted what was left of the five hundred crowns. He had enough to make the one last trip south, so late in December he and Virginia left for Florence. Again it was on the tip of his tongue to ask her if she'd come to London with him. But if she refused, he didn't think he could bear it.

The idea kept distracting him through their detour to Sabbioneta on the way to Florence, the sights of Florence itself, even in Siena, where he stood in the cathedral and studied the stained glass window depicting the seven ages of man. There they were: the infant, the schoolboy, the lover, the soldier, the justice, the slipper'd *pantalone,* and the old man approaching oblivion. He felt so pressed for time. If the world were a stage, how far was he from the end of his role? It was time to move on.

And past time to ask Virginia to come to London. He'd do it in Rome.

*E*dward returned to Venice to find five hundred crowns awaiting him from Cecil along with a plea to sell no more of his lands.

He fired off a reply at once:

> *I need to keep traveling because I have no hope of an*
> *appointment by the queen. She says I'm too young and*
> *somehow that renders me unfit. Yet she appoints others less*
> *worthy. I know she thinks it best not to appoint me because*
> *she wants me to write but to write I need education and*
> *travel. Books are crucial to my education and they cost*

money, too. If the queen ever does employ me I'll be so old my child will be the one to give thanks. To wait for her to appoint me is to watch the grass grow.

He and Virginia threaded their way through the streets and over the hillsides of Rome, Edward alternating Plutarch's *Parallel Lives of the Noble Greeks and Romans* with *The Fable of Menenius.* In the play he was going to write about the Roman military hero Coriolanus, he'd use Menenius, who'd likened the parts of the human body to types of people: brainy people, heart people, stomach people. He'd apply those images to people swept up in the corn riots of Coriolanus's Rome, which resembled the food riots in England.

His thoughts turned to *Antony and Cleopatra*—this one was but a mind sketch thus far, though he'd written a speech referring to her that clearly referenced the queen. Pleased with himself, he recited them for Virginia:

Age cannot wither her, nor custom stale
Her infinite variety;
Other women cloy the appetites they feed
But she makes hungry
Where most she satisfies; for vilest things
Become themselves in her.

"I can see you love those lines," she said, "but no woman likes to be reminded that she looks her age."

"You're right, but I can't bear to change a word. If the queen refuses to accept the facts of life, I must help her."

She laughed. "It's your head. Do with it as you will."

"*Julius Caesar* is the play I really want to focus on now. I'm making good progress on the outline. I need to study exactly where Caesar stood when he was stabbed to death on Capitoline Hill."

"Isn't that too gory for your queen?"

"Not if it's for a good purpose. I'll contrast the greatness of ancient Rome with the decadence of Spain, its Inquisition and so on."

Standing in front of one of Michelangelo's versions of *The Pieta*, he saw carved on a sash across Mary's bosom the words *Michelangelo Buonarroti facet*—Michelangelo made this.

"I don't have stone in which to chisel my name," he said, "but I can put proof in the titles and the plays themselves. I'll never forget your saying words endure longer than monuments."

He was ready to leave Italy now. In part thanks to Cervantes, he knew where his home was and what he must do when he got there: write his plays and stage them in England. The only question that remained: would Virginia come to London with him?

*T*hey sat together in the taverna in front of Venier's *palazzo*. It had been his favorite ever since his first night in Venice when he discovered it with Lewyn. Perhaps that was why he came here now, even in the dead of winter. Bundled up, they drank wine and talked.

"Virginia, you know I've decided to return to London. You were right—it's where I must live and stage my plays." He took a deep breath. "The thing is . . . I'd like you to come with me."

She sat silent for a very long time—too long, it seemed to him.

"Edward, I can't. As much as I love you, Venice is my home."

He wanted to scream. He had to convince her. "We could come back and visit, often. You'd be happy in England. I'll make a beautiful home for you—"

"Edward, you *have* a home. You have a wife."

"That doesn't mean we can't be together."

"It's not just that you're married. I don't want to be dependent, on you or anyone else. Besides, I have a goal here, to improve the place of women in our society. Venice is ready for change. England isn't."

Now it was his turn to be silent. Her answer left no room for argument. He wanted to cry.

In the silence that followed, a sweet, strong tenor reached them from the Church of Santa Maria Formosa. It was extraordinary, clear as crystal.

"Come, Virginia." He took her by the hand. "Let's meet the young man with that voice."

Without a word she followed him. They entered the church and took a seat in the last row of pews. They stayed until the music faded and the singers began to leave, two by two. After the tenor walked past them, Edward followed him, Virginia just behind.

"*Signor*, your voice is lovely."

The young man turned, his face streaked with tears. "Thank you, *signor*."

"*Milord*," Virginia said.

"Milord. I didn't know." He quickly wiped his eyes.

"It's nothing," Edward said. "Why are you crying?"

"My parents," he said. "The plague."

"They didn't lock you in the house with them?" Virginia said.

"I was in Padua, singing for professors."

She touched his sleeve. "Something similar saved me."

In that moment, Edward loved Virginia even more. So gentle. So understanding. He missed her already. They shivered—the day was turning colder. Edward turned back to the young singer.

"May I invite you to share a meal with us?"

"I don't know, milord." The boy glanced at Virginia. "I don't like to intrude."

"It would be our pleasure," she said.

Edward chose a tavern where they'd eaten before. He studied the young man as they waited for the fish they'd all ordered. He was as beautiful as his voice: milk-white skin, ebony curls, delicately carved features.

"How will you live now that your parents are gone?" Edward said.

"They left me something, and the church pays me to sing."

Edward ordered a bottle of wine and drank most of it himself. As he paid the bill, he had an idea.

"In a few days I leave for London," he said. "Someone left my entourage, and I have room for one more. Would you like to come along? In London you can live in my home as a page. I'll pay you, of course. And if you ever wish to leave, I'll pay your way home."

The boy glanced around the tavern and shifted in his chair.

"Milord, I don't even know your name."

"Edward de Vere."

"He's the Earl of Oxford, the premier nobleman of England," Virginia said, obviously not wanting the boy to miss such an opportunity. "The queen is his friend."

"My queen will love your voice," Edward said.

"She likes music?"

"Very much. She plays the virginal, as do I. And I have friends who are musicians and composers, and I use the lute in almost every play I write."

"Then you're a writer."

"I am. What's your name, young man?"

"Orazio Cuoco."

"Orazio, would you do me the honor of accompanying me to London? I'd be grateful."

For a long moment the boy didn't say anything. Then he nodded. "Thank you very much, milord. I believe I will."

*A*fter he'd given Orazio his address and arranged to meet him in the morning, Edward walked back to the church with Virginia. He wanted to see it one last time. He stood there, her hand in his.

"Why did you invite him?"

"The heart doesn't always have a reason."

But his did. He was drawn to the boy, his voice, his beauty. He was embarrassed to tell her that, though he had the feeling she knew.

"Perhaps I was also inspired by a fine madness. Socrates said madness is the channel by which we receive the greatest blessings—that it's nobler than good sense because it comes from God."

"Is that why you can be melancholy one moment, then explode with happiness and creativity the next?"

"Perhaps. Long ago when I read Aristotle, I decided to accept my condition. Aristotle asked, "*Why is it that all men who are outstanding in philosophy, poetry and* the *arts are melancholy?*" Of course he answered his own question. "*It's because they are tinged by the fire of madness.*" So I write, and invite Orazio Cuoco to London." He turned to face her. "Virginia, I want to thank you again. For everything you've given me. And . . . for giving me the strength to go home, even without you by my side."

"Edward . . ." She touched his cheek. "Even if you weren't married, even if you didn't live in London, . . . even if nothing stood in our way, I would still refuse to live with you."

He jerked back, but she grabbed his hands.

"Writing is everything to you," she said. "A woman wants to be the center of her man's world, but nothing will ever be more important to you than your work, and that's good. You're the most brilliant, imaginative man I've ever known." She smiled. "Sometimes I think I understand you better than you understand yourself."

Was he making a mistake to walk away from her? No—she was walking away from him. It had never been his choice to make. "I'll never forget you," he said. "Maybe one day I'll surprise you and return to Venice, properly dressed in black."

They laughed, but inside he was crying.

PART FIVE

Plays

16

But I will wear my heart upon my sleeve,
For daws to peck at: I am not what I am.

Shakespeare
Othello, the Moor of Venice

Three weeks after he left Venice, thoughts of Virginia Padoanna still flooded Edward's mind. Should he have pleaded? No, she wouldn't have come. Venice was her world, and London was his.

Forty-five miles south of Paris, he stopped for a night at the Count of Rousillon's chateau. He found it so agreeable that he stayed on for two more days to flesh out a play he'd been working on called *The History of the Rape of the Second Helene*. It was so optimistic he changed the title to *All's Well That Ends Well*. After two days and nights of writing, he slept half a day and then woke refreshed and resumed his journey.

As he neared Paris, he came across at least twenty thousand troops blanketing the fields on both sides of the road. He sent Russell ahead to ask the commander his intentions.

Russell returned almost at once.

"They're preparing to besiege Paris on behalf of Hercule, the

Duke of Orleans, milord. Catherine de Medici's sons are at it again."

"What does the Frog want now, besides his brother's throne?"

"Freedom for Protestants—and money. The Frog's as bankrupt as King Henri."

He should avoid Paris—he'd be a rich prize for anyone wanting a ransom—but he needed supplies. He'd been purchasing them himself for some time, having fired his offerer after the man admitted he'd spied on him for Cecil.

"Russell, will you help me purchase supplies?"

"Of course!" he said. "I've been looking for an opportunity to show my appreciation. This trip has been such a splendid adventure."

"It's not over yet," Edward said. "We'll be lucky to see Dover in one piece."

*I*n Paris, he stopped at the embassy to pay his respects. Henry Howard and Rowland Yorke, two of his old Steelyard drinking companions, happened to be in the ambassador's outer office.

Yorke greeted him with a smirk. "How was Italy, Edward?" He winked. "I hear the courtesans are something to see."

"Provocative, Rowland, but you've got them all wrong—as usual."

"S-s-some of us have been th-th-thinking about org-organizing a little trip there," Henry said.

"I highly recommend it. Mantua's interesting, as are the ruins in Sicily and the island of Volcano. And, of course, there's Rome."

Yorke moved closer. "Edward, you may as well hear it from a friend. . . . There's gossip going around back home."

"About what?"

"Nan," he said. "And the baby."

Edward felt his chest grow tight. "Are they all right?" Surely, Cecil would have written him if something had happened.

"They're fine," Yorke said. "But there's been questions raised about the little girl's birth."

Henry cleared his throat.

"Unless it t-t-takes eleven months to make an Oxford b-b-baby."

"That's ridiculous." He laughed.

"Afraid it isn't, old man. You bedded Nan in October after the party at the palace. The baby wasn't born until September."

"Gentlemen, you're mistaken. Cecil wrote me the baby was born in July. That's nine months."

"The fox was pulling your leg," Henry said. "The b-b-baby couldn't have been born in July, b-b-because she wasn't christened till September. No vicar waits two months to b-b-baptize."

"Cecil was probably waiting for my return." He'd begged him to come home, after all. "Such delays aren't so uncommon."

Henry and Yorke shared a quick glance, and Yorke shook his head.

"Whatever you say," he said. "But you'll hear it from others besides us by the time you get back."

"Go to hell, Yorke."

Nan, unfaithful? For God's sake, she'd quoted Scripture in bed. But that encounter had been far from pleasant. And he'd been gone a very long time. And she wasn't unattractive. Had someone else given her the attention he'd denied her?

*A*s they were crossing the channel, he spied a boat behind them, closing in fast. When it drew close enough for him to see its flag, his heart sank—Dutch pirates, at least thirty of them, armed to the teeth. His boat was slow and his entourage vastly outnumbered—when the pirates came alongside with grappling hooks and boarded, he ordered everyone to put down their weapons and offered the pirate captain his hand.

The captain growled something in Dutch. A Scotsman translated.

"Strip, milord. The same with the others."

"That won't be necessary," Edward said. "Take what you wish."

"Strip, milord. Everything. Off."

He removed his Italian shoes.

The captain growled again, and the Scotsman waved a dagger.

With a sigh, Edward took off his shirt and nodded at his men to do the same.

The boss shot his pistol into the air.

"Everything, milord," the Scotsman said, "or the next one's in your head."

He took off his clothes and stood there, naked, while the pirates pawed his garments. They took all the clothing and his purses but left his notes, drafts, and books, including the Hebrew Bible he'd bought in the ghetto.

He held back a sigh of relief.

The boss growled again and the pirates tossed a single article of clothing at each member of his entourage. Edward ended up with a shirt. Everyone was shivering. He was putting on the shirt when the boss growled again. The Scotsman spoke rapidly, gesturing at Edward, while the captain's face reddened. "Oxford," the Scotsman said.

The Scotsman handed his captain the perfumed gloves Edward had bought for the queen. The boss sniffed them, handed them back to the Scotsman, and said something that made the Scot laugh.

He seemed about to throw them overboard when Russell asked if he could have them. The Scotsman threw the gloves at him, and the pirates cast off. Wondering why they hadn't taken him hostage, Edward watched them sail away. Then he shrugged. Except for life and death, everything was speculation.

*T*hey landed on a beach several miles from Dover. Edward trudged from shack to shack like a beggar, offering peasants future payment if they'd part with a few rags. Almost none believed he was the Earl of Oxford—after all, he hardly looked it—but one or two accepted his promise, and after a day of scrounging he had clothing of sorts for everyone.

When he arrived in London, he stayed at Yorke's house. Settled in a comfortable chair with a glass of sherry, he tackled the subject that had been on his mind since he left France.

"I assume by now you've realized how little truth there is in those vicious rumors," he said. "Nan's the most faithful woman I know."

"I'm sure she is." Yorke kept his eyes on his sherry. "I'm surprised to hear you so defensive—it's no secret you've never cared for her."

Edward tightened his grip on his glass.

The drawing room doors opened. "Milord," the servant said, "there's a messenger here from Cecil House."

It was an invitation to stay at Cecil House with Nan and the baby.

Ever since Paris, Edward had brooded. He still thought the accusations were absurd, but there was an undeniable logic to them. He'd never loved Nan, and she'd as good as said she didn't love him. He'd found a lover in Venice—why shouldn't Nan have found one here in his absence?

He'd been granted a second chance. If he really wanted to free himself from Cecil, Nan's infidelity was the perfect excuse. He sent back his reply: "I shan't be coming to Cecil House, and you and Nan need not ask why."

*Y*orke found the whole thing endlessly amusing.

"Edward, did you notice who was standing in front of my house when we arrived?"

"Richard Worth?"

"Yes, and did you also notice what he did when we passed him by?"

Edward sighed. "I did not."

Rowland held his index fingers over his head to make a bull's horns.

"Better prepare yourself. You're a cuckold, my friend."

He never should have agreed to stay here, but he couldn't remain at Savoy House, right across the street from Nan. He had to find another place or he'd end up strangling Yorke.

*C*ecil's reply was swift. It said nothing of the circumstances, only entreated Edward to return to Cecil House. Nan added a postscript, saying that if he didn't come to her, she and the baby would come to him.

Edward responded just as quickly:

> *My lord, though I have forborne in some respect, which*
> *should be private to myself, either to write or to come unto*
> *your Lordship, now urged on by your letters and to satisfy*
> *you the sooner, I must let your Lordship understand this*
> *much . . . I am not determined, as touching my wife, to*
> *accompany her. I mean not to weary myself with such*

troubles and molestations as I have endured, nor will I, to
please your Lordship, discontent myself.

He refused to write to Nan directly, so he added a postscript to his own reply, rejecting her proposal and offering her and the baby the use of his apartment at Savoy House and his estate at Wivenhoe.

He'd move to Vere House in the meantime. No doubt Orazio Cuoco would prefer it.

*H*e received another letter from Cecil. This one insisted that Edward was the father of Nan's child.

Tired of all the back-and-forth, Edward went to see Nan's physician.

"Dr. Masters," he said, "what was Nan's reaction when you told her she was pregnant?"

"She didn't say a word," he said. "Just turned white as a sheet."

"And that was all?"

"Not entirely." He paused. He sighed. "She asked for an abortion."

He left the doctor's office in shock, went straight to Yorke's, and sent a note to Cecil requesting they meet at Savoy House.

It was high time he confronted the old boy face-to-face.

"*Y*our Lordship," he told Cecil as they sipped sherry in his rooms at Savoy House, "I want you to know I've changed my last will and testament. My cousins Horace and Francis will be my heirs."

Cecil frowned.

"I spoke with Dr. Masters," Edward said. "Did you know that once your daughter heard the happy news, she asked for an abortion? Is that the action of a wife who's just heard she's with child?"

Cecil shook his head.

"The doctor told me the same thing, Edward. *I* asked for an explanation. Did you?"

"The thing speaks for itself—"

"That's absurd. Nan's a young woman, and young women are often terrified to hear such news. It might mean their death, especially if the child's their first."

"You're the one who's being absurd. The baby was born eleven months after we were together."

"Little Elizabeth was born in July, just as I told you."

Edward slammed his glass on the side table.

"Then why wasn't she christened until September?"

"Because I refused to believe you didn't wish to be present!" Cecil shouted. "We waited until the vicar said he could wait no more. If the baby died without being christened, she'd go to hell!"

Edward stared at the bookshelves, silent.

"Edward, don't you see what Howard and Yorke are doing?" Cecil spread his hands. "Catholic zealots will stop at nothing to drive a wedge between Protestants, even if they ruin the life of an innocent child and destroy the reputation of an innocent woman."

"Yorke's not a zealot. He's a brave swordsman, and his father's master of the mint. And Howard's the only nobleman who's a professor at Cambridge."

"Don't talk to me about Yorke," Cecil said. "He doesn't even own an English broadsword. The man fights with a French rapier! As for Howard, he's a subtle serpent."

"With respect, Your Lordship, *you're* the subtle serpent in all this." Edward fought to keep his voice even. "You employed Lewyn to spy on me, and you hired my offerer to do the same."

"The queen and I were worried about you," Cecil said. "You had no idea how much such a large entourage costs, and your escape from the pirates was frankly a miracle. The Privy Council has sent Beale to Flanders to seek compensation for the damage to England's honor."

"And what of *my* honor?"

"Edward, please," Cecil said. "You've been different since you came back from the Continent. Come back to us. We love you—"

Edward stood. "I *am* a changed man," he said. "I'm withdrawing from court, as of now. I'm going to write."

And that's how things stood until the queen summoned him.

*A*pprehensive, he entered the presence room. He searched her face, white and still, but couldn't detect her mood.

"Welcome home, Edward."

"Thank you, Your Majesty. I have a present from Italy for you."

He removed the perfumed gloves from beneath his doublet. They were wrapped in silk.

"Gloves!" She pressed them to her cheek and inhaled. "Perfume!" She slid them on, smiling. "You knew my dimensions!"

"I've studied your hands."

"Dear boy." She patted the stool beside her. "Come here."

He climbed the three steps to the raised platform and sat.

"Tell me all about Italy, and don't leave anything out." Again she pressed the gloves to her cheek.

"That might be difficult," he said. "I was away for more than a year."

"If you grow weary, we'll take refreshment. Did you get ideas for plays?"

"More than I ever imagined, Your Majesty. I've set three in France and a dozen more in Venice, Verona, Padua, Mantua, Sicily, Illyria, Ephesus, the island of Volcano, Rome—"

"Just as I predicted—enough material for a lifetime."

"Two lifetimes, if you count the English history plays I revised, not to mention two long poems I have in mind. I'll need several secretaries just to keep my fingers from cramping."

"I asked your uncle to meet with you as soon as you returned—— Thomas is my Lord Chamberlain now."

"He was a bulwark against the rebels in the north."

"Now he's responsible for my well-being. I told him I need plays, but drama's not his forte. He'll need your help." She sighed. "Edward, the situation's ugly. My Privy Council's assessed a twenty-pound fine on anyone failing to attend Protestant services or traveling more than five miles from home. There've been assassination attempts from Rome."

"Rather cruel, don't you think?"

"I tried to dissuade them. My father expelled the church only thirty years ago and half of England still adheres to the old religion. But the council was determined." She clapped her hands. "Enough of that. I need distractions—you write the plays and Tom will stage them in the palace. Nothing religious—I need amusement that's witty and sophisticated."

"I'll do my best."

He told her everything he could about Italy except for Virginia. When it grew dark outside, they ate dinner. She seemed thrilled to listen to his every word, and he found he enjoyed retelling his adventures.

He was about to leave when she laid a hand on his arm and turned to the captain of the guards. "Clear the room."

∽

"*E*dward, go back to your wife," she said as soon as they were alone. "Nan needs you more than ever."

He stiffened. "I can't."

"Why?"

"It's a private matter."

"I'm your queen—there's no such thing."

"Your Majesty . . ." He took a deep breath. "Nan was unfaithful. The child isn't mine."

"Ridiculous."

"It's not. She all but admitted it to her doctor."

She shook her head.

"I don't believe it. There's some misunderstanding here."

"The child was born eleven months after I slept with her at Hampton Court—"

"The baby was born in July," she said. "Trust me, I was informed."

"But she wasn't christened until September."

The queen looked at him as if he weren't very bright.

"We were waiting for *you*. Though I did tell Cecil it was wasted effort."

He was silent.

"Edward?"

"Yes, Your Majesty?"

"What's this really about?" Her eyes narrowed. "What happened in Italy?"

He sighed. "I want to write, that's all."

"You *are* writing."

"I need to be free to write."

"You write because you're not free, Edward."

Again he was silent.

"I want you to think about it."

"Of course, Your Majesty."

"And I want you to speak to Nan, hear her explanation from her own lips. You owe her that much."

"All right," he said. "But I refuse to see the baby."

*T*he next morning he received a message from his uncle proposing that they meet at The Steelyard at eleven, but it was nearly noon when Tom burst into the tavern, white hair flying and his arm in a sling.

Ever since Edward had returned to London, he'd been behaving like an Italian nobleman, bowing and blowing kisses from his forefinger. But when Tom enfolded him in a hearty bear hug, he felt like a boy again, safe in his father's arms. But only for a moment.

"Come on," Tom said, "we've got work to do."

"Since when are you in charge of the queen's entertainment?" Edward said. "Didn't Dudley used to handle all that?"

"Not since the queen discovered he'd married Lettice Knollys in secret. Got tired of waiting for Her Majesty, I imagine." He settled into a chair and ordered ale for them both.

"I need plays, fast. I hope to God you have a few ready."

"More than a few."

"Whitehall's got a spare dining hall we can use as a theater, Edward. Twenty by forty, enough for the queen and her courtiers—she's down to twenty-five, you know, hasn't appointed a new nobleman since your father-in-law." He shook his head. "There's an endless line of ambassadors, though. I stopped counting at twenty. Seems we get a new one every day, all to convince her to marry their man." He drained his mug. "The long and short of it is that I'm pressed to find a way to entertain these folks. What have you got for me?"

"My *Famous Victories of Henry the Fifth* is ready, but the queen wants comedies. I suppose we could start with *The History of Error*. It's good as done."

"If it's a comedy, why not call it *The Comedy of Errors?*"

He shrugged. "I've no objection. I also have one about a nobleman who's always selling his lands and giving away the profits—"

Tom chuckled. "Sounds like you. What else?"

"*Love's Labour's Lost*, but it's not finished."

"Work on it."

"And I'm outlining a dozen others set in Italy."

"Wonderful—the queen loves Italy, talks about it all the time. Never been there myself. What are those about?"

"One's a love story—"

"Perfect," he said. "Her ladies-in-waiting are sure to swoon for that." He winked. "The newest is Anne Vavasour. I haven't seen her, but Raleigh says she's a beauty. Her uncle's Tom Knyvet."

"I know him," Edward said. "His family came over with the Norman invasion." He grinned and refilled his uncle's cup. "Glad to see old age hasn't hurt your appetite for pretty young things."

"Hah! Married twice and still no heir, you'd think I'd give up on the whole business. Hunsdon's sired *ten*, only two with his wife, and he's a decade older than me!" He sighed. "God's balls, it's good to see you. Up north I told myself I'd found a son."

Edward smiled. "I've missed you, too."

"How about the poems you wrote for the book, the one they printed before you left? Can you make plays out of them? The queen said she stayed up all night reading them."

"Puritans stopped the sales," he said. "They said the poems were pornographic. I'm bringing them out again, along with a satire on Hatton."

"I don't know what the queen sees in him. He knows how to dance but that doesn't make him a captain of the guard."

"I'm also working on a play about merchants in Venice."

"Good, good. No one here knows shit about any place but England. One day they're going to wake up and find the Spaniards are squeezing their balls. What else?"

"I started *Pericles, Prince of Tyre*. It won't be done for a while, though."

"Work on it." Tom's sword clanked against the table as he pulled himself to his feet. "Great to see you, Edward, but I'd best be off. Got a meeting to get to."

"I've got a few more I'm working on," he said. "One opens with a warning to Englishmen not to forget the bastard Prince Juan."

"Do me a favor? Finish that one, fast. Don Juan's the only one in the whole fucking barrel of Spaniards who knows how to fight."

"I will," he said. "There's also—"

"Look, I really have to go. The Privy Council wants to meet about getting compensation from the Dutch for robbing you." He sighed. "Sometimes I wish I were back in Ireland fighting Shane O'Neill." Tom started toward the door but stopped. "Damn, I almost forgot—the queen said she'll pay twenty pounds toward the cost of each play."

"That's barely enough for the actors! I can use my clothes for costumes, since all the leads are noblemen and royalty, but who's going to pay for sets, the musicians?"

"The queen says you will." He grinned. "She's tight as a mollusk's asshole."

"And thinks my pockets are hers, apparently."

"She's like that with everyone. No wonder no one wants to marry her."

"I *could* make simple sets, play the music myself . . ."

Tom moved to one of the piss pots lining the walls. "Whatever you have to do," he said over his shoulder. "Blast it, I'm going to be late. Look, I know it's a pain, but we've got to get these things on—you know how the queen is about her entertainment."

He finished relieving himself and marched out of The Steelyard, waving his hand over his head as if he were leading a charge.

*E*dward felt lighter than air. They were going to show his plays at court. Now all he needed was a place to sleep and work, somewhere far from Cecil House. Perhaps outside the city walls, near the new theaters.

While he was in Italy, he'd heard of an amphitheater a grocer and a carpenter built together in Shoreditch. It was so successful the carpenter started a second, The Curtain, with capacity for two or three thousand. Both were far beyond the jurisdiction of the Puritans.

Wouldn't it be grand to live near theaters? Instead of courtiers and bankers, he'd have actors and musicians for neighbors.

The owners of The Bull, the Red Lion, and the Cross Keys had turned their taverns into theaters. Blackfriars' enclosed hundred-seat theater was humming on land once owned by the church. Puritans had no jurisdiction there, either. Theater in London was finally coming alive.

When he reached Mark Lane, he saw a little girl with hair black as night standing alone on the corner. There were tears in her eyes.

"Little girl, why are you crying?" She couldn't have been more than seven or eight.

She glanced at his nobleman's ruff and sniffed. "Milord, my father is gone."

"I'm so sorry." He squatted so they were face-to-face. "What's your name? Is your mother about?"

"Emilia Bassano." She pointed to a house. "My mother's with

my uncles. I used to have five, but one died." The sounds of a violin, a recorder, and a lute drifted out of the window, a mournful pavane in a minor key. A man appeared at the window.

"Emilia, time to come in."

She gave a little wave and turned and ran inside.

Edward watched her enter the house. He thought of Nan and wondered if their daughter looked like him at all.

Of course not—she wasn't his.

On January 1, 1577, seven months after he'd returned to England, *The Comedy of Errors* was presented in the Great Hall at Hampton Court Palace.

Edward played the role of Aegeon. No one objected to his playing the lead—why did they object to his being the author?

Cecil and Nan were there, but he avoided contact.

The next month, *The History of the Solitary Knight* was performed at Whitehall Palace. He played Timon. The queen smiled from the audience when Timon sold his lands to help his friends.

Two days after *The Solitary Knight*, he staged *Titus Andronicus* at Whitehall. Again he played the lead.

"Thank you, Edward," the queen said after the performance. "You served notice on Philip."

Then, Sir Thomas died.

For days Edward had trouble believing it. Then for weeks he mourned—he slept, drank sherry, barely wrote. In time, though, he realized how much Sir Thomas would have wanted him to write. So he picked up his pen and forced himself to work. At first it took him a half-hour to come up with a single line, but soon he became caught up in the story and characters and the words flowed.

By the end of 1578, *Pericles, Prince of Tyre* was almost ready. He decided to see how it felt onstage.

As soon as the performance was over, he knew the play needed work. But what most surprised him was what it revealed about his own state of mind, his yearning to finally be united with his daughter. And who should corner him after the performance but Nan.

"Edward!" A strained smile. "How are you?"

"Working." He folded his hands behind his back. "And you?"

"I felt poorly for a long time after the baby was born, but I'm fine now." Her expression turned pleading. "She's a lovely child. You should see her. She looks just like you—"

"Please." He held up his hands and then lowered his voice. "We both know she's not mine."

"That's not true!" Nan looked as if she were about to burst into tears. "We waited for your return from Italy to baptize her—the vicar said we should—until he said we couldn't wait any longer."

"I spoke with Dr. Masters."

She paled, then flushed.

"I was terrified. Can't you understand?"

"I think I've understood quite enough."

And he walked away.

*H*e set *Pericles* aside when the queen asked him to accompany her on a progress.

Their first stop was Audley's End, the Howard estate in Essex. He sat beside her as Gabriel Harvey, a childhood friend who was also tutored by Sir Thomas, delivered the valedictory in Latin.

Gabriel's speech was filled with flowery phrases about the Earl of Oxford's writing. He pronounced it equal to the best of the

Greek and Roman masters. He reminded the audience of the Latin prefaces Edward had written for Bartholomew Clerke's translation of *The Courtier* and Tom Bedingfield's translation of Cardanus' *On Melancholy*. Finally he pointed to Edward.

"You flatter Pallas Athena, the Greek goddess of drama. You have written many Latin verses and even more in English. Thy will shakes spears!"

Edward rolled his eyes. He should have known Gabriel would do something like this, but he never dreamed he'd lay it on so thick. Since his appointment as a professor of rhetoric at Cambridge, he'd become a blowhard. Of course, he also wanted to be Edward's secretary—maybe this was his way of applying.

The queen squeezed his hand and wiped tears from her eyes.

"Keep writing, Edward—never stop." She pulled a roll of parchment from the leather bag she liked to carry. "Here's the deed to the Manor of Rysing," she said. "I confiscated the lands from the Duke of Norfolk when he was convicted of plotting with Mary Scots. They produce 250 pounds a year. Enjoy it."

Startled, he thanked her and looked around. Everyone—Cecil, Dudley, Hatton—seemed impressed by Gabriel's speech. Not him—he couldn't abide the man's excess. He decided to appoint Lyly his secretary.

*T*he next year was even busier. In January, *All's Well That Ends Well* was staged at court. He played Bertram.

Nan and Cecil weren't there.

Humor added to the play's success. Musicians played the "Earl of Oxford's March" William Byrd had written for him.

He had good luck finding composers. He paid Robert Hales twenty pounds a year to compose for him, until the queen heard

Hales' music and stole him away. He then discovered Thomas Morley and commissioned him to write a song he was planning to use in *Twelfth Night; or, What You Will*. He used Dowling and other composers.

In 1579, he met Anne Vavasour at a court performance of *A Moral of the Marriage of Mind and Measure*. He could see why Tom had raved about her. She truly was beautiful—and she had the largest breasts he'd ever seen in England.

When the duc d'Alencon—the Frog—arrived from France, the queen invited him to every play. She said she wanted to impress him with England's culture, though the *duc* himself seemed barely interested.

The first play Edward presented was *The Jew*. He played Antonio.

In *Twelfth Night*, Edward placed sheep's bells around Malvolio's neck. Hatton was mortified, but the queen only laughed.

The queen insisted she liked the Frog, though he wasn't attractive. So far as Edward was concerned, he was a fortune hunter, no different from Hatton. Edward told her the Frog was more impressed with the Portuguese crown jewels Drake delivered to her from his last raid than with her.

The Frog sent his aide Simier to negotiate a marriage contract. When he arrived, the queen played the flirt. Edward found his frustration with her more than he could bear. He could support her marriage to the Frog—it offered England an ally against Spain—but this was too much.

It was time for another prank.

When the queen announced her intention to marry the Frog, a Puritan writer named John Stubbs dashed off a pamphlet, *The Gaping Gulf*, that attacked her decision. Stubbs was convicted of treason, his right hand was chopped off, and all copies of the pamphlet were burned.

Edward thought a subtler—and safer—gesture was called for.

He commissioned a costume, excessively French. The feather on his hat all but dwarfed his horse, and the brim was so broad the slightest breeze threatened to blow it off. The streets were filled with spectators. As he rode through the city, they gasped, laughed, cheered. There was no need to say anything—they all saw the costume for what it was.

When he arrived at the palace and pranced into the Presence Room, everyone fell silent. The queen said nothing, a silence that spoke volumes.

It was only a matter of time before she threw the Frog back into the pond.

17

Do not presume too much upon my love;
I may do that I shall be sorry for.

Shakespeare
Julius Caesar

Virginia Padoanna had taught him how to touch. With
Anne Vavasour, he grabbed.

She was in the audience for *A Moral of the Marriage
of Mind and Measure*—he hadn't yet changed the name to *The
Taming of the Shrew*. She sat in the front row, laughing and
applauding wildly. She was a vision, and a vibrant one at that—
he could hardly take his eyes off her.

Before Anne Vavasour, every woman in England had painted
freckles on her face and dyed her hair red. Even after smallpox
scarred the queen's face, her *approved* image never changed. Yet
when she chose black-haired Anne as lady of the bedchamber, a
new template was born.

As the play progressed, Anne's enthusiasm dimmed. She
stopped applauding, and at many a moment he spied a frown on
her pretty face.

After the play, as he was removing his actor's paste, she barged
into his dressing room.

"Edward de Vere, how can anyone hate women as much as you?"

He continued to wipe his face, but his pulse quickened—already she reminded him of Virginia.

"The play's an innocent farce," he said.

"It's a celebration of female submission. Have you forgotten what Petruchio said? '*She is my goods, my chattels, my household staff, my field, my barn, my horse, my ox, my ass, my anything.*'"

"Yes, thank you. I did write the play, you know." He set his washcloth aside. "I was just demonstrating how *some* men treat women. *I* don't treat women that way."

"That's not what I heard!"

He winced. By all accounts, Nan remained an excellent mother—he hadn't thought how his own reputation might have suffered.

"And Petruchio *humiliates* Katharina," Anne said. "How can you write such things?"

"They're characters in a play." His face free of paste, he turned to her. "Have supper with me. I'll make it up to you."

"When?"

"Now."

She stared at him. Slowly, a smile broke across her face.

"All right."

*A*fter dinner, he took her to his apartment at the Savoy. In seconds they were thrashing about in bed.

She was a muscular lover. He'd never been with a woman who took the lead the way she did—not even the queen—but he enjoyed it. It had been four years, after all.

Afterward, she rolled onto her stomach and kissed him on the nose.

"Grumio did say something I respect. He criticized a man's excessive need for money. '*Give him gold enough and marry him to a puppet.*'"

"That was quite good." He stroked her back. "If Puritans ever permit a woman to act on the stage, you'd be outstanding."

For that, he got a sly smile.

"Tell you what," he said. "I'll add an introductory scene, make it clear the play's a farce. Would that please you?"

"It might," she said. "But right now I can think of something that would please me even more."

*A*nne wasn't as smart as Virginia, nor as sweet. She was a flirt, and not only with him. She was an Aeolian tempest—apparently one he couldn't do without. Every evening they supped at his apartment. Nan lived just across the street, and Edward wondered if she saw Anne parading into Savoy House. It soon ceased to bother him.

He taught Anne how to write a poem. She called it *Anne Vavasour's Echo.*

> *O heavens! Who was the first that bred in me this fever?*
> *Vere.*
> *Who was the first that gave the wound whose fear I wear*
> *forever? Vere.*

He was flattered, though the content of the poem was shallow. And she was so pleased with the thing. He told her the echo device reminded him of Leone de Sommi and Mantua.

She told him she was pregnant.

Every woman at court wore farthingales—they extended out all around, and even the shapeliest lady looked like a bell. For six months no one suspected a thing. At times he even enjoyed subterfuge when he could make himself forget the inevitable discovery and its consequences.

To distract himself, he focused on his plays.

Without an acting company of his own, he was forced to raid the companies of other noblemen. Knowing he couldn't go on like that, he bought the Earl of Warwick's Players for a pittance in 1580. At first Cecil fought the idea of his owning his own company, but the queen's enthusiasm for Edward's plays changed his mind.

As for the queen?

"Of course, you need your own company, Edward. Earl John had his. Why shouldn't you?"

So he changed the name to "The Earl of Oxford's Men."

The queen also encouraged him to buy two companies of boy actors to play female roles. He bought the Children of St. Paul's and the Children of the Chapel Royal and combined them into one group he called Oxford's Boys.

He couldn't have been happier.

*J*ust before Christmas, he sat in a cubicle on the second floor of the small building off Charing Cross Road where Catholic nobles prayed. Dark red drapes separated one pew from another, so he had no fear of being seen.

Eyes closed, he listened to the priest chant and wondered how much time he had before the queen found out Anne was pregnant. The penalty, he knew, would be stiff indeed.

Maybe they could flee to Spain. Let King Philip brag about how he acquired an English nobleman—so long as he was free to write, he didn't care. Money was only a distraction, his lands a burden.

"Edward," Anne asked when they were in bed one evening, "are you really sure you want to go to Spain? We could go to my family in the north. They'll take care of me till the queen is ready to accept us."

"She'll never be ready," he said. "Trust me, Spain is our best hope. If I'm writing I don't care where we end up, so long as it's well away from the queen."

He had no doubt Anne would go with him—she was wilder than he was. The only question was when.

As he listened to the chant in the darkness, he heard the high-pitched voice of Francis Southwell.

"When?"

"T-t-tomorrow." That could only be Henry Howard, his stutter barely a whisper.

"I agree." *That* was Charles Arundell. "No question about it."

What were they up to?

"Have c-c-courage, Southwell," Howard said. "Once the queen's d-d-dead, you'll wonder why you waited s-so l-l-long."

Edward froze.

Muffled footsteps—they were leaving. He waited until he heard a distant door open and close. Then he left the church and all but ran all the way to Whitehall.

By the time he reached the Presence Room he was gasping, his legs shaking. He straightened his back and forced himself to march—all the way to the throne, where he fell to his knees.

"Your Majesty . . ."

"Yes, Edward?"

"I've come on a matter of grave importance." He took a moment to steady his breathing. "I request privacy—please."

"Clerk, clear the room."

Within moments the Presence Room was empty of everyone but the queen, the clerk, and him.

"Your Majesty, I just overheard three men plotting to assassinate you."

He told her everything. As he spoke, she bit her lip so hard he saw a drop of blood. She dabbed it with a lace handkerchief and turned to the clerk.

"Fetch the guards at once."

As the clerk left, she regained her composure.

"I'd heard rumors," she said. "Southwell and Arundell are new to the mix, but eight years ago I ordered the execution of Henry's brother, the Duke of Norfolk. I'm not surprised to find him caught up in all this."

The clerk returned with the captain of the guards.

"I want you to bring these men here immediately." She gave him the names. "Edward, stay by my side."

The guards left and soon returned with Southwell, Ardunell, and Howard. All three were pale, and Henry was shaking in his boots.

"Edward's informed me of what you were up to," the queen said, "but I want to hear it from your own mouths. What do you have to say for yourselves?"

"Your M-m-majesty, everything he told you is a lie!" Henry said. "He's a b-b-blasphemer. You mustn't believe him—he's a h-h-homosexual! That choirboy was his m-m-minion—"

She raised a hand. "Enough. Guards, place these men under arrest in Christopher Hatton's house. They'll remain there until Walsingham completes an investigation. Edward, remain in your apartment. I assume you can write something to occupy yourself."

In due course, Howard and Southwell were sent to the Tower. Arundell escaped and made it all the way to France, where the Spaniards hired him to spy for them.

The charge was treason. They had no right to an attorney.

The only question was whether they'd be tortured—ostensibly against the law, but stretching racks, screwing bolts, and branding irons in the Tower told a different story.

*F*or Anne and Edward, time was running out, but if they fled now, people would think he'd been in league with Howard.

Three months later, Anne gave birth at the palace. She named the child Edward.

Edward was summoned to Whitehall.

As a lady of the bedchamber, Anne had broken a rule: any affair without the queen's permission was forbidden.

Anne entered the Presence Room just after Edward. They stood before the throne and waited. The queen entered—obviously angry, but he could see how hurt she was.

"This duplicity is beyond all tolerance." Her eyes blazed as she pointed to him. "You are banished from court. Leave—now."

What could he say? He withdrew without a word.

Early the next morning, guards arrived at his rooms on Broad Street. He barely had time to collect the script he was working on before they marched him to the Tower. It was within the queen's right to claim his life, but surely she wouldn't. After all, he'd saved her life not long ago. But who knew what she'd do, as hurt and angry as she was?

He wiped his sweating palms on his thighs as the guards prodded him onward—but not to the dungeon. Instead he was brought to a four-room suite with the Turkish carpet from his bedroom already on the floor. He stood there, astonished, as his desk was carried in, followed by stacks of fresh paper, by pens and ink. He even had a view of the Thames.

He collapsed onto a chair—the last item carried in—and

laughed. She was teaching him a lesson, one he planned to take to heart.

As he sat in this bizarre prison of his, he thought of Lewyn. He'd never have carried on with Anne if Lewyn had been there, watching over him. . . . No, he was a fool—Lewyn hadn't kept him from Virginia. He couldn't have kept him from Anne.

He had no one to blame but himself.

*A*fter ten weeks, he was released—and learned that Anne and the baby had been sent to the dungeon. For a time, he was worried sick. He bribed the guards for news, only to hear that Anne had fallen in love with the captain of the Tower, Sir Henry Lee. Lee was thirty years older, a kind man, a perennial tournament challenger with the physique of an Adonis.

He longed to see her and their child, but at least she was happy.

Eventually Anne married Henry, though she sent word that the baby would carry the name Vere. Edward was relieved—he might never have another son. He gave her a tract of land, two thousand pounds, and a promise: his cousins Horace and Francis would oversee the little fellow's military career.

*A*fter his release, the queen ordered him to remain in his apartment until the first of October. But the moment he awoke on the second, a beautiful autumn morning, he dressed quickly and rode through the streets of London heading for Suffolk. While he'd been in the Tower, his sister Mary had wed Peregrine Bertie, the son of an Oxbridge don and the Dowager Countess of Suffolk. He hadn't spoken to Mary in months, yet he'd received an invitation to come and meet her new family.

He was used to seeing soup lines and Cambridge graduates reciting poetry for pennies in London's streets, but now he saw Walsingham's men in the shadows, watching, writing down names. He knew that anyone might harm the queen, but poets?

He arrived at the Bertie estate as evening approached to find a dark-haired girl of twelve years or so perched on the fence by the gate. When she saw him she jumped down.

"Greetings, milord."

She looked familiar, but he couldn't quite place her.

"Good evening, young lady. Have we met before?"

"I'm flattered you remember, milord." She grinned and bobbed a quick curtsy. "I'm Emilia Bassano."

Of course—the little girl from London.

"How is it you're at the Bertie estate?"

"My father was the Dowager Countess's favorite musician. Before he died, she promised to employ me as her daughter Susan's companion." She glanced at the ground and looked up shyly. "When I heard you were coming I offered to be your escort. I thought you'd need a friend."

"How kind of you." He smiled and dismounted. "Though I'm sure I'll be fine."

He'd heard the Countess of Suffolk raised hell when her son announced his marriage. There wasn't a man in England who hadn't heard of his affair with Anna Vavasour—no doubt such scandal in the family was too much for the elderly countess.

He and Emilia walked side by side toward the house.

"Did you have a pleasant ride, milord?"

"I did. Does your family still live in Shoreditch?"

"They do." She clasped her hands behind her back. "Susan's getting married soon, so I'll return to London and live in the house my father left me."

"You like London, do you?"

"Wherever I'm free to write, I'm content."

He raised a brow and smiled.

"And what sorts of things do you write?"

"Prose *and* poetry." She scowled. "People laugh at me some-times. They don't think I can do it, because I'm a girl, but I don't believe them. I intend to convince women to respect themselves. After all, if it weren't for women there'd be no one at all, men or women."

He watched her for a long moment. "I don't believe them either," he said at last. "I think you'll be a wonderful writer if you work at it."

She beamed at him. "My father taught me to stand up for what I believe, milord. He said if I don't, who will?"

"I knew the Bassanos were fine musicians, but I didn't know they were so wise. Gave you a good education, did he?"

Her smile slipped for a moment. "He employed excellent tutors, milord. I miss him very much, but my education isn't over."

He patted her shoulder. "I miss my father, too. Emillia, you are remarkable. Have you met the queen?"

"Twice. She promised to look after me."

They reached the Bertie mansion. After dinner and the usual pleasantries, they retired to the drawing room for sherry. Edward found he liked Peregrine. His new brother-in-law struck him as an honest young man who wanted to be a soldier and a diplomat.

Finally the countess, who was about sixty-five, addressed him.

"Your play about the shrew caused quite a stir in the palace, milord."

"I'm sure it did." He took a sip of sherry. "And what did you think of it?"

"I didn't care for the shrew's name—Katharina." She eyed him over the top of her glass. "Did you name her after me?"

The room fell silent. For a moment, everyone seemed to be holding his breath.

"Not that I blame you," she said. "My objecting to your sister's marriage wasn't terribly kind."

Edward gave her his sunniest smile. "I named the shrew long before I staged the play," he said. "After my stepsister, Katherine Windsor."

The countess laughed. Mary and Peregrine breathed a sigh of relief. Emilia and Susan looked at each other and smiled.

He heard a high-pitched voice in the hallway. The double doors opened and in walked a governess with a girl of about five. She walked right up to him and held out a little handmade book.

"For you, milord," she said. "I wrote it myself."

"Thank you very much." He opened the book—there were only two pages—and read the neat handwriting. It was a story about an ox and a fox.

He closed the book and smiled at her. "What a wonderful present. May I ask your name? Mine's Edward."

"I'm Elizabeth," she said. "And if I may, I'd rather call you Papa."

His heart stopped. She had his nose, his mouth, his brows—but her hair, like Nan's, was a bouquet of brown curls. She was lovely.

It was all he could do not to cry. They were both shy at first, but as he asked her about her story, she brightened. Soon her words were tumbling out like a waterfall. He drank them in.

They talked and talked until it grew dark. Little Elizabeth yawned, and her governess knelt beside her.

"Time to say good night, my dear."

She nodded and looked back up at Edward.

"Papa, may I kiss you good night?"

His throat tightened. "Of course, my sweet girl."

After the double doors closed behind her, Edward excused himself. He went straight to bed and wept.

What a fool he'd been.

*W*hen he went down to the garden early the next morning, Emilia was there.

"Good morning, milord. I hope you rested well.

"I hardly slept a wink, Emilia," he said. "I don't know what to do."

"About what, milord? If I may be so bold."

"I couldn't sleep because I've been a fool."

"My father told me fools are what we mortals be."

"This fool would like to stop being one. Seeing my little Elizabeth last night . . ." He swallowed and pressed on. "I'd like to reconcile with my wife, but I don't know how. For years I insisted the child wasn't mine. Now I know I was wrong."

Emilia sat on a bench and propped her chin on her hands. "Is it very important to you, my lord?"

"More than anything."

"Then it doesn't matter *how* you do it," she said, "so long as you *do* it." She looked serious. "I know you don't want your daughter to suffer, milord."

She was right. And she made it all sound so simple. Always, children saw things simply—how could a man's judgment be so corrupted by a few years on earth?

*W*hen he returned to London, a letter from Nan was waiting for him. Again, she pleaded her innocence and begged him to consider his daughter.

He purchased a copy of the first English translation of the Greek sermons of St. Paul to the Ephesians and wrote an inscription in it: "*I have been unquieted by the uncertainty of the world and beg to be forgiven.*"

She replied with a short letter:

> *I received your gift for which I am grateful. As for your being unquieted by the uncertainty of the world, I myself am not without some taste of that. But seeing that you assure me, I will patiently abide the adversity which I otherwise feel. If God would so permit it, and if it would be good for you, I would make it my comfort to bear the greater part of your adverse fortune with you.*

She went on to invite him to Cecil House, but he wanted a truly fresh start, without Cecil hanging over them. He countered with an invitation to have supper with him at his apartment in Savoy House.

*I*t was an awkward meal filled with long silences—they went through the entire last course without speaking. When it was over, they retired to the drawing room. Once Nan was seated, Edward knelt beside her chair.

"I don't know how nor do I believe I have the right to ask you this," he said, "but it would mean a great deal to me—everything, in truth—if you could find room in your heart to forgive me."

She stood and gently drew him to his feet.

"Edward, in the book you gave me, St. Paul spoke of forgiveness, of the putting aside of sins. I take what he wrote to heart."

He was amazed at her graciousness. He'd made fun of her slavish devotion to Scripture, but now he saw her in a new light.

There was something to be said for structure, for putting aside one's own desires for a greater responsibility. Wasn't that what Lewyn had told him?

"Nan, would you and Elizabeth come live with me in my apartment in Savoy House? I've bought a house in Shoreditch, where I work and sleep. It allows me to separate my work—and my undisciplined friends—from my home. But at week's end, we could go to Wivenhoe. Is the arrangement agreeable to you?"

"Of course." She took his hand. "I've seen your plays. You have a gift, and I intend to nurture it. Before, I didn't know. Now I do."

He pulled her close and kissed her. As her arms closed around him, for the first time since he'd known her, he didn't think of her as his sister.

They went to his bedroom.

They had too much wine, but it helped. She exhibited none of the fear he'd seen at Hampton Court, nor did she recite the Twenty-third Psalm.

After that they made love regularly. He thought about teaching her some of Virginia's tricks but decided to be grateful for what he had and let Nan love him in her own way.

*A*t Wivenhoe they went riding with Elizabeth. He'd bought her a pony and she insisted on riding between them.

"Please, Papa—I feel safer between you and *Maman*."

Elizabeth, he knew, was the bond that had brought him and his wife back together. He didn't know what else he might come to feel for her and hoped his feelings would deepen, but he wouldn't try to force matters. Simply putting up with him and forgiving him were in themselves grounds for love.

And, truth to tell, Nan was rather attractive.

He felt so optimistic that he invested five hundred pounds in Edward Fenton's voyage to the Moluccas. He also contributed the *Edward Bonaventure*. As it turned out, Fenton sailed too late to round the Cape of Good Hope before the weather turned and had to alter course at Sierra Leone. While crossing the Atlantic to Brazil, he was attacked by Spanish ships—lucky to return alive even if he was empty-handed.

Edward decided he'd invested in his last voyage.

He heard that the Blackfriars lease was for sale and bought it—he needed a place for Oxford's Men to rehearse. He placed John Lyly in charge and leased the basement to Rocco Bonneti, an Italian fencing master everyone wanted as a coach. His assistance in the fencing scenes in *Hamlet* was invaluable.

When Peregrine returned from a diplomatic mission to Denmark, his description of Elsinor Castle was so vivid that Edward decided it would make a perfect setting. When Peregrine mentioned having met Rosencrantz and Guildenstern, he decided to use their names for Hamlet's schoolfellows. But when he said he was basing the play's verbose adviser to the king on Cecil, Peregrine insisted he change the name.

"*Corambis* is too heavy-handed, Edward. Everyone will recognize the play on Cecil's motto. You know the Archbishop of Canterbury and the Bishop of London must approve all plays. *Corambis* has to go."

"What about *Polonius?*"

"Better."

"Not that it matters," Edward said. "I can't present the play while Dudley's still alive. If he saw himself murdering the father in the play he'd poison me, too"

"Then put it aside until *both* Cecil and Dudley are dead, there's a good fellow. Discretion is the better part of valor, you know."

It wasn't long before Lyly proposed that he use Blackfriars not only to rehearse plays but also to stage them. Late in 1582 he opened it to public performances. Lyly also proposed he charge playgoers twice as much as they paid at The Theatre and The Curtain, but Edward hesitated. Who would pay that much for plays?

"Not to worry, Edward. It's a closed theater. On a cold night, the audience will be more than happy to pay for warmth."

And pay they did, not that he was getting rich from theater. If he wanted to be rich, he'd never have written a play as long as *Hamlet*. At nearly four thousand lines, it was twice the length of any play being staged, and he still wasn't finished writing it.

On top of all that, Nan was pregnant again. Perhaps a son this time.

For the time being, his life was proceeding smoothly.

One afternoon, Tom Knyvet—Anne Vavasour's uncle— accosted him in the palace.

"I can hardly bear to look at you," he said. "You're a cad, Oxford."

Edward sighed. "Then why have you waited so long to tell me? I haven't even spoken to Anne in over a year."

"That's right—haven't spoken, haven't written, cast her off like a damn pair of shoes."

"You *want* me to talk to her?"

"God's balls! If you had I'd have run you through already." He glared. "But I haven't ruled it out."

"Don't threaten me, Knyvet. It's not becoming for an officer in the queen's guard."

"I'll threaten whoever I like. Best watch your back, Oxford."

Knyvet turned and walked away. Maybe that would be an end of it.

*J*ust a few days later, as Edward and Oxford's Boys were leaving Blackfriars, Knyvet and his men attacked.

Luckily, Edward and some of the boys were armed. They fought to a draw, and no one was seriously hurt.

"Edward, I know Knyvet well," Walter Raleigh said when Edward met him for drinks the next evening. "He'll attack again unless you settle things."

"I'd like nothing more, but how?"

"He won't agree to anything less than a duel."

"Good idea." He'd never known Walter to lose a sword fight. "Will you be my second?"

"Absolutely."

*H*e challenged. Knyvet accepted.

They each got in several good hits, but the duel was inconclusive. The next day, again in the evening and just outside Blackfriars, Knyvet and his men attacked again. The fighting was fierce, but Edward gave as good as he got, and again nothing was resolved.

The following week, Knyvet and his men attacked again. Edward and Knyvet were each supported by three men. The slashing and shouting seemed endless. When it finally gave way to panting, someone suggested he and Knyvet finish it themselves.

Edward was tired. He'd been writing all morning and drinking sherry all evening. Still, he had to end this. "Very well," he said, and lifted his sword again.

Knyvet lunged, Edward deflected. They lunged and parried, lunged and parried, while their men stood around them and shouted encouragement.

Edward stumbled. All at once he felt an agonizing pain in his left foot, worse than anything he'd ever endured. He bit back a scream and glanced down.

Knyvet's blade had cut his ankle, now dangling at an odd angle. He left a trail of blood in the streets as his men carried him back to Fisher's Folly.

The neighborhood doctor was no help at all. The foot wouldn't heal, and while Edward was confined to bed, Knyvet came to see him.

"I wanted you to know my niece heard about your wounds and wrote to me. She told me you'd given her two thousand pounds, some land, and promised your cousins will take care of the boy's future in the army." He glanced down at Edward's foot, hidden beneath the coverlet. "I now consider that fair recompense."

Edward was as furious as he was helpless. "Didn't it occur to you to ask her before you lamed me?"

Knyvet shrugged. "I didn't come to say I'm sorry. I came to say I won't attack you again. But if I ever hear you've touched my niece again, I'll finish the job."

*T*hough he was still banished from court, the queen sent her physician. Edward was relieved—not only had he despaired of saving his foot, he'd nearly given up on salvaging his relationship with his queen. After two visits, the distinguished Dr. Rodrigo Lopez gave him the verdict.

"You'll keep the foot," he said, "but you'll always be lame."

"Can't you do something? What about bleeding me?"

Dr. Lopez raised his eyebrows. "I've done what I can." He

shook his head. "Be glad the foot is connected. It'll give you some support. The rest will come from a cane. In the meantime, keep the wound clean and don't lose hope. Attitude can be as important as medicine. Your body should respond to rest and nourishment."

At last, the wound was beginning to heal. And he was writing again.

Lyly sent word that the Blackfriars lease was up at the end of the year and the owner refused to renew it—neighbors had complained about the noise.

"If the queen doesn't allow you to return to court," Lyly said, "you'll have no place to present your plays."

"Something will come up," he said. "It always does. In the meantime I can talk to Burbage about showing my plays at The Theater and The Curtain."

*W*hile recuperating, he insisted his actors visit him at his new quarters for work, a grand mansion he'd bought called Fisher's Folly. It had a huge dining room for meetings and a grand salon for readings. In fact, the mansion was perfect for a project for English writers he'd been dreaming about, an atelier where they would live and write, something like what Raphael and Romano had created in Italy for painters and sculptors. He'd already made inquiries at Cambridge and Oxford, asking professors to recommend a dozen of their most promising writers.

He interviewed them all and then offered room, board, and a stipend to six of the best. After they were settled in their rooms, he invited them to the dining room for sherry and the opportunity to introduce themselves.

"Gentlemen, thank you for coming. You're participating in a grand experiment. If my plan succeeds, we shall lead English literature out of the Dark Ages into what people will one day call the golden age of Elizabethan culture. Henceforth, you shall be known as the University Wits."

A few snickered.

"I'd like each of you to introduce yourself. George, you begin."

"George Peele, bombastic son of a Hertfordshire curate, at your service."

The Wits grinned.

"I'm an Oxford man and an aspiring playwright. I'm translating *Euripedes* from the Greek and working on plays about Edward I. I married the daughter of a London salt merchant, but thanks to the Earl of Oxford, my father-in-law won't have to support me. Like our esteemed host, I have a weakness for pranks—though I haven't robbed a shipment of gold."

Grins gave way to laughter.

"Mr. Greene?"

"Robert Greene here. My claim to fame is my red hair. I'm a Cambridge man and a novelist known for clever pamphlets such as *Farewell to Folly*. I'm now writing a Greek romance I call *Pandosta*. After I squandered my wife's money, I sent her and our child to the country. I was leading a debauched life in London, but I'll be delighted to live on Willy's tab."

Edward rather liked the nickname.

"Mr. Spenser?"

"Edmund Spenser." He was a grave-looking young man with a quiet voice. "I've begun to write a book I call *The Faerie Queen*. If it's published, I'll dedicate it to the good earl. If not, I'll kill myself."

Edward studied Spenser. The young man was intense—he'd best give him extra encouragement. He'd paid to print thirty books already. He wouldn't go bankrupt if he printed another.

"Thomas?"

"Thomas Lodge, graduate of Oxford. As some of you know, my father was the Lord Mayor of London. He wanted me to follow in his footsteps. Instead, I write plays."

"Mr. Watson?"

"Tom's the name." A short, sharp laugh. "I have a reputation for violence. But the earl says I have talent, so here I am."

"Mr. Nashe."

"Tom Nashe, graduated Cambridge on scholarship. I'm writing a play called *The Isle of Dogs,* so critical of our corrupt political scene that I've no doubt I'll end up in jail." He grinned and patted his rather large paunch. "If you visit me, bring food."

Edward slapped his hands on the table and smiled.

"Gentlemen, thank you. Seated along the wall are my secretaries: John Lyly, who's also writing plays, and Anthony Munday, who's working on a narrative poem. I invited another young man, Christopher Marlowe, but he's on assignment in Rheims."

No laughter this time. *On assignment in Rheims* meant Marlowe was spying on Catholic priests returning to England from France to stir up dissent. One such priest had just been executed in London, and it was rumored that Walsingham's agents had assassinated the rest.

"I have a list of people who want to join our group," Edward said. "If I had more bedrooms, I'd invite them now. As it is, if any of you wish to leave, let me know."

There was a knock on the door.

"Come."

His clerk entered with a message. Was it Nan's time? She was nearly due.

"Gentlemen, I regret I must end our meeting," he said after scanning the note. "I've been asked to meet with the queen's secretary of state at once."

He reached for his cane and pulled himself to his feet.

"Don't forget to work, sleep, get drunk, find a whore, or whatever else your muse dictates. This meeting is adjourned *sine die.*"

18

There is nothing either good or bad,
but thinking makes it so.

Shakespeare
Hamlet, Prince of Denmark

Francis Walsingham shuffled to the empty booth at the back of The Pye, where Edward was waiting for him.

"I hope you don't mind meeting here." The secretary of state adjusted his Puritan-black robes. "My life's gray, and I seek levity wherever I can find it."

"The Pye's fine, Francis—if I may be so bold."

"Of course, Edward."

Walsingham never missed a single performance at the palace and always sat in the front row, but he called actors and playwrights sinful and blamed them for everything from poor harvest to the plague. Still, his choice of The Pye was considerate. The tavern was just down the street from Fisher's Folly. For someone tethered to a cane, it was preferable to walking all the way to Walsingham's office in Seething Lane.

"Edward, the latest reports confirm Philip will invade England as soon as his 131 galleons are fitted with cannons. He has thirty thousand assault forces already in the Low Countries waiting to cross. Drake captured every Spanish ship coming in from the New World in the last twelve months, but that hasn't deterred him. Philip borrows, now he's bankrupt—which gives him another reason to invade."

"If the queen would order our captains to stop raiding Spanish ships, maybe Cecil could make peace," Edward said. "Drake's a glorified pirate."

He watched Walsingham squirm. He was heavily invested in Drake's raids.

"The queen's father reduced her to penury," he said. "She never misses an opportunity to fill her purse."

"And as a result, England faces invasion by the strongest force on earth."

Walsingham glanced around, though they were alone in the tavern.

"Edward, at least half of England's still Catholic. If we don't stand together, we'll lose the war. I'm here to ask the question: how can we convince *all* Englishmen to unite and be loyal when three-fourths of the population can't read? The queen can only give so many speeches."

"Tell her to maintain better schools," he said. "Right now they're as useless as a Moslem *madrassa*."

Walsingham smiled. "Exactly. The people can't read, so we'll deliver our call to unity in a new way: through the stage."

"So you want me to write for you." Edward took a long swallow of ale. "Does this mean I'll be allowed to return to court?"

"No such luck, at least not yet. How's your foot, by the way?"

"Lame, thanks to Knyvet. What's he up to?"

"Prancing around court like a rooster." Walsingham folded his hands on the table. "The queen wants your *Famous Victories of Henry the Fifth* to be England's call to arms."

"It's five plays now, and I'm working on more."

"Excellent! An avalanche of patriotic plays, each one explaining that with unity, England always prevails." Walsingham drained his cup of ale and called for two more. "This is going to be easier than I thought."

"Would you like to read them?"

He waved a hand. "Not now. She'll be so pleased to hear you've agreed. Henceforth, Oxford's Men will be the Queen's Men."

Edward sat back and stared at Walsingham, trying to take in this conversation. Two cups of ale arrived.

"You'll be touring every summer until further notice." Walsingham drained his cup, stood on his spindly legs, and clapped Edward on the back. "If I hear her shout, '*Once more into the breach, for St. George and England!*' again, I'll grab a sword and charge myself." He chuckled and then turned and headed for the door.

"Francis!" Edward struggled to his feet. "Who's going to pay for this? Touring costs a fortune."

Walsingham stopped. "The queen said she'll work something out with you."

"Of course." He could hardly stand the bitterness in his own voice. "We've heard that before, haven't we?"

Walsingham gave a theatrical sigh. "Edward, I pay for the entirety of England's spy service out of my own pocket. Now it's your turn." He thought for a moment. "She did part with a thousand pounds for an anti-papist campaign. I'll give you half."

With that, he scurried from The Pye.

Edward returned to his seat, listening to the music and

rubbing his throbbing foot. He'd alert Tarleton to get the actors lined up.

But at the moment, it was time he checked on Nan.

*H*e reached Savoy House as Dr. Lopez emerged from Nan's room.

"She's having a difficult time."

"It's started?" Edward said.

"Yes. The midwife's with her, but I'm worried. Usually the second birth is easier."

"She'll be all right, won't she?"

"I don't know. She's petite but determined. She wants so much to give you a boy." Lopez picked up his leather bag. "Now I must go to the queen. She has another migraine headache. I'll be back this evening."

Edward crept into the room to find Nan asleep. He sat and watched her for a while and then went to his study. The place was cluttered with scripts. He had a habit of working on several plays at once, and parchment was scattered everywhere. He wanted so much to love his wife, and for her to love him. Yet they came from such different worlds, without and within.

He sat at his desk for a very long time, and at last he began to write.

Who taught thee first to sigh, alas, my heart?
Who taught thy tongue the woeful words of plaint?
Who filled your eyes with tears of bitter smart?
Who gave thee grief and made thy joys to faint?
Who first did paint with colors pale thy face?
Who first did break thy sleeps of quiet rest?
Above the rest in Court who gave thee grace?

He heard a knock on the door.

"Come."

The nurse entered. "Milord, her time has come. The midwife is with her, and I've sent a message to Dr. Lopez at the palace."

"How is she?"

"It comes hard, milord."

"Please call me if there's anything I can do.

"Yes, milord."

Tortured hours followed. He tried to return to the poem and couldn't. If she died, he'd be the proximate cause. How could he live with *that*?

He'd already drunk with the Wits and with Walsingham, but drinking sherry was all he could do. He tapped his cane on the rug: it made no sound. The quiet was maddening. He finished the bottle of sack, opened another, and finished that one, too.

The hours dragged. Another knock. He glanced out the window—it was dark.

"Come in."

Dr. Lopez entered.

"It's a boy."

He lost his breath. "Say again?"

"I said, it's a boy. Congratulations."

"You don't look pleased. What's wrong?"

"The baby's not well, Edward. He doesn't cry. He just entered the world and he's already tired."

"Nan?"

"She's fine. She lost a lot of blood, but she's young."

"Can I see her?"

"The midwife's preparing her for your visit."

Edward stood and gripped his hand. "Thank you, Ruy, for everything. How's the queen?"

"Migraines are her hell on earth."

"Please pass on our good news, will you?"

"I will. And again, congratulations. At last you have the eighteenth Earl of Oxford."

N an's room was dark and stuffy, all noxious outside air having been shut out.

The midwife greeted him and then left them alone. He bent over Nan's bed and kissed her on the lips. Dressed in fresh bedclothes, she looked pale and tired. She smelled of lavender.

She opened her eyes and managed a smile. "My prince is here."

"How are you, my sweet?"

"Better, now that it's over."

"Was it too terrible?"

"I'll survive." She bit her lip. "I hope the baby will. Dr. Lopez is worried. He didn't say so, but I could see it in his eyes."

"I looked in on the young fellow and he seems fine. He was sleeping. The nurse thinks he's all right."

She shut her eyes. "You have a boy, Edward."

"*We* have a boy, *and* a girl."

She squeezed his hand. "Thank you for saying that."

"I can never apologize enough for what I did—"

"I told you I forgave you."

"And I'm eternally grateful. But I can't forgive myself."

"Give it time."

He kissed her again.

"Edward, you're becoming sweet." Her brow furrowed. "And you've been working less. Is something wrong?"

"Not at all. The Wits elevate my mood, remind me of when I was young."

"My mother says youth's like a fine bragging."

"She's very wise."

"Would you find my father and tell him the news?" she said. "He'll be so pleased—a grandfather twice over."

"A veritable patriarch."

He kissed her one more time and headed for Cecil House.

*I*t was past midnight as he made his way across the Strand. Spring was finally here and the air was fragrant. He must remember to order some salve—Lopez swore it would lessen the pain in his foot.

He had a son!

It was late, so he used his key. He opened the door to Cecil House to find a servant dozing in a chair.

"Milord, it's late."

"I bring good news."

After a long wait, the old boy appeared at the second-floor landing in a dressing gown and a night hat.

"What is it, Edward? I was in bed."

"You're a grandfather again—and it's a boy."

Cecil's eyes lighted up. He began to make his way down the grand stairway, one step at a time, leaning heavily on his cane.

When he reached the foyer, he pulled Edward into a tight embrace—only the second he'd ever given in the twenty-one years he'd known him. When he released his grip, the two of them stood there grinning at one another.

"How's Nan?" Cecil said finally.

"She's fine. The baby, too. He's asleep. I'm sorry I disturbed you, but Nan and I wanted to be the first to tell you."

Cecil's eyes brimmed with tears. He brushed them away with his fingers.

"Let's celebrate. I'll pour something."

They hobbled on canes to the library.

"What a sight we are," Cecil said.

"But we soldier on, don't we?"

"We certainly do, my boy. Oysters?"

"Wrong season, isn't it?"

"These are from Belgium. *My* boat outran the pirates."

They laughed.

"Could you ask cook to bring something for after the oysters?" Edward said. "I haven't had dinner. Can't recall when I've been so hungry—or so happy."

*T*wo days later, the eighteenth Earl of Oxford died. They buried him in the family graveyard at Hedingham Castle. Afterward, Edward took Nan to Wivenhoe. He thought the sea air might be a balm to her spirits—his were beyond repair.

Together they stood at the shore, staring out to sea, her hand on his arm.

"When my father died, I thought nothing again could ever hurt so much," he said. "I was wrong."

She turned to look at him, a strange resolve in her expression he hadn't seen before.

"When you refused to accept Elizabeth," she said, "my tutor told me, 'I would not have thee linger in thy pain.' Now I say the same to you. And I promise, we'll try again."

He drew her closer. His son would never smell salt air, never visit the countryside, never play in the snow. He was plunged into a melancholy far greater than any he'd ever known.

After they returned to the house, he went to his study and wrote:

What plague is greater than the grief of mind?
The grief of mind that eats in every vein;
In every vein that leaves such clots behind;
Such clots behind as breed such bitter pain;
So bitter pain that none shall ever find
What plague is greater than the grief of mind.

The following month, Tom Radcliffe died. It was a heavy blow. In the seven years since Edward had returned from Italy, Tom had been like a father to him. And although the court doctors said his death was a mystery, Edward had no doubt: his uncle had been poisoned. There'd been talk again of Dudley's marrying the queen, and Tom had come out strongly—publicly—against it.

Of course, there was no proof, but Edward resolved to take revenge—with a play. Only not yet. It was too soon.

In time, he recovered enough from his melancholy to set about preparing for the first tour. He needed to purchase wagons, hire five more actors, and dredge up some decent costumes. Every major character was a king, a queen, or a noble, all of whom had to wear silks with faux jewels. The cost would be enormous.

He'd already sold forty-seven of his father's 103 parcels. Now he'd have to sell another.

*W*orcestershire blended with Warwickshire and then Derbyshire. Leicerstershire blurred into Gloucestershire, Norfolk into Suffolk. In every shire a different dialect, in every town a different bed.

He opened with *Henry V.* As the queen predicted, the play was wildly popular. People were on edge as more and more priests were arrested and tortured alongside the locals who tried to hide them. Confessions were followed by more arrests, and the details were terrifying, but *Henry V* calmed fears and inspired hope.

Edward grew weary of performing the role of Henry V on a cane. He asked Tarleton to take over the leads, starting with a new approach to Richard III.

Tarleton didn't disappoint. When he walked on stage with a clubfoot and a hump back, the audience went wild. Before now they'd had only the faraway Philip II of Spain to hate. Now they had a real live villain in the flesh. The approach was novel, and Edward embraced it— until it occurred to him the Cecils would be offended.

"Tarleton, you clown, you can't play Richard III with a clubfoot! Cecil will have my head."

"Where do you think I got the idea?"

"Nan will never forgive me."

"It was just an experiment. I won't do it again. But did you see how the people mobbed me afterwards?"

Ah, the people. Would he ever get used to them? The rags and filth, the belching and farting. But it was the Catholic countryside that would dictate the country's survival. London housed only two hundred thousand people—England had three million.

When his wagons entered a town, trumpets and sackbuts blared. Tumblers and acrobats did their tricks while Oxford-tawny and blue silks flapped in the breeze. It was almost as exciting as a cavalry charge.

A dozen wagons traveled behind him, transporting the Queen's Men and their costumes, props, and servants. Country people seldom saw aristocratic finery, so he ordered some actors to wear their costumes into town. People pointed and shouted and sighed.

The only thing they didn't bring along was food—there were plenty of taverns on the roads and he paid his actors well. Some grumbled and a few stole, but he turned a blind eye. He had enough on his mind.

Nan was pregnant again. Would the child live? Would she?

He came home to London to find Nan in labor. This time, everything went as it should: Nan gave birth to little Frances and the baby girl thrived. When he gazed at her, he thought he saw a smile.

Soon the queen summoned him.

She smiled as he entered the Presence Room. He smiled back— she was going to revoke his banishment, he saw it in her eyes.

19

And make her chronicle as rich with praise
As is the ooze and bottom of the sea
With sunken wreck and sumless treasuries.

Shakespeare
Henry V

T he second year of touring was easier. In 1584, Nan—
bless her—gave birth to Bridget, another beautiful
daughter. Cecil was so pleased he didn't even object
when Edward had to sell Wivenhoe to pay his actors and buy
wagons. Wivenhoe was a gem, and Cecil was impressed by the
price he got: 2,315 pounds.

The touring was even easier in 1585. Edward had come to
enjoy the rough-and-tumble crowds, and when he returned to
London he felt so optimistic that he invested in another voyage: five hundred pounds on Adrian Gilbert's attempt to find a
northwest passage to China across the top of the New World.

The voyage didn't succeed, but Captain Davis explored an area
he called Newfoundland.

Then little Frances, only two years old, died.

He was almost mad with grief. Nan saw him through it—she

was stronger than him. Was it faith? She said Cecil taught her to persevere.

All Edward could do was see toothless Frances smiling in her crib. He stayed in bed and cried for days until Nan persuaded him to return to writing.

*I*n June 1586, he was preparing to leave on another tour when Cecil sent him a message to come at once.

He left Elizabeth practicing the virginals and the maid cleaning up Bridget's food, which seemed to be everywhere, and limped across the Strand. His foot no longer pained him—Lopez had concocted something that killed the pain. He was now the queen's personal physician, a full-time job in itself, though he also continued to care for the ailing Robin Dudley and Francis Walsingham, not to mention Edward's family and Cecil.

Cecil was in the library, a broad smile on his face. The pain from gout was constant, but his eyes were sparkling. A royal decree with red ribbons and a seal lay on his desk.

"Sit down, my boy. Sherry?"

"It's a little early, but I believe I will." He accepted a glass. "Thank you."

"Edward, I have before me a resolution of the Privy Council granting you the largest stipend I've ever seen, and I've seen a few. Only the postmaster of England received one as large, and he's forced to account for every penny. All you have to do is write your plays. The council even approved it unanimously—now *that* is a rarity."

Edward was shocked. The queen seldom parted with a penny.

"A thousand pounds a year, Edward, payable quarterly, with no date of termination. Consider it a measure of England's appreciation for your work. Your generosity and talent earned the respect of a nation, the queen, and her council." Cecil slid the document across his desk. "Edward, Walsingham wrote the first draft—nothing about 'services rendered,' no reason stipulated for the payment." He chuckled. "No stigma of print dishonors England's premier earl."

Edward picked up the document and stared at it. "It seems excessive."

"Edward, thanks to you, the people—Catholics and Protestants—are finally united. Well, as united as they'll ever be. It took time, but at last England is whole." Cecil slid a bill of exchange in his direction. "Here's the first quarterly installment. The queen and Privy Council took note of the enormous sums you advanced on England's behalf. She wanted to present the document and money to you herself, but last night she suffered another migraine attack. Lopez is with her now."

"I don't know what to say."

"Don't say anything. Enjoy it, spend a quiet day with the girls.

"Quiet day? With the girls?"

*H*e was climbing into a wagon to lead the Queen's Men on the summer tour when a messenger arrived with a package. He opened it and found a book by William Webbe: *A Discourse of English Poetry.*

He was scanning the book, wondering who'd sent it, when a paragraph leaped from the page:

I may not omit the deserved commendations of many honorable and noble lords and Gentlemen in Her Majesty's Court, which, in the rare devices of poetry, have been and yet are most skillful; among whom the right honorable Earl of Oxford may challenge to himself the title of most excellent among the rest.

He shut the book and stowed it in the wagon. Talk about the stigma of print—he just hoped to God Cecil wouldn't see it.

A message from the queen found him in Derbyshire. She'd appointed him to the tribunal trying Mary Queen of Scots for treason. The captive Queen of Scots corresponded with a young Catholic named Babington who wanted to remove Elizabeth from the throne and replace her with Mary. A simple-minded plan, and the trial would be the usual farce—no attorney, no specific charges.

His brief? To sit on a panel of noblemen and find Mary Queen of Scots guilty.

The trial took place in the dead of winter at Fotheringhay Castle and lasted just a few hours. With thirty-four others, Edward convicted Mary of treason and sentenced her to death.

Her dignity was profound. She suffered from rheumatism and could hardly walk, yet her plea for mercy was so moving he took notes.

For weeks the queen delayed signing the warrant of execution. Afterward she claimed she hadn't known what she was signing. She imprisoned her secretary, saying she would never execute a fellow queen. But in February 1587, Mary Queen of Scots lost her head. The executioner had to swing the ax twice before he killed her, and her dog was permitted to lap her blood.

The whole thing sickened Edward. He had no doubt the Spanish invasion was only a matter of time.

∽

*I*n May 1587, little Susan was born. Now he was the father of *three* daughters. What riches! But celebration was impossible—he was scheduled to go on tour.

Then there was news: Francis Drake delayed things by raiding Cadiz and destroying thirty Spanish vessels, but Walsingham's spies confirmed that the Spanish armada was preparing to head for the Channel.

England possessed no formal naval force—the queen refused to spend the funds—but many Englishman owned boats. Edward demanded he be allowed to sail with a hundred other private boats against the Spanish galleons. To his surprise, the queen agreed.

Since Nan had been running a slight fever since the birth, Lopez was personally tending her in the queen's palace at Greenwich. Little Susan was flourishing.

Edward ordered the *Edward Bonaventure* fitted with guns and added more men to the crew. The cost was enormous, and he had to sell two more tracts of land. He arrived at the port of Plymouth prepared to resist the mightiest navy in the world. He was about to weigh anchor when he received a letter from Cecil.

Nan was dead. Puerperal fever had claimed her. Edward didn't even know what that was.

Grief tormented him. His sweet wife, his strength, his steadying force, was gone. Worst of all, now he'd never know what their growing closeness might have become. He walked up and down the pier, aimless, miserable. A small consolation was the news that Robin Dudley had died.

He knew the English boats could wait no longer—Spanish galleons had been sighted in the channel. Should he remain with his men or return for Nan's funeral?

The matter was settled by another letter from Cecil:

Edward, I know you are suffering, but I also know Nan would want you to sail against the armada. So I'm pleading with you. Take the Edward Bonaventure and help defeat the evil empire with every ounce of strength you possess. Nan would want it. So does the queen. We'll mourn in the Abbey. You fight in the Channel.

The Baroness and I will take care of the girls at Cecil House. As you know, we have a competent staff. When you return there'll be plenty of time to sort out their future and yours. Live for England. Live for the queen, the girls, Nan, and me.

So the *Edward Bonaventure*, along with the hundred other private boats that constituted England's entire naval defense, raised anchor in the port of Plymouth and sailed into the channel.

The Spanish fleet had size and number in its favor—137 of the largest galleons ever built. But in the confines of the channel, the advantage fell to England: their boats had more speed and maneuverability, could turn on a penny, rode low in the water, and offered a smaller target. Each boat towed a small craft devised by Francis Drake that was filled with explosives.

Drake called them fireboats. Edward called them floating missiles.

A storm arose. When the galleons found harbor in ports on the other side of the channel, the English struck. Clustered at anchor like a flock of ducks, the galleons were a perfect target. The English boats towed their fireboats into the galleons, also crammed with explosives and ammunition. Galleon after galleon sank.

The surviving galleons fled north around the top of the English isles, where they were ravaged by more storms. The Irish destroyed still more of them. Only a few made it back to Spain.

Spanish troops never set foot on English soil, and not a single English boat or soldier was lost.

*T*he queen proclaimed November 24, 1588, a day of thanksgiving for that year and every year thereafter. Edward escorted her into St. Paul's Cathedral and carried the royal canopy over her head.

The next day, Walsingham's spies reported that the Catholics in England still needed tending. So again, Edward prepared to tour the English countryside.

He was hurrying along Bishopsgate High, tending to a few final errands, when he saw Emilia Bassano walking on the other side of the street.

"Emilia!" he called. She was older now, perhaps nineteen, no longer a pretty girl but a beautiful young woman.

"Milord." She crossed the street. "I was so sorry to hear about the countess. How are you managing?"

"Melancholy is my permanent state. Why does one fail to appreciate the value of another until after they're gone?"

"I know what you mean."

"I'm glad to see you, but my company of players is touring in just two days and I have much to do."

"May I be of assistance?"

He looked at her and thought for a moment.

"I could help with the scripts, deal with the letters," she said. "And I play the lute."

He'd never taken a secretary on tour—Lyly came from a long line of humanists, not troupers. But he could use someone like her.

"Actually, Emilia, I'd very much appreciate it."

~

*H*e was heading for Warwickshire, seated in the first wagon of the caravan with Emilia Bassano by his side. The first performance was scheduled for Stratford-upon-Avon. When they crossed the river and entered the town, the trumpets blared.

The crowds cheered.

He breathed a sigh of relief. Stratford harbored pockets of Catholic resentment, and one failed Spanish invasion hadn't eliminated all dissent.

"Milord, is it always like this when you enter a town?" She glanced around. "The noise, the screaming?"

"Don't you like it?"

"I don't like mobs."

"I felt that way at first, but now I'm used to it." He waved an arm. "This is no less England than London."

The caravan had rolled up Henley Street heading for the square when he spotted a glove shop. His kid gloves had holes in them, and a reception at Whitehall was scheduled for his return to London.

"Pull up here, driver. Lead the caravan to the square and I'll meet you there."

He swung his good foot down and followed with the other.

"Would you like a pair of gloves, Emilia?"

"No, thank you, milord, but I'll be happy to accompany you."

*S*hakspere's Glove Shop was a dark little place that seemed sad. No one was there but a fellow in his early twenties, stitching gloves—small, unshaven, with thinning brown hair. He looked Edward up and down but didn't stand.

"Can I help ye, milord?"

"Yes, thank you. I require kid gloves."

"Don't have no call for kid gloves in Stratford. I'd have t' order skins."

"Very well, but they must be delivered to London in two weeks."

"That's a long way to go for gloves," he said. "I'd have t' charge extra."

"Perfectly reasonable, and I'll take six pair to make it worth your while."

The fellow's eyes narrowed. "Six pair of kid gloves? That'll cost a pretty penny."

"I think I still have a few left."

"I'll have t' ask Pa what to charge," he said. "He's not here just now."

"I'm sure he'll be fair. Just send the bill with the gloves. Mind you, I need them in two weeks. If they're late, I won't pay."

"Of course, milord. Can I get you and the lady a small beer?"

"That would be nice. By the way, I'd like my gloves to fit—you'd better measure my hands."

"I'll get paper." He rummaged under the counter. "Ye have to excuse me. An order for six pair of kid gloves comes as a shock. Pa'll never believe it."

"Work with your father, do you?" Emilia said. "That must give you a warm feeling."

"Yes, ma'am. With two brothers, Ma and Pa and me, it gets *very* warm."

"All of you in one house?"

"Milady, we're lucky t' have a roof over our heads."

"Would you mind if we sit down while you measure my hands?" Edward said.

"Please do, milord, and I'll get the beer." The young man scurried to the back room and soon returned with three mugs full of beer. "Sorry I don't got nothin' more comfortable than them stools."

"They're fine." Emilia smiled. "The bench in the wagon was harder."

The young man laid two pieces of paper on the scarred table and traced the outline of Edward's fingers.

"Married, are you?" Edward said. "With children?"

"Yes, milord, I've got three. Susannah's five, and Hamnet and Judith are three. They're twins."

"I've three daughters myself," Edward said. "That's a lot for someone so young."

"Yes, milord. Well, I got your measurements. We'll order the kid and get started soon as it's here."

"Two weeks, don't forget."

"Right, milord. What's the address?"

"Bishopsgate, just beyond the city wall. My house is Fisher's Folly. Everybody knows it."

"Fisher's Folly. Got it."

"Don't you want to write that down?"

He shook his head. "I'm not good at writing, milord. But I won't forget Fisher's Folly."

Edward extended his hand. "I'm the Earl of Oxford."

The glover's eyes widened. "I heard of *him*. You brought them perfumed gloves t' the queen!"

"As a matter of fact, I did."

The young man shook his hand. For the first time, he smiled. "My name's Will. Will Shakspere."

PART SIX

The Mask

20

I dare do all that may become a man;
Who dares do more is none.

Shakespeare
Macbeth

When he returned to London he went straight to Cecil House to see the girls. It was after nap time and they were in the library. Susan was playing on the rug with Bridget while Elizabeth, now ten, watched over them.

Cecil was already arranging Elizabeth's marriage. He had several promising wards, but Henry Wriothesley was the current prize. The new Earl of Southampton, twenty-year-old Wriothesley was under Cecil's control and his estate was enormous.

But for now Elizabeth was still his, as were Bridget and Susan. He was playing with them on the Turkish rug when Cecil entered.

"Girls, go to the kitchen. Nurse has treats. I must speak with your father."

Edward smiled as Elizabeth shepherded the younger girls from the library. She was so good-natured, even when her grandfather treated her like a toddler.

"Edward, the Court of Wards completed the appraisals of Earl John's properties. All your sales over the years made the task somewhat difficult, but with Nan gone, there's no reason to delay collecting your debt."

"How much do I owe?"

"Three thousand six hundred pounds."

"Good Lord! It'll take me years to assemble that sum."

"You have five. The queen concurs."

"What about Nan's dowry?" Edward tried to project a stern tone of voice. "You still haven't paid me."

"Nan's dowry is a different matter, Edward. What I refer to now is *your* obligation to the queen."

Such arrogance. But he could hardly sue the man—even more than the queen, he held the country's purse strings.

"That sum could take everything I have. Only twenty-five tracts remain."

"You'll find a way. You're a bright young man."

"In case you haven't noticed, I'm thirty-seven!"

"And in fine fettle. You've been writing and staging plays for twenty years and you still haven't prospered." He turned toward the bell. "Sherry? I have oysters."

"Why not? It's time for my last meal."

Cecil laughed and rang the bell.

"Why don't you find a wife with money?"

"Too soon," Edward said.

Just then a servant arrived with a package.

"For the Earl of Oxford from Richard Field, milord."

Edward unwrapped the package.

"Know Field, do you?" Cecil said. "He prints Walsingham's propaganda. Mine, too. Very reliable."

Edward examined the book. Written by George Puttenham, it

was titled *The Art of English Poesie*. He was flipping through the first few pages when a paragraph caught his eye.

> *In her Majesty's time . . . are spring up another crew of*
> *Courtly makers, Noblemen and Gentlemen of her Majesty's*
> *own servants, who have written excellently well as it would*
> *appear if their doings could be found and made public with*
> *the rest, of which number is first that noble gentleman*
> *Edward Earl of Oxford.*

"You're not going to like this," he said.

The oysters had arrived. Cecil speared one and popped it into his mouth.

"How's that?"

"Another member of our literati has let the cat out of the bag." He handed the book to Cecil, open to the page he'd just read.

Cecil scanned it and handed it back. "I wanted to censor it, but the queen said the comments are a tribute to you and insisted it be published," he said. "We had quite a spat about it, but you know how she feels about you and your plays."

*A*fterward, Edward went to Fisher's Folly.

"John, ask the Wits to come down to the dining room while the evening's young and they're still sober."

In ones and twos, the Wits thundered down the stairway and took their seats around the dining-room table. They were already laughing and drinking—they never seemed to get anything done until after they'd attained a certain state of inebriation.

Christopher Marlowe, the newest among them, had finally arrived. The young man was brilliant, admitted to Cambridge on a scholarship. His *Tamburlaine the Great* was taking London by storm. Edward rang the bell. A servant entered at once.

"Wine for the Wits, Mr. Christmas."

The servant soon returned with two carafes of wine.

"Gentlemen, I regret I am compelled to interrupt your labors. I'll get right to the point. As you know, I lost my dear wife, Nan. Now her father is calling in my chips." He paused. "I must pay his Court of Wards three thousand six hundred pounds."

Greene whistled.

"I have five years to make payment in full." The Wits glanced at one another.

"So, I have to sell some properties. The first will be Fisher's Folly. It costs the most to maintain and will fetch a good price."

Greene ran his fingers through his unruly red hair. The others sat in silence. He hated to turn them out. Until now his English atelier had been only a success.

Thomas Kyd, another new addition, laid his head on the table. A shy fellow, he roomed with Marlowe and had flowered in the hothouse atmosphere.

Peele sighed and shook his head. "What a blow, Willy."

Lodge, Watson, and Nashe remained silent.

Mr. Christmas knocked on the door. As was their rule, he opened it without waiting and entered. Emilia Bassano entered after him.

Greene whistled. Peele licked his lips.

Edward didn't blame them. He'd restrained himself on the long summer tours, not wanting to take advantage of his position. He'd been content enough to have her by his side.

"Gentlemen, permit me to introduce *Signorina* Emilia Bassano. Emilia assists me on my tours. She's also a fine writer. She has taken it upon herself to wage a writer's crusade in pursuit of respect for women in this land of ours. I'm sure you'll agree it's a worthy endeavor."

They laughed, though he hadn't intended his comment to be funny. Edward shook his head. She'd showed him her recent work, poetry and prose combined into a remarkable manuscript. She really was a fine writer, and he respected her goal.

She moved toward an empty chair along the wall, but he dragged out the chair next to his at the head of the table.

"Emilia, I was just telling the Wits that Cecil's calling in my rather large debt to the Court of Wards. I have to pay it within five years and it requires me to sell property. I'm starting with Fisher's Folly."

"Where will you live?" she asked. "You said you couldn't face living in Savoy House."

"I still have Bilton Hall, on the Avon River in Warwickshire. It's a lovely place, adjoins the Forest of Arden. After I sold Wivenhoe, I found Bilton Hall more than suitable for writing. Plenty of peace and quiet. Still, I shall miss Fisher's Folly and these fine fellows."

A few laughed. Good. They were young, they could handle a shock like this.

"How long do we have?" Nashe said. "Here, I mean."

"I'm not sure," Edward said. "But I plan to give you each a going-away present of twenty pounds."

The cheers were nearly deafening. He summoned Mr. Christmas for more wine.

By ten o'clock the Wits were back in their rooms and he and Emilia were alone in the dining room. She hadn't touched her wine, though he'd matched the Wits glass for glass.

He felt as nervous as a boy.

"Emilia, would you come to Bilton Hall with me?" He spoke quickly. "Nothing improper, mind you—you'll be my secretary. My fingers don't move the way they used to, and we could talk about writing."

She smiled. "I'd be delighted."

*H*e left the sale of Fisher's Folly to Russell and rode to Warwickshire with Emilia—him astride his old reliable, she on the young filly he purchased for her. Although she was a city girl she rode with ease, her carriage magnificent, as if she'd grown up riding through the country. Her black curls escaped her riding cap and her breeches clung to her shapely figure. The sight of her excited him.

She spotted Bilton Hall first and stood in the saddle to point. "How beautiful!"

Now he saw the place, handed down to him from the Trussell side of his mother's family, with fresh eyes. Bilton's structures were old, but he'd kept them in good repair. All that was left of the original 600 acres were the twenty that surrounded the main house. Still, they offered privacy.

He pointed to the north. "That's the Forest of Arden. Not another house for miles."

"It looks homey."

"I feel that way, too," he said. "I'm going to hold on to this one."

He kept no servants at Bilton. They bought eggs and cheese in the village, and he set the fire while she made omelets. They took their plates into the parlor and sat on the rug in front of the fire.

He saw her glance at the virginals in the corner.

"After dinner, we could play together."

"I'd like that very much," she said with a warm smile.

After they ate, he leaned over to fill their glasses. His lips brushed hers. She didn't turn away. He took her face in his hands and kissed her—a real kiss, his lips opening hers.

"I'll be right back," she said a minute later.

She went upstairs. He heard water splashing and soon she returned, wearing a robe. Her hair was wet, and the delicate fragrance of Nan's lavender soap teased the air.

*T*hey made love in front of the fire. As physical as Anne, as loving as Virginia, as innocent as Nan—and Emilia's passion outstripped them all.

Afterward, they lay together in the fire's dying light. He ran his fingers over her skin.

"I can't tell you how much I've thought about this moment," he said.

"I've always felt so attracted to you. But I thought I'd have to worship from afar."

"I'm nobody worth worshipping." The fire hissed and cracked. "Strange. I miss my wife, yet this feels right. I suppose that's a tribute to Nan—she always wanted what was best for me."

"I'm glad," she said. "When you invited me I felt guilty—though, of course, that only lasted for a moment."

They made love again. She was petite but curvaceous, and when their bodies locked together, she smiled. Love came naturally to her, as naturally as breathing.

He felt grateful he'd lived so many years before this moment. Otherwise, he might not appreciate it. He'd been given a second chance. Funny—when she slipped off her clothes and mounted him, he thought of the queen.

"Emilia, I tried writing about you in my book of sonnets, but I could never invent a moment like this."

"Are your sonnets like a journal?"

"I find sonnets the best form to express my secret thoughts. Some of them aren't nice, but a sonnet makes them sound almost acceptable."

"Were your thoughts about me acceptable?"

"Only if you find this acceptable." They laughed—he hadn't laughed in so long. "I'm always honest in my sonnets."

"I'd love to read them."

"I'll have to inspect them first. I wouldn't want you to be hurt by something I wrote in an unguarded moment."

"You could never hurt me. I love you too much."

"And I love you. Isn't it strange? I hardly know you, yet I'm as sure of my love as if I'd known you forever."

"At the Bertie estate when I told you to go back to your wife? I knew it was the right thing to do, but my heart ached."

*H*e felt as if he were twenty-five and in Venice all over again. Their time at Bilton Hall was delightful. They rode, he worked, and they made music together, literally and figuratively. He thought it would never end.

Once, after they made love in the drawing room, she went up to the bedroom. It was a long time before she came down.

"I've been reading your play," she said when she returned.

"*As You Like It?*"

"No, the one that's more finished. You were revising it."

"*Othello.*"

"You still feel so guilty. Edward, you didn't kill Nan. Puerperal fever did."

"If you think *Othello* reveals my sense of guilt, you ought to read my *Hamlet.*" He laughed, but he wasn't joking. "Every time I work on the play, it gets darker and darker."

"You mustn't keep torturing yourself."

"I'm not very nice."

*B*ilton Hall was the only place where he'd ever washed a dish, but with Emilia it was fun. After he put the dishes away, they settled onto a couch by the fire and read.

They both jumped at the blast of a horn. Not just any horn but the queen's horn, heralding her arrival. He went to the window and stared out. Emilia stood beside him, watching the enormous caravan approach. As they looked through the glass, he held on to her hand as if it were a life preserver.

When the queen entered he tried to look pleased.

"What a pleasant surprise." He was about to make introductions when she kissed Emilia on the cheek.

"I've known this young lady since she was a little girl. I promised her father I'd take care of her, and that's one reason I'm here."

The queen wasn't looking him in the eye.

"Your Majesty, Emilia's my secretary. She's been helping me with a play—"

"I didn't find you here by chance, you know. I had Walsingham's men follow you."

"After my tour I felt the need to get away, to write on site."

"I'm sure you did."

He offered wine. She must have a reason to be here, but what?

"When Walsingham told me you two were alone, I made arrangements. I hope you both take what I'm about to say in the spirit in which it's intended. You know I wish you only the best."

Dread washed over him—cold, sickening, overwhelming.

"I spoke to Elizabeth Trentham, my most loyal lady of the bedchamber of marriageable age. Her family's from Staffordshire and very rich. Her father manufactured drapes. Her brother

Francis invests in real estate. I can't think of a better family for you to marry."

Edward stared at her.

"She also writes and her poems are superb. She's been with me ten years and is mature enough to live with someone . . . creative. I told her all about your personal history and she's seen every one of your plays at court. She assures me she's ready, willing, and able to cope with your, ah, complexities. And she's not yet thirty, so she has ample capacity to bear children."

If she weren't the queen, he'd have hit her.

She turned to Emilia. "I also spoke to Henry Carey. Lord Hunsdon's my dearest cousin and most faithful courtier. He assured me his wife is tolerant of his mistresses. When the time comes for you to marry someone of your class, which I'll also arrange, he'll help establish you in a manner befitting a lady of means. Now, I've said what I have to say and don't wish to discuss it further. They're expecting me at my next stop by nightfall, so I'll say goodbye."

And out swept Her Majesty.

I won't stand for it." Edward paced the room. "She's the queen, but I have my limits."

Though she was standing by the fire, Emilia rubbed her arms as if she were cold.

"One arranged marriage is enough. It took me years to accept it—I don't have that kind of time now!"

He stopped pacing and took Emilia's hands, warming them in his. He racked his brain. Why was she doing this? Did she feel slighted? Was she still angry about Anne Vavasour? With the queen, you never knew.

"She doesn't care about my marriage—or your future," he said.

"If she did she'd have done something about it before now. She's jealous of us. She—"

Emilia put a finger to his lips and spoke softly but firmly.

"Edward, you can't defy her. She'll take the Queen's Men from you and throw you in the Tower."

"I don't need my own company. I'll leave court and take my chances in the public theaters."

"What about your freedom to write? The queen's censors permit you to write whatever you want, but if she orders them not to approve, they won't."

"How can you accept what she's proposed?"

Emilia sat down and drew him into the seat beside her.

"She's not *proposing*. She's the queen. She's ordering. You may not see it that way, but—"

"I should have fought back when she was here."

"Edward, don't berate yourself. She's *the queen*."

"You're willing to be Hunsdon's mistress?"

Emilia's expression turned to stone. She stared at the fire for a long time. "First and foremost, we must think of you."

"Dammit, don't you want us to be together?"

"Of course I do, but you're a great writer."

"Why should that—"

Again she put a finger to his lips. "Edward, I hoped I'd play a large part in your life, but your life means more than mine, and your writing means more than your life. I've seen how people respond to your plays."

Now he was the one who turned to stone.

"Remember when I told you once that my father said his Bible was his connection with his soul?" she said.

"Yes."

"Well, on those tours, I saw how your plays provide a connection for Englishmen and women to *their* souls. They responded to your characters, they laughed, they cried, they *thought*. Through your plays, they learn about their humanity. And your plays will be helping them learn long after you and I and the queen are gone."

"I won't give you up," he said. "We'll go to Italy—"

"Your place is here, in England."

"What's that got to do with me? With us?"

"Edward, don't you see? You give people another way to consider morality, love, hate, loyalty, righteousness, politics, kings, queens—themselves."

"Does that have to mean I can't live my own life?"

"In Elizabeth's England it does. If you rebel they'll crush you just as they have other writers. You have power over people's minds, but the queen has power over you. It's as simple as that."

No, it wasn't simple. A queen who helped him with one hand and slapped him down with the other wasn't simple. But Emilia was right about who had the power. He had power over words and minds. The queen had power over him.

"How can you go to bed with Hunsdon? He's an old man, likable enough, but he doesn't *read!*"

"You think I want to?" Her cheeks flushed. "I have as little choice in this as you. The difference is that you haven't accepted it." He pulled away, but she grabbed his hand. "Edward, we can still see each other, you know. When your plays are presented at court, I'll be there. And I don't know Elizabeth Trentham as well as I know other noblewomen, but she's educated and refined—broad-minded. Maybe we can be together sometimes. But above all, your life as a writer will *not* be ruined because of me. I couldn't bear it."

"I refuse to let you to go to bed with that boor."

"Don't worry about me." She forced a smile. "I can take care of myself."

"Emilia, I *was* going to marry you. I was." He looked at her, hoping against hope. "You really think we'll be able to see each other?"

"We'll find a way."

"I'm not ready to give in. I'm going to fight. She can't always have her way. I'll convince her she's wrong."

"Fight if you must, but don't fight the queen. She can be vindictive."

She was right. She was right about everything.

21

In the old age black was not counted fair
Or if it were it bore not beauty's name;
But now is black beauty's successive heir,
And beauty slandered with a bastard shame.

Shakespeare
Sonnet 127

For a long moment after the queen left they stood looking at each other. Edward could think of nothing to say, no words to express his anguish.

"I'm going to pack," Emilia said.

He followed her, silent, watched her gather her belongings and then opened his arms.

They made love. It was no less passionate, but something had changed—they clung to one another, intense, desperate, committing every second to memory.

Afterward, he ordered a carriage for her. When she climbed in and closed the door behind her, he feared he'd never see her again. Not unless she was tethered to Lord Hunsdon, and he didn't think he could bear that.

He dragged himself to his study, where he scanned the latest draft of *As You Like It*. He wanted to finish it here, while the Forest of Arden was nearby and the Howard-family tragedy fresh in his mind. Yet his mind wandered—for the first time, his plays and poems seemed thin, insubstantial. What pleasure would he take in their success without Emilia by his side?

Down the road was Plaistow House. He knew it was for sale. It would take years to pay off his debt—what difference would a few more pounds make?

*H*e hired two servants to close up Bilton Hall and arrived in London a day early for the meeting with the queen. His rooms in Newington Butts weren't far from Shoreditch, so he walked to The Theatre, where his players were presenting *Richard III.*

He was limping along Bishopsgate High when his good leg began to ache. As he paused to rest he saw a poster for the play nailed to a tree. Tarleton had died, and now Armin, who usually played a clown, was the lead. Edward wondered how he'd handle the role.

He resumed his tortured pace. Trumpets blared, announcing the show. He pushed on. Soon he was trapped in the crowd, with gallants, merchants, prostitutes, and housewives all trying to enter the amphitheater at the same time. A ticket-taker recognized him and waved him in. He struggled up the steep stairway to the gallery, where he saw another poster. The author was listed as anonymous.

He sighed, took his seat in a box, and surveyed the house. In the cockpit below, a gallant and a commoner were arguing—it looked like the gallant was refusing to remove his wide-brimmed hat. The commoner threw a nut, which struck the gallant square in the back of the neck. Along the wall, a commoner relieved himself in a piss pot. His pound of flesh was so large it caught the attention of a prostitute who sidled over and whispered something. The man laughed and nodded, and together they left the theater.

Edward sighed again but caught himself. This might be a far cry from the palace theater, but at least his work was being shown. Good thing he'd sent *Henry VI* to The Rose, in Henslowe—the neighbors here were already complaining about the trumpets.

The play was beginning. "Now is the winter of our discontent . . ." He leaned back, closed his eyes, and smiled.

The next day he went to Westminster. He marched through the Presence Room and straight into the queen's private quarters, where he sat to wait. She still worked through the night, but she slept later these days.

At last the door opened. The queen entered, leaning on Elizabeth Trentham's arm. A tall man he'd never seen before followed them.

Edward rose. "Good morning, Your Majesty."

"Good morning, Edward. You know Eliza—this is her brother, Francis."

"Hello," the Trenthams said in unison.

In the ten years Elizabeth Trentham had been a maid of honor, he'd spoken to her only once. She seemed to be the only lady in London who didn't flirt.

Her brown hair wasn't striking, but her silky complexion made her look younger than her twenty-nine years. Not that her age bothered him—he was forty-one. And at least she was shorter than him.

Her features were plain, but that was just as well. Presumably she'd be more apt to be faithful—though you never knew with women. Her gaze was knowing, which he liked. And her posture suggested restraint—he could use some of that.

The queen sat on the sofa and patted the place next to hers. The Trenthams took seats facing him.

He managed to come up with a smile.

"Edward," the queen said, "you and Eliza need time together. But before Francis and I go, he has some thoughts to share with you. I understand he's been meeting with Cecil, the better to understand your finances."

"Your Grace," Francis said, "I've reviewed your properties. I haven't inspected them, but it's clear that Cecil's knowledge of London values is outdated. You owe the Court of Wards thousands, but your lands and buildings are worth much more."

Francis pronounced *lands* and *buildings* as if they were eighth notes. It was all Edward could do not to laugh.

"Your Grace, after you pay off the Court of Wards, I suggest you protect your future heir," Francis said. "You wouldn't want them abusing Oxford Eighteen the way they've abused you."

Edward glanced at the queen, but her eyes were closed.

"I also suggest you develop your ten acres in Covent Garden— at least 130 town houses." Francis paused. "Are you with me, or do I go too fast?"

"Not at all. I know you have an eye for land. I also know I haven't devoted myself to my real estate as much as I should, but—"

Elizabeth Trentham placed a hand on her brother's arm and turned to Edward.

"Edward, please don't apologize. Your plays are far more valuable than lands or buildings. Francis is pleased to assist you, but you'll always make the decisions."

"We'll make the decisions together, Eliza—you, Francis,

and I." He smiled at her. She smiled back. Francis reached for Eliza's hand.

"Every time I'm in a meeting with her, I understand again why Father put Eliza in charge of his estate. Of the eleven of us, she's the smartest."

"You really think we could build 130 town houses on ten acres?" he said. "London clerks are conservative."

"Covent Garden's in the center of London, largely ignored. We'll have no problems."

"How do you suggest I protect my future heir?"

"Place the property in trust. Every nobleman's doing it. That way the Court of Wards can't touch it."

He glanced at the queen. Was she really asleep? He turned back to Francis.

"I'd like to spend the rest of today with your sister. Will you join Eliza and me for breakfast at The Pye, tomorrow at nine?"

"I'd be delighted. One more thing—we understand your situation's not liquid. May our family contribute ten thousand pounds to the marriage?"

He saw the queen's eyes open and then close.

"I'd very much appreciate it—anything that leaves me free to write."

Francis chuckled. "Elizabeth's seen all your plays, you know. Maybe one day I will."

"It'll be my pleasure to take you."

*H*e took Eliza to The Steelyard. It was midmorning, but the crowd was already raucous. She ordered a small beer and then touched his hand.

"Edward, I'm happy to be marrying you. I never thought I'd wed a writer."

"I'm happy you feel that way."

"The queen impressed upon me that writing's your life, and there won't be much room for me—"

"Eliza . . ." He thought of Emilia and then forced her out of his mind. "I've not been the best husband. But I promise you I've learned from the experience." He took her hand. "I'd like us to make the best of this."

*T*he wedding took place on the palace lawn at Greenwich. The July heat was extreme, but a breeze from the Thames kept things tolerable. Four-year-old Susan was their flower girl, and Elizabeth, Bridget, and the five Trentham girls were maids of honor. Trentham brothers were ushers. The Archbishop of Canterbury officiated.

Eliza walked down the aisle on Francis' arm, her bright smile shining through the lace. Edward's secretaries—he had three now—sang a madrigal composed by John Dowland. He'd invited all the former Wits, who drank steadily throughout the reception. Edmund Spenser read a portion of *The Fairie Queene*. The real queen, to whom it was dedicated, nodded and smiled.

Eliza danced with Francis, Hunsdon danced with the queen, and Edward and Cecil limped over to chairs with a good view of the Thames.

Cecil raised his glass.

"To you, Edward."

"Thank you, Baron. And thank *you* for taking care of the girls all these years. I'm sorry Lady Cecil isn't here to share the moment."

Cecil shed a tear. "Kind of you to remember. I've arranged for Bridget and Susan to live with Countess Bedford in South Buckinghamshire. Two young girls is too much for one new

wife. I think she'll have her hands full just taking care of you."
Cecil nodded toward the dance floor. "See how nicely our
Elizabeth dances with Southampton? I'm trying to convince
him to marry her, but he's a hard nut to crack. Would you
have a word with him, my boy? I'm told he attends The Theatre
every day."

"Won't my advice be as biased as yours?" Edward said.

"Do it anyway. They say he's sweet on your work."

He raised a brow and looked back at the Earl of Southampton.
Henry Wriothesley had delicate features, a lithe yet muscular
frame. He couldn't tell if his daughter liked him. Her gaze had
ever been guarded, more so as she grew older.

"I suppose I could pen a few sonnets to impress on him the
importance of marriage in perpetuating his name and securing
his property. He's handsome, don't you think?"

"Not really," Cecil said. "That curly, long hair makes him look
like a girl. How well do you know him?"

"Not at all. When's his birthday?"

"He'll be seventeen in a few weeks."

"I'm sure I can put together a few sonnets by then."

That night he and Eliza consummated their marriage. Eliza
was efficient. She also bled a lot. He liked her but hoped
they'd made a boy. He didn't fancy making love to his wife more
than he had to.

"I have a confession to make," she said after it was over.

He tensed.

"I write," she said. "Nothing like you, of course—only sonnets—but may I show them to you sometime?"

He relaxed. "I'd be delighted."

"I've read a few of yours, the ones you pass around court."

"I didn't pass around many."

"Still," she said, "they were lovely."

A few days later, Edward was drinking with the Wits at The Steelyard. They were raucous, as usual, but he couldn't match their frivolity.

Spenser ordered another round and glanced at Edward.

"Gentle Willy, why so sad?"

Greene brushed his long red hair from his eyes. "Upset about Alleyn's performance?"

Edward pulled himself together. "What about Alleyn?"

"Edward Alleyn played the Duke of York in your *Henry VI* last week," he said. "He jumped on the stage like a *shakescene*, trying to steal attention."

"Ever since he married Henslowe's stepdaughter, he insists on playing every leading role," Lyly said. "Edward, I know *you* can't protest, but *I* intend to."

"When that ungrateful bastard jumped on the stage, he shattered a plank," Spenser said. "Here's to our Lyly shattering his neck."

Edward chuckled, but his heart wasn't in it.

He wished he were here with Emilia.

*H*e dragged himself back to the large suite he'd rented in Newington Butts until he and Eliza could find something suitable. The new cook served him hot soup—already his wife knew how to settle his stomach.

"Where was I this morning?" he asked her. "I feel as if I'm in a fog."

"You'd started *Antony and Cleopatra*." Eliza nodded to the

cook. The empty bowl was removed and his favorite—pasta—was served.

"Edward, please be thankful you're alive," she said. "A brave and talented writer just died."

"Who?" He twirled the pasta on his fork like an Italian, the spoon in his other hand.

"Veronica Franco."

He thought of Virginia. A lump formed in his throat.

Eliza tilted her head. "Did you meet her when you were in Venice?"

"I did," he said. "She was everything you just said. Brave as well as talented."

"So are you, Edward. Focus on your writing and you'll come right with yourself."

22

*I have of late—but wherefore I know
not—lost all my mirth; . . . this goodly
frame, the earth, seems to me a sterile
promontory; this most excellent canopy,
the air . . . appears no other thing to me
than a foul and pestilent congregation of
vapors.*

Shakespeare
Hamlet, Prince of Denmark

*H*e wrote all day, through the night, and into the next morning. Now he needed to walk.

He was making his way along Bishopsgate High when he saw her, that black, curly hair bouncing about her shoulders and her hips swaying as she glided down the street. His good leg was stiff and his bad leg worse, but somehow he managed to catch up to her.

"Hello, Emilia."

She turned. There was a smile on her face. "Edward! Hello."

"How are you?"

"Slightly pregnant."

His stomach twisted. Should he congratulate her?

"May I walk with you?"

"Of course."

"Where are you going?"

"To see my future husband, Alphonse Lanier."

"In your condition?"

"It's been arranged," she said. For a moment, she looked bitter. "He was happy to marry a woman carrying another man's child—for a price."

"Isn't he the fellow who plays the recorder at court?"

"For years, he's wanted my father's seat in the Consort of Recorders. Now, Hunsdon's giving it to him. A marriage of the Bassano and Lanier musical dynasties, so Hunsdon's baby has a proper father."

"Emelia, you must be—"

"I'll get over it." She lifted her chin. "I could have said no, but I won't make my child a bastard."

"I'd give anything if—"

"It's not your fault, Edward. Noblemen don't marry commoners."

His face burned.

"The queen said it was the best she could do," Emilia said. "So much for women's solidarity."

"I'm so sorry." The truth was, he couldn't bear it. He loved her, and she was in so much pain.

"If anyone's to blame it's my father. *He* arranged for me to live with the countess, and in the process I fell victim to hope." She shook her curls as if to cast off her woes.

"How's the writing?"

"Coming along."

"I heard you married. How's that going?"

"She puts up with me. I'm sure it isn't easy. I'm not sure marriage ever is."

"I won't find it difficult," she said. He wished she hadn't.

They walked in silence for a while.

"I paid off the Court of Wards," he said. "I'm free at last."

"Don't take anything for granted," she said. "Now I know why a Jewish man thanks God every morning he wasn't born a woman."

He laughed. She didn't.

They stopped in front of a modest house.

"This is where I leave you," she said.

"Can we meet again?" He couldn't bear to leave her here, now, like this.

"We'll both be married. To others. Hunsdon wants me to name the baby after him. It's his tenth child."

"Henry's not a bad name."

"I just hope it's not Henriette." She entered the house. The door closed behind her.

He stood there a few minutes, staring at the "Chez Lanier" sign. After a while he heard the faint sound of a duet for recorder and virginals.

He'd give anything to be the keys on her keyboard just so he could feel her touch.

*H*e penned seventeen sonnets for Henry Wriothesley's seventeenth birthday and sent a message inviting him to meet at The Rose. When Edward touched the door, it swung open. He entered and saw Henry standing in the cockpit. He was even more handsome than he remembered, more beautiful than Orazio Cuoco.

"Hello, Henry."

"Hello, Edward." His smile was radiant. Just looking at him made Edward feel young.

"I thought I'd give you an insider's view of The Rose. Well-done, don't you think?"

"I love the faux marble," Henry said. "I usually hate green, but here it suits. Is it because the playhouse is open to the sky and green's the color of spring?"

"Very perceptive. And it was half the cost of Burbage's Theatre." Since when did he care about cost? Such stuffy details wouldn't impress a man like Henry.

"How many patrons does The Rose hold, Edward?"

"Twenty-five hundred, same as The Theatre."

"I could never write a play, but I do love beautiful language." He looked around at the seats, the stage. "It makes the world seem sweeter."

Edward held out the package of sonnets. "Seventeen sonnets," he said, "to sweeten your seventeenth birthday. May you always enjoy good health."

Henry's eyes lighted up like a child's as he grabbed the packet. Charming.

"Thank you so much, Edward."

And he had such a lovely way of speaking—musical despite courtier affectation. He eagerly tore the paper off the package and read aloud the opening lines of the first sonnet:

From fairest creatures we desire increase,
That thereby beauty's rose might never die.

Henry looked at him, his face still alight.

"That's *so* beautiful."

"I have a confession. When I wrote those sonnets, I promised Cecil to try and convince you to marry our Elizabeth."

"That's so *sweet*, but I can't marry. When I lived in Cecil House she was a sister to me."

Edward smiled. "I understand how you feel—completely."

"It's just that I want to live. You understand that, don't you?"

He tucked his curls behind his ears. "Of course you do. You're a writer." Henry read aloud from the next sonnet:

When forty winters shall besiege thy brow,
And dig deep trenches in thy beauty's field.

He looked up, eyes wide. "Are you *forty?* Ever since I saw your *Romeo and Juliet*, I think of you as timeless. When I saw that play, I lost my heart."

Edward was fast losing his.

"I'm so flattered." Another dazzling smile. "I promise I'll marry one of your daughters, just not right now. Essex promised to take me on one of his raids on Spanish ships. You've no idea how much I long to go. It sounds thrilling."

"Indeed it does." Edward smiled. "Come, let's walk. You can tell me all about your plans."

*W*hen he arrived home, Eliza greeted him with flushed cheeks.

"Edward, I saw Dr. Lopez."

"Are you all right?" He took her hand.

"I've been unwell in the mornings—sometimes I can be so stupid! Edward, I'm pregnant."

He hugged her.

"I'm so happy!"

"Dr. Lopez said he can't tell if it's a boy, but Elizabeth knew a midwife who says she can, so we went to see her, and she says it *is!*"

After twenty years and two marriages, would he finally have an heir?

"Eliza, I'm going to buy you the most wonderful present in the world. What would you like?"

"Being your wife is all I want. That and for you to write to your heart's content."

He felt a surge of warmth toward her, something very like love.

"I insist. What can I do?"

"Just pray the baby's healthy."

He clapped his hands. "I know. I'll buy you the King's Place. It's in Hackney, once belonged to Henry VIII."

"My love, you just paid off the Court of Wards."

He kissed her forehead. "Let me worry about money. I'm going to see the queen tomorrow and ask her permission to publish something. I could use a few thousand pounds."

"She'll be so pleased. Dearest, let's give her a present."

"Of course." He pulled himself to his feet. "Now I must work."

"You know you needn't ask the queen's approval," she said. "She loves everything you write."

He thought for a minute. "In this case, I think I do. Eliza, you know the queen and I—"

"You don't have to tell me about *that*." She stifled a giggle. "You weren't the only one. Whenever some courtier refers to her as the Virgin Queen we always laugh."

"That's why I must ask her permission. I've never written a long poem, but they're popular these days. I'm told mine should sell a dozen editions or more." He took a deep breath. "It's about her and me, disguised as the story of Venus and Adonis."

"I see," Eliza said. "You could lose your head."

"That's why I'll get her permission."

"She'll never give it."

"I think she will. She'll laugh at the audacity and love the idea of an older woman taking advantage of a younger man."

"What about the Cecils? Robert's the principal secretary now, in everything but name."

"When the queen and his father agree, he goes along."

"Have you forgotten that she had John Stubbs' hand cut off for writing a *pamphlet*?"

"Don't worry, my dear. I have an idea they'll be sure to accept, one that will shield me completely and please even Robert Cecil."

Eliza gave him a long, hard look. "If you say so."

"Let's make a wager." Edward grinned. "I say Robert will go along. If I lose, I'll buy you King's Place. If I win, I'll buy you King's Place. Now, let's toast Oxford Eighteen. Sherry?"

"Dr. Lopez says I mustn't drink wine. No doctor in England agrees with him, but he says it's the latest view in Padua."

"Then what will you have?"

"Apple cider. Elizabeth and I bought some on our way home. It's lovely."

"As lovely as my wife?"

"Lovelier."

"Impossible." He kissed her.

When the queen entered, Edward got to his feet. "Your Majesty."

"I regret I had to keep you waiting. Dressing me takes so much longer these days. How are you?"

"Good news, Your Majesty. Eliza's pregnant. The midwife says it's a boy."

She beamed and clapped her hands. "I'm thrilled to hear it."

"Your Majesty, Eliza and I can't thank you enough for bringing us together. Will you be the child's godmother?"

"I'd be delighted." She blotted her eyes, careful not to smear the paste. "What does Lopez say about the sex of the child?"

"He says no one can predict gender."

"Lopez never lies." She fingered her hair arrangement. "I don't know what I'd do without him. Now Edward, your message said you wanted the Cecils to be here so I could approve something you'd written. I admit you've piqued my curiosity."

"It's a long poem that was . . . inspired by our relationship. If there's anything you don't like, or if you want me to burn it, just say so. But if you could permit it to be published, I'd be grateful."

"I can't read an entire manuscript—my eyes aren't what they used to be." She sighed. "Read me the parts you think I should hear."

He leafed through the pages. "It's called *Venus and Adonis*."

"I read it in the original."

"This is my own version. Venus is talking to Adonis—they're naked, in bed. She describes her body as he caresses it.

> *'Fondling,' she saith, 'since I have hemmed thee here*
> *Within the circuit of this ivory pale.*
> *I'll be a park, and you shall be my deer;*
> *Feed where you wilt, on mountains or in dale . . .*
> *Graze on my lips, and if those hills be dry,*
> *Stray lower, where the pleasant fountains lie.'*

He looked up. She wasn't even blushing, though he couldn't be sure with all the paste. All he saw was a single tear.

He waited.

"Publish it at once, Edward, and promise you'll always think of me that way."

He was relieved but not all that surprised. He'd been right about her.

"Eliza thought you'd throw me in the Tower," he said.

"Don't be ridiculous. It's art."

"Still, the Puritans—"

"Require enlightenment."

"But Cecil and his son—"

"I'll take care of them."

"*Y*our Majesty." Cecil bowed when he and his son Robert were ushered into the queen's private chambers.

"How's my Spirit?"

"The usual aches and pains, Your Majesty."

"You're so brave. And Robert—how's my Bosse?"

Robert cringed and shifted from his clubfoot to the other.

"I'm well, Your Majesty. Thank you for inquiring."

"I know my Cecils are busy, but our favorite playwright asked me to approve the publication of a poem. I found it touching, but he wants to be sure you agree. He values your judgment so much."

Cecil and Robert glanced at each other.

"Edward, read the passage."

When he finished it, Cecil took a lot of time settling himself and shaking his head before he spoke. "Your Majesty, . . . I don't know what to say."

"Then don't say anything. Let it be published."

"But, Your Majesty—"

"No buts. Robert?"

"Your Majesty, the passage is offensive." Robert's body was perfectly still, his eyes on fire.

"It's not offensive, it's life. Where's your sense of humor?"

"Your Majesty," Cecil said, "may I make a suggestion?"

"Of course."

"Such a poem might prompt . . . curiosity about you and the Earl of Oxford. Perhaps his authorship could be hidden by a pen name?"

"What say you, Edward?"

"I have no objection."

"Then it's settled," Cecil said. "*Venus and Adonis* will be published under a pseudonym—"

"Just a moment." Robert limped closer to the queen. "In light of the . . . *vivid* language, I think Edward should also employ a go-between to whom authorship can be attributed."

"You mean hire a dumb man?"

"Exactly, Your Majesty. Someone to deliver the manuscript to censors, thus further insulating Edward from any possible repercussions."

"Edward?" The queen seemed tired now. "Are you agreeable to employing a go-between as a part of your mask?"

He, too, felt tired.

"Why not?"

"Do you have someone in mind?" Robert said.

"When I do, you'll be the first to know."

23

Heigh-ho! Sing! Heigh-ho unto the green holly:
Most friendship is feigning.

Shakespeare
As You Like It

*E*dward went straight to Richard Field's print shop and told him he'd be using a pen name for the long poem and would let him know what it was as soon as he picked one.

"How long will it take to set the type?" he said. "I'm told it will sell many editions."

"Many editions for a poem about Venus and Adonis?"

"Field, don't try my patience. If you must know, the poem's about the queen and me—at least that's the way it will be received."

"You're sure she'll approve? I don't fancy losing my hand."

"She's already agreed."

"Very good, milord, I'll get to work at once. By the way, milord, there's a fellow looking for you. I sent him down to the The Theatre. He's working with Burbage now."

∽

*W*hen Edward entered the amphitheater, he saw a young man sweeping up leaves and dust as if his life depended on it.

"Hello, Will."

"Milord! How'd you know I was here?"

"Richard Field said you were looking for me. I'm glad to see you made it to London."

"Thank you, milord. Sorry I never delivered them gloves. Pa said the kid was too expensive, and he never asks for an advance."

"Don't worry about it. How do you like the city so far?"

"I like it fine, though them carts with bodies kind of gets t' me."

"Found yourself a place to stay yet?"

"Field found me a room at the Mountoys that don't cost much. And Mr. Burbage promised if a better job comes along here with more money, he'll give it t' me." He swept the leaves into a pan and dropped them into the bucket. "I'm saving up to send the money home."

What a stroke of luck.

"I don't have much time now, but I wanted to ask you something," Edward said. "How would you feel about being my mask?"

"Not rightly sure what you mean by that, milord."

"It's not considered proper for a man in my position to sign his name to something for sale—like, for example, a manuscript. So I need someone to let me put their name on my work, to act as a go-between with the printer and a few other people."

Will looked thoughtful.

"I know such matters are complicated, but—"

"I understand all right, milord. You're playing hide-and-seek."

"In a manner of speaking, I suppose I am. Of course, I'd pay for your assistance, not that you'll have much to do. I'll need you to bring my poem to the printer and to persons who approve publication—the Archbishop of Canterbury, the Mayor of London, the Stationers Registry. I'll give you their addresses. And should anyone ask if you're the author, just say yes. And that's all there is to it."

"Milord, I read a little, but I can't write much."

"They won't care, Will. If you say you're the author no one will challenge your assertion. Are you interested?"

"Would my name be on the poem?"

"It would."

"I suppose I ought to ask, milord, how much? I mean, what exactly did ye have in mind t' pay for my services?"

"I don't want to take advantage. Give me a price, and if it's within reason, you've got a deal."

Will looked at Edward for a long moment. Edward waited.

"When I got t' London and discovered luck was with me, milord, I decided the first thing I'd do with any real money I got would be to thank Pa by getting him the coat of arms he always wanted."

"What a novel way to say thank you."

"I heard there's a man at the College of Heralds who looks the other way. All I got t' do is pay 'im sixty pounds, milord. So that's what my fee would be for being your mask. Sixty pounds."

"I could buy the best house in Stratford for that."

"Like I said, milord, I don't know what t' charge. But I know this is important t' you, so I'm trying to be accommodating."

"All right," Edward said. "I'll pay you sixty pounds if necessary, but I'd like you to ask your man at the College of Heralds if you can get away with less."

"Be happy to, milord. How do I find ye?"

"Burbage knows. Just tell him you need me."

With that Will returned to sweeping the floor and Edward left The Theatre, musing over the scene that had just taken place.

A few weeks later, he met with Will again. He said his man at the College of Heralds "won't come down none on it." Edward gave him sixty pounds and the Cecils the name of the go-between. Who, he'd decided, was cunning if uneducated.

*T*he eighteenth Earl of Oxford was born in June—the first Henry in the Oxford family in five hundred years. Edward didn't tell Eliza that Henry Wriothesley was the reason he chose the name.

About the same time, *Venus and Adonis* was published. Two editions sold out at once, and Field was already printing a third. Edward used the proceeds toward the purchase of King's Place in Hackney. It cost a fortune and needed work, but Eliza liked it. And Emilia would be right down the street.

In the middle of all this, Dr. Lopez sent a message: "Please come at once. Need your advice."

"Ruy, my friend, how are you?"

Lopez looked thin, his usually rosy cheeks pale. Even his hair seemed whiter.

"As well as can be expected," he said.

Edward steered him toward a chair. "Let me get you some wine."

"Thank you. There's sherry on the table behind you."

He poured a glass and handed it to the doctor. "You said you wanted my advice. What can I do for you?"

"I'm afraid it may be past the time anyone can help me."

"Why? What do you mean?"

"Kit Marlowe's been murdered."

"No!" Such a promising talent! "What happened?"

"They claim he had a dispute with three of Robert Cecil's agents over who'd pay for wine, but Kit surely knew no one fights with Robert's men and lives to tell the story. They stabbed him in the eye."

"I don't know what to think," Edward said. "Why on earth—"

"Edward, . . ." Lopez rubbed his eyes. "Kit discovered Mary Scots was framed, by Robert's men. That's why they killed him."

Edward nearly spilled his sherry. "If that's true, they'll never get away with it—"

"Of course they will," Lopez said.

The room was warm, yet Edward shivered. He refilled Lopez's glass and poured one for himself. "Good sherry."

"My father-in-law imports it from Spain." Lopez forced a smile. "I suppose I'd better enjoy it while I can."

"Ruy, what's wrong?"

Lopez stood up, walked to the window, and looked out at the garden. "I suppose there's no harm in talking about it." He walked back to his chair and collapsed into it. "Just before he died, Walsingham asked me to be a double agent for England. He wanted to trick King Philip into thinking I'd kill the queen. Then he planned to reveal the plot so Catholics would see Spain for what it is—an evil empire. I love the queen, but this intrigue went too far. I refused."

"Francis had his mad side, didn't he?" Edward said.

"When Francis died, Robert got his files. He stumbled across Walsingham's plot, and now he's saying *I* plan to kill the queen."

"Surely he sees it was only one of Walsingham's plots," Edward said. "Can't you convince him?"

"I've tried," he said. "London's gone wild—conspiracy is everywhere. The queen might have saved me in the past, but now . . ."

"Ruy, this is absurd. I know how the queen feels about *you*. I'll talk to her."

*H*e decided to walk back to Newington Butts. It was farther than he usually went on foot, but he needed to clear his mind.

He was almost home when he saw her.

"Hello, Emilia."

"Edward!" She smiled at him. "Congratulations on your son. What's his name?"

"Henry," he said. "What brings you to Newington Butts? I thought you and Lanier lived in Hackney."

"The house isn't ready." She tilted her head. "You look sad. What's happened?"

"I just saw Dr. Lopez."

"Did you hear what happened to Marlowe?"

"I did." He swallowed. "Kit was so promising . . ." He shook his head. He couldn't bear it.

"Emilia, could we meet?"

She looked away. "I never dreamed England would be like this." She practically spit out her next words. "*This scepter'd isle, this other Eden, this demi-paradise, this precious stone set in the silver sea, . . . this blessed plot, this realm, this England.*"

"You made a few mistakes in your recital."

She frowned. "Don't you understand what's happening?"

"Too well," he said. "If Lopez is found guilty of treason, they'll hang him, cut him down alive, slash his bowels, cut off his testicles, and chop his body in quarters—"

"Stop it!" She put her hands over her ears. "Have you gone mad?"

"No, but I can't speak for the rest of the world." He stared at her, eyes pleading. "Emilia. I need you."

"That's never been the issue." She sighed. "Where and when?"

"Your house, now. I assume no one's home."

"Lanier insists on a servant. He thinks Hunsdon's made him rich."

"Then we'll go to The Theatre." He offered her his arm and she took it.

"Congratulations on *Venus and Adonis*," she said. "I assume it's yours."

"The idea doesn't bother you?"

"Why should it? The countess told me bedding the queen made you a national hero. Many hoped she'd marry you."

"You don't resent my being with her?"

"Would it matter if I did?" She shrugged. "Only women pay the price for that sort of behavior."

They reached The Theatre.

"Let's talk about something else," he said.

She smiled. "Did we come here to talk?"

They laughed.

He tried the door—it was locked. Good, Will was gone for the day.

He pulled out his key, unlocked the door, and led her to Burbage's office behind the stage. She fell into his arms—he marveled all over again at how perfectly she fit there. They undressed each other and plunged onto the sofa.

He began to move slowly—they might not be able to steal another moment like this. He closed his eyes, imagined that they were married, that it was early morning on a day like any other, that they'd make love again and talk all day and into the evening.

"I've missed you so much," he said.

"And I you."

"How do you pass the days? Are they too long, like mine?"

"The baby takes up most of my time," she said. "And I worry. Lanier went through nearly everything Hunsdon gave me. Now he's selling my jewels."

"I can help you."

"Thank you, but I didn't tell you that because I need the money. I can always take care of myself and the baby. I'm going to open a school, teach noblemen's children."

"You'll be a good teacher," he said. "Just look at all the things you taught me." He held her even closer. "I love you, Emilia, and I always will. Never forget that."

"And I love you."

"I've been writing sonnets about you at night. It keeps me sane."

"I'm glad something does."

They both laughed. Next to making love, he enjoyed their laughing together more than anything.

"I'm finally writing again," she said.

"About?"

"The usual—a plea to women to reject the way the Bible portrays us, starting with the Fall. If anyone's to blame for that, it's not woman."

He made love to her, again as if this time were the last. Afterward they lay side by side, his arm around her and her leg thrown over his. He told her about his new plays—and his mask.

"It's killing me, seeing Will Shakspere's name on my work. I've used pen names before, but this is different. It feels like someone's stolen my writing."

"Edward, he can barely read. No one will believe he's a writer, much less the author of sophisticated plays."

"What about a hundred years from now? He'll be remembered and I'll be forgotten."

"You're worried about a hundred years from now? I'm worried about next week."

He laughed.

"I saw you dedicated *Venus and Adonis* to Henry Wriothesley."

"I'm trying to convince him to marry my Elizabeth."

"You were very passionate."

"You should see the dedication in my next long poem, *The Rape of Lucrece*."

She studied him. "Why such feeling?"

I'm not sure." He stroked her hair. "Except for you, I seem to have a habit of falling in love, then forgetting why."

She gave him a penetrating look. "Well, *I* think you're infatuated with Henry."

"Maybe I'm hoping he'll invest in my plays. The queen pays me a thousand pounds a year to write, but she could stop at any time. And you know how I am. Money slips through my fingers."

"Is that why you wrote, '*What I have done is yours; what I have to do is yours, being part in all I have, devoted yours*?" She rolled her eyes, but she was smiling.

He buried his face in the space between her shoulder and neck. He felt her fingers—the ones that made such beautiful music—stroke his cheek. "Maybe I do love Henry Wriothesley."

"I know."

He pulled back and stared at her. "You do?"

"It's hardly a shock," she said. "You always write about two men who love each other—then a woman comes between them."

He frowned. "Am I so transparent?"

"Perhaps only to me." She smiled. "Edward, what's your wife like? You haven't said a word about her."

"She's a good woman and I care for her, but it's not the love I feel for you." He sighed. "But she looks after me sweetly, and—"

"You do need a lot of looking after."

They both laughed.

"The Wits tell me I've become a recluse, but they haven't seen anything yet.

When I'm settled in King's Place, I'm going to write tragedies—no more comedies or English history plays—and no one will see me but you and my family."

She grinned. "What about Henry Wriothesley?"

"Touché. Last night I described him in a sonnet as the

master-mistress of my passion. I wrote that his body parts are superfluous for a man in love with a man." He sighed and looked down at the floor.

"Edward, you're ashamed of too many things—who you love, how you write—"

"You're not the first to tell me that. Kit Marlowe said I should let my feelings out."

"And look what happened to him."

*T*hey got dressed. He let her leave first. When he opened the door of Burbage's office, the theater was deserted.

He felt as if a weight had been lifted from his chest. But didn't he always when he was with Emilia?

24

How many ages hence
Shall this our lofty scene be acted over
In states unborn and accents yet unknown!

Shakespeare
Julius Caesar

The queen had signed Dr. Lopez's death warrant—
Edward had to confront her.

He'd sent a message requesting an appointment, but
there hadn't been time to wait for a reply. He took a sedan chair
to Westminster.

Usually she didn't emerge before noon. He drew up a chair and
sat down to wait. To his surprise, her clerk appeared at eleven,
ushered him into her private chambers, and left him alone with
the queen.

"Your Majesty."

"Edward. What's so urgent?"

He was a good four feet from her, but still he could smell her
breath. Ruy had pleaded in vain with her to let the surgeon
remove the black teeth.

"Your Majesty, you signed Ruy Lopez's death warrant." He
waited a moment. "Please tell me there's some mistake."

She stretched out her hand, palm down, fingers spread, and studied the diamond-and-ruby ring on her finger.

"Do you like it?" she said. "Ruy gave it to me. King Philip sent it to him when he agreed to poison me. We laughed when Ruy told me about it."

He glanced at the ring. "It's beautiful."

"He said he'd put the poison in my syrup. So clever—he knows I can't *stand* syrup."

He began to relax. Perhaps signing the warrant had merely been another one of her gestures, one she had no intention of enforcing.

She looked up, her eyes fixed on some point beyond him. "I told Ruy to save the ring for his daughter, but I changed my mind. I sent a message to him in the Tower that I needed something to remember him by."

"Your Majesty—"

"Parliament's unyielding, Edward. I have to comply."

"But the trial's a farce! The panel didn't let Ruy call a single witness. Your mother received a better hearing than that!"

She stiffened. "She was as innocent as Ruy. It's Parliament who's got him, not me."

"But you can stop it!"

"No one can stop a mob. If I don't kill Ruy, Parliament will kill me."

He took a deep breath and forced himself to let it out slowly. "With respect, Your Majesty, that makes no sense."

She looked at him and shook her head. "Poor Edward, you really don't understand. When they're in a group, people aren't rational. Ruy's a Jew. They need someone to burn, and I can't be the one in their path."

"At least postpone the execution!" He was shouting. He forced himself to lower his voice. "Once people cool down—"

"I hate delays," she said. "They make my heart flutter and my stomach twist."

"Ruy could give you something for that."

She smiled. "He always made me feel better." Again her eyes seemed to be fixed on some distant point. "Do you remember your first tournament? When you won again the next year I loved you even more." She began to cry.

He seized her hand. "Your Majesty," he said, "if you won't stand up for Ruy, who will?"

Her face went still. She drew back her hand. "Earl John would be proud of you." She stood. "I'll make my apologies to Ruy in heaven. There they have no trouble remembering Jesus, too, was a Jew. Now, Edward, I must ask you to leave."

*O*utside, he waved away the sedan chair. The queen's words still rang in his ears as he limped down the street toward The Theatre. Londoners all around him raced toward the killing field at Tyburn, drunk though it was still morning, singing, waving flags, eager to be as close to the scaffold as they could.

That night he felt as if he'd witnessed Ruy's execution a hundred times over. At last he got out of bed and wrote.

Hath not a Jew eyes? Hath not a Jew hands? Organs, dimensions, senses, affections, passions? Subject to the same diseases, healed by the same means, warmed and cooled by the same winter and summer as a Christian is?

He achieved no catharsis. He should have gone to Tyburn to protest, but he was as much a coward as the queen.

When he finally fell back asleep, his dreams were a parade of the dead: Earl John, Nan, Uncle Tom, Sir Thomas, Kit Marlowe, now Ruy Lopez.

Was there no end to bigotry and hatred? After the doctor, who was next?

The next morning he went to The Theatre. The front door was open, and the wind crept in to stir the dust and leaves. He heard the soft swish of a broom from somewhere past the stage.

"Will?" he called. "Will Shakspere?"

The sweeping stopped and Will stepped out, brushing a strand of hair from his eyes. "Good to see you, milord."

"I wrote a poem, *The Rape of Lucrece,*" he said. "I'd like you to deliver it to the censors. Do you remember the addresses?"

"I remember 'em, milord. What sort of payment did ye have in mind?"

"I already paid you sixty pounds."

"That you did, milord, and thank you again. But a new poem's a new task, isn't it?"

Too weary to argue, he handed Will the package.

"What did you have in mind?"

"Being as you're a good customer, milord, I'll keep the price same as before."

"Another sixty pounds?"

"I'm still wearing the clothes I was wearing when I come t' London a year ago, you know. And I got a wife, kids, Pa, Ma, a sister, three brothers—"

Edward held up a hand. "I find your argument persuasive."

"Glad we could come to an agreement, milord."

"I don't have that much with me," he said, "but last week Burbage and I were getting ready for The Theatre to reopen and came up with a plan. I think I could include you in it. To your profit, of course."

"Sounds good, milord. How would that work?"

"Sir Robert Cecil tells us he's limited the number of companies permitted to perform in London. The Lord Chamberlain's Men, under Lord Hunsdon, will stage my plays here. The Admiral's Men will likely stage some of them at The Rose. How would you like to be a shareholder in the Lord Chamberlain's Men? We've six already, but I see no reason why we couldn't add a seventh. In return for delivering my poem, I'll buy your shares for you."

"What exactly would I get in money?"

"It depends on the number of performances and how many attend. Over the course of a year, I'd think, you'd receive as much as five pounds a week."

"Would I have t' pay taxes?"

"Most people do. It's the law."

"Sounds good t' me, milord." He grinned. "Count me in."

"Mind you, I'll require more than a single manuscript delivery."

"How much more, milord?"

"You'd start by helping with the move to the new location. Burbage may lose his lease here and he's trying to get Blackfriars."

"Blackfriars is smaller, isn't it? That'd cut down on my share."

"True. It's only a hundred seats," Edward said. "But it's enclosed, so he'll be open year-round, which will increase your share. Did you obtain that coat of arms for your father?"

"Dethick's kept me hanging. Milord, when could I expect the first payment out of my shares?"

"Sometime in the spring."

*I*n the fall, Edward's daughter Elizabeth became engaged to William Stanley, the Earl of Derby. The Stanleys were always fighting among themselves, but with only twelve earls left and most of them married, there wasn't much to choose from. Besides, Stanley's brother had been the patron of the Earl of Derby's players, and William wrote plays.

Edward had personally delivered Henry Wriothesley's invitation to the wedding, but Henry tendered his regrets. Essex had asked him to be his aide on a raid on Spanish ships. To Edward's surprise, he was relieved. He was too old for fantasies. Besides, he was immersed in a play for Elizabeth's wedding, one he'd been thinking about since Italy. He'd never forgotten Sabbioneta, that grand villa he visited en route to Florence. He was setting the play, *A Midsummer Night's Dream*, in the Sabbioneta's private theater.

*F*our months after the wedding, he slipped five pounds into Will's pocket.

"Thank you, milord."

"Perhaps now that the theater is doing so well you'll bring your family to London."

"Later, milord. I got somethin' cooking."

"What's that, if I may be so bold?"

"Sorry, milord. I'm not at liberty t' tell ye."

He felt a sense of unease—the whole point of employing a mask was to maintain a low profile. He didn't fancy having to get Will out of trouble if some hare-brained scheme went sour.

*H*e stopped by Emilia's house—he went there often. She seemed even happier than usual.

"Essex took a fancy to the recorder, Edward, and invited my Will to come play for him on the voyage to the Azores. He said music will help pass the time."

"Last night I wrote a sonnet about all the Wills in my life," Edward said. "I call them my Wills in Over-plus. There's Will my mask; Willy my nickname; Will your husband; Will Cecil; Elizabeth's husband, Will Stanley; Will Lewyn—"

"Well, *my* Will finally spent the last of Hunsdon's gifts, so I went to see Dr. Formon to find out if he'll gain anything from the voyage. Essex promised to knight him."

"And what did your astrologer-cum-physician predict?" Edward started undressing.

"He said Will won't become a knight, then he asked me to climb into bed with him."

"He *what?*"

"He offered to waive his fee, so I got in." She saw his face and rolled her eyes. "Don't give me that look—we didn't fuck. I lingered a while, then I left."

"What do you mean *lingered a while?*"

"He threatened to tell everyone about the mole on my breast," she said. "Then people *would* think we'd been together. What could I do?"

He felt sick to his stomach. "It didn't bother you?"

She shrugged. "No more than being sold to Hunsdon and Will."

Her practicality nauseated him. He pulled his shirt back on. "I'm going."

"Very well," she said with a sigh.

"That's it? You don't even want to know why?"

"I'm sure I'll read about it in one of your sonnets. What a troubled life the seventeenth Earl of Oxford leads."

"You're outrageous."

She spun around to face him. "What about you? Have I ever accused you of faithlessness because you sleep with your wife?"

"That's different, and you know it!"

"Get out, Edward. And don't come to see me again."

He stormed out. Did he expect her to keep herself for him? Of course not—that would have been impossible. But whatever he'd loved in her was gone.

No. Emilia was, as ever, being herself. Love had blinded him.

*T*hat night he couldn't sleep. His work was no longer his own, the woman he loved slept with other men, and the young man he cared for was risking his life on a madman's voyage.

He threw off the blankets and got out of bed. Eliza was asleep. Awake or not, she always had peace of mind. How?

He prowled the halls of King's Place, walked through the dancing gallery-turned-library and into the moonlit garden. He stalked the paths between the fruit trees. Emilia confounded him.

> *A woman that is like a German clock,*
> *Still, a-repairing, ever out of frame,*
> *And never going aright, being a watch,*
> *But being watch'd that it may still go aright!*

Work on his tragedies the following year improved his mood so much he almost looked forward to giving Will his payments.

"Hello, Will. I've got five pounds for you."

Will stopped sweeping. "Thank you, milord."

Edward looked around. The lease was about to expire here and the deal with Blackfriars had collapsed. Soon he'd be out of places to perform, save The Rose and the hall at court.

He glanced back at Will, halfheartedly swiping his broom across the floor.

"What's wrong?"

Will looked up. He looked weary, lost. "My son, milord. I just got word—he's dead."

Edward slung his arm over the younger man's shoulders. "I'm so sorry, Will. What happened?"

Will took a steadying breath. "My brother says he drowned in the creek."

"I lost a son, years ago," Edward said. "It's a terrible thing."

"What happened to him, milord?"

"Died in his crib." Old grief overtook him. He patted Will's back. "If there's anything I can do . . ."

Will shook his head. "Thank you, milord, but I don't figure there's a thing in this world to be done about it."

Edward nodded and handed him the pouch. "Again, I'm sorry. Please give your wife my condolences."

"Thanks. I'm up to my ears with Gardiner and Wayte, so this might help."

"The South Bank judge and the owner of The Swan?"

"Judge got a court t' serve me this writ." He pulled a grubby piece of parchment from his pocket.

"Let's go inside. You can sit down, I'll get you some beer." He steered Will toward a chair near the theater entrance. "May I see the writ?"

Will handed it to him. "I got t' give the court a bond t' guarantee me and Wayte and Dorothy and Annie don't disturb the peace."

He studied the writ. It contained no reason for its issuance. "Tell me about it, Will."

"Wayte had a deal with Annie Lee and Dorothy Soer— they're prostitutes and they make good money. Him and me was going t' help them, if you know what I mean. But the Bishop of Winchester and the judge own brothels, and they don't like competition. They shut us down. Your five pounds'll keep me out of the clink at least."

Edward checked his anger—however unfair, there was nothing he could do about the writ. Will had broken the law.

"I have more scripts for you to deliver," he said. "They're a little more complicated. Every actor needs his own copy. I planned to pay you three pounds per delivery." He looked directly into Will's eyes. "But I can't have you getting in trouble with the law. I hope that's clear."

"It won't happen again, milord, I promise."

"What if you were to move back to Stratford? Whenever I have a job for you I'll send a message, you'll make the delivery, then return home. You'd be well away from all the temptations of London, and I'm sure your family needs you right now. What do you say?"

"Oh, I'll go back t' Stratford, milord. I'm not happy here anyway. Any time you need me, you can find me at that shop on Henley Street or at the house I'm buying. It's called New Place. By the way, milord, do you think you could give me an advance for the next two or three deliveries? I'm a little short of the purchase price, y'see."

"How much do you need?"

"Thirty pounds, milord."

"Thirty!"

"Milord, with ten actors a play and a script for each, I figure that's what you'd be paying me for one job anyway."

He hadn't thought of that. If it weren't so frustrating, he'd have laughed. For all his troubles, Will was better with money than he was.

"I'll pay you half now and half when the scripts are ready."

"That's very kind, milord. Very kind. I won't forget."

∽

*T*he next year, 1597, Ben Jonson wrote a play with Tom Nashe called *The Isle of Dogs*. A satire on corruption in London, it attacked everyone from Robert Cecil on down a long list of courtiers. After one performance, Robert threw Jonson and Nashe in Marshalsea Prison.

Mary Sidney, impressed by Jonson's brilliance, used her Pembroke influence to get them out of jail, but the damage had been done. Robert Cecil ordered all copies of *The Isle of Dogs* burned and shut down every playhouse in London.

The timing was terrible. Edward had just completed several plays and he'd already sent word to Stratford. So far, the system worked beautifully—whenever he called, Will came. The actors accepted their scripts and never said a word about the "author." Edward's plays were the golden eggs, and they were smart enough to spot the real goose.

On one of Will's visits to London, Edward invited him to have a drink at The Steelyard.

"How're you keeping?" he asked.

"Lending money, milord. If blokes don't pay I go t' court. But it's not too often, and the money's good."

"I hope you're not drawing attention to yourself?"

"No one cares about a lawsuit filed for a few shillings, milord. Besides, I spend most of my time trading grain and investing in real estate. I'm buying a 107 acres in Welcombe. Pa knows all about farms. And I got my eye on a cottage on Chapel Street—"

"You get into a lot of things, don't you?"

"I learn my lessons, milord. Ye got t' have more than one iron in the fire."

"How true." He gave Will the five pounds he'd earned before Robert Cecil closed down the theaters, along with a little extra with which to enjoy his new home.

∽

*T*he next troubling bit of news about Will came from the heavyset Ben Jonson on an evening when they met for drinks.

The young playwright wiped foam off his lip. "Milord, the town of Stratford cited Will for hoarding grain in a drought, and the city of London cited him for not paying taxes. I'm no goody-goody, but hoarding *grain* in a *drought*?"

Edward frowned. "Are you certain?"

"I am," Ben said. "And since Robert Cecil reopened the theaters, Will parades around in fancy clothes and brags about his *coat of arms*. Folks will start to wonder where he gets his money."

"I'll have a word with him, Ben. Thank you for telling me."

"Of course, Will's behavior *did* give me an idea for a play." Jonson grinned as he ordered another beer. "I call it *Every Man out of His Humour*."

"I'd like to see it. Perhaps I can get Burbage to put it on at The Theatre."

"I'd like that, milord. In my play, a country fellow buys a coat of arms with money he claims came from someone important. But the best part of the script is the motto."

"Which is?"

"When the College of Heralds first denied Will's father a coat of arms, they scrawled 'No, Without Right' across the top of his application. But after Will bribed Dethick and the application was approved, they altered the words to *Not Without Right*."

"I didn't know heralds were so creative." Edward chuckled. "But what's the motto in the play?"

" 'Not Without Mustard.'"

Edward laughed so hard he peed his pants, something he was doing on occasion now. He'd ask Ruy—

Damn. He sighed.

*H*e summoned Will to meet him at The Pye. Edward got there first and chose the booth he and Francis Walsingham had shared fifteen years ago.

He studied his reflection in the mirror behind the bar. His hair was gray, his face lined. What did he expect? He was probably lucky to be alive. Thank goodness for Eliza and little Henry. They were another kind of love, without passion but satisfying nonetheless. The boy was beautiful, and Eliza's care and attention to his health enabled him to continue writing. He'd finally finished *Hamlet* and started *King Lear*. He was pouring himself a second glass of sherry when Will arrived, out of breath.

"Sorry I'm late, milord." He took off his expensive cape and enormous hat and plopped himself down on a bench.

"Everything all right?"

"Trouble with tax collectors, milord. They say I live in London even though I told 'em I live in Stratford. This is the third time they cited me. Said the parish needs money." He grinned. "Everybody's hurting but me."

"Doing well, are you?"

"I am, milord. I'm lending money, trading grain—"

"I heard you were cited for *hoarding* grain. In a drought."

"I weren't the only one, milord. They cited about ninety of us, all told."

"And nothing about this strikes you as wrong?"

Will dropped his eyes to the table.

Edward sighed. "What would you like to drink?"

"Small beer's fine. One of these days you ought t' let me pay, milord."

Edward ordered a small beer and another sherry. "You've been causing quite a stir when you come to London."

"Doing what exactly, milord?"

"You flaunt expensive clothing, smoke expensive tobacco. The public will wonder how you got all that money. I can't have them knowing I pay you to be my go-between. There'd be a scandal at court."

Will looked troubled. "Hadn't thought of it like that, milord. 'Preciate you warning me."

"The warning's born of self-interest. You'd be out of a job, but I'd be disgraced."

"Sorry, milord. I didn't mean t' cause trouble. I ain't never had no money to show off before."

"Just don't let it happen again."

"You got my word, milord. You been good t' me, I won't forget."

"Good boy." He smiled. "Though I suppose you're not a boy anymore."

"Not hardly, milord. I'm near thirty-four."

"Good Lord! My time's out of joint."

"Nice way of putting it, milord." He drained his beer.

"Can you keep a secret?" Edward said.

"You can count on me, milord."

"Burbage built The Theatre, but he doesn't own the land beneath it. Now his landlord refuses to extend his lease."

"You told me, milord. Them trumpets is hard on neighbors."

"So are the crowds. The scene's colorful. I like it, but others don't."

"What will Burbage do?"

"Remember, you're sworn to secrecy."

"Mum's the word, milord."

"He's going to take apart the theater plank by plank, move the pieces across the river, then construct a playhouse in Southwark under a new name. He's calling it The Globe."

"The whole place, piece by piece? Can he *do* that?"

"His lawyer says the pieces are his property, though I have my doubts, since they're affixed to the land. But he says the lawyer told him to do it and pay a fine when they catch him. He's asking all the shareholders to help."

"What's the landlord do while all this moving goes on?"

"We're waiting till he goes north for his winter vacation. What do you say? Will you help us?"

Will grinned. "Have you ever knowed me to run away from a good thing?"

Edward smiled. "Burbage intends to make The Globe the personal playhouse for all my plays."

"I'll keep a lid on it, milord. My head got big, but it's down t' size now."

25

Death once dead, there's no more dying then.

Shakespeare
Sonnet 146

*E*dward received word: Cecil was confined to bed and failing fast.

He left King's Place by sedan chair. At Cecil House he hurried up the stairs as best he could. He'd worked all day and most of the previous night—he was exhausted, yet increasingly he felt driven of late by a burning compulsion to finish everything he could.

He entered Cecil's bedroom and found the queen trying to push a spoon between Cecil's lips. Soup dribbled down his chin. The physician in the corner made no move to challenge her.

He limped over to the bed and touched Cecil's hand. He was as cold as ice. Edward laid a gentle hand on the queen's shoulder, but she wouldn't look up from her task. He left the bedroom and hobbled down to the library. Robert was waiting for him in Cecil's chair.

"Edward. Take a seat."

It had taken forty years to win Cecil over. He didn't have a hope of winning Robert, who didn't look troubled in the least by the fact that his father was dying, most likely already dead.

"Your mask seems to be working well, Edward. Don't you agree?"

He didn't. This farce would bury him, but he felt too weak to resist. Had he ever been strong? No. Sooner or later he always gave in. Like Earl John, he was all bark and no bite.

"I was thinking of publishing eight of my plays now," he said, "before the pirate copies are published unannounced."

"Good idea. Francis Meres, an author up north, requested permission to publish a book naming contemporary writers and their works. He calls it *Palladis Tamia,* 'Wit's Treasury.' I'll have him include *Shakespeare* as the author of your previous plays."

"How thoughtful of you."

He must work faster. No time to mourn the man he'd loved more than he hated.

*H*e returned to Hackney and went straight to the library. .
A law forbade comment on royal succession, but after today he had to say *something.* To be safe, he had set *Julius Caesar* 1,500 years earlier in ancient Rome.

He was also working on *King Lear.* The transfer of Hedingham still rankled, especially now that he had a son. Like Lear, he had given away his castle when he was alive. He was thinking of transferring Hedingham to a trust for the three girls.

He took comfort in what was happening with "his" theater. On a snowy night in December, Burbage and the shareholders took apart The Theatre and carried the pieces to the south bank. Two months later, The Globe was standing between a brothel and a bear-baiting pit. Not one neighbor complained.

Bridget, now fifteen, married Francis Norris, the soon-to-be

Earl of Rycote. Cecil was barely in his grave, but they went ahead with an understated wedding. Several weeks after the wedding, he met Ben Jonson for drinks at The Steelyard.

"Did you know your man Will is going around town asking nobles if he can be their mask?" Jonson said.

"I'm taking care of him in my own way. I give a line to a character, Touchstone: 'to have is to have.' In Italian, it's *avere e avere*. A Vere is a Vere."

Ben shook his head. "You'd better find another, less subtle way to handle him," he said.

*B*en Jonson tells me you're offering your services to other noblemen," Edward said the next time he saw Will. "Just because your name's similar to my pen name doesn't mean you're *me*. You're my mask, Will, and that's all. Do you understand?"

"Guess I got carried away again," Will said. "I'll do better, milord."

"There's a good fellow." He leaned back in his chair. "Now, how are those children of yours? I heard the school in Stratford only has one room."

"I didn't put 'em in no school, milord. Working was good enough for me, so I figured it was good enough for them."

*R*ather than fight the Irish, Essex lost most of his men to illness. Then, without warning or authority, he declared a truce and came home. The queen and Robert were so furious they canceled his only income, a monopoly on the import of sweet wine. Essex called the queen crooked, said she must be replaced, and, with only three hundred men, including Henry Wriothesley, marched on the palace.

Essex and Wriothesley were captured and charged with treason. To Edward's surprise, the queen appointed him to the jury of lords hearing evidence. When Henry entered the courtroom, he walked up to Essex and kissed him. Edward caught his breath as old feelings surged.

The trial was over in time for lunch. Both men were sentenced to beheading.

Edward went back to King's Place and dreamed of Henry that night. They were naked, in bed, just as he'd described in those steamy sonnets years ago.

He woke, startled, aroused.

He couldn't bear to let such a beautiful young man die for such a stupid mistake.

*H*e went to see the queen. He sent no warning, made no formal request. He simply arrived at the palace early one morning and waited.

Finally, the clerk brought him before the queen.

"Your Majesty, I've come on a matter of grave importance," he said. "I'm sure you're aware that Henry Wriothesley is to be beheaded tomorrow."

Her breathing was heavy, the silence interminable.

"I beg you to commute his sentence to life imprisonment, Your Majesty. He's young, he was under Essex's influence. He deserves your mercy."

She fingered the hairpiece woven with pearls. He thought of Lopez—hardly a day went by that he didn't.

"Last night I read your preface to your tutor's translation of *The Courtier*." She looked directly at him. He was glad she couldn't see his clenched fists. "You said a monarch must be merciful."

"I did, Your Majesty."

She sighed, and he thought he'd never heard a wearier sound.

"I'll commute Henry's sentence," she said. "Now go home and write."

He limped out of the palace. He should have been ecstatic—he'd saved Henry's life.

This was the second time he'd pleaded with a capricious queen to spare the life of a man who should never have been condemned to death in the first place. He could only hope it would be the last.

*T*he next time he saw Will, he was pleased to see him in modest clothes. He handed over his scripts for *Hamlet*.

"Morning, Will. How's the family?"

"Morning, milord." Will sighed. "Pa passed on this week. Family's going t' miss him."

"I'm so sorry," Edward said. "I know how much he meant to you."

Will thrust his jaw out. "Milord, I'm going t' show 'em. I'll erect a statue for Pa in Holy Trinity Church."

Edward leaned in. "What of?"

"It near killed Pa when they made 'im stop trading wool. I'll have his bust mounted on the wall, with a woolsack in his lap."

It was almost poetic—Edward liked it.

"Would you permit me to make a contribution?"

"I'd sure appreciate that, milord, but it's going t' take time."

"I'm sure dealing with the leaders of a small town is difficult."

Will hesitated. "Milord, Ben Jonson asked if I want t' act in one or two of his plays." He almost looked bashful. "He's got some short parts, so I don't need t' read."

"Well, that was kind of him." Though he strongly suspected an ulterior motive.

"He said you was behind it, so I wanted to thank you."

*T*he first performance of *Hamlet* was staged in the auditorium of Middle Temple, one of the Inns at Court. At four thousand lines, the play was twice the length of any other play he'd written—too long for The Globe, Burbage said, but not for the audience at court filled with law students and courtiers.

Edward sat between Eliza and the queen, Robert Cecil on her other side, behind them Bridget and Elizabeth with their husbands.

"Father," Elizabeth whispered in his ear, "I'm glad I never married Wriothesley. William and I fight, but at least my William doesn't start revolutions."

His daughter Susan entered with her fiancé, Philip Herbert. Philip's brother William was the Lord Chamberlain now, thus in charge of the queen's entertainment. His favorite cousins, Horace and Francis Vere, on furlough from their army unit in the Low Countries, entered behind them.

He wished Uncle Arthur were there. In his sixties now, Arthur was failing. So many had gone now.

Sic transit gloria mundi—thus passes away the glory of this world.

James Burbage's son Richard played Hamlet. Edward always thought he'd play the part himself, but he could hardly make it to his seat now, let alone drag himself across the stage.

Not once during the entire four-hour performance did the queen close her eyes. She seemed riveted. At play's end, bodies littered the stage but the applause was thunderous.

He took a bow. To hell with anonymity.

At the reception that the people at Temple Inn put together, the queen surprised everyone, chatting and laughing, more alive than she'd seemed in years. But the greatest surprise was Robert.

"I enjoyed it immensely," he said with a smile. "Heartiest congratulations."

William Russell was next.

"Edward, my boy, I loved it, especially the part about the pirates. Those were the days, weren't they?"

Edward laughed. "If you like wandering the beaches of Dover for hours, begging for clothes, then, yes, I suppose they were."

After everyone had moved to the refreshment table, Susan and her fiancé approached. She kissed Edward on the cheek—she hadn't done *that* since she was a little girl.

Before Nan died, discussion of his playwriting had been kept to a minimum at Cecil House—Lady Cecil saw to that. But after she died, he'd begun inviting the girls to his performances. Susan in particular was fascinated.

"I can't wait to act." She clung to his arm. "Philip asked his brother William to stage more of your plays at court. William said the queen was too tired, but we're wearing him down, aren't we, William?"

"Tonight the queen surprised me," William said. "I've been too protective. I shall put plays on her agenda once again."

"The next thing I'm going to do," Susan said, "is convince you I should be allowed to act in all Father's plays at court. A woman can't perform in public, but why not in the palace? A woman can be queen—why can't she be an actor?"

At last he had a child to follow in his footsteps. He was so proud of her.

Horace and Francis approached, swords gleaming, their leather like mirrors.

"Edward," Horace said, "Francis and I want to thank you for

putting us in your play. What a treat for us to be Horatio and Francisco."

"And don't worry," Francis said, "we're going to take the last lines to heart. The world shall know your story, never fear."

He glanced over his shoulder, wondering if Robert had overheard, but he was on the other side of the room, laughing for the first time in years.

Ben Jonson stumbled over. He reeked of beer. "Much too long, Willy," he said. "You could've blotted a thousand words."

"Didn't you like any of it?"

"Of course." He grinned. "But if you want to entertain the public, do yourself a favor and ask your gardener if you can borrow his ax."

"The world of drama is changing," Edward said. "I think the people can afford to elevate their tastes."

The queen walked over. "Edward dear, thank you for waiting until Robin was in his grave. I couldn't have borne it if he'd tried to take revenge on you." She cocked her head the way she had a million years ago at Hedingham. "And it's past time he had a little punishment for what he did to your father and Tom."

She turned and walked away, leaving Edward astonished.

One afternoon Robert arrived at King's Place escorted by a company of guards.

Edward greeted him at the door and brought him into the library. Robert settled into an easy chair.

"What I'm about to say must be kept in strictest confidence. Do I have your agreement?"

"You do."

"I have been in contact with King James in Edinburgh. Half a dozen claimants to the throne are polishing their armor. If we don't arrange a peaceful path to the throne, we'll have civil war. I saw your *Julius Caesar*, so I know this troubles you, too."

Edward waited. This could be a trap. As soon as he agreed, he'd be violating the queen's own edict not to discuss the succession, at which point Robert's guards would drag him off to the Tower.

"I've asked James to be our king."

"And?"

"He's suspicious. After what we did to his mother, who could blame him? But he's the logical choice. He's descended from Henry VII and he agrees to keep England Protestant despite his mother's Catholic vows. We must encourage him."

There was the cheese. Should he bite?

"What have you in mind?"

"I'd like you to write a letter to James," Robert said. "Anonymously, of course." Robert smiled. "Just sign the letter *forty*. I'll supply the courier."

"*Forty?*"

"*Four zero.* Thirty-nine others are already in contact with him. You're next. When I see him, I'll reveal your identity personally."

Edward took a deep breath.

"How do I know I can trust you?"

"We've had our differences," Robert said. "I can understand why you'd be hesitant. But Edward . . ." He leaned forward and lowered his voice. "I'm begging you. If you won't do it for me, do it for England."

"I'll offer my encouragement."

Robert stood up and balanced himself on his twisted frame. "Thank you, Edward. You won't be sorry."

*H*e wrote to King James and held his breath. James replied. Formal letters grew into a warm correspondence. All the while Edward, hearing time's hooves at his heels, worked on his plays.

News from the palace turned ominous. The queen refused to eat. She insisted on sleeping on the floor. The end was surely near.

He couldn't bring himself to go and see her. They'd laughed together too many times—he wanted his last memories of her to be happy.

A week later, on March 24, 1603, at two in the morning, the queen died. He left for Richmond Palace as soon as he heard. Sitting in the sedan chair, he was numb—frozen, body and mind.

When he arrived at Westminster, Robert hugged him.

"I had to cut the coronation ring off her finger." His voice trembled. "In the forty-five years she reigned, she never once removed it."

"Where is it now?" Edward asked.

"On its way to Edinburgh." His voice was even shakier now. "With any luck, James will be here in sixty hours, put the damn thing on his finger, and we can put this all behind us."

*E*dward returned to King's Place, the depression coming over him now too dark to bear. The queen was gone. Her death was more than a void—it was a sword through his heart. He remembered holding the canopy over her head to celebrate England's first day of thanksgiving for the victory over the Spanish armada. That day he'd walked beside her. Now he'd walk behind her casket.

He sat in his study. He wanted to write, but what could he say?

He'd long since stopped *blaming* her for their failed affair, for Nan, for Ruy Lopez, even for what she'd done to Emilia. But he couldn't find it in him to forgive. Yet there were a thousand things she'd done *for* him. Her unwavering support of his writing. Italy and the plays he wrote there. *Venus and Adonis.* All the plays he'd staged in her palace, without which nothing meant anything.

He reached for his Bible.

And underlined a passage in Revelation 14:13: *"Blessed be the dead for they rest from their labors and their works follow them."*

*E*ighteen days before the queen's funeral, by order of King James, Henry Wriothesley was released from the Tower.

Edward was working in his library when Henry came in unannounced. They embraced. As Henry's body pressed against his, for an instant he was back in the cockpit of The Rose, the day he gave the boy those seventeen birthday sonnets.

"Edward, I'm free." His face was wreathed in smiles. "My jailer said I have you to thank."

"I only wrote a letter or two."

"That's not all you did. I heard about your meeting with the queen. Edward, I owe you my life."

Henry's affection warmed him but came too late. Those feelings were only a bittersweet memory.

"I've been unkind," Henry said. "I never thanked you for those lovely dedications. I was caught up in my infatuation with Essex. Can you forgive me?"

He felt so weary. What did Henry want from him? "Of course," he said. "I'm just glad to see you free."

"So's my wife. She just gave birth, you know. I can hardly believe I'm a father."

"I'd heard," Edward said.

"I'm happy. I hope you are, too." Henry glanced around the library. "I'd like to meet your son if that's all right. I heard you named him after me."

"He's with his tutor." He felt uneasy for some reason, but Henry showed no indication of leaving. "I'll summon him."

Waiting for his son, he struggled to remember. Why had he written those dedications, those sonnets? He must have cared deeply— he just couldn't recall why.

His son entered the library. Young Henry was nearly ten now. Indeed, time *was* out of joint.

"My boy, this is your Uncle Henry." He watched the two shake hands. He felt a mild wash of nostalgia, nothing more.

"Henry, I hope you and my son will be friends."

"Of course we will." He smiled. "Won't we, Henry?"

Little Henry was holding a small sword. He assumed the stance Rocco Bonetti had taught him and then made a perfect riposte and lunge.

"Till death, won't we, Uncle Henry?"

"Indeed we will." Henry glanced up at Edward. "And that's a promise I intend to keep."

It should have cheered him. Instead he felt only a quiet dread. "Henry, return to your tutor. I'll let you know when lunch is ready." He watched his son run down the hall, toy sword dragging the ground behind him. "I'm trying to be a better father to Henry than I was to my daughters, though one of them does seem fond of me."

"One out of four. Not bad at all."

"There you go, Henry. Always the gambler."

"Some people never learn." He laughed.

"Try, Henry. You might live longer."

*H*enry finally left. For the first time since the queen had died, Edward cried—not a tear or two but a torrent of them. He cried as he remembered the day he'd met the queen at Hedingham, when he first smelled her musk. He cried as he thought of her constant encouragement. He'd done everything she wanted, play after play, a never-ending reciprocation. Even when she took Emilia from him, even when she executed Lopez, his affection for the queen hadn't ended.

He had to forgive her—he'd made too many mistakes of his own.

But now that she was gone, who would forgive *him?*

26

My train are men of choice and rarest parts,
That all particulars of duty know,
And in the most exact regard support
The worships of their name.

Shakespeare
King Lear

The queen was interred in Westminster Abbey. Edward had his name removed twice from the list of official mourners—he didn't think he could bear it—but relented. He had to march behind her casket. He was Lord Great Chamberlain of England.

The succession, like everything Robert had a hand in, went smoothly. When King James promised that he and England would remain Protestant, opposition crumbled.

A gala coronation was planned, but the king delayed entry into London until the bout of plague subsided. In the meantime, death bells tolled, body carts rumbled, and passersby sniffed healing herbs.

Edward was summoned to Whitehall two months after the coronation. Once more he entered the palace, climbed the steps, and limped down the corridors. Every day, walking was more difficult, and today was the worst—there'd be no queen at the end of it.

Thirty-seven-year-old King James was seated on the throne. Edward had learned much about the man during and after their correspondence. James had taken his mother's death hard, as well he might. Since then he'd learned to play off one Scottish lord against another. Every day, he was terrified of being assassinated. Although he yearned for peace with Spain and aspired to religious tolerance for English Catholics, he knew those goals were not Parliament's and he'd have to struggle. On the personal front, though his marriage was a success—he had several sons—he'd lost his heart to George Villiers.

"Welcome, Great Oxford." King James' voice was strong. "I want you to know that waiting for a letter from Number Forty was often the high point of my day."

"Thank you, Your Majesty."

"Now then," he said, "here it is. Your annual thousand pounds shall continue so long as you live. Robert presented the decree and I've signed it."

"Very generous, Your Majesty. You have my thanks."

"I'm also informed the queen delayed returning to you the Forest of Essex and Havering-atte-Bower. That, too, has been accomplished."

That really *was* generous. Edward could only bow.

"Henceforth," James said, "I shall personally be the patron of the Lord Chamberlain's Men. The company's name is being changed to The King's Men."

"You've no idea what that means to me, Your Majesty."

"Now then." He clapped his hands. "Mary Sidney invited my wife and me to visit her family's country estate—Wilton, I believe. Her son, my Lord Chamberlain, suggests a performance of *As You Like It*. But I think the evening would hardly be complete without the presence of the playwright."

"I'd be delighted to attend."

"Mary told me she already erected a sign over the door to the room at Wilton where you will stay. It reads 'Shakespeare's Room.'" James smiled. "I hope her enthusiasm is acceptable."

"It is, Your Majesty." He found the king's willingness to ignore his anonymity refreshing.

"Now I have a request, Great Oxford."

"Anything, Your Majesty."

"May I call you Willy? I've been informed your writer friends do, and since I intend to organize an English-language version of the Bible, that may justify my being called a writer, don't you think?"

"I believe it does, Your Majesty." He swallowed a smile. "I'd be honored if you call me Willy."

Susan played the role of Cordelia in a court performance of *King Lear*. She was sixteen and a natural on the stage.

King James attended the performance. Afterward, Edward asked if they might meet in private.

Again he was ushered into the room where so often he'd met with the queen. The king had already refurbished it in bright colors and rich fabrics.

"Willy, you don't look well."

"I'm feeling poorly, Your Majesty. It's that foot of mine."

"Shall we sit on this love seat? You'll feel more comfortable."

"Thank you, Your Majesty. I want to talk to you about my daughter."

"She was remarkable. Before I was introduced to your plays,

my interests inclined to philosophy and theology. But now I'm an aficionado of drama, and a performance like Susan's only adds fuel to the fire."

"I'm so pleased. She tells me she wishes to be married next year during the Christmas season. Why she wants to wait a year and a half is beyond me, but she loves Philip, he loves her, and I want to invite you to be my guest at her wedding. I'm taking the liberty of making my needs known far in advance since your schedule is so crowded."

"When the date is fixed, let me know and I'll be there—on one condition. I'd like six or eight of your plays to be performed on the days before and after the blessed event."

"You're too kind, Your Majesty. To stage so many different works so close together will be an enormous undertaking, especially before the king himself, but it will be my honor to try."

*H*e selected *Othello, The Merry Wives of Windsor, Measure for Measure, The Comedy of Errors, Henry V, Love's Labour's Lost, The Merchant of Venice,* and *The Tempest.* He also chose two plays by Ben Jonson, *Every Man out of His Humour* and *Every Man in His Humour* to give Ben a boost.

Then he returned to *The Tempest.* He added some personal lines, an adieu to the world in dialogue.

My charms are all o'erthrown . . . and what strength I have's mine own, which is most faint. . . . Let me not . . . dwell in this bare island. . .release me from my bands. . . . Let your indulgence set me free.

*H*e'd written what he had to write. There would always be more to say, but for now, for himself, he'd said enough.

He summoned Eliza to the library.

"When the wedding is over I should like to go and live in Hedingham," he said, "but it's fifty years since I lived there and the caretaker tells me it needs work. Would you take Henry and all the servants to supervise the renovations?"

She studied him. Theirs had never been a passionate marriage, but she knew him intimately.

"Please, Eliza—I need you to do this for me."

"Aren't you coming with us?"

"Not immediately. I have a few more works to finish here."

"Edward, don't you think cook should stay here with you?"

"That won't be necessary. Take everyone with you—I can fend for myself."

*I*n two days Eliza and Henry were ready to leave with the servants. Edward kissed her and hugged Henry. The boy was muscular, getting taller every day. Oxford Eighteen would win tournaments.

He worked all day and that night slept soundly. The next morning, he limped into town to buy bread, eggs, cheese, butter, and milk. The walk felt longer than usual—his foot pained him constantly. If only Lopez were there.

In the market, he said hello to people out and about—fewer than he expected, thanks to the current devastating bout of plague. His presence was a curiosity, most of the nobility having fled to country houses. The villagers wished him well or bowed or shook his hand. He slipped a few pounds into one old man's pocket.

He limped home and wandered through King's Place, appreciating how tastefully Eliza had furnished everything. He walked about in the garden, smelled the roses, and then came in and sat down at his desk in the library.

He stared at the bookshelves. He knew every book, had read them all in the original Greek, Latin, French, Spanish, Italian. They were his oldest friends.

He thought about Sir Thomas' library, what a treasure and a comfort it had been to him. He thought about the happy hours he'd spent learning French at Cecil House and translating Ovid's *Metamorphoses* with Arthur. Between kisses with Virginia he'd even improved his Italian.

His life had its bright spots. His plays would last, and Cervantes was right—he shouldn't whine about anonymity, the compromise that had made performing them possible. A line in one of his sonnets expressed how he'd felt about it: "My name be buried where my body is. . .though I (once gone) to all the world must die."

For days he followed the same routine. He worked most of the night, napped all morning, and in the late afternoon took a walk in the village.

One evening he leafed through his manuscripts. The pile was huge: thirty-seven plays, 154 sonnets, two long poems, and his prefaces to Bedingfield's and Clerke's translations. Also the short poems he'd written, some published, some not, and the Henry VII play he'd begun. He was satisfied with his oeuvre, if not always with his life.

A week later he realized he needed to add something to *Macbeth*, the title character a fellow much like himself: basically decent, determined to do the right thing but unable to because he hadn't the strength. He fell asleep thinking about Macbeth and in the morning wrote a soliloquy for him:

> *To-morrow, and to-morrow, and to-morrow,*
> *Creeps in this petty pace from day to day*
> *To the last syllable of recorded time,*

And all our yesterdays have lighted fools
The way to dusty death. Out, out, brief candle!
Life's but a walking shadow, a poor player
That struts and frets his hour upon the stage
And then is heard no more: it is a tale
Told by an idiot, full of sound and fury,
Signifying nothing.

Two more weeks of writing, wandering in the market, shaking hands. Then one night he felt the lumps in his groin and armpits.

He put himself to bed and waited.

In a few days, black dots surrounded by red circles appeared. The plague took no more than three days, for which he was grateful. His plays would live even if his name were buried with his body.

He prayed his daughters and son would be well. He wished he could have been at Susan's wedding. Still, the reception would be full of people he'd spent his life dodging. Given his current frame of mind, he'd probably insult one of them, and he didn't want to spoil her day.

He thought of Francis Trentham. His brother-in-law had made him rich again. After he'd given away almost everything, they developed Covent Garden. How many working writers did something like that?

He thought about the queen. Had she found another kingdom to rule? He laughed out loud at the thought of her trying to boss her way around heaven.

The chills came, followed by pain. He heard himself scream Emilia's name. She was incredibly strong. She'd endure anything, including his death.

It wouldn't be long now. Another day, another night. In the morning he heard young girls singing in the garden. They must have slipped in to play.

He listened. It was that song children sang whenever the plague came.

> *Ring around a rosie,*
> *Pocket full of posie.*
> *Ashes. Ashes.*
> *All fall down.*

On June 24, 1604, Edward de Vere, the seventeenth Earl of Oxford, died.

AUTHOR'S NOTE

Six months after Edward died, King James gave away Edward's daughter Susan to Philip Herbert, Earl of Montgomery. The king added substantially to her dowry and celebrated her wedding by having ten plays performed, eight by *Shakespeare* and two by Ben Jonson.

Five years later, *Shakespeare's Sonnets* were published. No one claimed authorship. The printer dedicated the *Sonnets* to the "ever-living" poet, a term used to honor someone deceased.

The *Sonnets* state that the author is lame, "carried the canopy," and was forty years old when the *Sonnets* were written. Will Shakspere was not lame, never carried the canopy, and was in his twenties when the *Sonnets* were written.

Eliza Trentham Vere, the Countess of Oxford, died eight years after Edward's death. In her last will and testament, she instructed her executor to pay "my dumb man." Will Shakspere was still alive in Stratford, investing in real estate, trading in grain and malt, lending money, and suing his delinquent borrowers. In London, Will also joined with others in purchasing the Blackfriars gatehouse, played two small parts in Ben Jonson's plays, and was described as an actor by Ben Jonson in *The First Folio of Shakespeare's Plays*.

In his last will and testament, Will made no mention of owning any books, unpublished manuscripts, or unperformed plays. Nor were any writings by him of any kind, even letters, ever found. A few years after Will's death, a monument to his father containing a four-cornered woolsack was erected in Holy Trinity Church in Stratford.

Seven years after Will's death, *The First Folio of Shakespeare's Plays* was published, Ben Jonson the editor. It did not contain a biography of the playwright. It did not contain Edward's long poems with their passionate dedications to Henry Wriothesley. It did not contain the sonnets, which, through their references to the author's lameness, age, and role as the Lord Great Chamberlain of England, all but named the Earl of Oxford as author.

Jonson inserted a frontispiece to *The First Folio* that he described as the "figure" for Shakespeare. Prepared by Martin Droeshout, the frontispiece is not a likeness of Will, who died when Droeshout was a child. Jonson admonished the reader to look "not on the picture but the book." He also included his poem that referred to Shakespeare as the "swan of Avon." (Will lived in Stratford-upon-Avon; Edward owned a home—Bilton Hall—on the Avon.) And he included a poem by Edward's childhood friend Leonard Digges that referred to the playwright's Stratford "moniment," with the "i" in *moniment* set in boldface type. A moniment is an archive of work, not a statue erected to honor a man.

Two years after *The First Folio* was published, Oxford Eighteen and Henry Wriothesley went to the Low Countries to fight for Protestant rights. The "two Henries," as they were described in a contemporary cartoon, died of wounds incurred in battle. Edward's son inherited his father's love of Venice—before he died, he was fined for riding in a Venetian gondola with a courtesan.

The same year the two Henries died, King James died. After his son Charles succeeded him, a bloody civil war broke out. The Puritans overthrew Charles and ruled for eleven years, during which they closed all theaters. By the time the monarchy was restored, 156 years had passed since Edward's death, 142 years since Will's. No one alive knew them, their children, or their friends. Many theater records were destroyed.

No original scripts of Shakespeare plays have ever been found. *The First Folio* states that it was prepared from copies.

*I*n 1709, the Reverend Nicholas Rowe, a curate in a town near Stratford, was preparing an edition of Shakespeare's plays for publication. He reported that when he tried to write a biography of the playwright, he could find no evidence that Will from Stratford had been a writer, only that he was an actor and was poorly educated even by the standards of the day.

The curate's experience was repeated in the 1760s by an authority on English literary matters, Samuel Johnson. He made a similar investigation of Shakespeare for an edition of the plays he was preparing and reported finding next to nothing about Will. But he decided to equate Shakespeare with Homer, there also being next to nothing known about the legendary Greek author.

When David Garrick, Johnson's friend and a celebrated actor, organized a Shakespeare festival in Stratford in 1765, the myth of the Stratford man known as Shakespeare was born. Stratford town boosters "beautified" the monument to Will's father by converting the four-cornered woolsack into an unlikely writing cushion, placing a sheet of writing paper on top of the cushion, and inserting a pen into the hand of the effigy. Today, Stratford is the second-largest tourist attraction in England.

Until the 1800s, the sonnets, with their evidence pointing to Edward as Shakespeare, were largely ignored, although William Wordsworth, the poet laureate of Britain, did describe them as the way by which Shakespeare "unlocked his heart." The question remained: who was Shakespeare? But another issue had captured the people's imagination: why must all great people be noblemen?

A host of commoner heroes emerged, from the Three Musketeers in France to Sherlock Holmes in England. The next step was predictable if not inevitable. Why not a commoner playwright? Why not Will, a common man who dreamed up sophisticated poems and plays without the education, knowledge of foreign languages, travel, and other experiences upon which the plays and poems were based? Surely he was the commoner genius with a magical imagination they were looking for.

Still, many had doubts. By 1850, more than 250 published titles by established scholars and writers had taken on the question "Who Wrote Shakespeare?" Charles Dickens was particularly articulate on the subject. So was Benjamin Disraeli, the prime minister. In America, John Greenleaf Whittier, Ralph Waldo Emerson, Walt Whitman, Herman Melville, Henry James, and Mark Twain joined the many who doubted Will's authorship of the plays. Whittier wrote, "I am quite sure the man Shakspere neither did nor could." And Walt Whitman said Shakespeare's were "plays of an aristocracy."

Henry James expressed outrage: "I am 'a sort of' haunted by the conviction that the divine William is the biggest and most successful fraud ever practiced on a patient world." Mark Twain applied common sense to the issue: "A man can't handle glibly and easily and comfortably and successfully the argot of a trade in which he has not personally served."

But faced with sixty candidates, scholars stayed with the man from Stratford. To accept anyone else meant scrapping a century of scholarship. Careers and reputations have been built on the assumption that Will from Stratford wrote Shakespeare's plays—despite the "beautified" Stratford monument, *The First Folio* references to Avon and Stratford, the references in the sonnets that point to the Earl of Oxford, a pamphlet by "Wit" Robert Greene with a "shakescene" these scholars insisted was Will, and much other evidence to the contrary.

The latest research reveals details I believe further establish Edward de Vere, the seventeenth Earl of Oxford, as Shakespeare. Much of this novel is based on those details. Mark Anderson's *Shakespeare by Another Name*, Charlton Ogburn's *The Mysterious William Shakespeare*, and Richard F. Whalen's *Shakespeare: Who Was He? The Oxford Challenge to the Bard of Avon* are a few of many books that make the case.

Literary figures, writers, and scholars, joined by Royal Shakespeare Company actors and directors including Derek Jacobi, Vanessa Redgrave, Michael York, Jeremy Irons, and the late John Gielgud have also raised their voices in support of the Earl of Oxford as Shakespeare. Thousands more have signed a "declaration of doubt about Will" that is circulating on the web.

After twenty-three years of study, John Paul Stevens, retired associate justice of the United States Supreme Court, announced that he, too, was convinced that the Earl of Oxford wrote the works of Shakespeare and said his conclusion was "beyond a reasonable doubt." Justice Stevens reiterated that no original scripts have been found, but circumstantial evidence can be as reliable as hard evidence where, as in this case, there is so much of it. Justice Stevens was joined in his view by Associate Justice Antonin Scalia, which in itself is noteworthy. Having practiced law in Washington, D.C., I know that the two justices seldom agreed on other issues. Retired Associate Justice Sandra Day O'Connor and the late Associate Justices Lewis Powell, William Brennan, and Henry Blackmun concurred.

Hard evidence with strong probative value was uncovered in the twentieth century. Charles Wisner Barrell reported in *Scientific American that* an X-ray of a painting of Shakespeare in the Folger Shakespeare Library, in Washington, D.C., revealed an underpainting of a nobleman wearing a ruff collar and a ring with a boar's head. In Elizabethan times, only noblemen were permitted to wear ruff collars, and the boar's head was the insignia of the Earl of Oxford.

The underpainting also contains *CK*, the initials of Cornelius Kettel, who painted a portrait of the Earl of Oxford in 1580. Listed among the possessions of Oxford's great granddaughter Henrietta Stanley of South Yorkshire as a portrait of Shakespeare, the painting went missing and was later renamed *The Ashbourne Portrait*. The face fits perfectly the face in another portrait of the Earl of Oxford, *The Wellbeck Portrait*, painted in 1575 and given by Edward to his wife Nan on the birth of their first child.

More hard evidence was uncovered by Professor Roger Stritmatter, for which he was awarded a Ph.D. by the University of Massachusetts at Amherst. He found that the red velvet-covered Geneva Bible in the Folger Shakespeare Library known as *Shakespeare's Bible* contains the Earl of Oxford's coat of arms embossed in gold on the cover. It also contains hundreds of mult-colored underlinings and manicules—hands with pointing fingers—next to words and phrases used in Shakespeare's plays.

Yet biographies, many by respected scholars, continue to claim Will is Shakespeare. Professor Colin Burrow of All Soul's College, Oxford University, described the most recent one as "the literary biographical equivalent of Coca-Cola. The sweetness gets too much, . . . and after a while it starts to produce a buildup of gas."

It is understandable that scholars fear to admit a mistake. Jobs in the humanities are hard to obtain. No one wants to jeopardize a career. But the Cambridge Encyclopedia of English Literature issued a warning: Writings that claim Will is Shakespeare are filled with terms like *perhaps, must have, could have,* and *should have* and should therefore be read with caution.

To my mind, the issue is settled. The Earl of Oxford predicted in Sonnet 72 that "my name will be buried where my body is."

But as he wrote Robert Cecil, "Truth is subject to no prescription, for truth is truth though never so old, and time cannot make that false which was truth."

Edward de Vere had to hide his authorship. But we don't, and the time will come when we won't.

ACKNOWLEDGMENTS

*T*his historical novel, dramatizing one of the world's great literary mysteries, has a history of its own. I'd just completed *1492: The World of Christopher Columbus* when the publisher asked if I'd be interested in writing a sequel. I began to trace what happened to several families who had populated Columbus' world and discovered that some had fled to London and maintained contact with the man who wrote the works of *Shakespeare*.

My research into their lives led me to doubt that William Shakspere of Stratford was "the" Shakespeare. I also learned I was in good company.

I labored for fifteen years, an investigation that took me to England and Italy several times. Hardly a morning dawned when I didn't sit down at my computer to be greeted by news from other researchers. I thank each and every one of them. This book could not have been written without them. Here are some of their names—if I have omitted anyone, it is not intentional.

Nina Green's web site was invaluable, especially for details about the Earl of Oxford's financial affairs. Stephanie Hopkins Hughes, former editor of *The Oxfordian*, also maintains a valuable web site. I thank her for her insights on Elizabethan theater and Emilia Bassano Lanier (now recognized as the first feminist writer and activist), as well as her manuscript on the life of Sir Thomas Smith.

The work of the late Dr. Noemi Magri of Padua was very helpful in connection with Oxford's travels in Italy, his visit to Titian's atelier, and his writing of *Venus and Adonis*. The late Cecil Roth's classic *The Jews in the Renaissance* was crucial in appreciating Leone de Sommi of Mantua's contribution to commedia dell'arte and Shakespeare's works. The late Richard Paul Roe's *The Shakespeare Guide to Italy* is indispensable to anyone wishing to know how, where, and why Oxford wrote a third of his plays in and about Italy. Richard F. Whalen's research on the alteration of Will's father's monument by the Stratford town boosters was an eye-opener. Professor Kay Redfield Jameson's *Touched by Fire* contains valuable insight into the Earl of Oxford's likely bipolar condition. Eva Turner Clark's *Hidden Allusions in Shakespeare's Plays* is a gold mine of evidence about the early versions of Shakespeare plays the Earl of Oxford performed for the queen when he returned from Italy. I found Kevin Gilvary's *Dating Shakespeare's Plays* a sound guide to the periods during which the Earl of Oxford wrote the plays.

The research of Philip Johnson, Alex McNeil, Marion Peel, Eddi Jolly, Derran Charlton, Sally Hazelton, Alastair Everitt, John Rollett, Richard Malim, the late Scott Brazil, and Ramon Jimenez was indispensable, as was Jeremy Crick's investigation of Elizabeth Trentham and her brother Francis. Richard Malim has also written a fine new work on the Earl of Oxford.

I also thank Naomi Czekaj-Robbins of the Wellfleet Library for her resourceful assistance.

Edward de Vere's descendant Jason Lindsay and his wife, Demetria, who live in Hedingham Castle, were most gracious to my wife and me. They showed us around the castle keep and permitted us to walk the grounds of Edward's childhood home. A recent article in *Shakespeare Matters* by Jack A. Goldstone was helpful in my understanding the ambiguous inscriptions on the Stratford monument.

The research of Robert Detobel, Hank Whittemore, John Michell, Diana Price, Charles Beauclerk, Dennis Baron. Ron Hess, Gary Goldstein, Dr. William Waugaman, Dr. Paul Altroochi, John Shahan, Matthew Cossolotto, Professor Rima

Greenhill, Ruth Lloyd Miller, John Hamill, and the late Sir Frank Kermode was also helpful, as was that of Charles Bird, Charles Murray Willis and Michael Llewellyn. David Riggs' *The World of Christopher Marlowe* helped me understand the Earl of Oxford's contemporaries. For Edward's correspondence, William Plumer Fowler's *Shakespeare Revealed in Oxford's Letters* was indispensable.

Professor Margaret F. Rosenblum's *The Honest Courtesan: Veronica Franco, Citizen and Writer in Sixteenth Century Venice* brought to life the world the Earl of Oxford entered during his year in and around Venice.

For those interested in a greater understanding of Shakespeare's plays, I recommend *The Oxfordian Shakespeare Series*, fully annotated from an Oxfordian perspective by Richard F. Whalen.

I want to thank my editors, Renni Browne—founder of The Editorial Department and co-author of *Self-Editing for Fiction Writers*—and her colleague Shannon Roberts for steering me away from taking on the Shakespeare academic establishment. Her and Shannon's painstaking editing and probing questions helped bring this odyssey to a sound conclusion.

I thank my son-in-law Dr. Moshe Wurgaft for holding my hand throughout the many computer challenges. I thank his wife, my daughter Dr. Nina Wurgaft, for her constant encouragement. I thank my son, Professor James Ron, for helping me find compassion for scholars in today's hard-pressed academic world. I also thank his wife, Emma Naughton, for her encouragement.

To my wife, Dr. Martha Frohlich, author of two books on the creative process of Beethoven, I say thank you for fifty years of marriage, for her help in thinking through this book, for so much more that words can never express. And to our four grandchildren, Mia, Tessa, Leo, and Sacha, I want to pass along the words of the Earl of Oxford, my companion over these many years, in the hope that they will offer inspiration during difficult times ahead. As he wrote in *Hamlet*, "The very substance of the ambitious is merely the shadow of a dream." So to you, the people I love, and to my readers, I say never stop dreaming.

Newton Frohlich

Wellfleet, Massachusetts

ABOUT THE AUTHOR

Newton Frohlich, a former lawyer in Washington, D.C., is the author of *1492: The World of Christopher Columbus* (also translated into Spanish and Dutch), and *Making the Best of It: A Common Sense Guide to Negotiating a Divorce*. He spent fifteen years traveling and researching for *The Shakespeare Mask*, and is a member of the Shakespeare Oxford Society and the DeVere Society. He has lived in Washington, DC, the south of France, and Israel. He makes his home on Cape Cod with his wife, Martha, a musicologist.

CPSIA information can be obtained at www.ICGtesting.com
Printed in the USA
BVOW04s1856210714

359966BV00002B/3/P